IN THE THRONE ROOM, ONE BY ONE, THE TORCHES WERE TRAMPLED OUT

From outside, in the halls and the streets beyond, from over the whole city, rose an animal howl, mingled with the thunder of fighting and the saw-edged whine of Banning shockers.

After a time there was silence. In the darkness of tattered flags and forgotten glories, one torch still burned in a high sconce, spilling a red and shaken light over the man pinned by knives against the stone wall. The Venusians and the apes withdrew, taking their dead. Outside fighting still continued, but the sound of it was distant, muffled. Mayo had not moved from the place where she pressed close against the wall, touching Rick's feet.

Jaffa Storm came and stood before them.

He smiled and stretched his giant body, muscle by muscle, as a panther does. His black eyes held a deep pleasure.

" 'The wind is rising,' "
blown itself out! These
Mars. What's left is noth

The Tor Double Novels:

A Meeting with Medusa by Arthur C. Clarke/*Green Mars* by Kim Stanley Robinson

Hardfought by Greg Bear/*Cascade Point* by Timothy Zahn

Born with the Dead by Robert Silverberg/*The Saliva Tree* by Brian W. Aldiss

Tango Charlie and Foxtrot Romeo by John Varley/*The Star Pit* by Samuel R. Delany

No Truce with Kings by Poul Anderson/*Ship of Shadows* by Fritz Leiber

Enemy Mine by Barry B. Longyear/*Another Orphan* by John Kessel

Screwtop by Vonda N. McIntyre/*The Girl Who Was Plugged In* by James Tiptree, Jr.

The Nemesis from Terra by Leigh Brackett/*Battle for the Stars* by Edmond Hamilton

*The Ugly Little Boy by Isaac Asimov/*The [Widget], the [Wadget] and Boff* by Theodore Sturgeon

*Sailing to Byzantium by Robert Silverberg/*Seven American Nights* by Gene Wolfe

*Houston, Houston, Do You Read? by James Tiptree, Jr./*Souls* by Joanna Russ

*forthcoming

LEIGH BRACKETT

THE NEMESIS FROM TERRA

A TOM DOHERTY ASSOCIATES BOOK
NEW YORK

THE NEMESIS FROM TERRA

Copyright © 1961 by Ace Books, Inc.
Reprinted by permission of the author's estate and the estate's agent, Blassingame-Spectrum Literary Agency.

A TOR Book
Published by Tom Doherty Associates, Inc.
49 West 24 Street
New York, NY 10010

Cover art by Tony Roberts

ISBN: 0-812-55960-6   Can. ISBN: 0-812-55961-4

First Tor edition: May 1989

Printed in the United States of America

0 9 8 7 6 5 4 3 2 1

CHAPTER 1

RICK STOOD PERFECTLY still in the black blind notch of the doorway. The thunder of his own blood in his ears drowned any other sound, but his eyes, cold pale amber under tawny brows, watched the narrow tunnel of the street.

Three shadows came slipping through the greenish pools of moonlight on the age-worn stones.

Rick's left hand rose and steadied. Harsh echoes rolled and slammed between the packed, still rows of houses. Two of the shadows fell without a sound. The third stood upright in a shaft of Phobos-light and screamed.

Rick saw him clearly—a black anthropoid from the sea-bottom pits, one of the queer inhabitants of an evolutionary blind alley you were always running into on Mars. Some said they had once been men, and degenerated in their isolated, barren villages. Others said they were neither man nor ape, just something that got off on a road that went nowhere. Rick didn't care much. All that interested him was that the black apes were trained now like hounds to course men for the press-gangs of the Terran Exploitations Company.

Rick had no wish to slave in the Company mines until he died. He hit the black boy hard in the midriff and shut him up for good. After that, there was silence.

Rick had never heard silence like that before except on the dead worlds. The Company press-gang was beating the whole Quarter, from the stews on the Street of Nine Thousand Joys north into the angle of the city wall, but the noise they made doing it didn't seem to touch the silence of Ruh. It was like the alloy skin of a spaceship, that you couldn't touch with fire or acid or steel.

He went on, down the narrow twisting street. Doors and windows in thick walls, like gouged-out eyes. There were people behind them, all right. You could smell them. Hundreds of centuries of people, too many of them, living there. But it was like walking through the catacombs in the Terran Moon.

That was because there was a new law on Mars—a world

worn threadbare and weary with the weight of time, where the little laws of the city-states had been enough since men could remember. Ed Fallon had come from earth with his Terran Exploitations Company, and now the Company was Law—at the frontiers, beyond ordinary law, making its own rules and breaking men's backs over them. The floating Terran population fought the Company when they could, feebly. The human Martians of the city-states like Ruh barred their doors and windows and prayed destruction on every alien head.

Quite suddenly Rick was up against the city wall, and there was no longer any place to go.

Back of him the crimpers were working in. On the other side of the wall, even if he could climb its enormous bulk, was a three-quarter-mile drop straight down, to the bottom of the dead sea.

Rick turned. His eyes held a green glint.

Two Martian miles away across the sea-bottom, a rocket ship went up from the Company port, slamming like a bullet into the black sky. Southward the broken towers of King City stood high over the flat roofs. A good mile beyond that, hidden in a shallow valley, was New Town, the brawling frontier gateway to half the world whence Rick had come. There were no lights anywhere.

Unseen men fought and cursed and screamed, but the silence didn't go away.

Rick settled his thick wide back against the wall and let his left hand swing free with the weight of the blaster.

Somebody yelled. They had found the dead anthropoids. Rick heard boot-heels hitting the stones, coming closer.

Quite suddenly there was light.

If he hadn't been flat against the wall he wouldn't have seen it. He realized then that the houses on the left didn't run flush to the city wall. There was a gap about two feet wide, and about twenty feet along it somebody had opened a door, a thin, dim crack.

Rick slid into the tunnel, sideways, and fast.

A woman's harsh, angry whisper snarled something in Low Martian. A squatty shadow moved across the bottom of the light. The door began to close. Rick's shoulder hit it just before the bar dropped. Something tumbled away from it with a whooshing gasp. Rick went in, kicked the door shut behind him, and dropped the bar with his right hand. The left held the blaster.

Nobody moved.

The room was cut in the thickness of the city wall. It was little. It stank. The roof touched Rick's rough, tawny head. There was a shelf bed covered with musty blankets, a table of ancient Martian work, hand carved from "yrl-wood" and worth more Universal Credits than Rick could make in ten years of sweating in a glory hole, two worn matching chairs, an old woman, and a dwarf.

The dwarf was curled up in the ashes of a dead fire, gasping. He was no more than a child, thin, with green, slanting eyes. The old woman lay on the shelf bed. Rick took her for just a dirty old woman, until she looked at him.

Her eyes were like moonstones, and Rick would have believed she was blind, had he not noticed her brilliant, deep red pupils.

"Just take it easy," he said in crude Low Martian.

They said nothing. They watched him. Rick's skin crawled.

Back in the street there was noise, but he could tell that they had lost him.

He squatted down against the door. His chest heaved, and his shirt, of iridescent Venusian spider-silk, stuck to his body.

"I'm staying here until they go," he said.

The dwarf hugged his knees. His eyes burned like green coals in the smoky lantern light. The old woman didn't move or speak. From somewhere out of the tangle of blankets a small red lizard appeared and flicked down onto the dirt floor.

"I will read your future," the old woman said slowly.

Rick laughed. "I'm strapped. I got kicked off my ship for slugging the mate, and my pay is all in the pockets of girls I met afterward. If they have pockets."

"I will read your future."

He scowled at her, and then shrugged. There was no way in or out but the door at his back, and certainly nothing to fear from them physically. The noise in the street was no nearer.

"Suit yourself."

"You do not believe?" said the old woman.

"That stuff's all right for women. Me, I believe in what my hands make."

She smiled, showing needle-sharp teeth like a snake's fangs

in the wrinkled dark leather of her face. Her eyes stayed on Rick, with that queer intent stare.

She got up slowly and went to the table. She lifted away a cloth and revealed a silver bowl filled with clear water.

Rick laughed, without malice.

The old woman's blood-red pupils flared wide. "You're a spaceman."

"I was born in a tramp-hull, and I never been out of them since."

"The spaceship is built on a certain world. Is it chained to that world?"

"Gosh, no! What are you driving at?"

"The mind is not chained to the body, Earthman. Thought is like a ship. It can go anywhere. It can open the Gate and walk along the roads of Time. Time is real, as real as this Mars you stand on and as easy to reach, once you know the way."

Rick was scowling, his yellow eyes intent. "Maybe. But I don't believe in a future laid out for me like a treadmill. I make my own as I go along, and too many things can happen."

"Yes. But only one thing does happen. Tonight you ran away from your fellow invaders. You would have been taken for the mine gangs had not my misbegotten grandson opened the door to hear the excitement. And so, for the moment, you are safe. You came to a crossroad. You took one fork. All your possible futures stemming from that moment of choice recede onto another plane in favor of the actual one. Life, Earthman, is a series of crossroads."

"And you think you can shoot your mind up the line a-ways and sort of look over the next one?" Rick asked her.

"Yes."

Rick laughed. "Not bad. Then a guy could always know in advance which road to take, so he'd find the pot of gold and not the mud puddle."

"You still don't believe."

"I've always liked to gamble, myself. Anyway, it doesn't matter."

"No," she said slowly, "it doesn't matter."

She was looking at his face again, his hands, his eyes.

"Contradictions," she murmured, as though Rick wasn't there. "Work has made him thick and coarse, but the bones are fine. The jaw, the nose, the cheekbones, showing through the flesh as the iron ridges show under the moss of the sea-bottoms. But the mouth has yet no shape beyond self-indulgence, and the eyes—the eyes sleep!''

Rick laughed again, easily. ''Is that why you want to read my future?'' His muscles were relaxing. The noise in the street outside had blurred into distance again. The recent strenuous business of getting rid of his roll was catching up to him. He yawned.

He wasn't going to sleep. His mind was still on top. But he felt comfortable. The red lizard skittered across his feet suddenly like a tiny comet.

The old woman's voice had dropped to a whisper. ''Perhaps,'' she said.

She bent her head over the water in the silver bowl.

It got quiet. The air was warm and close. The dwarf hugged his knees in the ashes. The old woman's breathing rose and fell with a slow deep rhythm, like the breathing of the sea. The red lizard moved in silent little rushes over the stone floor, going nowhere.

Rick's mind played idly with the picture of roads stretching ahead in an infinite network. If you got onto one road, and didn't like it, why couldn't you simply cut across the hills to another?

The roads gradually took on a scarlet color. They moved and shifted. He tried to keep track of them, but they flowed around too much. His eyes began to ache. He shut them.

''Yes, this is better,'' he thought. ''Pull down a nice dark curtain. Wake me at seven, Ma.''

The weight of his own head jerking against his neck muscles brought an instinctive grab at slipping consciousness. He opened his eyes, starting half erect.

The old woman was standing by the table, still half bent over the looking-bowl. Her mouth was open, the breath going in and out snakily over her sharp teeth. She was staring at Rick.

The dwarf was on his hands and knees, motionless with fear, like a fly stuck in amber. The red lizard ran and ran and ran, with a terrible silent purpose, getting nowhere.

Rick's body felt as cold as a toad's belly in the rain. He started to get up. The crazy pattern of the lizard's movements drew Rick's attention. Yet without looking at them he could still see the old woman's eyes—whorls of pale cloud caught around a blood-red star.

"What are you trying to do?" he asked her thickly.

He tried to forget the lizard. Part of his brain was already trapped in the scarlet maze. His face twitched.

"Hypnotize me, you shriveled hag! All that bunk about the future! Hypnotize me!"

Sweat ran out of his hair. He braced his feet. His left hand rose, bringing the atom-gun up.

"You'd put me under and then throw me out to those crimps!" he accused her.

Her gaze pressed against his, beating back his strength. Her crimson pupils blazed. Little red suns, burning and terrible.

"You cannot fire, Earthman," she snarled.

He fought his own finger on the blaster's firing stud. The red lizard ran and ran, winding blood-bright threads around his mind.

Suddenly, from somewhere, the old woman caught up a knife.

The force of her thought hammered at him. "You cannot fire!" it said. "You cannot fire!"

Rick's muscles stood out like thick ropes. He sweated heavily, crying with weakness.

The old woman started across the room.

"I saw your future, Earthman," she whispered. "Your future, if you live."

She set the point of the knife against his throat. "I saw your shadow over Mars," she mumbled.

Rick's veins swelled. His face twisted into a death grin. The knife point bit. Then his finger pressed down on the firing stud.

As her face fell away from him, he could still see her eyes, burning red. He laughed, hoarsely, a beast sound without humor. Blood ran hot down his neck, but the knife had clattered to the pavement and she hadn't cut him deeply.

Rick turned. After a while he got the bar up and the door open. He went out. The cold night air shocked some of the dizziness out of his brain, but it felt sluggish in his skull like it had been stunned.

"My shadow," he whispered. "My shadow over Mars."

He went back down the street. The anthropoids still lay where he had shot them. The invulnerable silence of Ruh hung heavy in the moon-shot dark.

He began to shake suddenly with reaction. Weakness overcame him. He leaned against a wall, his chest laboring.

Four black shadows came slipping on silent paws from a side turning. He didn't hear them soon enough. Whirling around, he fired, but they were already on top of him. He went down, under a weight of sinewy bodies, beast-quick, strong, with the musky smell of the furred animal.

Rick's head cracked hard on the stones. He fought for a while, a blind instinctive thrashing of the body. Presently he became quiet.

One of the anthropoids stayed flat on the street. The other three drifted away into the silence, bearing his heavy weight with ease.

Some time later a small, hunched shadow slid out of the narrow space under the city wall and went swiftly south, toward the broken towers on the hill.

CHAPTER 2

PHOBOS HAD SET in the east. Diemos was no more than a red ember, low over the desert. The King City of Ruh lay silent under the sullen glow, its empty towers open to the wind. The moonlight was like a splashing of old blood on the stones.

Only in the lower tiers, that had been the rooms of state, the public offices, the libraries and treasure-houses, were the walls still sound. There was life there.

One flaring torch burned in the throne room, where kings of the line of Karadoc once sat, when there were salty blue seas on Mars, and green hills above them. Only the high seat and the people around it were in the light. Surrounding them was spacious, empty darkness, rustling with old flags, heavy with the ghosts of old glories, breathing out the dry sharp taint of death.

Llaw the dwarf crouched on the ceremonial rug, woven from the long bright hair of virgins whose dust had long since been blown away by wandering winds. The dwarf had been talking for a long time, half chanting, his voice ringing thin against the stone walls. His green eyes were crazy and wild in the torchlight. Suddenly he had ceased to be a child.

From the left side of the throne a woman watched him. She was not old in years, but she was ancient in pride and sorrow, as though some inner fire, banked but unquenchable, had sapped and dried her.

At the right of the throne stood a man. His tough, sinewy body was half bared in the harness of a common soldier, much worn, but his arms and accouterments were bright. His face was lean, scarred, sullen, and savage, and his eyes were the eyes of a caged wolf.

This was Beudach, chief of the fighting men of the Ruh—a warrior without a battle. His soul hung with the tattered banners in the hall. To his King he had given his heart, and his whole knowledge of harms and the way of using them. Now he watched the grandson of the seeress as a prisoner watches the turning of the key in his cell lock.

On the throne itself sat a boy.

He was dark, and bright, and beautiful. He was like a sword-blade, or a new spear, and the fire that smoldered in his mother blazed in him. He was Haral, last of the line of Karadoc, with the plain, ancient iron Collar of Ruh locked proudly on his young throat.

Llaw the dwarf stopped speaking.

For a while there was silence. Then Haral spoke.

"His shadow over Mars," he said slowly.

"My grandmother saw it, Lord," insisted the dwarf. "She was a great seeress."

"The Rule of Mars to an Earthman," mused Haral. "The outland yoke hammered on our necks to stay."

The woman cried out, but the wolf-faced man was before her, bending over the throne.

"Now, Lord! Now is the time to strike, if there's any blood or pride left in the men of Mars!"

The boy rose, slowly. The torchlight crimsoned his white skin.

"Beudach."

The wolf-faced man dropped to one knee. "Send Parras to me."

Beudach went away, smiling.

"Do you know where this Earthman is?" Haral asked Llaw.

"No, Lord. But I will find him." He licked his lips. "There is a blood debt."

"It shall be paid."

The woman set her hands on the arm of the high seat and laughed, once, silently.

Beudach returned. There was a man with him, a plump, smiling, youngish man in a sky-blue robe. His eyes were like those of the dead seeress, moonstones flecked with red.

"I want word given to the leaders of every city that pays seizin to Ruh," Haral said to him. "Say that the old Banner of the Twin Moons is raised again, this time against the tyrants of Earth. Tell them to gather what strength they can, and hold it in readiness, and to send their chief warriors here to Ruh, secretly, for a council of war. Llaw!"

The dwarf sprang up.

"Go with Parras. Give him the description of this Earthman, Rick, so that he can warn the cities to watch for him. Then go yourself and spread the word through Ruh."

Llaw and Parras bowed and started out. Haral stopped them.

"Wait. You must give them a slogan." He laughed, boylike, his face aglow with excitement. "Give them the old one, the oldest one on Mars—the cry of the sailors and the sea-board men when the oceans rose out of their beds, and after that the cry of the people who live in the deserts and the wastes where the seas were. Tell them, Parras—'The wind is rising!' "

The dwarf and the seer went out. Haral sprang down from the high seat. He caught his mother and whirled her around and kissed her, and then pulled Beudach's sword from the scabbard behind his left shoulder.

He shouted and threw it high in the air. The blade turned over and over in the torchlight, hurling red sparks at the darkness, and fell. Haral caught it deftly by the hilt.

Beudach watched him. There were tears in his eyes.

Ten days later Ed Fallon, head of the Company, was standing at his high window, gazing out at the vast panorama of Mars. He heard the door of his office open, but he didn't turn his head. He didn't have to. Only Jaffa Storm's tread had that particular strong, uneven rhythm.

"Come over here," Fallon said. "By gosh, it's worth looking at."

Storm put down his sheaf of reports on Fallon's desk and went over to the wide glassite window. He was a big man, nearly seven inches over six feet, with a body like a gladiator's under his black, close-fitting coverall, and his slight limp gave

no impression of weakness. There was a "Mickey" holstered
on his lean hip.

He stood beside Fallon, dwarfing even his thick-chested,
powerful build. He said nothing, but his black eyes saw everything with a sombre, rather terrible thoroughness.

"My baby," said Fallon. He struck his red-haired hands
together and laughed. "She's growing up, Jaffa. Pretty soon
she'll have all of Mars to play with."

His eyes had sparks in them, watching the surging strength
of his baby—the Terran Exploitations Company, called simply,
the Company.

Fallon's office was on the top floor of the Administration
Pylon. It was walled with glassite, and gave a full-circle view
of the Company world—laboratories, processing division,
foundries, forges, tool shops, the vast pit-head housings with
their train sheds, and beyond them, far enough away to be safe
from the rocket-blasts, the Company spaceport, whence the
cargoes of Fallonite went Earthward.

Apart from all these, behind charged walls of metalloy,
were the barracks where the Company work-gangs lived, while
they lived.

The pylon was high enough to show other things, too. The
sea-bottom, spreading away into pale distance under the Martian sun, its gaunt ribs showing naked through the blue-gray
moss. And to the south, the Old City of Ruh, like the broken
crown of a dead king dropped and forgotten on its soaring
crag.

Death was out there. Age and cessation. Fallon thought no
more of it than he did of last year's worn-out shoes. He watched
the life of his Company, the thunder and sweat and surge of
machinery and the men who bossed it, and it was his own life,
his own blood and sweat and surging energy.

Young, that baby, like Earth's intrusion onto dying Mars,
but already stretching out muscular hands to close around a
planet. A planet whose central government was no more than
a feeble token, with the real power scattered wide among the
city-states still clinging to the deserts and the sea-bottoms and
the barren hills. A planet practically untouched by outland
hands until the discovery of Fallonite. It was disunited, in-
grown, weak, an easy touch for the first strong man who could
see wealth and power springing out of its fallow fields.

"By gosh," said Fallon again, softly, "it's worth looking at."

"Yes," said Storm, also softly. He limped over and sprawled his huge length onto a couch, pulling cigarettes from his breast pocket. His thick hair was blacker than his coverall, his skin hardly lighter. He was Terro-Mercurian, born and bred in the blazing, thundering valleys of the Twilight Belt, where legend had it that the babies came with horns and tails, and with all the heart burned out of them with the heat.

Fallon turned back to his desk, looking with distaste at the stack of papers.

"Bah! I'd rather be back in the foundry than mess with this stuff."

"You're a liar," said Storm. "You're a conniving, crafty old fox, and you love it. You never were a laboring man at heart, anyway."

Fallon looked at him. He decided to laugh.

"You're not a comfortable guy to have around." He sat down. "How you coming with those new men?"

"Like always. There's one big yellow-eyed devil I may have to kill. I hope not. He's strong as a horse."

Fallon chuckled. "Nothing like a cheap labor supply! And as long as I pull the strings that make the New Town go, it'll be jammed with the best supply there is—floaters, homesteaders, placer men, space-hands, bums—guys who can vanish with no kicks but their own."

"Until the law moves in."

Fallon roared with mirth. "Yeah! That worries me a lot!"

"Uh huh. Just the same, I hope they don't get leery about going into the Old City. I'd rather take 'em there. Not so tough on our men. The Marshies just sit tight and hope we'll kill each other off. In the New Town, they don't like crimpers." Fallon shrugged. "That's your worry, Jaffa. Just keep those pits open, that's all I want."

"You'll get what you want."

Fallon nodded. He sweated over the papers for a time in silence. Storm sat still, smoking. Outside, the Company hurled its rude and alien noise against the quiet of Mars.

Presently Storm spoke. "I was in Ruh last night. Old Ruh."

"Have a good time?"

"Fallon, I smell trouble."

The red-haired man looked up. "Trouble?"

"The city feels different. It has felt different, since that last raid ten days ago."

"What the devil! Are you going psychic on me? The Marshies won't even say good morning to us. And besides, those ancient, washed-out little twerps wouldn't have the getup to make trouble."

"Listen, Fallon.'' Storm leaned forward. "I spent four seasons in the cliff-caves of Arianrhod, down on the edge of Darkside. The people aren't human, but they know things, and I learned a few of them."

His dark face twitched slightly. "I walked through Ruh last night, and I felt it, through the walls and the darkness and the silence. There's a new feeling in the people. Fear, restlessness, a peculiar urgency. I don't know why, yet, or what it will lead to. But there's a new thing being whispered back of those closed doors. They're telling each other 'The wind is rising!' ''

His sombre black gaze held Fallon. After a while, in the stillness, Fallon repeated the phrase.

"The wind is rising."

He laughed suddenly. "Well, let it! It'll take a bigger wind than any old Mars has left to blow my walls down!"

The telescreen hummed, calling for attention. Fallon flipped the connection.

"Kahora calling—Mr. Hugh St. John," the operator said.

"Put him through." Fallon winked broadly at Storm and then composed his face to a friendly smile. The screen flickered and cleared.

"Hello, Fallon," Hugh St. John said. "Are you busy?"

"Not for you. What's on your mind?"

"Mind? I'm beginning to wonder if I have one!" St. John's sensitive, aquiline face looked tired and discouraged. He had untidy fair hair and blue eyes that were unexpectedly shrewd and penetrating.

"Things not going so well, huh?" Fallon said.

St. John laughed bitterly. "The whole purpose of the Unionist movement is to promote understanding between Earthmen and the Martians, so that each can give his best to the other without hurting either. And what have we done so far? We've caused a complete break between the Pan-Martians and the Moderates, and the feelings between our two races get worse every day. No, Fallon. Things are not going so well."

"Are there any new rumors of—well, trouble? Rioting, let's say?"

"We have contact now only with the Moderates, and there aren't many of them, as you know. They're shunned as bitterly as we are. And of course here in Kahora we don't know much about the Outside. You know what a Trade City's like. I should think you'd have more chance of hearing than we."

"There's nothing that I know of," Fallon said innocently. "Look here—you need more money?"

St. John nodded. "Well, if we could carry on our work in the Polar cities, there's a bare chance. The Thinkers are re-vered all over Mars, and if we could win them over they might swing native opinion our way. But you've already given so much it seems wasteful."

"I still got plenty. How much?"

"Well, about five thousand U.C.'s ought to be about right."

"Make it six, and let me know when you need more. I'll send the draft through right away."

St. John's eyes glowed mistily. "Fallon, I don't know what we'd do without you!"

"I'm not giving away anything. Mars means as much to me as it does to you." Fallon raised his hand. "So long pal."

"Good bye. And thanks."

The screen went dead. Fallon leaned back in his chair and grinned.

"The fool," he said. "The dear, sweet, lily-livered fool!"

Storm watched him with faint amusement. "Sure of that?"

"What do you mean?" snapped Fallon. "I've brought that Union Party up practically by hand. Give them something to focus their opinions on, and they start tearing each other's heads off in no time, never knowing it's what I want them to do."

Storm shrugged. "I wonder?" he said.

"By heavens, Jaffa, you're so suspicious I wonder you trust yourself."

"I don't," said Storm quietly. "That's why I've stayed alive."

Fallon stared at him. And then, for the second time, the telescreen hummed—emitting a series of short, nervous sounds. The "urgent" signal.

Both men went to it, quickly. The screen sprang to life. A man in greasy coveralls leaned forward as though he were trying to come through physically. There was blood running down his face.

"Trouble in Number Five drift. That new gang has gone wild."

"How bad is it?" demanded Fallon, his tones sharp, hoarse.

"They took the guards. Beat 'em down with their shackle chains. That big guy Rick, he's leading them. After grabbing four Mickeys, they dug in behind some ore cars, and they got four Mickeys."

"A Mickey never gave you that."

The man wiped blood off his face with his fingers. "They're throwing ore fragments. My guess is they'll make a rush for the shaft."

"Very well, I'll be right down." Fallon killed the screen and turned to his companion. "How many men in that gang, Jaffa?"

"Thirty-two."

Fallon made another connection and spoke briefly to the huge white Venusian on the visaplate. The picture showed racks of arms and other huge men in the background. It had been Jaffa Storm's idea to have an all-Venusian corps of Middle-Swampers for his strong-arm work. Being outlanders and fairly savage, they had interest in two things only—food and fighting. Storm saw to it they had plenty of both.

"Vargo send fifteen men down to Number Five drift," Fallon said. "Take a high-power Banning shocker. There's thirty-two guys down there want to play rough, and they're all yours!"

CHAPTER 3

MAYO McCALL LOOKED down through the glassite wall of her booth ten feet above the floor of Number Five drift. Thirty feet to her right was the shaft where the Fallonite ore went up to the surface. To her left was the brilliantly-illuminated tunnel that followed the vein out under the waste of the dead sea-bottom.

Mayo McCall watched the men running back and forth below. Quite calmly she reached out and closed the switch that controlled her testing beam—the ray that spanned the head of

the drift and checked every carload of dull red rock for Fallonite content, the chemically amorphous substance that was already beginning to revolutionize the Terran plastic industry.

Mayo was alone. No one on the drift floor was paying any
attention to her. She folded her arms on the table in front of
her and peeled back the sleeve of her dark green technician's
overall. She pressed a hidden stud on her wristwatch.

The lens and half the silver case rose, revealing a micro-
scopic two-way radio. Mayo counted five slowly, watching the
men below. Her brown eyes held a deep glow. She had a strong,
supple body whose curves even the coverall couldn't hide, and
hair of a rich, warm mahogany color that made her skin look
like cream.

"Go ahead," the radio whispered.

Softly, distinctly, without moving her lips, Mayo McCall
spoke.

"There's trouble with a new gang, here in my drift. Set the
amplifiers and recorders. I'm going down . . . Wait. A bunch
of Venusian guards just arrived with a Banning shocker. This
looks big. It may be just what we've wanted."

"Be careful, Mayo. You know what they'll do if they discover what you're doing."

"I know. There goes Fallon and Jaffa Storm. This ought to
be good. Stay with me."

She pulled her sleeve down carefully. The loose cloth covered the radio. She opened the door of the booth.

The drift was empty now for as far as she could see. She
went quickly down the plastic steps and turned left, going silently and keeping close to the red rock wall. The rails of the
dilly road glinted burnished silver in the white glare.

From up ahead, around a bend in the tunnel, came the sudden brittle whine of a heavy-duty shocker cutting in.

The first beam was low power. Crouched behind an ore car,
Rick felt the shock run through him like liquid fire. It made
his heart pound, but the pain wasn't too much to take.

There were twenty-two men spread out beside him along the
rail. The other nine had been put to sleep with the Mickey
shockguns of the guards, in the first scrimmage. The focus of
the Banning was widened to take in the lot.

"Jimminy! We can't take that!" one of the men cried shrilly.
"They'll step up the power."

"Shut up," Rick told him. The Venusian, Vargo, called to

them. He looked innocent and happy, incongruously like a nice
old lady with the dead-white hair coiled high on his head.

"You come out now, eh?" he said to the miners.

No answer. Vargo looked around. Jaffa Storm had just come
up, running easily with his odd, limping stride. Fallon was
some distance behind him. Fallon waved his hand.

"It's your show, boys!" he shouted.

He stopped, not too close, and lounged against the wall.

"Advance your power at the rate of one notch per second,"
Storm said quietly. The Venusian with the Banning grinned and
took hold of the small lever. "I will count to ten," Storm said
clearly, to no one in particular.

It grew very still under the cold brilliance. Rick peered
around a wheel. The manacles clashed softly as he raised the
Mickey in his twitching, jerking hand.

He didn't fire. The little guns had a shorter range than the
distance a strong man could throw an ore fragment, which was
why the rebels still had opposition. The Company men moved
back beyond the ore fragments.

Rick watched the lever click forward on the Banning. Little
blue lights began to flicker on the rim of the wheel in front of
him. His body began to jerk with the same erratic violence.
Each separate nerve stood out in coruscating agony.

Jaffa Storm began to count.

Jaffa Storm's voice echoed under the stone vault with the
rhythmic impersonality of a clock tolling.

When he said, "Five," one of the rebel miners began to
scream.

"I'm coming out!" he shrieked. "I'm coming out!" Jaffa
Storm stopped counting. He held his hand out, flat. The cur-
rent stayed level. In the dead silence the man crawled across
the rock, his shadow black and inhuman beneath him. His
wristchains dragged, clashing.

Six others followed. Rick watched them. Once he tried to
raise the Mickey, but his hand was like an old man's, palsied
and without strength.

Storm began to count again.

Three times the advancing lever was stopped while men
crawled and whimpered across the rock. When Storm said,
"Ten," there was only one man left beside Rick. He must have
had a weak heart. He was dead.

"Cut your power," Storm said.

The Venusian looked surprised, but he thumbed the stud. The whining stopped. Rick's body went lax. He lay face down, breathing in hoarse animal gasps. Sweat lay like thick oil on his skin.

"Rick," Storm said. "Are you ready to quit?"

After a long while Rick laughed.

"I suppose," said Storm, "you think I'll kill you anyway."

Rick's words had no shape to them, but their meaning was plain.

Storm nodded. He gestured to the Venusian. The man got up, and Storm sat down behind the Banning.

The guards and the dough-faced exhausted men moved back, against the wall. They didn't speak. Their breathing sounded harsh and loud. A still white glare filled the drift.

Storm lighted a cigarette, without haste. He placed matches in the pack, weighted it, and threw it. He didn't appear to strain at all, but the pack struck the wall behind Rick with audible force.

Presently Rick got his knees under him. He picked up the cigarette and sat back against the rock, dragging smoke deep into his lungs. It was quiet enough so that the faint sizzling of the illuminating tube sounded very loud. Rick looked up at it.

It was sunk in a trough in the ceiling and protected with heavy wire screen. There was no way to break it. Rick knew that. He'd already tried every way there was. The main switch for the whole length of the tube was back near the mouth of the drift. There were also switches for the individual sections, but they were not within his reach.

He sat almost at the peak of an oblique bend in the drift. To his left the tunnel ran into a dead end, without side galleries or even cover of any kind. Most of it, because the bend was shallow, was in clear range of the Banning.

Almost directly in front of him, in the opposite wall, was the dark opening of an abandoned side gallery. It probably led into a cul-de-sac, although it might, just possibly, cut into one of those endless mazes left by the giant mud-worms of prehistoric Mars, whose tunnelings remain fossilized under the sea-bottoms. In either case, it would mean only the difference between a fast death and a slow one, and as for reaching it, it might as well have been on Phobos.

Off to his right, across the naked, pitiless stone, Jaffa Storm dropped his cigarette and stepped on it.

He leaned forward. His hands touched the Banning with gentle delicacy. He tilted the muzzle high and flashed an experimental beam. This time the focus was tight, the power-whine hysterically high.

A thin stream of pale and crackling fire licked out, touched the opposite wall, and was gone. The smoking surface was fused like glass.

Quite suddenly one of the chained men turned his face to the wall and began to vomit.

Rick crouched down behind a metal wheel. His yellow eyes had the cold cruelty of those of a cat. His body was relaxed and still.

Jaffa Storm leveled the Banning, his dark face betraying neither pleasure nor interest.

He laid the beam on the disc of Rick's wheel and let it stay.

The nearness of the charge sent fire shocking through Rick's flesh. The wheel began to heat. Blue flames danced on its rim. Sweat poured down Rick's face, and dried, and the skin reddened angrily. His eyes were tortured.

He sprang suddenly, sideways along the rail, toward another wheel. The beam flicked over his head and came down ahead of him. He leaped back, making a dash the other way. Again the beam was quicker.

He dropped behind the wheel again. The beam found the disc and stayed.

Rick measured the distance to the gallery opening. He laughed silently, without humor, and gathered himself.

From the empty drift, beyond Storm and the men and the Venusian guards, beyond Ed Fallon, leaning white-faced against the wall, came a woman's voice.

"Stop!" it said.

Hasty footsteps rang against the tunnel vault. Voices broke loose in a nervous babble. The heat and the blue fire went away from the wheel. Rick looked around it, cautiously.

He saw the girl and she was beautiful. Even in that technician's coverall she made a lovely picture as she hastened to Jaffa Storm. Her hair clung in deep sorrel curls around her face, her brown eyes were blazing. She was so full of fury that she actually seemed to give off light.

"Stop that," she said. "Stop it!"

Fallon was coming up behind her. He looked rather sick.

"I've stopped," said Storm, mildly.

"It isn't enough for you to take these men off the free streets and chain them up and make slaves of them. You have to murder them, too!"

Storm rose lazily, motioning the Venusian back to the Banning.

"Do I do all those things, Miss?"

"Don't try to be funny! You know it's the truth."

"How do you know I do?"

"Everybody knows it!"

"Do they. Do they really." Storm's hand shot out so quickly that it was only a blurred flash. He pulled her close and said with friendly curiosity, "Or are you just trying to make me admit it, perhaps for someone else to hear?"

His free hand went over her with impersonal swiftness. She struggled, striking at him with her left arm. He laughed. He caught her wrist, and there was a faint snap of metal. He held her tight and peeled the sleeve back.

"Yes," he said. "Yes, I thought so."

He stripped off the watch-radio and crushed it under his heel.

Fallon whistled softly. "I better take her up to the office."

Storm nodded. His black eyes were warm. The girl lay quiet in his arms. The neck of her dark-green coverall had been torn open, and her throat and cheeks were smooth like new cream.

"You're awfully strong," she whispered. She shivered and let her head roll back against him. Her eyes were closed. "I guess I'm caught."

"M-m-mh."

"Are you going to kill me?" she asked him.

"That might depend."

She raised her lashes. "I don't think I want to die yet."

He laughed. He held her off, facing him, so he could look into her eyes.

"That's awfully quick work, baby."

"Time doesn't mean much in a spot like this."

"You're a liar, precious. A most beautiful, lovely liar."

She said nothing. Her lips were warm, rosy and alive.

"I can read your mind," Storm said.

"You're awfully smart," she murmured. "Because I can't read it myself."

Storm laughed again, softly. He bent his towering height and kissed her, taking his time.

In the middle of it, with her mouth still pressing his, she brought her knee up, hard, with deadly accuracy.

Rick shouted. Jaffa Storm doubled up, his face twisted with stunned agony. The girl kicked him again, on the knee, and broke free.

"I've trained my mind, too," she yelled, and ran.

The Venusians burst into a sudden raucous howl of laughter at Storm, who was huddled over on his knees, retching. The manacled men joined in.

Fallon made a grab for the girl. He missed, but some of the guards ran out and her back to the shaft was barred. From behind the ore car Rick bellowed.

"The light switch!"

Her gaze flicked from him to the switch near the tunnel mouth, all in the instant between one step and the next. The switch was on the opposite wall, away from the guards. She moved.

"Don't fire!" Fallon yelled. "I want her alive." He began to run, with half a dozen big Middle-swampers loping past him. The girl was going like a dark-green comet.

Jaffa Storm got up. He kept his body bent, but his feet were steadier than Rick knew his would have been. There was no expression on his face, not even pain. He struck the Venusian away from the Banning. He laid him out cold, and never glanced at the body. He fired. His beam went between two Venusians, close enough to singe them, and hit the wall five feet to the girl's left. She didn't falter.

"Stop that!" Fallon yelled furiously. "She's got to be questioned!"

Storm fired again. The Venusians had scattered out of the way. The girl dropped flat, rolling. The beam missed her by the minimum margin, and then Rick was on his feet, running fast across the stone pathway.

He shouted. Storm's attention wavered slightly. Without breaking stride, Rick threw what was in his left hand.

It was an ore fragment. It was heavy, and jagged. It took Storm across the left side of his face and knocked him flat.

The light went out.

The Banning was still on. Its beam made an eerie unreal shimmer in the blackness. Rick's eyes adjusted quickly. He was heading for the tunnel mouth before Storm hit the ground, and in the bluish glimmer he made out the girl's shadow, racing for the same place. Elsewhere, pandemonium was on a holiday.

Nobody chased them. They were afraid of the Banning. There was a heaving and profane commotion back against the wall. Somebody got hold of the Banning finally and screamed, "Watch out!" and started to flash the beam around. Rick and the girl collided at the tunnel mouth and fell. The tongue of flame licked the air, crackling, where their heads had been, and flashed past. Before it could come back they had plunged into the pitch darkness of the gallery.

It turned. They crashed the blind wall and clawed around the corner, and behind them the Banning beam hit the rock and chewed away in a baffled fury.

"Come on," Rick said.

They went, faster than any sane people would have dared. They fought the rock walls and the trash of abandoned digging on the ground, the darkness, and themselves.

Three times Rick thought, "This is it. End of the tunnel. Dead end!" Then his groping hands would slide around a corner, and they'd go on.

Suddenly, quite suddenly, the drift changed. The floor was round, like a huge pipe, instead of level. There was no debris. The walls were curved, with a curious regular smoothness under the hand.

After a while they slowed, and then stopped. The silence lay as dead and heavy as the darkness. Their hoarse breathing had a quality of sacrilege, like noise in a tomb.

Instinctively they moved close together, close enough to touch. Rick's wrist-chains clashed softly.

"They haven't followed," the girl whispered.

"No. They'll send the black boys. The anthropoids."

Silence. Blood drumming hot behind their ears.

"We're in one of those mazes I've heard about, aren't we?" the girl murmured. "Where the big worms used to crawl before the sea-bottoms hardened."

"That's right."

"Is there any way out?"

"I don't know. Sometimes worm tunnels lead into a pit, or a cliff face. Sometimes the roof has been cracked. About this one, I don't know."

"Not a very good chance, is it?" But her voice showed no fear.

"I wouldn't give odds."

Silence. Their breathing, their body heat, their fear, mingling in the thick dark.

"What's your name?" Rick asked the girl.

"Mayo McCall. What's yours?"

"Richard Gunn Urquhart, but Rick's enough."

"Hello, Rick."

"Hello, Mayo." He found her shoulder and shook it. "You have courage, baby. Ha, I hope you ruined that big scut for life."

"That rock of yours didn't do him any good."

"I got a hunch it didn't finish him," said Rick. "I hope it didn't. I'd like to see that guy again, some day."

"And Fallon?" she asked him.

"Fallon and the whole blasted Company," Rick's voice was vicious. "I'd like to boot them clean to . . ."

After a while Mayo whispered, "Maybe you could, if we're lucky," Mayo whispered, after a while.

"What do you mean?" asked Rick. "Go on, explain."

"If we live, I might show you how," said the girl. "We'd better go now. Which way?"

"Which wrist am I holding?"

She moved it slightly. "The left."

"That's the way we go, then. And baby, you better be lucky!"

CHAPTER 4

WIND MOVED SIGHING through the broken walls, and the dusk came down to join it. Far out across the western wastes Phobos rode the last pale glow of the sun edging the rim of Mars. Ruh lay silent, barred and shuttered, but not asleep.

With night shadows crept through the streets. Some of them came drifting in through secret portals in the city wall and then sought the heights of the King City, where they vanished. Upon entering the flaring torchlight in the throne room, however, they became men.

Fighting men. Of different ages, sizes, coloring, in the harness of different city-states, but all alike in one thing—the look they bore. The look of wolves in a cage.

They sat around a table of blood-red wood worn hollow by the arms of centuries of war chiefs. Haral the boy king leaned forward like a bent blade from his high seat, and the eyes of Beudach, who stood always at his right hand, were as steel in the fire.

Only one shadow remained in the Quarters. It was small and hunched and swift-moving, and its eyes burned emerald in the Phobos-light. It went from door to door, whispering, asking, and the name it said was "Rick."

High up against the stars, in the ruined Tower of Destiny, Parras, the Seer, bent his fresh young face above his looking bowl. His mend reached out across the sea-bottoms, the sand deserts, the age-worn hills. It touched other minds, asking, and the name it said was "Rick."

To the green-eyed shadow and the mind of the seer came an unvarying answer.

"Not yet."

"Wait, then," Parras would tell them. "Keep watching. There is a blood debt to be paid. 'The wind is rising!' "

Down in the mine gallery, Rick put his hand on Mayo's shoulder. "Hold it," he cautioned the girl. "I thought I heard something."

They stood still. Presently Rick heard the noises quite clearly, somewhere far behind them in the stale blackness of the wormbore. The soft scrambling noises of many creatures, running.

"What'll we do?" Mayo asked.

"Keep going, I guess. I've only got one Mickey, and that won't even slow 'em down. Tired?"

"I'm all right. What happens when they catch us?"

"Ask me then."

They went on again. The going was fairly easy, the floor smooth and the turns gradual. Rick knew they must have left their original bore long ago, branching off into only the stars knew how many intersecting tunnels. He had no idea how long they had been wandering, only that it was too long. They simply kept going because there was nothing else to do.

The anthropoids, fresh and running easily by scent, drew closer by the minute. Rick hung back a little, behind the girl.

Quite suddenly Mayo gave a strangled cry and fell heavily.

There was a dry sound of something splitting. Rick tried to
stop, tripped, and went sprawling.

There was a smoothly serrated surface under him. It tapered
upward, widening to the sides. He scrambled up and followed
it, with Mayo beside him.

"The tunnel's blocked," she gasped. "Rick, it's blocked!"

"Sure. Here, climb up." He pulled her onto the top of the
obstruction and began to crawl. Presently his head hit the roof.
He reached out, groping. The obstruction curved into the side
of the bore, sealing it completely.

Rick let his breath out, hard. He lay still, utterly relaxed,
and listened to his heart. It was like thunder. The sweat felt
cold on his skin. Mayo lay beside him, breathing unevenly.

Behind them, another sound grew louder, closing in.

After a while Rick pushed himself backward and turned
around. He got the Mickey in his hand and sat waiting. His
body was like lead. He slid his right hand out the length of the
chain and found the girl's slender palm.

She gripped his fingers, and her grasp was cold, like ice.
They sat listening to the soft rushing footsteps.

Suddenly she spoke, rather loudly. "What is this thing,
Rick?"

"Don't know." He ran his knuckles over the smooth ser-
rations. "Hey! Yes I do, too! It's the guy that built this tunnel—
the old crawler himself. He died here, and turned to stone."

He laughed, not because it was particularly funny. He gave
the fossil a crack with the barrel of the Mickey.

It rang hollow.

Rick hit it again, harder, and then he remembered the brittle
cracking sound when Mayo fell. He got up on his knees, balled
his fists together, and struck down with all his strength.

It nearly jarred his teeth out, but he knew. "Oh, cracky!"
he whispered. "If I only had a pick, or a big maul!" He
laughed again, sharply. He slid the heavy manacles as far down
as they would go on his hands, wrapped the chain around them,
and went to work.

He had a crack started when the anthropoids began to swarm
up over the slope of the worm's tail.

Mayo took the Mickey. Rick went on pounding. They were
so far back in the cleft between the fossil and the roof that the
brutes had to come at them from the front only, and not many
at a time. Mayo did all right with the Mickey, for a while. The

shock-charge put the leading anthropoids to sleep, and their bodies rolled back to trip the ones coming up behind them. It was a blind fight. The blackness was choked with the sound of feet and moving bodies, and a rank animal smell. The anthropoids worked silently.

Rick drowned everything else with the smashing thunder of his manacles on the echoing stone.

"The Mickey's dead, Rick," Mayo reported at last. "The charge is gone."

"Come here. I've made a hole." She found it. "Can you break the edges back?"

"I think so." He heard her kicking, beating and straining. Things snapped. Anthropoid paws found his leg and pulled him backward. He swung. He didn't have hands any more, only a numb mass bound together with metal. The mass hit something, and for the first time there was a scream.

"It's coming!" Rick heard Mayo say.

He swung again. The blackness was full of bodies. Every time Rick swung he hit something. There was a new smell, warm and dank and sweetish. His arms were wet.

There were too many bodies. They weighed him down. He went on swinging until his arms were held tight. He kicked. Things smashed and fell away from his boots, but they came back again. Presently his legs were held, too. He heaved and twisted. Some of the paws were shaken loose. For a moment he was almost free. He got in a few good ones, and then he was down again. From a great distance Mayo's voice was calling out.

"Rick! Rick, come on!" it said.

He tried it, but it was no good. And then suddenly a cyclone hit the heaving mass on top of him, and there were gaps in the paws that held him. Mayo screamed and tugged at him.

He used strength which he didn't know he had left, to thrash free. Mayo plunged down the hole, dragging his feet after her. An anthropoid grappled with him. He slugged it with his irons and dropped through into the inside of the fossil worm. Two of the brutes tried to get through the hole at once and jammed there.

Mayo helped him up and they staggered away down the worm's interior.

They were knee deep in dust. The intestinal structure had fallen away, crumbled, and dried, while the outer shell hard-

ened. The clouds that rose behind them slowed the anthropoids. Rick and Mayo went on, far beyond their physical
strength driven by a raw, primitive urge for survival.

It came to Rick dimly, after a while, that something was
happening.

"Falling in," he said thickly. "Vibration—cracking it."

It was horrible in the dark. Smothering dust, the noise of
splitting destruction everywhere. Parts of the shell had become
homogeneous with the hardened mud, and apparently that was
caving in, too. The miners always feared the treacherous strata
away from the true rock that held the ore veins.

There were screams again behind them.

"When we reach the head there won't be any place to go,"
Mayo said suddenly. "Solid rock."

The cracking ran forward over their heads. A falling mass
grazed Rick's shoulder. He pushed the girl on faster. Dust rolled
strangling against their lungs. There was a terrible, crushing,
bottled-up thunder.

Their heads struck the top abruptly. They dropped, crawling. The space narrowed in on them. The dust thickened. Mayo
whimpered hoarsely. There was a ripping, splitting crash!

Dead end . . .

Several days later, Hugh St. John was standing on the terrace
of his apartment, well up in the tallest building in Kahora, the
Trade City for Mars. His sensitive young face was drawn and
grim. He nervously was smoking a slender Venusian cigarette.

Kahora was halfway around the planet from Ruh and Fallon's
Company. It was night. Diemos rode low in the purple-
black sky above the glassite dome that covered the city, shielding its polyglot inhabitants from the naked weather of Mars.

Down below, the streets of Kahora lay like a little web of
jewels. St. John listened to the city's pulse. It was a slow, quiet
beat. The business that went on here was the sterile handling
of things already made and done, figures added up by sleek
men who spent their idle hours in the Dream Palace and the
exotic night clubs. Even the air was artificial, carefully cleaned,
scented, and kept at an even temperature.

He had been in Vhia, the Trade City for Venus. That hadn't
been so bad. Venus was a young planet, lusty and strong. Even
the glassite dome hadn't been able to keep out the savage beat
of the rains and the sense of hot jungle just outside. Men were

busy there, too, the heart and brain of the commerce of a thrusting, aggressive world. Where there was enmity with the Venusians, it had been a healthy one.

Here everything was old, passive, faded and worn out. Even the Martian hatred of the Earthmen, the invaders, was a silent thing, festering in barren darkness. The stream of Martian trade flowed through Kahora like the chilling blood of an old man already three-quarters dead.

St. John's mouth twisted bitterly. The only living thing on Mars was Ed Fallon and his alter ego, the Company. Alive, he thought, like an evil beast—hungry, independent, and fatal.

Presently the robot servant at the door identified and admitted the man St. John had been waiting for.

"Mak," St. John cried. "Mak, did you find out anything?"

Eran Mak shook his head. He was Martian, a Low-Canaler from over Jekkara way, and he looked like what he was—a civilized bandit. The dubious fame of his people went as far back into Martian history as the history itself. He was small, tough and wiry, with a slender dark face, a friendly smile, and eyes like drops of hot gold. He wore a cluster of tiny bells in his left ear, and his clothing, the fashionable white tunic of the Trade Cities, gave him the satanic look.

"I'm afraid there's not much hope, Hugh," he said quietly. "I finally made connections with Christy. Since they found out about Mayo, he's scared green. She and this fellow Rick got away all right, into an abandoned drift, but heaven only knows what happened after that. Christy says they sent the black boys after them, and only a few came back. Some of them were all messed up—crushed arms and such, as though they'd been caught in a cave-in. So I guess they're both done for."

He lifted his lean shoulders. St. John turned away.

"Were you in love with her, Hugh?" Eran Mak was one of the few who could venture to ask such a question. He was St. John's best friend.

"I don't know. I don't think I could have sent her there if I had been in love with her. And yet, when I knew she was caught, and her radio suddenly stopped sending, my heart turned to ice." Suddenly he shivered. "Mak, if she's dead, then I killed her!"

"She knew what she was doing," Mak consoled him.

St. John shuddered again. He sat down and put his face in his hands.

Eran Mak crossed the terrace and also seated himself, the little bells tinkling faintly as he moved. He smoked a cigarette in silence. Then he frowned.

"This is going to make Fallon awfully suspicious," he said.

St. John drew a long breath. "That's true. Well, I'll stall him as long as I can. Anyway, I cashed his last draft!" He rose abruptly. "I don't know how we can manage to continue the work without the rat's money."

"It may not matter. There's a storm brewing, Hugh. One devil of a big thundering storm. It's all under cover, but here and there a little puff of breeze warns of a gathering tornado. It may blow us all clean off Mars."

"And this world's last chance for life will be gone. I've failed, Mak. My whole plan has been a fool's dream from the beginning."

He gripped the rail of the terrace, looking out over the jeweled city.

"Think what we could give them, Mak, if they'd only let us! The strength, the new ideas, the new roads to travel! But they won't allow it. They slam their doors in our faces, and the Martian Planetary Government only refrains from kicking us off into space because they don't want open trouble with Earth and Venus.

"Only Ed Fallon gets anywhere. He's going to own all Mars in a few years, because of that cursed ore he discovered. Money will make such a big noise in the Government's ears that any yelling the people do won't amount to a penny whistle in a hurricane. And Mars will be just as dead, either way it goes."

He hit the rail hard with his hand and started pacing.

"My only chance of getting rid of Fallon failed when Mayo was caught before she could get proof of what he and Storm are doing. With that, I might have gone to the Interplanetary Coordination Authority—their Labor Board would have made an investigation. But now it's too late!"

He sat down again.

Eran Mak set the tiny bells chiming with his fingertip.

"You know what I think?" he answered. "I think the job needed a bigger man than you, or me, or any of us. It would take a whale of a big man to unify Mars—all the scraps and pieces of us from Jekkara to the Pole, withdrawn into our little city-shells, sitting in the dust and hugging our memories. If we could find a Goliath like that, there might still be a chance."

"You might as well ask for Phobos to balance those bells in your ear." St. John leaned back and closed his eyes. He looked indescribably bitter and tired.

"Besides," he added, with a faint smile, "if we found a Goliath, someone else would find a David to slay him."

CHAPTER 5

THERE WAS FRESH air. There was pain. There was darkness threaded with a greenish glow. Rick stirred.

After a long time he was on his hands and knees, coughing in the dust. Back of him about three feet he was aware of a solid mass walling him in. Ahead there was a ragged rift in the blackness, through which seeped moonlight.

In the moonlight, he saw Mayo's face, still and white as stone.

He put his hand on her throat. It was warm. There was a pulse-beat. The discovery brought him happiness and relief.

He spoke to her. She moaned faintly, and that was all.

Rick crawled past her and shoved against the stuff barring his way. It was rotten, already half gone from the shaking of the slide. Presently the hole was big enough to get through.

It came to him to wonder why the worm's fossil head had not collapsed with the rest of it. There was enough moonlight coming in now to show how close they had come to dying. He looked at the upper surface, almost touching his face.

Then he understood. The worm's digging end had been sheathed with armor plate like the point of a drill, and it was still as strong as a granite arch.

Rick patted it and smiled. Then he crawled out, backward, dragging Mayo's dead weight.

He found himself high on the face of a crumbling cliff. The worm had died with its head not two feet from open water. Now there was no water. There was a lonesome, aimless wind and a maze of shadows racing under the swinging moons, and the cold dry smell of dead land.

At the foot of the cliff was a tumbled slope covered with gray-green moss, and then the desert began. It stretched as far

as Rick could see, in bleached waves of sand that rolled like
surf under the wind and the moon-shadows.

Out across it, far out, there was a city.

The city lay in the bed of the dry sea, thrusting its marble
spires to the sky in a stricken gesture of prayer. Even while
Rick watched it, it flickered like a breaking dream, obscured
by drifting veils of dust.

It was the only thing in the whole landscape that held even
a suggestion of human life. Rick got stiffly to his feet. His
whole body ached, but he could make it work. He went down
the cliff, sliding, half falling, dragging the unconscious girl.
His shackle chain made a loud ringing jangle against the rock.

He got Mayo up into his arms. Her throat and arms were
foam-white in the moonlight, her thick hair falling dark against
Rick's skin. They were both half naked, dusty, stained with
blood.

He walked out across the sand, setting one foot doggedly
before the other. The swinging chain tolled in the silence like
a cracked bell.

He was close to the city when little winged people appeared.
Rick remembered having heard legends of them. Like the anthropoids, they were end-products, the left-overs of a race
incredibly ancient, once powerful, now reduced to a mere forgotten handful clinging to empty cities lost in the sand—cities
that had once been island kingdoms in a blue sea.

The winged ones drifted out from the white towers, out
across the little racing moons. They were light and indescribably beautiful, and their wings shimmered with soft secret fires
like opals under mist. They clustered round and followed Rick,
who tramped on doggedly. They tossed on the wind like huge
petals, making no sound. Rick could see their eyes, glowing
with a faint phosphorescence.

Presently a marble wall loomed up in front of Rick and
halted him.

He laid the girl carefully on the sand and turned around. He
had no particular idea of what he was going to do. The gossamer creatures fluttered down onto the blowing sand. They
were human in body, slender and graceful, wearing only short
kilts. There were both men and women. Their skin was covered with a fine silky fur, almost like bird-down, and they were
no more than four feet tall.

One of the men landed nearby. His handsome little face held

neither friendliness nor enmity. "You are Rick," he said in a clear, soft voice. Then he whipped a pencil-tube from his girdle and fired.

Rick slid down into utter darkness. The last conscious picture he took with him was not of the man with the tube, but of a tiny woman, poised like the Winged Victory of Samothrace in the greenish moonlight, watching him with huge, still eyes.

It was the eyes most of all he remembered.

He lay on his back, comfortably, on a pile of silks and furs. He was rested and without pain, except for a slight stiffness. His hands were still chained.

The little woman sat beside him, her slender body shining like new gold in a flood of sunlight from a huge arched window high in the wall. A second glance told Rick she was little more than a girl, with all the beauty that blossoms just across the threshold from childhood. Her hand lay small and warm on Rick's bare chest.

"I have been finding out if you live," she said. "You live strongly."

Rick laughed and sat up. "What's your name?"

"Kyra."

He stirred her hand gravely. It was like a doll's hand.

Somebody near stirred and yawned.

"Your mate is awake," Kyra said. Her speech was pure High Martian, and a little difficult for Rick to follow.

"Mate?" He shook his head. "No. Just a swell girl I almost died with." He got up. Mayo was sitting up on a second heap of furs and bright cloths. She smiled.

"Hello, Rick. For heaven's sake where are we, and how did we get here?" She stared at Kyra.

Rick told her what he knew. "The city is called Caer Hebra," Kyra explained. "We have lived in it always, since the world was. There were many of us, once."

Rick looked around him. They were on a sort of broad terrace, inlaid magnificently with colored stones Rick had no names for. The pattern had a curious infinite quality, without beginning or end. It did strange things to anyone who looked too long. Above them, the roof soared in a pure arch of veined marble.

Only one great window could be seen. There were bas-reliefs on the walls, alive and almost breathing. They showed men and women like Kyra, only they were as big as Rick and

Mayo. There were trees in the pictures, birds and beasts and once a sea with ships on it.

Rick also noticed a low, carved railing, and in the center of it, steps. They were wide enough to march an army down, and they descended majestically into blue shadows and—sand!

It choked the vast hall below, flowing around the waists of sculptured figures, leaving here and there an impotent pleading hand or a half-smothered head where the statutory had been set lower. It crawled out from the high window, lapping at the steps.

Rick became aware of a peculiar rustling sound, like the breathing of a sleeping giant, the rubbing of the desert against the outer walls.

"There are many levels below this," said Kyra. "When my father was a child he played here, and there was no sand." She looked up at the window. A feathery plume blew in and sifted down to the terrace. Rick shivered.

He realized presently that both he and Mayo had been washed and treated with ointments. Kyra set food before them, bringing it from a table beside a massive bronze door. They ate.

"Kyra, what goes on here?" Rick said. "I remember some guy rayed me. How did he know my name?"

Kyra explained, and Rick's face hardened.

"A blood debt!" he said. "By golly, if they think they're going to sacrifice me, they're wrong!"

"My people will come at dusk to carry you back to Ruh." Kyra's luminous eyes held a shimmer of tears. "They will kill you," she whispered. "And you live—so strongly!"

She caught his hands suddenly, stretching her little self up to him. "I've heard them talk. I know the prophecy—your 'shadow over Mars.' They hate and fear you." Her next words were almost choked by tears and eagerness, and came tumbling out in an incoherent flood.

"I think you would bring life to Mars instead of death," she said. "You have life in you, so much life, and we are dying. Don't let them kill you, Rick!"

He smiled and stroked her feathery soft hair. "Better not let your people hear you talk like that. They know you're here?"

"No. Oh, Rick!"

She looked up at him. He bent and kissed her small trembling lips and suddenly she pulled away from him. For the first

time she was shy. Spreading her wings, she darted away up the
shaft of sunlight and was gone.

Rick sat down, rather helplessly, and looked at Mayo. There
were tears in her brown eyes.

"Yeah," said Rick softly. "Isn't it!"

"Rick, I don't understand. What prophecy?"

He told about the seeress.

"I didn't mean to kill her! But she had me crazy. Also she
tried to knife me." He tilted his head back so Mayo could see
the half-healed cut on his throat.

She didn't say anything. She sat staring at him with such an
intent and yet distant look that presently he moved restlessly.

It wasn't so much her look that disturbed him. It was because her hair was afire with sunlight and her skin was like
Venusian mist at dawn, lucent pearl flushed over with sultry
warmth. A muscle began to twitch in his cheek.

She rose and put her hands on his arms and studied him.

"The old woman was right," she said. "Kyra's right. There's
strength in you, Rick. It's sleeping, but it's there. You've never
done much with your life, have you?"

"I've enjoyed it, most of it."

"But you haven't built things. You haven't been going anywhere. Have you thought, Rick, that maybe there was something in that prophecy?"

He laughed. "I'd look fine, wouldn't I, as a shining savior!"

"I think," she said quietly, "you might look very fine."

He didn't move for a long moment, didn't breathe. Then he
took her in his arms and kissed her. Presently, they drew apart.

"Rick, we must have a talk," she said then. "There isn't
much time, and we've got to do something!"

"There's nothing to do, baby. Maybe later, there'll be a
break. But right now, unless we can sprout wings like the kid,
we've got to wait. Anyway, they've got nothing against you.
You're in the clear."

"Don't tell me that!" Mayo stirred impatiently against the
white fur on which she was lying. "Listen, Rick. Back there
in that tunnel you said you wanted to drive Fallon and his gang
off Mars."

Rick nodded. His cat-eyes blazed.

"Then will you come in with us, with Hugh St. John and
me?" she asked him. "Rick, I tell you union is the only hope
for Mars. Maybe you're the man who can bring it about. That

old woman didn't talk like a hysteric, an ordinary crystal-gazer. She talked sense. That conception of a fan-shaped future is fundamental even on Earth. Many scientists accept it as sound theory.''

She sat up, flushed and shaken with excitement, gripping his arm with hurtful strength.

"Take hold of your future, Rick! Mold it, build it, make it a great, towering thing that people will remember as long as they have tongues to talk about it!"

He stared at her, through her and beyond her. He began to tremble.

He rose abruptly, pacing the inlaid terrace. "My shadow," he whispered. "My shadow over Mars."

Mayo straightened slowly, watching him. An odd look came into her face—a faint, uncertain fear.

"Why not? By golly, why not!" He stopped, talking to her not as an individual but only as a point on which to focus his voice. There was a fire in him suddenly. The blaze of it spread through him until, in the sunlight, he looked to her like legendary Talos, still hot from the forges.

"Why not?" he repeated. "Fallon, St. John, Storm—why not me? Take hold of my future. Sure. My future, and a world. A whole round world just waiting for somebody to pick it up. Some guy's hand will grab it. Why not mine?"

Silence, with the marble vault still echoing.

"Rick!" Mayo whispered.

He only half saw her. "You know who I am," he said slowly. "Richard Gunn Urquhart." He pronounced it as though it had a tremendous cabalistic meaning. "I never realized that before. I guess I never really knew I was alive."

He threw back his head and laughed.

Silence, and the ringing echoes. The sunlight faded from the window. Mayo sat on the heap of furs and bright silks, unstirring.

He knelt beside her and took her in his arms.

"We'll go up together," he said. "You're the woman I need—a strong woman, to go beside me like a sword. Together, Mayo! And I'll give you Mars to wear on a chain around your neck!"

He kissed her. Her lips were cold and unresponsive, and there was a bitterness on them, a taste of tears.

He drew back, suddenly chilled. "What's the matter?"

She looked up at him. Tears welled and ran down her cheeks, shining palely in the dying light. She was not sobbing. There was an emotion within her too deep for sobs.

"I love you, Rick," she told him.

"Sure. And I love you."

"No. There's no love in you, Rick. Not the kind of love I mean. Part of you has come awake—the sleeping thing the old woman saw and was afraid of—your strength. But it hasn't any soul."

His eyelids narrowed. "What are you talking about?"

"I thought you were the man we needed, just as Kyra did. A strong man, to bring life to a dying world. But you don't even know what we're talking about. You'll bring death, Rick. Death and destruction, if you live."

He released her slowly and stood up. "I don't get it. You wanted me to take Mars, didn't you?"

"I wanted you to save Mars. To build, to restore, to create."

"Have I said I wouldn't?"

"Will you?"

He tried to hold her gaze and then turned away irritably. "Bosh! Give me time! I haven't even started to think yet."

"Will you give Hugh his chance to work, as he's dreamed of working?"

He turned on her, with a look of feral ugliness.

"Listen Mayo. I've never worn anybody's collar. I'm not making any promises, or any guesses. I don't know how anything's going to shape up. But whatever I build I'll build in my own way, on my own plans." He swore furiously. "If that isn't just like a dame! For the first time I realize what a chance this offers. After a lifetime of taking the boot from the guys higher up, I see a way to maybe get a little higher than anybody else. And right away you start tying my hands, shutting gates on me!"

He went over to the rail and stood scowling at the sand below. Then he came back.

"All right, I'll be honest with you. All this is a pretty new idea, though I guess I've been thinking about it in the back of my mind ever since the old woman said that. But I don't give a hang for Mars, or the Martians, or Hugh St. John. I care about Richard Gunn Urquhart, and it's good that I do because nobody else does or ever has. I want two things—to pay Storm and Fallon back what I owe them and to see what I can make for myself out of a world nobody else can handle. You got that?''

She nodded. ''Yes, Rick. I've got it.''

He watched her silently. Then he laughed.

''All this rowing, when I'll maybe be dead in a couple of days anyhow!'' He dropped down beside her. ''Look, Mayo. We found each other. We'll always belong to each other, because two people can't go through what we did without fusing a part of them together. But there's more than that with us. We don't know each other yet, and there's lots of ways we won't agree. But somewhere, somehow, we click, and that's the important thing. I never felt that way with anybody else. It's as though a part of me had been missing, and suddenly it just slipped into place.''

He stared at her with a sort of comic wonderment. ''Hey! You know you're the first dame I ever stopped to explain to? Anybody else, man or woman, until a couple of minutes ago, would have got their teeth slapped in!''

Mayo laughed suddenly, a shaken sort of laughter that ended in a sob. She put her arms around him.

''You're just a kid, Rick,'' she said. ''You never grew up.'' She drew his head down. ''Maybe,'' she whispered, ''there is a soul there somewhere. Maybe it just needs love to wake it up.''

Their lips met. And then, in the dim silence, the brazen doors crashed open.

CHAPTER 6

UP ABOVE, THE little racing moons seemed close, frighteningly close against the starshot sky. The wind cut like a knife. Rick lay motionless in the cradle of broad straps and watched four pairs of wings beat the night above him, at the ends of four stout ropes.

Off to his right Mayo McCall lay in a similar cradle, carried by four more of the little men of Caer Hebra.

The Mars landscape slid by silently, far below. There were endless reaches of sand, flowing under the restless wind and the shadows, chains of mountain peaks, worn blunt by the feet of uncounted millennia, and the desolate wastes of the sea-bottoms. Here and there a marble city gleamed under the moons, like the face of a dead woman half concealed by vines and creeping verdure.

Presently, far off to one side, Rick saw the great sprawling blaze of the Terran Exploitations Company. The winged men began to drop in a long arc, and then the towers of Ruh lifted darkly into the night sky.

Jagged fingers of stone shot up as though to grasp them. Rick's heart stuck in his throat. Blurred light and shadow flickered past him, carved monsters brushed his flesh—and then, with no more than a slight jar, he was lying on a broad terrace, with Mayo not far off. Kilted warriors stood with drawn swords in the shadows. The men of Caer Hebra folded their wings and bowed with the easy grace of men who give respect but not servility.

The man they bowed to was lean and sinewy, harnessed in the worn leather of a common soldier. A wolf-faced man, with eyes that caught the moonlight in points of brilliant greenish flame.

"Loose their feet," he said.

He gave Mayo one slow look that sent the blood up into her face, and then turned to Rick. He watched while the Earthman got to his feet, his chained hands clasped in front of him.

Rick waited, not speaking. His eyes had the same remote and deadly look of a captive tiger.

After a long time the lean man laughed softly and nodded.

"I am Beudach," he said, as one speaking to an equal. "My master waits."

He bowed ceremoniously to the men of Caer Hebra and motioned them to precede him. The guards closed in. Mayo moved close to Rick. Her hands were bound, but their elbows touched.

They followed Beudach into the tower. No one noticed the shadow sliding down the moonlight on silent moth-wings; a small shadow that swooped in and clung trembling to a stone gargoyle, hidden in heavy darkness.

Far below in the deserted streets of Ruh, a man walked restlessly. A huge man clad in black, whose boot-heels struck the worn stones in uneven rhythm. He walked alone. Men watched him from behind locked shutters, but no one moved to touch him. The polished butts of twin blasters glinted on his lean hips. His course was aimless, his expression strangely remote.

Quite suddenly he stopped. He raised his head slowly, turning a bit where he stood, like a hound questing.

His black eyes lifted to the towers of the King City. The light of the twin moons caught in them and burned, a phosphorescent green. Then he smiled and limped swiftly away toward the city wall. . . .

The throne room blazed with an extravagance of torches behind bronze-shuttered windows. Smoke hung in a blue haze under the carven vault. Through it faded banners and tarnished shields caught the shaking light in glints of dull crimson, purple, and gold.

Twelve men sat around the blood-red table, war chiefs from the twelve principal city-states that owed homage to Ruh. The boy-king Haral was in his high seat, and his dark, worn mother sat at his left, watching them all with bitter rage.

The hall was still when Beudach came in with guests, guards, and prisoners. But Rick, looking at their proud, sullen faces, knew that there had been trouble a moment before—high tempers, with words to match them. Jealousy was here—the scramble for precedence. They were fighting for that, before they thought of the battle of Mars.

Beudach took his post at Haral's right. The men of Caer Hebra bowed and moved to places at the table. Rick and Mayo were left alone before the high seat, the guards withdrawn somewhat behind them.

From a dense patch of shadow near Haral's feet came a quick harsh sigh, like the hiss of a coiling snake. Llaw the dwarf moved out into the torchlight, smiling.

Rick faced them all, erect and easy, his elbow touching Mayo. His hard face was impassive. Inside, he was tense.

"You know why you are here?" Haral inquired.

"I do."

The boy-king stood up. He trembled with excitement.

"You men!" he cried. "You fighting men of Mars! Here is the Earthman of the prophecy. Through him alone can the invaders gain dominion over our world."

He flung out his hand. The gesture was theatrical. It might have been funny. It wasn't. There was a great blazing dignity in the boy. Rick nodded to himself with a reluctant admiration.

Haral's voice rang like a silver trumpet. "Look at him, you

men of Mars! Tonight we stand at the crossroads. Tomorrow there will be only one highway, leading straight to victory—and freedom for Mars!''

A shout went up, and on the heels of it Parras the seer stepped out of the shadows behind the high seat.

"Lord," he said. "I must tell you this again. I have sent my mind into the future, and I have seen a third road. A black road, Lord, not far ahead. I can only say—be quick!''

Haral laughed. He was young. Very young. "We have destiny by the throat tonight, Parras!" He turned to the dwarf. "The debt is yours, Llaw. And according to the blood right, you can choose your own way to collect it. There is the Earthman. See that he pays!''

The dwarf leaped down from the dais, silently, with the deadly grace of a cat pouncing.

"Wait a minute!" said Rick.

Beudach's wolfish eyes flickered with disappointment. Haral stared at Rick in wonder. "Would you plead for your life?" Haral asked.

Rick laughed. "That would do me plenty of good wouldn't it! No." He nodded to Mayo. "It's about this girl."

Haral frowned, almost as though he hadn't noticed her before.

"I want her turned loose, not touched," Rick said. "You have nothing against her."

Beudach was not disappointed now. He was pleased.

"Lord, she is his mate," Llaw said.

Rick ignored him. "We met in a tight spot, and got out of it together. She hardly knows me." He didn't look, but he hoped she wasn't blushing.

"It's not important now," Haral gestured. "Llaw!"

Rick opened his mouth angrily. Llaw gestured. The guards moved in. Rick shut his teeth together, leaving them bare, and shoved Mayo carefully out of the way.

He put three men down with his shackle chain and two more with his feet before somebody slammed the flat of a sword blade down across his temple. He felt two more blows before the darkness closed in. Through the last of the light he saw Beudach's face, set in an expression of disgust. Beudach was looking at Llaw. . . .

When Rick again regained consciousness, there were jagged streaks of crimson across the black. They came with a strangely

regular beat. Somewhere far off a woman was screaming. It
was not a fear-scream, or hysteria. It was the angry shriek of
a clawed animal.

Rick opened his eyes.

Red waving curtains hid the throne room. There was movement beyond them, distant and unreal. The shrieking came
from beyond the curtains, and a swinging clash of hammers
on metal that seemed very close.

Presently he realized that the redness was pain, pain so in-
tense that he almost could see it.

It seemed to him that he was high up, very high, looking
down upon the crimson, hazy sea.

The screaming stopped.

There was darkness again for a period of time. When it lifted
he could hear only a sort of uneasy mutter. The pain had shifted
for his mind had slipped free into dimensions where it was
aware of the pain but was disconnected from it. He opened his
eyes again.

His head was hanging forward. He saw his own body, erect,
stripped naked, shining with sweat like polished bronze,
streaked with blood. His feet rested on a transverse ornamental
beam of some dark blue wood, cracked and darkened by age.
The hilts of two heavy daggers stood up through his arches.
The daggers were bright in the torchlight. Very bright.

Far below him was the stone floor.

Slowly he turned his head. It was heavy and took a long
time to turn. He saw his left arm stretched out against the wall.
The fingers of his hand were curled laxly around the hilt of a
third dagger, driven through his palm into a crack between two
blocks of stone.

He knew without looking that it was the same on his right.
He let his head drop forward again.

Mayo knelt on the stones. Her face was turned up to him.
He smiled.

Llaw the dwarf crouched, hugging his knees, almost in the
attitude of a man worshipping. He was alone. His gaze fixed
on Rick, unwinking, burning with a deep, insane light.

Back further, the twelve war-chiefs and the men of Caer
Hebra sat at the blood-red table, drinking, talking low in a
desultory way. They avoided each other's eyes and did not look
up. Haral slumped in the high seat, staring at the rug of virgin's
hair. His face was white, sick. Beside him the Queen-Mother

sat unmoved, watching the man on the wall. To her he was not human, not worthy of the sympathy she would have given to a beast. He was an Earthman.

Beudach rose suddenly from the dais. His face held a cold fury and his hand twitched over his dagger hilt.

"By the gods of my people!" he snarled explosively. "Isn't this enough?"

Llaw smiled faintly. He didn't move. Parras spoke out of the shadows.

"Lord, I beg you," he said. "Finish this!"

Haral raised his head, carefully not looking at Rick. "Llaw?"

"By the blood right, Majesty," said Llaw softly. "This is my choice."

Haral fell back in his high seat.

Beudach stared upward. His eyes met Rick's dark amber gaze, and gradually a silence came over the hall so that the slow splashing of blood-drops onto the stone floor was clearly audible.

"I am ashamed," said Beudach. "For my people I am ashamed."

He turned and suddenly moved forward, set his foot under Llaw's chin and threw him flat. Then he drew his dagger.

"Blood right or not, Earthman, you deserve a man's death!" he cried. His hands swept back for the throw.

Llaw yowled like a mad cat and flung himself at Beudach, incredibly swift. Beudach staggered. The knife whirled, glittering, through the torchlight, struck wide, and dropped clanging onto the stones. Beudach snarled and got his hands around Llaw's throat.

Suddenly, out in the vaulted halls beyond the bronze doors of the throne room, a man screamed. And as though that sound were the trigger, a perfect fury of noise burst out.

Every man in the throne room came to his feet. No one spoke. Blades flashed out of scabbards. Beudach raised his head, and between his wide-spread feet the heels of the dwarf drummed a diminishing tattoo and were silent.

Beudach dropped the body. He didn't look at it. He went to Haral, drawing the sword that hung behind his shoulder.

Mayo was standing now, pressed against the wall. By stretching her bound hands high she could reach Rick's feet, but not the dagger hilts. She looked up into his face. She tried to speak, but nothing would come. His sweat and blood dropped onto her white skin, shining in the red glare.

Rick's lips formed the words, "I love you." He smiled. And then the bronze doors crashed open and Jaffa Storm was standing there, with his Venusians and the black anthropoids crowding in behind him.

CHAPTER 7

FULLY CONSCIOUS, RICK watched from the high wall. His mind was clear, detached, perfectly sane. But in his eyes, in his face, something had changed. It was like the chilling and tempering of the weapon from the soft hot steel. Never again would he be careless and happy-go-lucky.

He watched the Martians fight and go down under the blasters of Storm's men. Guards came. The hall was choked with warriors. The huge white-haired Venusians, the blasters, and the black apes cut them down.

From outside, in the halls and the streets beyond, from over the whole city, rose an animal howl, mingled with the thunder of fighting and the saw-edged whine of Banning shockers.

In the throne room, one by one, the torches were trampled out.

After a time there was silence. In the darkness of tattered flags and forgotten glories, one torch still burned in a high sconce, spilling a red and shaken light over the man pinned by knives against the stone wall. The Venusians and the apes withdrew, taking their dead. Outside fighting still continued, but the sound of it was distant, muffled. Mayo had not moved from the place where she pressed close against the wall, touching Rick's feet.

Jaffa Storm came and stood before them.

He looked upward for a long while without speaking. Then he smiled and stretched his giant body, muscle by muscle, as a panther does. His black eyes held a deep pleasure.

" 'The wind is rising,' " he quoted softly. "Bah! it's blown itself out! These men were the leaders of Mars. What's left— a few barbarians and the Thinkers at the Pole—are nothing."

He laughed quietly. "I knew they were here. I knew you were here. I have as much knowledge as their seers. Perhaps more."

Mayo had slid silently to her knees, her bound hands on the shadowy floor.

Storm studied Rick. "There was some prophecy, wasn't there? And a blood debt." He nodded. "You've caused me a lot of trouble, Rick. That stone hurt. You made me look foolish when you got away, and you inspired a lot more men to try it. Besides, there was something—else."

Rick laughed, a harsh whisper of sound. "That's true. I saw you take the boot from a girl."

Storm nodded. He leaned over and caught Mayo by the shoulder.

She came up fast. She had Beudach's knife in her hands. Storm let his breath out, hard. There was a blur of motion and sound. The dagger rang on the stones and Mayo was lifted in Storm's arms.

"You're a strong man, Rick. You'll live for quite a while. I don't think anyone will come here just yet—there's no one left in the King City, and they're still busy down below—and if anyone does, I don't think they'll take you down."

"Such an idea pleases you, doesn't it," sneered Rick.

Again Storm laughed. "It does," he said. "You were to rule Mars, weren't you, according to the prophecy? They cling to the belief of the fan-shaped future, the infinite roads. Somewhere, Rick, you took the wrong turning!"

He went away. Rick watched the warm sheen of torchlight in Mayo's hair as far as he could see it, and then listened to the limping tread of Storm's boots fading down the hall.

He was alone.

He tried, once, to see if he could move the blades that pinned him. After that he hung motionless, breathing in deep, harsh sighs.

Presently, somewhere in the dimness, something stirred.

It was Beudach, dragging himself from under a heap of bodies by the high seat. He crawled among them on his hands and knees, searching the faces. Save for his labored breathing, he made no sound, not even when he found what he sought.

In the guttering torchlight, Rick saw the ivory gleam of Haral's body as Beudach raised it in his arms. Rising slowly to his feet Beudach walked, erect and without swaying, to the dais and laid the boy in the high seat, his dark head propped against the carved back, his hands along the arm rests. The red light caught in his open eyes, and on the worn bosses of his collar.

Beudach found a sword and laid it across Haral's knees. Then he sank down on the dais.

After a while he raised his head and looked at Rick. There was a light of prophecy in his eyes.

"You will not die," he panted, solemnly.

In a whisper, fully as hoarse, the man on the wall answered, "No."

"You will rule Mars."

"I—will—rule—Mars!"

Silence. Presently Beudach nodded. "For good or ill, the road is taken. And you're a man."

"Beudach," Rick said.

"Yes?"

"With my own hands, Beudach—my own hands!"

Beudach looked from Rick to the dead boy and back again. He smiled. Then he let himself down from the dais and began to crawl slowly and painfully across the floor toward Rick.

Suddenly he stopped.

"Someone's coming," he muttered.

Out in the darkness of the corridor there was a soft rustle of movement, and then a faint scream—shocked and strangled.

"Rick! Rick!"

The quick silken rustle of wings in the dusk, and then Kyra was clinging to the carved stones beside Rick, her great eyes wide, stunned, and tearless.

"I followed them, Rick," she whimpered. "I thought maybe there'd be something, something I could do to help you. Oh, Rick."

He smiled at her. "You can, baby." His speech was slow and thick. "You can pull out these knives."

Her tiny face whitened, but she nodded. From the floor Beudach spoke.

"Wait. He'll fall. The ladders are still here. Help me."

She fluttered down. Between them they raised one of the light metal ladders that had been used to get Rick up there.

Very, very slowly Beudach climbed it and pulled the daggers from the Earthman's feet.

After that, Rick was only partly conscious when they pulled the blades from his hands. He knew that Kyra's wings beat rapidly as she held him up. He sensed Beudach's wiry, dogged strength. He tried to help them, but there was a coldness on him, and a roaring in his ears.

Presently there was a hot sting of wine in his throat. He lay propped against the wall at the foot of the ladder. Beudach crouched beside him, with a goblet. Shaking with exhaustion, Kyra was binding strips of cloth around his hands and feet.

Beudach dropped the goblet. There was a cold sweat on his face. He raised something from the floor beside him.

The iron Collar of Ruh.

"Listen, Earthman. Our time is finished. Whatever time is to be on Mars will be new, and different. And it will be your time."

He stopped to fight for breath.

"This collar is the symbol of kingship over half of Mars. Where Ruh and the Collar lead, Mars follows. I'm going to put it on your neck. There's a hidden blade in the lock. Only one or two men in each generation know the secret, and when anyone else tampers with it he gets death from the poison on that blade, and the lock stays locked. The collar will be your key to the loyalty of the Martians. What you do with that loyalty will bring your own destiny upon you."

He stopped again.

"Why do you give me the collar?" Rick whispered.

"Because that's the way the road leads. Because you will destroy the Company, and the men of the Company. Because there is no Martian left with strength to wear the Collar—now. Things may not be that way always, but the future will have to take care of its own."

He placed the iron collar around Rick's throat. It was still faintly warm from Haral's young flesh.

Beudach looked a long time into Rick's cold, fathomless yellow eyes. Once his hand moved, almost as though to take the collar back. Then he closed the lock.

"There's a secret passage leading to safety out of this place," Beudach went on. "Press the sixteenth boss to the left of the main hall, up, then down. More than one lord of Ruh has gone that way to safety. And hurry." He looked once more at Rick. "Remember, Earthman—that collar won't save your life if you betray it."

Rick's eyes held no emotion.

Kyra came back. She took hold of Rick, half dragging, half carrying him to a narrow black rectangle in the wall.

Beudach sighed. Slowly, as though he were settling down to
sleep, he fell sideways and lay still, with his head on Haral's
feet.

Then came a grating sound as Kyra sealed the secret passage
with a block of stone, and cold dry black closed around
Rick. . . .

Many hours later, in the glassite-walled office on the top
floor of the Company's Administration pylon, Jaffa Storm was
sprawled lazily on a couch, smoking. He did not appear to be
paying much attention to Ed Fallon.

Fallon was moving with short angry strides up and down in
front of the desk. His blocky face was ugly.

"Blast it all!" he burst out finally. "To pull a stunt like that
over some dame was reckless folly. Do you know how many
men you got killed?"

Storm shrugged. "They were Venusians. They like to die
fighting. I've got more coming."

"Sure, that's easy. But what about the Martians you left dead
all over the streets? You fool! Don't you realize it may get us
kicked straight off the planet?"

Storm's eyebrows went up derisively. "Who'll do the kicking?"

"The Martian Planetary Government will complain to Earth,
and the Interplanetary Coordination Authority!"

"You don't say?" Storm sat up. His black eyes were remote
and faintly contemptuous. "I've already lodged a complaint
with the MPG. It won't go any further."

Fallon stood still. His eyes grew narrow.

"They had two Earthlings prisoner, didn't they?" Storm
went on. "One a woman, and both employees of the Company.
They pinned the man up on the wall with knives, didn't they?
The devil only knows what they were going to do with the
woman. All right. We had to rescue them, didn't we? And
where could we go for legal protection? Besides, we have evidence the Marshies were getting ready for a massacre. The
Planetary Government doesn't want trouble, Fallon. They've
got nothing to back up their trouble with."

He laughed. "Along with the complaint I sent a big fat
check to be used on one of their restoration schemes!"

Fallon smiled, without humor. "Clever kid. And what about
Ruh? What about all the Marshies this side of Kahora? How

are they going to feel about you blasting their king and their top men to Kingdom Come?''

"They can feel any way they want to," said Storm evenly. "I've got blasters. I've got a ring of Bannings around the walls, and plenty of Venusians, with more coming. There's no law on Mars but strength—and I've got that, too."

There was a new and insolent note in Storm's voice which worried Fallon. He turned back to the desk and sat down.

"All right, Storm," he said. "Maybe you're so smart you can get away with it."

"You bet I can get away with it. Listen, Fallon! Those men in the throne room were plotting to get your scalp. We'd have to fight them sooner or later. I preferred it sooner."

"You preferred it. Yeah. You use my men and equipment, you risk my company and everything I've put into this dustball of a planet, just because you had a personal grudge to satisfy. And all of it without saying a word to me. Maybe you think you'd be better off running this show."

Storm's gaze slid speculatively over Fallon.

"You've got it so it practically runs itself." He leaned over and crushed out his cigarette. He went on casually, "You're getting flabby, Ed. Physically, I mean. You're turning into the typical tycoon, the guy who sits behind the desk and grows a veranda, and only gets a kick out of doing tricks with his brain. I've watched you, when I've had to take some of these tough boys to the wall. You don't like it, Ed. It makes you sick. What happened in Ruh made you sick, and you were so scared you almost passed out. You're getting old, Ed, beginning to slow down and get cautious. I've put over the first blow, but there'll be other blows. Other companies, hijacking, throat-cutting, all the rest of it. Mars isn't a world you can afford to get old on, Ed."

Fallon sucked his breath in, softly. "You're a liar, Jaffa."

"Take it any way you want," retorted Storm.

"I'll take it the way you mean it. You want the Company for yourself."

"The Company means Mars, Ed. I want Mars."

Fallon nodded. He did not seem particularly surprised. He let his red head drop forward, crumpling slightly upon himself where he sat.

His movement, when it came, was very quick. Jaffa Storm was a little quicker. The blaster echoes faded quickly into the

soundproofing. There was a seared spot on a pillar next to
Storm's head. Fallon still sat behind the desk. He had now
neither a face nor any further interest in the future of his Company.

Storm rose and limped over to the telescreen. He called
Vargo and gave instructions. Then he went out, fastening the
door behind him.

A few moments later he let himself into a locked apartment
in another part of the compound.

Mayo McCall rose from the couch where she had been lying
and stood back against the wall. She did not tremble or cry or
become hysterical. She said nothing. There was something
deadly in her brown eyes.

Storm smiled and sat down. He admired her frankly. Her
clothing had been brought to her from her old quarters. In
place of the ragged coverall, she was wearing a simple draped
tunic of dull bronze cloth that made her hair look like fire. The
cut of the garment emphasized the supple magnificence of body
that the coverall had only hinted at.

"I've taken over the Company," Storm said quietly.

Her brows rose slightly. She watched him, speechlessly.

"Don't you want to know what I'm going to do with you?"
asked Storm.

"Does it matter?"

"Maybe. Because I'm not going to do anything."

She stared at him.

"Well, perhaps I should say anything—for a while." He
studied her for a long moment, half smiling. "You made me
an offer once, Mayo."

She laughed. "Don't tell me it's still open!"

"It could be." He leaned forward. "Listen, Mayo. I own
the Company, and the Company will own Mars. This is a fallow world. The ploughing of it will grow a crop of wealth and
power that hasn't been known since the development of the
frontier continents centuries ago on Earth—and wasn't known
then, really, because they were only playing with pieces of a
world."

His black eyes held a deep, smoldering heat.

"I've never seen a woman like you, Mayo. I don't know
what it is. I've seen plenty of them with as much looks, maybe
more. But you've got something different, something that's you.
And I want it. I want it so much that I'm not going to pay off

what I owe you—unless you make me. Those are the cards, Mayo. Play 'em any way you want to."

He stood up. "I've got plenty of time. I don't mind waiting. In fact, I rather like it. Just remember that I'll get what I want, one way or the other, in the end."

CHAPTER 8

QUIETLY RICK LAY on a shelf-bunk covered with silks and skins. There was a small window above him. Greenish moonlight fell through it, giving shape to the tiny cell-like room. It was, ironically, almost identical with the room in which Rick had met the seeress and her blood-thirsty grandson—and the prophecy. It was hollowed in the thickness of the City Wall, and from above or far below on the dead sea-bottom the window would show merely as an irregularity in the stones.

There was one door, leading into the passage that came under the streets of Ruh from the throne room. The passage branched here. Kyra, exploring cautiously, had found that it led through a balanced stone into a back street of the Thieves' Quarter.

The little hideout had been thoughtfully provisioned, evidently as a traditional duty rooted in more turbulent days of the city's history. There was clothing, food, wine, weapons, and everything necessary to the care of wounds.

Rick held his hands up in the shaft of moonlight and flexed the fingers. Already, in the four days he had been here, the wounds had begun to heal well. It was the same with his feet. The daggers, fortunately, had been razor sharp and had slid through between bone and tendon with a minimum of damage.

Rick smiled faintly. He dozed again. He had been sleeping a great deal. His body, naturally strong and toughened by the hard life he had led, was almost normal again.

Presently there was a flutter of wings outside, and Kyra pulled her tiny, little self through the window.

Rick woke immediately. "Did you find her?"

"Yes! Oh, Rick, she was so happy to learn you are safe. She said that only to know that was enough."

"How was she? Has Storm bothered her?"

"She's in no danger, right now," Kyra explained. "I gave her the knife. She tells you not to worry, to be careful, and—and she sends you—this!"

She placed her soft little lips against Rick's. Then, quite suddenly, she was crying, curled against his chest. He stroked her.

"You're tired," he said. "You've done too much for me, and I've put you in too much danger. You've got to go home."

Her wings rustled sharply. "Oh, no! Rick, you need me!"

"Not that much. You saved my life, kid. Now go home, where you'll be safe."

"Rick, I can't go home! They—I don't know what they'd do to me. Besides, there isn't anything there I want, any more."

He tilted her head back. The moonlight gleamed on her young face, the slender curve of her throat.

"You know what you're saying, Kyra?" he asked her.

"I know."

"And you know what I have to say back to you."

"I know." Kyra nodded her pretty head.

"It isn't any use to tell you that this isn't love the way you think it is, and that you'll get over it."

"I won't go home, Rick. You can't make me. You can make me fly away a little but I'll come back." She spread her wings and stood up. The moonlight made her delicate fur glisten like hot silver and touched a dim opaline fire from her wings.

"I love you, Rick, but it's more than that. I love Mars. You're going to make Mars a world where people can hope, and look forward. You don't know what it is, Rick, to be young in a dead city, with nowhere to look but back! And I want a part in the building. Even if it's just a little tiny part, to know that I've helped will be enough. You can't take that away from me."

He looked at her for a long moment, without speaking. A strange, stony look hardened his face briefly. An expression almost of cruelty came into his eyes as he squared his jaw. Then he shrugged.

"No, I don't suppose I can, short of killing you," he said quietly. "All right, Kyra. We'll play it that way."

She dropped cross-legged by the low bunk, smiling, triumphant.

"Anybody around the Company see you?" Rick went on.

"No. Not any of the times I've been there."

"Learn anything more about Storm, or the defenses of the place?"

"No more than I've told you. Rick, I don't think anybody would live through an attack! On our side, I mean."

"Probably not. How does Ruh look, Kyra?"

"I saw torchlight in the streets when I came back. I think there will be trouble, very soon. Oh, Rick—there was one thing I overheard while I was hiding on a roof tonight. Storm has raided the New Town twice for men, already. The pits are working on a triple shift. Men have died."

Rick nodded. "Storm's not wasting any time." He sat up, swinging his feet over the side. "Get the bandages, baby, and tie these up, tight."

She started to protest, and then went obediently to work.

"I can't wait any longer," Rick said, half to himself. "Once they start it'll be too late, for all of us!"

The balanced stone moved silently, a few minutes later, and they stepped out warily into a narrow rat-run, hugging the foot of the Wall. It was densely shadowed, deserted except for varied smells. From somewhere ahead came a low, confused, but angry murmur.

Kyra darted off into the air and came back presently to say that there was a mob gathered in the Thieves' Market, with more people coming steadily from the better Quarters of the city.

She caught Rick's arm. "They'll kill you," she whispered. "They'll tear you to pieces."

Rick smiled. It was a strange smile, without humor or humanness.

"Go on," he said. "Lead the way."

Kyra turned obediently, but her wings trailed on the dirty stones.

They went along narrow, twisting streets between buildings so ancient that the dust of their erosion lay heaped in the sheltered corners. There was nothing human in sight, nothing but rags of washing hung bannerwise from the black windows to show that people lived there at all. But Rick could sense them, in the reeking air of the place. People among whom evil was as commonplace as breathing. Phobos had set in the east, but Diemos hung low over Ruh, so low that the towers of the King City seemed to have impaled it.

The crowd roar grew steadily louder.

There was an odd quality in it. There was fury, but it was
the fury of a dirge rather than a war cry.

They came to the end of the street. The mob roar, the mob
smell beat back at them. The tossing glare of torches blotted
out the moon. They looked into a broad square, jammed solidly with people. The leaning, settling houses shouldered up
around it, and here, too, were people—hanging out of windows, clinging like swarming bees to every balcony and over-
hang that would give them footing.

The noise burst suddenly into a great shout, and then tapered
off to silence. The voice of one man rang out, thin and bitter
like a trumpet call across the field of a lost battle.

Rick began to work his way forward. No one bothered to
look at him.

The man stood on a scaffold in the center of the square—
the gibbet where the thieves of the Quarter meted out their own
justice. He was small and wiry and grizzled, dressed in the
rags of a gold-mesh tunic. His face was twisted, lined with
scars, his eyes a slanted reddish topaz that burned like the torch
flames.

"You know why you're here," he was shrieking. "You know
what has been done. You know the men who would have freed
us are dead, and our young king with them."

He paused, to let the sombre snarling response of the crowd
die down.

"You know," he said quietly, "what there is left for us to
do."

The yell that answered him was a pure blood-cry.

"You know they have the weapons, the walls, and the
strength. All right! But they can't stop us. We won't come
back—we know that, too—but before we die we'll wipe the
Earthman's Company from the face of Mars!"

In the instant of silence before the shout, Rick raised his
voice.

"Wait!" he bellowed.

An angry mutter spread across the square. The little man
looked down at Rick. His eyes dilated. His breath sucked in
harshly, and suddenly he flung his hands out to silence the
crowd.

The quiet spread out from his urgent hands, crawling across
the upturned faces, lapping the walls like still water, until the
snapping silken rustle of the torches sounded plainly.

Rick began to climb the steps onto the scaffold.

He went slowly, but erect and without limping. He wore a purple cloak that swept from his big shoulders to his heels, held at the breast with the symbol of the Twin Moons in burning emerald.

He walked onto the platform, under the swinging chains of the gibbet. He raised his bandaged hands to the clasp and let the cloak slip down.

No one voiced a single word. Only a breath, one huge indrawn sigh, swept from wall to wall and was silent.

Rick stood perfectly still. His supple, thick-muscled body was half bared in the plain leather harness of a soldier, and around his throat, dull and battered and worn with centuries, the Collar of Ruh gave back an iron gleam to the torches.

The thief in the golden tunic goggled at him. "Who are you?" he asked.

Rick didn't raise his voice, but it rolled back off the walls.

"Richard Gunn Urquhart, the leader of the prophecy."

A sort of moan rose out of the crowd, a beast cry before blood. The thief flung his arms out.

"Wait! Wait, you people!" He stepped close to Rick, his fingers curled hungrily on his dagger hilt. "How did you, an Earthman, get the Collar of Ruh!"

"Beudach himself took it from Haral's neck after the massacre and put it on mine. You know the story of the lock. You know I'm telling the truth."

"Beudach!" whispered the thief. The name ran eerily across the square, half voiced—Beudach . . . Beudach!

"An Earthman," said the chief. "An Earthman, with the Collar of Ruh!"

He drew his knife.

Rick's face was impassive. He didn't look at the knife. He stared out over the crowd with a steady gaze.

"Listen, you people," he said. "When Beudach locked the Collar on me, he said, 'For good or ill, the road is taken.' And it is. This, out of all the roads Mars might have walked, is the one that came topmost on the wheel. You can't change that. Nobody can change it. They tried to. They pinned me to the throne-room wall with knives, but they couldn't change it."

His voice had a queer ring in it. Not fierce, or threatening, or pleading, but as though he were so completely confident that he had stopped thinking about it, and was only rehashing what they must already know.

"I'm not an Earthman. I was born in deep space, and the Jekkara Port was the first ground I ever set foot on. I belong to no world, and no race. I belong to myself, to give my loyalty where I will."

He waited, and then went on.

"Mars isn't lost, unless you go ahead and lose it," he said. "You will, if you tackle the Company this way. Kyra! Kyra, come here and tell them what you saw."

The sea of faces turned to watch her as she rose out of the dark street and came fluttering down beside Rick on the scaffold. She touched him, timidly, afraid of the crowd. Rick put his hand on her gently. Then he faced the crowd again.

"The Earthman of the Company left me hanging on those knives, to die," he shouted. "It was Kyra who saved me—she and Beudach. I owe my life to Mars."

He smiled down at Kyra.

"Tell them, baby," he whispered.

She told them. "You would die," she finished, "and never touch them."

An uncertain mutter of talk ran across the square. The thief leaned forward. His knife was still raised, but he seemed to have forgotten about it. His topaz eyes held a curious, unwilling respect.

"You," he said. "How would you do it?"

"If I tell you that, Jaffa Storm will know it almost as soon as you do. He has powers as great as your seers—stone walls don't stop his mind. How else do you think he knew your leaders were here ready to be killed? If he hadn't been so busy, and felt so safe, he'd have been back to spy on Ruh before this."

"Then we would just have to trust you," the thief said softly. He began to balance the dagger idly in his hand. "Beudach was a dying man."

"Tell them, Kyra," Rick said.

She stretched herself in the torch-flare, her wings spread wide.

"Listen, you Martians," she cried out furiously, "Jaffa Storm put chains on Rick and tried to make him be a slave in the mines. When Rick wouldn't submit, Storm tried to kill him. Four nights ago he left Rick hanging on the wall to die, and he took Rick's mate back with him to the Company. What more reason could a man have to want revenge?''

There was a sort of light shining out of her. Her soft young voice carried like a flute.

"Rick will lead Mars to greatness," she told them. "He will bring life back to the dying. He will give you unity, and strength.''

For a long time there was silence. Then the shout came—a crashing thunder of salute that shook the stones.

Rick turned to the thief in the golden rags.

"Keep them ready," said Rick. "It won't be long. I'll send word back by Kyra when to strike.''

The thief nodded. Rick held up his hands to the crowd. He smiled, but his eyes remained cold and remote, untouched. Then just as silently and mysteriously as they had appeared, Rick and Kyra departed. . . .

Out across the sea-bottom, in the office that had been Fallon's in the Company Administration pylon, Jaffa Storm was busy—busier than Rick dreamed. He was not doing anything physically. He was sitting perfectly still, elbows on knees, his eyes closed, and his knuckles pressed in a certain curious way against his temples. He had been in contact with Rick's mind before. Now that he had the wave-length, so to speak, it was much easier to tune in. He laughed softly when Rick made his statement about Storm's mental powers and the danger of telling the battle plan.

Storm did not move until Rick was through speaking—until he had examined the unspoken things inside the Earthman's head. Then he rose, stretching, and nodded.

"A good plan," he said. "Very shrewd. It has even a fair chance of succeeding. Opposing brute force against brute force is always a gamble . . . Let's see.''

He flicked on a light under a sort of table of thick frosted glass, and spun a selector dial. Presently a three-dimensional full-color miniature of the Polar area—a glorified relief map—took shape on the screen.

Jaffa Storm sat down again, taking the same position. He stared at the screen, but his eyes were looking into some other place, much farther away.

CHAPTER 9

HUGH ST. JOHN sighed, stretched out in a long chair, and closed his eyes.

"Well, that's that," he said to Eran Mak. "The last shot in my locker, the last credit in my bank account. I'm finished."

Eran Mak said nothing. He was sitting on the balcony rail, smoking, watching the easy life of Kahora under the sun-lighted dome. His swarthy piratical face was shadowed and sombre.

"I hoped maybe you, as a Martian, would have better luck," St. John said dully. "But they didn't let you any farther than they did me."

The bells in Eran Mak's ear chimed as he shook his head.

"Well, there goes Mars. Mak, just who and what the devil are these Thinkers, that they're too blamed good to see any-body?"

"Nobody knows, really, except that they're the First Race, supposedly the original Martians, which would imply that the rest of us came from somewhere else," Mak answered. "Or else they're non-human and preceded us in evolution. I suspect they're just a bunch of smart people who liked to live in peace and comfort, and so withdrew themselves behind a wall of legend, glamour, and fear."

St. John found the strength to smile at that. "What I love about you, Mak, is your simple faith in everything. But these Thinkers have done a lot of good from time to time."

Mak nodded. "Sure. Theoretically at least they guide the viewpoint of Mars—when they feel like bothering. It has to be some big important split, like the inter-hemispheric war back in Sixty-two Thousand and Seven, when the Sea Kings had trouble."

"Wouldn't you think this was important?" inquired St. John.

"I suppose," said Eran Mak quietly, "the Thinkers have aged with the rest of us."

There was a long silence. The city whispered below. Warm sunlight fell through the high dome, bringing a soft jewel lustre

to the buildings of colored plastic, a delicate shimmer to the
web of walks and roadways arching between them. The air was
soft, neither warm nor cool, pleasantly scented.

Eran Mak swore with a deadly calmness and got up, sending
a shower of music from the bells.

"I'm going back to Jekkara, Hugh!" he growled. "I want
to breathe air again, and wear something that doesn't make
people look twice to see if I'm male or female. Want to come
down with me?"

"Yes, thanks, I may as well." St. John looked up and
laughed, rather sheepishly. "I don't know why Mars should
mean anything to me. But this is like giving up hope for a
friend."

He looked down at the plastic pavement. "If I only knew
what happened to Mayo."

Mak put a hand on his shoulder. St. John rose and followed
him inside, to start packing.

The telescreen hummed.

"The devil with it," said St. John. He went on into the
bedroom. The buzzer continued to hum stridently. Presently
the tempo changed to the short insistent "urgent" signal.

St. John swore and hit the switch. The screen flickered and
cleared, showing the interior of a crude public booth, liberally
scrawled, carved, and initialed. The man in the booth was a
stranger, big and tawny and yellow-eyed, dressed in the usual
gaudy silk shirt and tight pants of a space-hand on earth-leave.
His hands were bandaged.

He was not a usual space-hand. St. John suppressed a shiver
of excitement.

"Hugh St. John, here," he said.

"Urquhart," answered the man. "Richard Gunn Urquhart." He pulled the bright shirt open at his throat. "You
know what that is?"

Eran Mak, standing behind St. John, let his breath out in a
startled curse.

"By the planets! The Collar of Ruh!"

Rick nodded. "For Mars. A united Mars. Mayo says that's
what you're after."

"Mayo!" St. John gripped the edges of the screen. "Where
is she? Is she all right?"

"Jaffa Storm's got her, but she's not been harmed. It's a
long story, and I'll tell you later. Right now I want to know

something. Do you want union enough to risk your neck for
it?''

St. John drew a long breath. His eyes met Mak's briefly.
"Go on," he said. "I'm listening."

"All right." Rick sketched in the details of the massacre at
Ruh. "The Marshies are all set to go. The men of the New
Town will be, too, when I get through with 'em. Storm has
been crimping here already, and the people don't like it. But
frontal attack won't be enough. Somebody's got to help us
from the inside. If we can get Storm, the rest will be easy."

St. John frowned in a worried manner. "What about Fallon?"

"Storm killed him four days ago. Nobody but Storm and
Mayo know about that, and probably the Venusian, Vargo. Do
you think you can work it with Storm to get permission to land
on the Company's 'copter deck?"

St. John frowned. "I don't know whether Storm has definitely connected Mayo with us or not, but I think he was always suspicious of me. I'll be honest with you. He'll probably
let us land, all right, and then he'll blow us to Kingdom
Come."

"You willing to try it?"

"Mayo's there—you're sure of that."

"I'm sure. I'll tell you about that, too."

"All right." St. John leaned closer. "There's just one thing.
Who the dickens are you, and what do you want out of this?"

Rick held up his bandaged hands. "To get these around Jaffa
Storm's throat."

The bells in Eran Mak's ear rang faintly. "I know you.
You're Rick, the man Storm was trying to kill, the man who
helped Mayo to get away, down there in the mines."

Rick stared past St. John at Eran Mak. "Well."

Mak's hot golden eyes dwelt on the iron Collar. "I'm a Jekkara man myself. But if Beudach of Ruh put that on you himself, it means plenty." He shrugged, smiling. "What have we
got to lose, Hugh?"

St. John's hands trembled slightly on the edges of the screen.
He was still studying Rick, with an odd intentness.

"Not a thing," he said softly. "Not a blamed thing. All
right, Rick. I'll fix it with Storm somehow. Then what?"

"Then fly down to the New Town. I'll be waiting, with

everything set to go. And make it fast, St. John! Fast, before anything gets to Storm."

In the meantime, Jaffa Storm had finished his mental exploration—an effort that left him exhausted, despite his physical strength. He, of all the creatures on Mars, human, semi-human and sub-human, had seen beyond the veil of mystery that hid the Polar Cities and the Thinkers who dwelt in them.

Jaffa Storm was pleased with what he saw with his mind's eye. He gave instructions and took off northward in a one-man flier. He returned less than a full day later, tired, exultant, and bearing in his arms something wrapped in a curious shining cloth—a something that, for all its small size, bent Storm's knees with its weight. . . .

After finishing his talk with Hugh St. John, Rick walked down the main street of the New Town. It was night again. He had waited purposely until the life of the place was going full strength.

Ochre dust rose in clouds from Rick's boots. The unpaved streets, marked out at random by lines of shacks and lean-tos, were crowded with men—space-hands, placer miners, homesteaders, drifters, bums, thieves, con men—and women to match. They were predominantly from Earth, but Venus, the Asteroids, and every planetary colony was represented.

Most of the buildings on the main street were saloons and crude copies of expensive amusement places. Dream Palaces, joints dealing in exotic drugs at cut-rate prices, a couple of three-dimensional cinemas showing films several years old, and numerous girl shows featuring, "The Exotic Beauty of a Hundred Worlds—No Minors Allowed." The noise was terrific.

Rick steered around a developing brawl in mid-street and stopped in the comparative shelter of an archway. He watched for a while. There was tension about the crowd. An ugliness that had, as yet, no direction to it. Every man was armed, most of them with blasters.

He glanced up at the sky, measuring the distance between the two moons. He nodded and went on. Presently he turned into the swinging red plastic doors of "The Furnace—Hottest Spot on Mars." And the biggest spot in the New Town of Ruh.

A bunch of tired-looking Venusian girls were putting their polished-emerald bodies mechanically through a routine Rick had seen five years ago in Losanglis, back on Earth. Hard-looking men, in various stages of drunkenness, leaned on the

ringside tables and carried on loud one-sided conversations
with them. The long bar, backed up by an interplanetary array
of liquors, mostly, and a cheap Florent mirror—the type that is
sensitive only to the infrared heat rays given off by living
bodies, transforming them into visible reflections with interesting results—was jammed from end to end.

Rick elbowed his way in. He ordered thil, a potent cold-
green liquid from the Jekkara Low-Canals, and sipped it,
studying the mirror.

Suddenly somebody down the line let out a bellow.

"Rick! Rick Urquhart!"

The volume of other noise lessened a bit, for others nearby
had been startled by the tone, and the next words rang
clearly.

"My stars! I thought you was dead in the Company pits!"

At the word "Company," a brassy silence descended upon
the Furnace.

Rick scanned the mirror. He saw a gangling, sinewy shape
gesticulating frantically at his reflection. "Texas!" he yelled,
and pulled himself up on the bar.

He was aware that he had the attention of everyone in the
place, including the tired chorus girls.

He walked down the bar, past rows of mugs and glasses,
reached over and pulled "Texas" up beside them. They
pounded each other. Texas had a tough, good-natured face with
the bones sticking through his leathery skin, bad teeth, high-
heeled boots, and a liquor breath that could stand by itself. He
had herded meat-animals on three planets and an asteroid, and
was the closest thing to a friend Rick had found in his wan-
derings.

"For Pete's sake, yuh old sheepherder!" yelled Texas. "I
thought the crimpers got yuh, last time we was over in the Old
Town."

"They did," answered Rick. "But I started a small riot in
the mine and was lucky enough to get away." Rick's voice
carried quietly all over the room. "I hear Storm's coming here
for his men now."

An animal snarl from the crowd answered this last remark.

"Nobody gets away from the Company," somebody near
Rick said. "How come yuh managed it?"

Rick held out his wrists. "See those marks? You think I was
wearing shackles for the fun of it?" He spoke to the crowd.

"Yeah, I was lucky. I got away down an abandoned drift. But the others didn't. You know what they used on us? A Banning, full power. I've seen what happens to the guys the Company takes! I've lived in the barracks and sweated in the mines and had the living blazes kicked out of me, right along with them. I was lucky. Now I'm telling you. Unless we do something about Jaffa Storm and that gang of his, we'll all die in the pits before we're through!"

"Sure," said Texas, after the noise had died down. "But Storm holds all the aces, Rick. I'd shore like to tromp his head in, but can anyone get inside to do it?"

"I can," Rick said.

He watched the men lean forward hungrily. "Listen, you guys! Maybe you know there was some trouble in the Old Town a few nights ago. Well, I was there. I saw Storm march his men in and blast down their king and a bunch of Marshie leaders. The Marshies are going to hit the Company tonight, with everything they've got. Are you going to let them have all the fun?"

He waited until he could make himself heard again.

"And I'm telling you this, too! Unless we fight along with the Marshies, we're done. And why shouldn't we? Gosh, they're human too, and we've both taken it from the Company long enough! We're going to have to fight the Company sooner or later. How long do you think the little guys like us can last on Mars, fighting Storm and the Marshies both?"

He let them think about that, for a moment.

"I've got it fixed to get inside the compound tonight," he said quietly. "I owe Jaffa Storm a big debt, and I aim to pay it off. How many of you guys want to be there when we open the gates?"

The air was full of waving fists and a great harsh roar.

"You take 'em, Tex," Rick said. "'Get 'em there fast, and quiet. Keep separate from the Marshies until the fighting begins, but work with them. I got that end all fixed. Get volunteers to take up what 'copters and atmoplanes there are in this dump and clean out the Bannings by the gates. Take every weapon you can scrape up; if I don't manage to do what I'm planning to do, you and the Marshies can kick the gates down, anyway, together!"

At the same moment Kyra had been trying to win cooperation from the Martians with but meager results. The thief in

the golden rags was scowling sullenly. He was proving stubbornly antagonistic.

"Earthmen!" sneered the thief. "When men spill blood together in the same cause, it makes them brothers. Should we
become brothers to them?"

The men around the table let out a yell.

"No!" they shrieked. There were five of them, representing
every Quarter and class in Ruh.

Kyra beat the air impatiently with her wings.

"These Earthmen have done you no harm," she said. "They
mean you no harm. They've suffered from the Company as
much as you have, and they have a blood debt. By our own
laws, can we deny them the right to pay it?"

The men thought about that. The thief started to say something. Kyra spoke first.

"Together, Martians and Earthmen both, we can destroy the
Company. We'll have weapons, and strength. Alone either one
of us would fail. This, even if—if Rick should be killed, we
can go ahead and win." She waited a moment, and then cried
out, "The Earthmen will go, whether we do or not! Will you
let them have all the glory?"

The men around the table rose and howled that they would
not.

"We'll fight!" they bellowed. "Down with the Company!"

CHAPTER 10

AFTER A SEARCH Rick found St. John and Eran Mak on the
'copter field just beyond the shacks of the town.

"You fix it with Storm all right?" Rick asked.

"Yes," answered St. John. "Told him I had news from the
Polar Cities—something so important to him and Fallon that I
was scared stiff. Don't know whether he believed me or not."

"Doesn't matter, as long as we get there."

More time passed. Noise, movement, and light died in the
New Town. St. John threw down the stub of his cigarette.

"Time now, Rick?"

"Yeah. Let's go."

They climbed into the neat little flier. Eran Mak took one last look at the sky.

"The moons are right together, Rick," he said. "Favorable omen for Mars. Chance, or did you plan it that way?"

"What do you think? Shut the door, for Pete's sake, and let's go!"

Because he was looking for them, Rick saw the crowds of men moving across the sea-bottom from Ruh. They went without lights, spread out widely, hugging the shadows. Rick hoped that owing to the rough terrain and the confusing moonlight they could get close to the Company walls without being spotted.

The Company compound was blazing with light, everything going full blast. While they watched, two ships went up from the port, trailing comet-tails of flame across the night. The little 'copter trembled in the air-wash the rocket-liners left behind them.

"Wait a minute!" Rick said suddenly. The others looked at him, startled. He was watching the rocket-flares. "How do I know?" he muttered. "Storm read our minds before. How do I know?" He burst without warning into a rowdy ballad about a spaceman's daughter and a lonesome comet, shoved St. John away from the controls, and took over himself. His eyes blazed with excitement.

"Have you gone crazy?" St. John snapped.

But Eran Mak studied Rick shrewdly.

"There are more things in heaven and Mars than you Earth-born people know," he said. "Telepathy, for one." He glanced quickly at the way the 'copter was heading now. "Come on, Hugh. Let's sing!"

Using the ballad as a screen for his thoughts, Rick shot the 'copter toward the spaceport and brought it low over a dark and deserted area on its outskirts. Then he handed the controls back to St. John.

"Storm may not have been as busy as I thought," he explained. "He may have picked my mind clean, for all I know, and set a trap for us all. Anyway, I got a better idea, and a better chance of getting by with it. Get back to the men, double quick, and tell 'em to stay way back from the Company until I'm through. Then come in swinging!"

"How will we know when you're through?"

"You'll know!"

St. John frowned, looking quickly at the spaceport. Rick's
jaw hardened.

"He isn't running out, Hugh," Eran Mak said quietly.
"Let's go."

"Sorry," St. John said curtly.

Rick grunted and dropped out the door, ten feet or so to the
ground. The 'copter sped away. Rick stood still, looking
around him, and then headed for the loom of a row of launching racks about a half mile away. Apparently no one had noticed the furtive landing. There was no reason why anyone
should have, at that distance from the field.

From the small size of the racks he judged the ships cradled
there were private jobs belonging to officials of the Company.
That was exactly what Rick wanted. Everything was dark
around them, too, which meant that nobody was going anywhere just now.

Rick crawled face downward for the last few hundred yards.
That was fortunate, because he avoided the electric-eye warning beams, which were set to catch a man knee-height from
the ground. Presently he was in the shadow of one of the huge
tilted tubes. The racket of the port itself, where men slaved to
load Fallonite and unload supplies, was close to him.

The rack was not locked. There was no reason to keep it
locked. Rick slid inside, through the double-lock into the cradled ship. A nice, opulent, easy-to-handle baby, convertible
for atmosphere travel. Sweating with the need for haste, Rick
found a bulger in the locker and put it on. Then he strapped
himself into the pilot's seat and got busy.

The thunder of the warming motors must have brought people running, but Rick didn't wait to see. He took off long
before the tubes were safely heated, and once a spaceship has
begun thundering there isn't much anyone can do about it.

He made a long screaming arc upward clear of the thin air-
blanket. Then he flipped over, got the rotos going, and swooped
back toward the Company compound. On the way he dumped
fuel, watching the gauge carefully. Mayo's bungalow prison
was way off from the Administration pylon, but he was taking
no chances.

He came in high and pushed the ship's nose downward, aiming it like a bomb over the pylon and the north wall. Then he
locked the controls, pushed the ignition wide open, and bailed

out, blasting blue blazes out of the bulger-rocket to get away from there.

The force of the explosion threw him around, even so. It was beautiful. The pylon crumpled down like a dropped wedding cake, and the walls flattened outward. After that everything was hidden by smoke and flying debris.

Rick smiled, his teeth glinting wolf-like in the moonlight. Then he changed his course, shooting away toward the far side of the compound where Mayo was.

On the way he saw men pouring up out of the folds and creases of the sea-bottom, flowing toward the breached walls. Earthmen and Martians, running together over the gray moss, blasters and slice-bars swinging beside sword-blades and the spiked knuckle-dusters of the Low-Canals. Just men, now, carrying the same hate in their hearts, charging the same barricade.

Rick nodded. "Make 'em bleed together," he thought, "and you've made brothers. For a while, at least. And a while is all I need."

He dropped down, into the dark and quiet back lot of the compound, and found Mayo's bungalow from Kyra's verbal map. He climbed out of the heavy bulger, laughing at the weakness of his knees and the way his heart pounded. Excitement of the ship and the wrecking, sure, but there was more to it than that.

The bungalow was unlocked. He knew the minute he opened the door that it was empty. He went through the rooms, calling Mayo's name, and then he saw the blood on the carpet, a trail of it, fresh and wet. He turned cold, and very quiet.

He followed the erratic spatter of red drops across the paving outside, to a little shed that might have housed a 'copter, kept secretly for an emergency. The trail ended there.

Rick ran back. He yelled for Kyra, but there was no answer, though he had sent her to watch, to help Mayo escape if she could. There was a tremendous roar of fighting now, where Storm's Venusians were standing off the Terro-Martian rabble. Rick ran toward it, more slowly now because the wounds in his feet were making themselves felt. On the way he saw the prison-barracks of the work-gangs had been thrown open according to his instructions.

Things were a little confused for Rick after that. He was caught up in the fighting, but he only half saw the men he blasted down. He was looking for St. John and Eran Mak—not because he wanted them, but because he wanted their 'copter. He was thinking of Mayo and Jaffa Storm, and he was not quite sane.

Between the men of Ruh, New Town and Old, and the liberated slaves, the Company resistance was crushed, utterly. Rick's stunt with the crashing ship had almost done it alone, and without Storm to egg them on the Venusians were weakened. It was quiet again in a surprisingly short time. At last Rick found St. John and Eran Mak standing at the edge of the enormous crater made by Rick's ship. The ruined pylon lay like a giant scrap pile over one edge. The two men were bending over a twisted metal object.

"Heaven only knows," St. John was saying. "I never saw anything like it before. But it's probably just as well we didn't have to face it."

Eran Mak touched it, shivering slightly. "It was made for death. You can feel that." He saw Rick then, started to hail him, and changed it to a startled, "What's wrong?"

"Mayo. Storm's taken her—had a 'copter hidden out. Where's yours?"

"Won't fly," said St. John briefly. "Debris hit the prop." His face was white and strained, suddenly. "We'll find a telescreen and get the MPG busy right away. Also the Interplanetary authorities. He may get away from Mars, but he'll be caught when he lands." He caught Rick's look of leashed fury and flinched. "It's all we can do right now! Come on."

They found a screen in the laboratory, which was untouched by the blast. While St. John made his reports, Rick paced restlessly, limping with pain but unable to sit down. They were alone in the office, the three of them. Eran Mak leaned against the door, smoking, watching Rick with hard, speculative eyes.

St. John switched off the screen. "Now. Let's talk business," he said.

"The blazes with business," snarled Rick. "I'm interested in Mayo."

Rick's mouth twitched in a half smile. "They're my men. I brought 'em together, and I control them." He hit the Collar of Ruh with his knuckle. "There's no law on Mars but strength. Storm knew that, too. Now I've got the strength. I'm willing to play along with you, unless you get under my feet too much, and I'm not going to run things the way Storm did."

"Until you have to," St. John said, "or until you feel like it. Mars is your plaything now, is that it?"

Rick's face hardened, his cold cat-gaze turned inward.

"I told Mayo I'd give her Mars to wear on a chain around her neck," he said. "I don't know what I'm going to do with it, yet, aside from that. Whatever looks the best to me. But the devil with Mars, and you, too!" He limped over to the screen, reaching for the switch. "Maybe I can get a 'copter from the field."

He heard Eran Mak's bells chiming faintly, and then in a sudden jangle of music. He turned around. The wounds in his hands and feet made him clumsy, but even so his blaster was almost drawn when Eran Mak took him across the temple with the heavy barrel of his own weapon. Rick sagged to the floor and lay still.

St. John licked his lips. "You shouldn't have done that, Mak," he said hoarsely.

"Why not?" The Martian was perfectly composed, tying Rick with brisk efficiency. "The big boy is as irresponsible as a child and just about as safe to play with as a tiger. Think for yourself what Mars will be like in five years, under his rule."

St. John nodded slowly. "A barbarian emperor has never brought anything except war and cruelty. But without Rick we'd never have won."

"No. But he did that for himself. Not for you, nor me, nor Mars." Mak rose and stood scowling at Rick, swinging the bells back and forth with his fingertip. "What to do with him is the sticker. I don't want to kill him and there is his personal following to think about. That cursed Collar!" Mak snapped his fingers suddenly. "Get me some acid out of the lab. I can get the lock open with that. Without the Collar Rick is nothing to the Martians, and if we tell the Earthmen that Rick ran out on them with several million credits of the Company funds, it'll finish him for good."

"That's dirty, Mak!" St. John protested.

"Sometimes," said the Martian patiently, "a dirty blow wins a clean fight. Think of Mars, not Richard Gunn Urquhart. Go on, Hugh! Move!"

Hugh St. John moved.

CHAPTER 11

IT TOOK RICHARD Gunn Urquhart a long time to collect himself. He came to slowly, in a series of mental jerks. From that, and the pendulum sensation in his head and the dead-frog taste in his mouth, he knew he'd been drugged with tsamo, a Martian narcotic.

The roof over him, when he could see it, turned out to be the ceiling of a spaceship's cabin. Through long training, Rick's subconscious did a quick weighing and sorting of the sounds filtering in from outside. The ship was in port, lading, and not yet cradled.

He felt shaky. He was in no rush to wake up—until he discovered that his right wrist was manacled to the bunk stanchion. After that, things began to come back to him. The tsamo made him stupid. Connected thinking brought the sweat of physical effort to his skin, but finally he had the pieces put together, well enough. He sat up, yelling, shaken and blazing-eyed with fury—and desperation.

No one answered. The cabin door was closed, and he was alone. He fought the cuff-chain for a while, gave it up, and subsided into a quietness that had nothing of peace in it.

He saw the letter, propped on the table beside the head of his bunk.

It was addressed to him. He tore it open.

> Rick:
> This is admittedly a dirty trick, but you left us no choice. The future of a world was more important than you, or us; so—
> Fifty thousand credits have been placed to your account in the New York Main Office of the First Interplanetary Bank of Earth. Perhaps that will help to poultice the bump on your head. Don't try to come back to Mars. Both Martians and Terrans have been given a slanderous but logical account of your actions and will probably shoot you on sight. Moreover, as you said, there is no law on Mars but strength—and now we have the

strength. Be sensible, and keep your head where it will be of use to you. Good luck.

Eran Mak.

There was also a postscript.

    Don't worry about Mayo. We're moving heaven and Mars to help her.

Rick's lips pulled back from his teeth in a snarl. He crumpled the letter and threw it away. Quite suddenly he was violently sick. He lay quiet for a while, cold yet dripping sweat. The dulled racket of lading flowed past his ears, engines, winches, men yelling, the thump and crash of heavy loads.

He pulled himself up and began bellowing again.

Presently a boy came in, carrying a tray. He was like a million ship's boys on the Triangle. His ragged slops flagged loosely on his ankles and his face had a look of habitual wariness, like that of a hunted but vicious animal. He set the tray down, keeping out of Rick's reach.

"Where am I?" Rick asked.

"Jekkara Port." The kid studied him, obviously impressed by Rick's size and mature toughness.

"What ship?"

"The *Mary Ellen Dow*, outbound for Earth. We take off in three-four hours."

Despite the handcuff Rick stood up. "That means they start cradling in just a few minutes, and after that I'm stuck! Get me the skipper."

"Not a chance. No one ain't comin' in here but me, till after take-off. That's orders. 'Sides, they're busy." The boy turned toward the door again, but his attention lingered on Rick's bandaged, big brown hand.

Rick relaxed. He pointed to a purple bruise under the kid's eye and grinned. "I see you got some battle scars, too. Over a dame, I'll bet."

It was no dame. The cook had a hangover. But the kid expanded with pride.

"Yeah," he said. "Some dish, too. Happened at Madame Kan's. Ever been there?"

"You bet. Best place on Mars."

"It's okay," said the kid condescendingly. "But I don't like these Martian babes much. Too skinny."

"That's right. Bad tempered, too." Rick winced. "Golly, what a head I got! Who doped me?"

"I dunno. You was out cold when they carried you in. That was three days ago. You musta taken a deep breath, all right!"

"I guess so." That wasn't hard to figure. Eran Mak had knocked him out and then kept him that way with drugs. It must have been Eran Mak, then, who had taken the Collar of Ruh. Rick gave the boy a sudden look of intimate intentness. "Kick that door shut and come over here. I want to talk to you."

"I ain't got the key to that cuff on me."

"I know that. Listen, pick up that letter and read it."

The boy obeyed, warily. His eyes began to bulge. "Fifty thousand credits!" he said hoarsely. "My stars!"

"You could buy Madame Kan's, with that."

"No," said the kid softly. He was looking way off somewhere, and his face changed. "No. I'd get my master's ticket and then I'd buy my own ship—or part of it. A ship that would maybe go out—clear out to The Belt and even Jupiter."

"You can have it, kid."

The boy turned around and looked at him. His mouth twisted sullenly. He started to go out.

"I mean it," Rick said. "Listen, you fuzz-tailed sap! I'm playing for something bigger than fifty thousand measly credits. If I don't get off this ship before she starts cradling, I'll lose something plenty important. I'm offering to buy the key to this handcuff for fifty thousand credits."

The kid stared at him. He tried three times before he could get the words out. "Ain't got the key."

"I've been a ship's boy myself. You can get it."

The kid ran his hands through his hair and across his face. He seemed to be having trouble breathing. "I ain't fallin' for no bunk like that!" he cried out suddenly. "I'll get eight bells beat out of me for lettin' you go, and that's all I'll get."

"Gimme that letter." Rick went through his pockets and found a stub of pencil. The boy tossed the wadded paper on the bunk, still not coming close. "What's your name?"

"Yancey, William Lee Yancey."

Rick smoothed out the letter and wrote carefully on the back of it. Then he tossed it back. The kid read haltingly:

To whom it may concern. William Lee Yancey has done a job for me worth fifty thousand credits. My account in the First Interplanetary Bank of Earth, New York Main Office (see other side), is to go to William Yancey.

Richard Gunn Urquhart.

A slow, hot glow came into the boy's eyes. He rolled the paper tight and hid it on him.

"Wait," he said, and went out.

Rick waited. He waited a thousand years, and his heart wore a hole through his ribs. He stared at the cabin wall, but all he could see was Mayo's face the last time he remembered it, with the sweat and blood of his impalement glistening, jewel-like, on the white skin and the dark eyes full of sorrow and terror and love.

The kid came back, and he had the key.

"Swiped it out of the Skipper's extra pants," he grinned. "They're hookin' the tugs on. We got to hurry."

Rick could hear the powerful electro-magnets of the roaring tugs clamping onto the ship's skin, ready to wrestle her into her launching cradle. The job would take several hours, but after it was started there was no way on or off.

The lock clicked. Rick flung the cuff off and they went to the door. There was no one in the corridor. Officers were on the bridge, crew strapped into their launching hammocks. Sometimes the cradling was tougher on the crew than the take-off.

The warning bell rang through the ship. Air locks were already shut. The boy pulled Rick's sleeve. "Waste chute," he said. "This way." They ran. Rick's feet were still stiff and sore, but he could use them all right.

They found the chute, slid in, and let the compressed air blow them gently out. The tugs made a deafening clamor, heaving and straining to shift the huge bulk. Nobody noticed the two men running from the shadows under the hull of the *Mary Ellen Dow.* It was not quite dawn, with Diemos dying in the western sky and the sun not born yet in the east.

Rick paused in the shelter of a towering empty cradle, and saw that the boy had disappeared. Rick smiled crookedly.

"Didn't trust me not to clip him and take my letter back," he thought. "Yeah. Well, he's smart, at that."

He promptly forgot the kid and the fifty thousand credits in deciding what was the safest and quickest way to steal a 'copter. In his spaceman's dress he could get by all right unless Eran Mak and St. John had plastered his description around too much on the telescreen. Finally he shrugged. That was a chance he'd have to take.

He walked on, erect and not too fast, acting as though he belonged there. He only stopped once, to pick up a piece of heavy scrap that fitted nicely into his curled-up fingers. There was about him a cold, withdrawn look—of ruthless concentration.

The 'copter field was a good mile and a half from the rocket field. Jeeps sped back and forth between them and the huge warehouses, sheds, and repair shops. Even at this early hour Jekkara Port was awake and hustling. Before long, one of the jeeps slowed down and the driver offered Rick a lift.

Refusal would have been more dangerous than acceptance—spacemen never walk if they can help it. Rick climbed aboard.

The driver, an indistinct dark shape in the gloom, talked as he sent the little car bucketing across toward the 'copter field.

"You just in, pal?"

"Yeah."

"Then you ain't heard the news, I guess."

"No."

"Well, the Terran Exploitations Company has had the blinking stuffings knocked out of it. Some of our guys finally got smart and took the law in their own hands. Looked like for a while the Company was gonna own the whole cussed planet, but now us little guys are gonna have a look-in. Swell deal, all around. This new gover'ment they're putting together is all right."

He burst into sudden laughter. "Only thing is, we got to get in harness with the Marshies. Well, it's their world—and if they let me pick my own, I won't mind!"

"Yeah," said Rick. "That's fine."

"Suits me." The light was getting stronger now, with the suddenness of Martian dawns. "Funny thing about that Urquhart bird, though. Rick, they call him. Fed everybody a lot of pious bunk about the future of Mars. Got the fight going, and then ran out on his pals with about everything in the Company's safe. Took a collar with him, too—some gimmick that's sacred to the Marshies, or something. He better never come back to Mars if he wants to stay healthy."

Rick said nothing. The 'copter field was still too far away.

The driver rattled on. "Lots of guys is going to buy land here. Build cities, make the earth good again. Yeah, there's a great future from Terra. There'll be a lot of work to do, and it'll mean something when we get through. Why, my boy might be President of the MPG some day!" He turned to Rick. "Why don't you grab yourself a piece of this? Ain't no future in space except old age and the grav-bends . . ."

His voice trailed off. His eyes got wide. "Hey," he said. "Hey, you're—you're—Rick!"

Rick hit him with his loaded fist. But the driver was tough, too, and quick. He was half stunned in spite of his rapid twist, but he fell across the horn and made it bleat like a scared goat—a goat enlarged to the size of a small spaceship. Drivers in other jeeps began to slow down and look around.

Rick kicked the guy clear out onto the ground and grabbed the wheel himself. Somebody yelled. More horns began to blare. Jeeps circled around, whipping red veils of dust behind them. Rick jammed his foot down on the throttle.

The dregs of the tsamo in his system wiped out all the emotions in him other than his main determination to get where he was going. Only a complete lunatic could have got away with it. He did. He shot full speed toward the 'copter field, horn and throttle pressed wide open, and left it to the other men to get out of his way.

They did. Some of them so narrowly that a sheet of tissue paper would have been torn between the passing wheels, but they did. They weren't quite crazy enough to stand against the driver who didn't care whether they stood or not.

Rick crashed through onto the edge of the 'copter field. By this time there were alarms ringing and men running around, but nobody was quite sure yet what the trouble was. There was a sleek, fast little ship warming up out on the tarmac. Rick went for it. Three startled mechanics scattered away from his jeep. Rick jumped out and let it tear on by itself.

The owner of the 'copter came from the other side of the ship. The mechanics closed in. There was a lot of noise. Rick hunched his shoulders, still cuddling the hunk of scrap in his fist. He knocked two of the mechanics cold. The third was too

dizzy to get up, and the owner took one look at Rick and ran
away.

Rick was clear of the ground before anyone else could get
close enough to do anything.

He pushed the motor wide open, heading for a low range of
hills in the distance. Other 'copters, six or seven of them, were
shooting up from the field behind him in furious pursuit. Rick
spared one hand for the telescreen. He listened briefly and then
smiled, not because anything was funny.

His escape from the *Mary Ellen Dow* had been discovered,
and the skipper was screaming to high heaven about it. The
driver of the jeep had been revived sufficiently to tell who
slugged him, and the field dispatcher was sending out a general
alarm over the theft of the 'copter.

Such calls were addressed variously to the Martian Planetary
Patrol and to Hugh St. John. Rick had never known anything
on Mars to move that fast. The driver had been right—there
was considerable feeling about that Urquhart guy, and none of
it was friendly.

Rick left his screen on as an aid to keeping track of what
Mars was doing about him. Angry, red-faced men tried repeatedly to make him answer direct calls. He left his transmitter off and didn't even bother to curse them privately.

The pursuing ships hung right on his tail, but he had played
in luck. There wasn't anything there good enough to overhaul
him. The hill swept up under him, worn and red and barren,
scarred with hollow canyons like cavities in an old man's teeth.
Rick's tawny brows got a deep cleft between them.

His pursuers couldn't catch him, but he couldn't get away.
His position had been radioed all over Mars, and pretty soon
there would be MPP ships circling in, and probably a few of
St. John's. All landing fields where he might go for fuel would
be warned and closed against him. The 'copter didn't look like
it was going to be much help to him.

He thought all that over, studying the landscape—screwed
up tight inside but not panicky. Just coldly weighing his
chances.

There began to be calls in quick Martian rattling through
his receiver. MPP men signaling position, and getting close.

Far away down the tired line of hills Rick was a red cloud
rolling in from the desert. He let his breath out in what might
have been a laugh and kicked the rudder bar. The little ship

made a tight arc across the sky, fled screaming, and plunged a few moments later into the heart of a sandstorm.

CHAPTER 12

DEEP INTO THE sandstorm plunged Rick's 'copter! It was one of those howling, angry khamsins that burst up from nowhere when the lonesome winds meet each other and start quarreling. They had swept up over the hills now, swirling their dusty cloaks in each other's faces. Anything less scientifically stabilized than the 'copter would have been smashed into the ground within ten minutes. But the little craft took the punishment bravely, bounding wildly in the twisting currents, going where they pushed her, but riding them, her automatic stabilizers keeping her level. Rick set the controls and locked them. She'd fly on all right, all by herself.

There was a standard emergency escape kit in the rack. He strapped the harness around him, tied a thick cloth tightly over his face, and dropped through the hatch.

He fell into stifling sheets of sand. They wrapped themselves around him, crushed and beat and tore him, worked into his clothes and into his eyes and mouth and nose. He pressed the plunger on the escape rig. He was dropping fast, too fast. In the roar of the storm he couldn't hear whether or not the lighter-than-hydrogen synthetic gas was going into the balloon or not. Seeing anything much was out of the question.

After a while his rate of descent slackened and he was conscious of pressure by the harness. Relief brought a quick cold sweat on him. He thought about back in the old days when a guy had to depend on a chute for a low altitude jump, and thanked Providence whoever it was that thought up the synthe-silk balloon which could be inflated in three seconds from a pressure tank and a man could live through almost anything there was in the sky.

The 'copter would head empty out of the storm and with any luck the hounds would waste a lot of time chasing her. By that time Rick could have lost himself in the hills—providing the wind didn't slam him flat against a cliff he couldn't see.

It didn't, quite. The balloon bobbed out suddenly toward the edge of the storm. Noting the difference in the light, Rick uncovered his eyes, shielding them with his hands and peering through the merest slits. Dimly, very dimly like the shadow of a submerged rock under his feet, he saw a ragged pinnacle, and then ahead of him a vast looming shape that looked solid.

He doubled his knees into his chest and took the impact as he would have taken a fall, on his flexed legs. It jarred him badly, but no more. He pulled on the cord that let gas out of the bag, clinging desperately to the eroded rock. The wind dragged at the balloon, and the balloon dragged at his harness, and pretty soon his fingers were bleeding with hanging on, but he hung. In a minute or two the deflated bag flapped down around him.

It didn't weigh much, only a couple of pounds. Rick eased with infinite care out of the harness and let it drop. Then he just hugged the rock and waited.

The storm went away as suddenly as it had come, leaving drifts of red dust in the sheltered places—partly from the desert, partly dropped in the wind's fresh gnawing of the eroded cliffs. The sky was empty of ships. Down below him there was a ravine, with little tangled canyons leading out of it—leading to anywhere you wanted to go, to nowhere, to death.

Rick judged the position of the sun with great care, and began to climb down.

He reached the floor of the ravine without trouble, chose a canyon that extended in the direction he desired to go, and started to walk. He walked as silently as possible, stopping frequently to listen. In his former visits and his association with Martian space-rats, he had picked up a working knowledge of who—or what—lived where on the planet.

This was Shunni country, and had been vaguely something else before. "Before," on Mars, means a long, long time. Somewhere ahead, beyond the foothills, was the Low-Canal town of Valkis, and the whole area had been intensely Pan-Martian. Rick didn't know how they'd feel about the Collar of Ruh, here on the other side of the planet. He could guess their sentiments about an Earthman, however. Any Earthman, but especially one named Richard Gunn Urquhart.

The canyon twisted aimlessly. It was hot. It was dry. Rick's tongue began to swell, with a taste like moldy feathers. There had been no water on the 'copter—evidently the mechanics had not finished servicing her. His feet began to throb. It was quiet.

Under the high walls of the canyon, with a narrow strip of sky overhead, it was like being dead and in the grave, but not yet buried. As time wore on, Rick began to expect a shovelful of dirt in his face any minute. The dregs of the tsamo in him did queer things to his mind.

He came finally to a sharp elbow bend. There was a cleft in the left-hand wall, like a window, and he looked out across foothill slopes at a town huddled, like an old, old woman in ochre rags, beside a sluggish, dull canal.

That was Valkis. Valkis was a bad town. It was the thieves' market, a hideout for wanted men, a sinkhole of vice, a place where a lot of women and quite a few men went and were never heard of again. But it had something, or was supposed to have something. A landing field and a couple of camouflaged hangars that concealed ships such as no honest men ever possessed. Sleek things with souped-up motors that even the MPP ships couldn't touch.

Rick studied it with hard cat-eyes. He could afford to rest a while, now. Go down the slopes with the night and the shadows, later on, and hunt. And after that—well, there'd be time to plan.

He turned around, thinking about a safe place to hide and sleep, and discovered men had silently surrounded him. He hadn't heard so much as a breath or the whisper of a sandal on rock, or the rubbing of leather harness. But they were there.

They were on both sides of him. Tall, hard-faced solemn men with blank, hard, solemn eyes, with barbed spears in their hands and knives in their belts and the animal sheen of strength in their olive skins and olive-purple hair. Shunni barbarians.

Rick and the Shunni studied each other without speaking for some time. Finally one huge man pointed his chin at Valkis beyond the rock-window.

"You want to go to Valkis, Earthman-called-Rick?"

"You know me?"

"Every man on Mars knows you. The seers have sent into every village the picture of the man who united Earth and Mars."

Rick nodded. "I want to go to Valkis."

"We are like brothers to the men of Valkis," he said. "You will go there."

Rick's eyes flickered. The men began to close in, still quiet,

still solemn. Rick raised his hands slowly and leaned back
against the canyon wall.

"Look," he said. "I'm tired. I'm unarmed. I've had all the
roughing up I want for a while. Just take it easy, and I'll be
good."

They took it easy. Very easy, for barbarians with a deep and
ancient hate in their souls. Too easy.

And they were as brothers to the men of Valkis.

After a while, as they wound their way down the barren
foothill gorges, Rick got the idea that there was some deep
emotion behind the blank solemnity of their eyes. He got the
idea that they were very happy men.

They came to Valkis in the quick thin dusk. Because of the
condition of Rick's feet, the Shunni had carried him most of
the way, on a rude litter of spears and skin robes. It was as
though they wanted him to rest and regain strength. They kept
him bound.

Rick guessed that some telepathic message hd preceded
them. The narrow streets, the roofs of the flat stone houses
and the mouths of the dark alleys between them were crowded
with people. Lithe rat-faced little men dressed in gaudy rags,
and their lithe little women with bells in their black braids and
their ears and around their ankles, making a wicked, whispering music up and down the shadowy streets.

There was no talk, no jeering nor cursing. Rick walked erect
between his Shunni guards, and the Martians watched him with
their eyes of emerald and topaz—slanted eyes that showed no
white around the iris—and nobody made a sound. The last of
the light ran westward out of the sky, and then, in the darkness,
a drum began to beat.

It came from somewhere ahead, in the center of the town.
It boomed out six times with crisp authority, and was silent.
As though it were a signal, the crowd began to flow into the
street behind the Shunni, following, without speaking. The tinkling of the bells ran like canorous laughter in the stillness.

The drum sounded again, six more single blows. Then,
abruptly, harps came thrumming in, the queer little double-
banked things they play along the Low-Canals, that have such
an unhealthy sympathy with human nerves that they act more
like drugs than music. The drum began an intricate throbbing
to an offbeat rhythm. As one man, Valkis sucked its breath in,
and let it out in a long sigh.

Richard Gunn Urquhart walked steadily, his face blank, his eyes hooded. His hands, tied behind his back, were cold. Sweat trickled over his skin and presently, along the right side of his face, the muscles began to twitch.

As they entered the town, he had seen the landing field, to the north along the canal.

They came to the water suddenly, running black and sluggishly between banks of sunken stone. They turned north, and up ahead there were torches flaring orange against the night. The houses faced upon a square, the pavements of which had been worn hollow by countless generations of sandaled feet.

The drummer and the harpers were there. They were old women, wearing only a semblance of clothing, all of their bodies that were uncovered, without paint or ornamentation, even their heads shaved clean. They were lost in a ritual dance, their eyes glazed, their leathery shoulders twitching sharply as they breathed.

They crouched in a semi-circle around a gigantic slab of stone, raised no more than twelve inches above the ground level and polished black as though many hands had stroked it. Stone steps led down, under it.

Rick's gaze stabbed briefly around, looking for a way out and not finding it. Too many people, too much strength. He would have to wait until they untied his hands and removed the long hobble that let him walk, but not run. The Shunni had not, for one second, given him the slightest chance to escape.

They took him down the steps.

He began to remember things he had heard about the gods of Valkis. Just talk, the idle scuttlebutt of the space ways. Valkis kept its secrets well. But people talked, anyway, and what they said wasn't pretty.

They went down a long way in the dark and came out in a long square-roofed place that looked like a temple. The roof was supported with squat stone pillars. The first thing Rick noticed was the heat. Mars is a cold world, and down here it was as hot as Venus. Fires burned on round brick platters between the lines of pillars, tended by more of the shaven hags.

There was something more than fire. There was steam. He could hear the hiss of water over hot rock somewhere, from a hidden inlet from the canal. Stifling clouds of it drifted around, making the stones and the people glisten with sweat. The music was faint now, hardly more than an echo.

The mob flowed on around a huge pit sunk in the floor of the temple. It was about twelve feet deep. It was empty. It was clean. There were four doors in the walls, closed with curtains of crimson silk.

The Shunni halted Rick at the edge of the pit, and then for the first time somebody spoke.

A man, who might have been the mayor of Valkis, or the high priest, or both, came and stood in front of Rick. He looked the Earthman up and down, and the sheer distilled hate was almost like a visible aura.

"Look at him," the man whispered, staring at Rick. "Look at him!"

The stone walls took the whisper and played with it, so that every person in there could hear. They all looked.

"The Shadow over Mars! The shadow of outland rule, the shadow of death for our world and our people. Look at him! A thief and a liar—the man who put the yoke on our necks and nailed it there! But for him, there would have been no union."

A sound ran through the place like a wolf licking its teeth.

Rick smiled, not because he felt like smiling.

"It's too bad for you, isn't it?" he said. "As soon as the new government is set, they'll clean you out of here like a nest of roaches. I don't wonder you're sore. The old way of no law at all was so much nicer."

The little man stepped back and kicked Rick with a diabolical accuracy below the belt.

"Untie the Earthman," he said. "Drop him into the pit. Drop him gently."

Once more, the Shunni were very, very kind. . . .

CHAPTER 13

GIDDY AND WINDED, Rick crouched on the stones, getting his wind back. Faces peered down at him, wreathed in the coiling steam. Once again there was silence. This time it was a hungry thing, crouched and waiting.

It was hot, with the heavy oppressive heat of a low jungle. The air was dead, unstirring, acrid with sweat. Now there began to be another odor under that. A rich dark smell of rotten earth—earth fattened with other things than dirt. A smell utterly alien to the dry thin air of Mars, where cactus and brittle scrub is all that grows.

Then he discovered the perfume.

It stole through and over the coarser smells clear and poignant as the single note of a violin above the basses. It was faint, as though with distance, and yet it set all Rick's nerves to quivering.

It was like the perfume the girls wear on the Street of Nine Thousand Joys, if you could take it off the body and put it on the soul. It promised all the sensual pleasures he knew, and a few he didn't know, and still there was nothing crude about it. It was the kind of perfume angels would wear while they were making love, spreading sweetness from the shaken silver feathers of their wings.

He was still all alone in the pit, and there was still no sound. The crimson curtains hung motionless.

Rick's mouth tightened angrily. He glanced, without letting them see that he did, at the faces rimming the pit. They were expectant, waiting, the eyes unwinking, the mouths sucking shallow breaths over teeth bared and glistening to the firelight. They'd been here before, and they knew what was coming.

It was the waiting that got you. The silence, and the wondering. The muscles began to jerk again along his right cheek. He stood erect, and walked deliberately to the center of the pit. Then slowly so that they could see that his hands were steady, he put a cigarette in his mouth, lighted it, and drowned the match-flame in a long, easy plume of smoke.

That impressed them, a lot more than he'd dreamed. There was no tobacco on Mars, no climate nor soil to grow it. Smoking was still a new and startling thing.

A few of the Martians began to cough. The fumes were clinging heavily to the misty air, and their throats weren't used to it. Rick grinned and blew some more their way.

A sharp sigh sped around the pit suddenly, and the faces swayed inward. It had nothing to do with the cigarette. They were looking at something behind Rick.

He whirled and saw Mayo McCall standing there across from him, as though she had just stepped through the silken curtains.

She wore the torn, green coverall that bared her throat and shoulder, the dregs of the firelight poured red glints into her hair. There was sweat on her face, and drops of blood. She looked at him, and all her heart was in her eyes.

Rick's lips parted, but no sound came. He stood staring for a moment, and then he moved toward her—slowly at first, then more rapidly, until he was almost running. His bandaged hands reached out, and all at once there were tears on his cheeks.

"I love you, Rick," Mayo whispered, and stepped back through the curtains, and was gone.

Rick cried her name and ripped the crimson silk away. There was a shallow niche beyond it. It was empty, and the solid stones mocked him with the sound of his own voice. He beat on them.

"Mayo!" he screamed, and the Martians let go a feral howl of laughter.

Rick turned around, half crouched and snarling. His eyes blazed crazily. That was what they'd been waiting for. That was part of the game.

"Mayo, Mayo!" his soul seemed to cry. "Where did you go, how did you get here, why did you run away?"

The sides of the pit were swimming before his eyes, as though he were drunk. The heat, cursed heat! The perfume!

"Steady down, Richard Gunn Urquhart!" he heard himself say. "Steady—or you'll make a fool of yourself!"

He was swaying on his feet, but he didn't know it. He discovered he was still holding the cigarette. The bandages held his fingers close together so it hadn't dropped out. He took another drag on it. The smoke did something—he didn't know whether it was better or worse. Anyway, it killed the lovely effluvium of that wretched perfume.

He saw movement out of the corner of his eye and turned to find Kyra standing in the second doorway.

She stood on tiptoe, her wings outspread. They, and her huge dark eyes, held deep opaline lights. She was smiling, and in her hands was the Collar of Ruh.

A thin animal wail went up from the watching Martians— sheer hate made vocal. It touched an answering chord in Rick. The Collar grew large before his eyes, dwarfing Kyra, dwarfing the pit. It became as large as Mars. It was Mars.

"I know the prophecy—your shadow over Mars," Kyra said. "Life to Mars, instead of death. Your life—you live so strongly."

Rick hardly heard her. His blood beat thunderously inside

his skull. Kyra, Mayo, everything was drowned in a hot flood of desire. Mars, power, wealth, Richard Gunn Urquhart the space-rat made into the guy at the top of the heap.

He laughed up at the Martians, savage laughter, and taunted them with the filth of three worlds and a dozen dialects. The dull iron bosses of the Collar blinked redly, like somnolent eyes. Dying Mars, awaiting the conqueror.

He reached out to take the Collar.

It slipped through his fingers. Kyra smiled and vanished through the curtains.

Again Rick cried out and wrenched the hangings down. Again there was nothing but a shallow niche and emptiness, and hard stone under his hands.

And once again the Martians laughed.

Rick staggered back to the center of the pit. He did not cry out now, nor curse. He looked with narrow, empty eyes at the faces peering down, the dark fresco of them above him in the steam, studded with hot jewels and the white glitter of teeth. He was afraid.

The perfume stroked his olfactory nerves with fingers of soft flame. It was pleasant. It sent ripples of sensuous delight through him. Yet because it was a part of what was being done to him he feared it, and especially so because it was pleasant. The animal was close to the surface in Rick, and it spoke.

"Bait for the trap," it said.

He raised the hand that held the cigarette, and it was not until then that he realized he was on all fours. That frightened him most of all. He dragged hungrily on the butt, burning slowly in the wet air. It made him dizzy and sick, but he could stand up again.

He did, and there was a naked girl poised in front of the third door—a green-eyed wanton with coppery hair curling on her white shoulders and her red lips brimming with secret laughter. She twitched the curtains aside and beyond them Rick saw the Street of Nine Thousand Joys, bright with lanterns and the warm light spilling out of familiar doorways, human and safe with voices, quarrels, music, the smell of wine.

The Street of Nine Thousand Joys, where Richard Gunn Urquhart was just Rick the space-rat, without a prophecy, with no enemies and no destiny but tomorrow's hangover. Escape.

"Go back and be just Rick again," something was telling him. "Forget Mars and the Collar and the woman named Mayo.

Get good and drunk and forget, and stop tearing your head out. Above all, escape!''

The girl tossed her head and moved away, watching him over her shoulder. Rick followed. He called to her to wait, lurching unsteadily, fighting down a childish urge to cry. She shook her curly head mockingly and fled before him down the dappled shadows, and Rick ran after.

He heard the wicked scream of laughter from above him just an instant before he crashed headlong into a blank wall of stone. He dropped, stunned. The girl, the Street, vanished, and there was only an empty niche like the others.

Rick lay still. Presently he began to sob, his mouth relaxed and wet like a child's.

The Martians grew silent. They were waiting again.

The perfume soothed Rick. It was like a woman's fingers, comforting. His mother's fingers. Into his mind came a picture of the fourth door. Beyond that he would find rest. That was where the perfume came from. He could go beyond that curtain into the darkness, alone and in peace. He could sleep. He could forget.

Quite slowly, he got to his hands and knees and began to crawl toward the fourth door. There was no sound anywhere now. The Martians seemed to have stopped breathing.

Something kept trying to jar Rick's mind awake again. A smell, an acrid familiar reek that clashed with the perfume. He didn't want to wake. He ignored it and went on crawling.

He came to the fourth door and thrust the crimson hangings back. Before him was a dark passageway, slanting sharply down. The perfume breathed from it, and under it, suddenly strong, the rich smell of earth. A latent memory made Rick reach out and feel the emptiness, not quite knowing why he did. The passageway was really there.

He crawled into it. The last thing he heard as the crimson draperies closed behind him was the laughter of the Martians like the spring cry of wolves on a hilltop.

It was easy to crawl, half sliding, down the slope. Presently he could sleep, and forget. . . .

Pain, a savage, searing stab of it between his fingers. It shook through the drugged clouds in his brain. He tried to push it away, but it slashed and stabbed and wouldn't go, and the involuntary reflexes of his body fought to do something about it. He raised his hand, and again the acrid smell assailed him. There was a little red glow in the darkness.

The cigarette stuck between his fingers had burned down and was searing the tender flesh. The bandage was smoldering.

He pushed the butt out and hugged his hand to him. The pain helped to clear his head. Memories came back to him— the cryptic torture in the pit, the Martians watching him. Rage boiled up to help the pain. He was aware suddenly that the perfume was stronger, and a clear terror of it came to him. It was a drug, and it was going to get him under again.

Slowly he was sliding down the shaft.

He pressed his boots hard against the opposite wall and peered down. Far below was a phosphorescent glimmer, a glimpse of space. And—flowers!

White flowers, pale and lovely, swaying as though a vagrant breeze blew over them. Infinitely beautiful, breathing perfume, calling to him . . .

Yes. Calling to him. In his mind.

"Come!" they whispered. "Come and sleep!"

"What are you?" he asked. "Where do you come from?"

"There were many of us when the world was young," droned the answer. "We grew in the green jungles. We ruled Mars before man could walk erect."

The men of Valkis had found them, then, some time in the ancient past, a handful of them clinging on beside some sheltered volcanic spring. And they built a temple, and the flowers lived on.

They were beautiful. They were friendly. They smelled nice.

Rick slipped farther toward them. His head was swimming again.

"How did I see Mayo?" he asked the flowers. "What were those things out there?"

"We take the images uppermost in a man's mind and let him see them, the things he wants most."

The thought broke off short. "Why?" Rick asked drowsily.

"Come," said the flowers. "Come and sleep."

Sleep. The smell of the fat black earth came strong under the perfume, and the animal instinct of his body told Rick what it was fattened with.

He braced his feet frantically to stop his sliding. He was afraid. He knew, now. But it was too late. The drug had him, and he couldn't fight.

He began to slip again.

His burned hand hurt him, rubbing the rock. Cigarette burn. Tobacco. Out there in the pit, it had helped, a little. Even a little— Perhaps, being a drug, it fought the other drug. It wouldn't hurt to try.

He fumbled the pack out. His hands were clumsy from the bandages, and they shook. He dropped the pack. It slid away down the shaft and dropped among the flowers.

"Come," they said. "Come and sleep."

He hunted through his pockets. Feverishly, panting. He found one crumpled cigarette, dropped out of the pack and forgotten.

He was careful not to drop it, nor the matches.

He filled himself with the smoke, over and over. It nauseated him, but it fought the perfume a little, enough so he could think. Not clearly, but enough. Enough for him to claw his way back up the shaft, inch by inch, pressing his boots against the stone and inching his back up, digging with his nails into the irregularities of the rock, climbing with his muscles the way a snake glides on his scales, because he had to or die.

The flowers were angry. They were hungry. They hurled the perfume at him in drowsy clouds, but the harsh smoke fought it back. He reached the level space behind the curtains and lay there, shaking and exhausted. The cigarette was used up. He took to slapping his own face violently, pressing the raw burn, anything to keep his mind awake.

There was no sound outside in the temple but the faint crackling of the fires. Rick peered through the curtains. The gloating faces were gone from the pit rim. They hadn't waited. There was nothing to wait for. Nobody had ever before come back up that shaft. Rick went out and studied the walls.

The old women who tended the fires would not be watching the pit, either. They would be huddled over their bony knees in the heat, dreaming of the days when they wore little bells in their hair and had chimed the hot-eyed men into dusky chambers beside the Low-Canal.

The walls were old, old beyond counting. The blocks had settled and moved a little, so that their surface was not even. The walls could be climbed. Evidently, because the Martians were not affected, atmospheric pressure kept the perfume lower than the pit edge. He'd be safe, when he got up there.

He climbed, biting his lips to keep his drowsy brain awake.

After an eternity he reached the top and lay panting on the stones, covered with cold sweat. He began to shudder, violently. Gradually his head cleared.

It was very still in the temple, full of steam, full of shadows and wickedness. The old women crouched by their fires, dreaming, the wrinkled skin twitching across their shoulders, now and then, as though a hand stroked it. Rick began to move, through the quivering darkness behind the farthest line of pillars against the wall.

He reached the stairs and crept up them. The drummer and the harpers were gone from the square. The cruel, noisy life of Valkis was going on in the surrounding streets, but apparently this place was sacred to religion. It was deserted now.

Rick slipped quietly into the black water of the canal and began to swim northward. Lights blazed across the water here and there. Men and women thronged the bank in front of the canal-side houses. But Rick was a good swimmer, and no one saw him. He hauled out on the edge of the landing field.

There was nobody around, no reason for anybody to be around. Rick found a scrap of iron and pried the lock off the nearest hangar. There was a 'copter inside, a sleek wicked little thing with an illegal motor.

There was only one place on Mars Rick wanted to go. He went there, like a comet rushing to perihelion.

He went to Caer Hebra.

CHAPTER 14

CAER HEBRA CAME into Rick's view, just before sundown, its marble spires almost drowned and lost in the drifting sand. He set the 'copter down on a massive terrace, stained and cracked but still retaining its perfect symmetry, and climbed out.

Before his boots touched the ground he was surrounded by the little winged men of the island kingdom. No women greeted Rick this time. The small ivory faces of the men were stern, and their small furred hands held pencil-tubes.

Rick was not conscious of fear. He was not conscious of anything but the need in him.

"Is Kyra here?"

The leader nodded slowly. No one spoke. Many wings made a sad, silken rustling in the lonely wind. Sand etched light feathery patterns on the marble beneath their feet.

"I will see her," Rick said.

The leader nodded again.

"It is her wish, and the wish of the dying must be heeded," he said. "For that reason, Earthman, you will live to go away from Caer Hebra. Come."

The word "dying" shocked Rick. It cut through the numbness of his inner mind. He started and cried out, "Kyra!" There was no answer. The little men motioned him on. He obeyed.

She lay on a heap of soft furs, high up in a tower where she could look out across the dry sea. She held out her hands to Rick and smiled.

"I knew you would come," she said.

Rick took her hands, gently, as though they were flowers and easily crushed. "What's wrong?" he asked. "Baby, what's wrong?"

"The black Earthman burned her," said the leader, behind him. "She will not live."

Kyra's fingers tightened on him. "I followed them, Rick. You sent me to watch Mayo, and I did. I couldn't stop him from taking her, but I followed their ship. It went very fast, and I lost it, but I kept flying north and after a long time I sighted it again. I went down to it, and Jaffa Storm came out from the ice dome and saw me. But I broke the controls, Rick. With a stone I broke them, so his ship couldn't fly. And it was dark, very dark for an Earthman's eyes, so I got away."

She was drawing him down to her, as though he were too far away for her to see him clearly.

"I tried to get back to Ruh, to the Company, to find you, Rick. But I couldn't fly that far. I couldn't. I knew you'd come here, only I was so afraid it might be too late."

Rick knelt down beside her. He looked over his shoulder at the men.

"Get out," he said.

They were angry. For a while they didn't move. Rick's yellow eyes took on a peculiar, almost phosphorescent glow. Kyra had forgotten that her people existed. Presently they turned and left.

"North," said Kyra. "North, in the Polar Cities under the ice dome."

"I wouldn't have had you do it," Rick whispered.

The rosy light fell across her face from the sunset, warming the ivory pallor. Her great eyes held a soft brilliance.

"Don't be sad for me, Rick."

He said nothing.

"I'm not sad. I haven't lived many years, but there isn't anything more I could have had from life. I've loved you, Rick, and in a way we've been mated, haven't we? I helped you to create a new world, even if it was only a little bit of help. Not many women have given life to a planet, have they, Rick?"

"No."

"I'll live in that new world. We believe in rebirth. Some day my soul will have a new body, and it will remember. It will say to me, 'I did this. With Rick, I did this.' And I will be happy."

She fumbled suddenly at the zipper of his shirt, drawing it down. She thrust her hands inside, against his chest.

"So strongly—I can feel it beating. That's Mars, Rick. So much life and strength, and we were so tired."

He bent over and kissed her. Then he stretched out beside her, holding her like a child in the curve of his arm, her head against his shoulder. She went to sleep, smiling.

The sun went down in the dry waves and Phobos came up from the western horizon as though borne on the afterglow. By the time Diemos had marched from the east to his nightly mating, Rick knew that Kyra would not be disturbed if he arose and went away.

He laid her back in her nest of furs. From some forgotten corner of his childhood the sign of the cross came unbidden. He made it and went out.

Silently the little men of Caer Hebra stood in the wind and the moonshadows and watched him take off. It was not until he had flown north for some hours that he realized why his eyes and throat had dried sea-water. . . .

He had been flying for a long, long time. He was cold and cramped, and the fuel gauge needle kept fluttering over to pat the terminal E.

The terrain below was a desert forgotten of God and man. Now, in the Martian spring, the gorges ran full with the thaw-water that fed the canals. There were mosses and lichens and a few tough flowers. But the black rock was rotted and split by time, ice, wind and water, and it looked as untouched by humanity as the Moon.

Far ahead he could see the soaring edges of the ice cap—the

core that remained through every summer. He checked this course against the location of the Polar Cities, which were mapped but seldom visited. When a curious visitor did drop in, he returned with a weird tale of voices that spoke in his brain and told him, gently but with unmistakable firmness, to go away again. Nobody, except in ancient legend, had ever found the entrance to the ice domes under which the Cities were hidden.

Since these domes were regular in shape and never melted, even slightly, in high summer, it was assumed by some that the mysterious Thinkers kept them that way artificially. The Terran invasion of Mars was too young and too much interested in money to bother with half-legendary cities that no one had ever seen. A Martian, of course, observed the tabus with strict etiquette, and most of the few Earthmen who had heard of the Polar Cities put them down as a legend growing around a natural freak.

Rick's motor began to miss. He nursed and coaxed it onward, toward the glittering rim of ice knifing the pale sky. Presently it died altogether and no amount of cursing or praying could start it again. Rick pulled the glasses from the locker beside him and scanned the ground.

He saw the domes, three of them clustered together in a circle. They were far off, glistening like drops of water on a stone.

He still had altitude. He played the light 'copter like a glider on the wind, fighting for every inch of headway. He made it, almost. Just before he was forced to make a landing he sighted Jaffa Storm's ship on the ground, a tiny speck beside one of the domes.

He landed safely on a broad strip of rock ground flattened by moving ice, well out of sight of the domes. He was not sure that that made much difference for he was by now thoroughly convinced of Jaffa Storm's telepathic powers. But instinct and training made him go cautiously, just the same.

An area of tumbled boulders offered cover. Rick slipped and stumbled between them until, after a long time, he could look out onto the level space before the domes where Storm's 'copter was.

He had no weapon except the scrap of metal, which he had dropped into his pocket. There had been no blaster in the ship, and no way to get one.

Neither could he discover any cover. Rick walked out across the open ground. The lean Martian sunlight touched the domes. They were huge and perfectly round, and the light shone through them, pellucid and pure, like lite through raindrops. High above

them, shearing off half the sky, was the pale ice-green blade of
the polar cap.

Nothing stirred. There was no sound. The 'copter had a desolate and forgotten look until he got close enough to see that
someone had been working on it, repairing the controls. He studied them. The job had been competently done. The ship would
fly.

Yet the ship was still there.

Rick looked around him, standing still beside the little ship.
His ears, his eyes, the nerves of his skin were tuned so acutely
that they ached.

Silence. Empty earth and the enigmatic domes like huge ani-
mals asleep and not telling their dreams to anybody. Over all the
crushing impersonality of the ice and above that, the cold pale
sky.

Rick shivered. His cheek muscles twitched and the lids narrowed cat-like over his yellow eyes. He went toward the nearest
dome.

There were footprints in the bare ground. Many lines of them,
going both ways. The mark of the left boot was light. There were
no signs of Mayo's prints.

Rick followed them, walking steadily but without haste. The
stories of the mental compulsion to go away returned to him. He
felt no compulsion whatsoever. Either the legends lied, or something had been changed inside the domes.

He followed the footprints up to the curving clear wall, and
nothing happened. Nothing at all.

He found the entrance. It was a hallway half-closed with inter-
meshing sheets of crystal that slid back into the ice and could not
be told from it. A man could be caught between those crystal
panels. He could be crushed and cut apart, or trapped unhurt to
die slowly in a little shining cell.

He stood for a moment or two, listening to the stillness. Then
he went in.

His footsteps rang back at him like echoes in a bell. Several
times, through tricks of light and perspective, he thought the doors
were sliding in. But he reached the interior safely. In spite of
himself he was shaking and covered with sweat.

He was looking at a city.

It was sunk below ground level, so that he was even with the
spires. It was not very big, limited to about ten thousand inhabi-

tants. But it was the most beautiful thing Rick had ever seen, and the most unpleasant.

He'd been in the Lunar cave-cities. He'd walked through the fantastic monuments of an unknown race on Phobos, and on Venus he had seen a drowned empire under the silver sea. But this beat them all. It turned his stomach over.

The buildings were all made of the same material—a colorless plastic that took the prismatic sunlight from the dome overhead and played with it, so that the walls seemed to be full of drifting jewels. That was all right. It was the shape of the things that got you.

Wherever the Thinkers came from, whatever they were, they had either brought with them or discovered an alien geometry. The buildings swept the eye along curves and angles that veered sickeningly toward another universe. The shapes of them, the meaning of them, gave the mind a shock. It was like the dream of a crazy surrealist painter brought to life, unhealthy and fascinating.

There was a swift musical clashing behind Rick. He turned around, and found that the way had closed behind him. There were no controls of any kind, so far as Rick could see.

He went down transparent steps to the city.

It was dead. He could feel that. The silence had been there too long, and the streets had stopped waiting. The leaning walls looked at him malevolently, not liking the echoes his feet called forth. Rick's eyes began to smolder.

He stopped abruptly, filled his lungs. "Mayo!" he yelled.

The cry broke into a million fragments and tinkled back at him with a sound of subtle laughter. He went on, holding a course for the far side of the city. From up there by the entrance he had seen another flight of shining steps and a hall, leading into the adjoining dome.

He wondered if Jaffa Storm had let him get inside and then gone out by another way with Mayo.

It was about then he heard the music.

It came softly, and in some strange way it was linked with color, so that Rick saw and heard it at the same time. The harmony was like the buildings. It was not born in a normal mind—normal, at least, by human standards. It came from everywhere, like the air. Rick supposed the system resembled a public address system of some kind, serving the whole city.

He could feel his brain crawling around in his skull, trying to hide.

The colors came stronger, pulsing like veils of mist through the eerie streets. They kept sliding off the edges of the spectrum into something else. They did things to the emotions, the nerves, even the intestinal functions. The music plucked at Rick's mind, stimulating it with notes and rhythms it was never meant to hear.

He began to think, suddenly, that he could understand the symbolic meanings of the buildings and where the curves led.

After that, for a while, he lost track of things, or very nearly. Some stubborn piece of his consciousness ran over the nightmare hills behind him, crying out, and nothing could stop it. Abruptly its cry got through to him and dragged him back, balanced delicately on a hairline between two worlds.

He was stark naked, and he was embracing a crystal pillar of no shape that he knew under the sun.

He sprang away from the pillar in shuddering nausea, clawing and clinging to his sanity.

"Wait," he thought. "Storm's doing this. He pushed a button somewhere to start this concert, like the guys that lived here used to do. He's looking in your mind and laughing to beat the devil, watching you fall apart. You going to let him laugh?"

Rick straightened up. That would mean Storm was still here, to be caught and killed. Things might yet work out.

Cords knotted up under the sweat on Rick's face. He pulled his strength, every bit of it, together, and sheathed his mind against the music and the colors. He started walking toward the nearest wall of the dome. He watched his feet and counted the steps, carefully, one by one.

If he were wrong, and Storm had gone away, it would mean disaster! But wait! He had to quit thinking things like that.

He reached the wall. He was not steady on his feet, but he was still counting. Far away along the curve he saw the steps again and went over and climbed them. Suddenly he realized that the hellish concert was over.

He sat down on the top step and waited until he had stopped shaking. Then he went into the next dome.

CHAPTER 15

NO BUILDINGS WERE here in this dome, no houses. In the center was a gigantic structure of metal and plastic. It hummed faintly, and a pale, shimmering radiance came out of it.

Ranged around it were row upon row of soft couches covered, coffin-like, with the transparent plastic. People lay upon them, either dead or asleep.

Rick could find no sign here of Storm and Mayo. He looked for the entrance to the dome beyond, found it, and started out across the floor.

The creatures under the plastic shields were not human. They were anthropoid but, somehow, in the texture of their flesh and the shape of their features, there was something alien. They lay quietly. If they breathed or stirred, Rick couldn't see it. But they were not dead, for their flesh was warm-looking and was not decayed.

He supposed that there were the Thinkers, who had built the city he had just left behind him. They seemed to be sexless. Their nude bodies were all alike. They had a perfection and beauty of form as unpleasant as their buildings.

Rick walked steadily toward the archway leading into the last of the three domes. He was not frightened. A man such as he came to the end of things, and one way or another, that was that. He looked around for a weapon, anything that could be used as one. There was nothing. He flexed his bandaged hands and went on.

There was no shelter, no cover of any kind around the steps and the archway. Rick did not try to hide. It was no use hiding from a telepath like Storm. What Rick wanted now was the finish, as quickly as possible. He wanted Storm.

There was no thought of death in his mind—for himself.

He climbed the stairway. He caught a glimpse of what looked like a vast laboratory and machine shop, and then Jaffa Storm was standing above him on the top step, his heavy blaster leveled at Rick's muscular body.

Rick stopped. Storm smiled at him, quite pleasantly.

"Where's Mayo?" asked Rick.

Storm jerked his head slightly, backward. "In there. She's quite safe. She won't be able to help you, and keep her that way. She's a wildcat." His black eyes looked Rick up and down. "Too bad you're going to miss the fun of seeing me break her."

Rick said nothing. His hands hung limp beside his naked thighs. His face was expressionless, his eyes veiled. He was halfway up the crystal steps, something less than his own height below Storm's feet.

"How did you like the concert?" Storm said.

Rick didn't answer.

Storm laughed. "Don't bother. I know. I was watching your mind every second." He indicated the sleepers beneath their coffin lids. "Curious tastes those birds had. I still don't know what they are or where they came from. I can't get through to their minds. I think that mentally they're not here any more, but have gone on into some realm of pure thought. The bodies, I think, are synthetic."

He broke off and stood studying Rick, as though he wanted to impress every feature, every line on his memory.

"I never want to forget you," he said. "I have never before met a man I hated as much as I do you. I think I hate you because you're nearly as strong as I am, and that makes me afraid. I'm not used to being afraid. I don't like it."

"You've lost Mars," said Rick. "I took that from you."

"No," Storm said slowly. "No, you haven't. You messed up my plans, all right. You came blamed near killing me, too. Very smart of you to realize at the last minute that I had probably read your mind and would be ready for you. I was mighty busy, as you can imagine, and I didn't get the switch until it was too late to do anything but jump out of the way. As it was, I received a nasty cut from some flying metal, and my disintegrator was smashed to glory."

He swore abruptly, though softly. "I wish I could think of a way to kill you that would really satisfy me."

Rick's mouth twisted in what was almost a lazy half-smile. "You can't kill me, Storm. This is my road, not yours."

Storm stared at him a moment. Then he laughed. "By Jupiter, you believe that, don't you?"

Rick nodded. "You knew I was coming."

"Yes. I kept track of the little one—what was her name, Kyra?—of her mind, until I knew she couldn't do me any harm, and I kept pretty close check on yours, too." He chuckled. "St. John and the Martian pulled a fast one on you, for fair! I always told that thick-headed Fallon he underestimated them.''

Rick's eyes, after the mention of Kyra, had become deadly in a peculiarly cold way, as though no ordinary human emotion could express what he felt. He still had not moved.

"But you've lost Mars," he repeated.

"No. That's the difference between us, Rick—the difference that's going to cost you everything. I trained my mind. It works for me, not I for it. When I found out what you were planning to do, uniting the Martians and the Earthmen against me, I knew you had a fair chance of succeeding. So I used my head.

"I'd been curious about the Thinkers for some time. The Martian seers, who might have discovered the truth, were forbidden to pry by their hereditary tabus. No Earthman had the power. But I did, and to blazes with tabus. I found out that the Thinkers' thought-barrier—the mental compulsion felt by anyone trying to enter the domes—was merely a broadcast by a mechanism similar to a televisor. It was automatic, and gosh knows how long it's been running. I cut it off, of course, for your benefit.

"Anyway, after I forced my mind against that barrier, I found out that the Thinkers have simply—gone away. They're still alive, because I can feel the vibrations from their brains, but they've withdrawn somewhere beyond this world. I suppose they reached the point in their peculiar evolution where pure thought was the only unconquered realm left.

"But they left things behind them, Rick. An armory of weapons and machines such as men have dreamed of but never been able to produce. Disintegrators. Mental amplifiers. Energy projectors that make our Bannings look like children's toys. The Thinkers were named for a reason, you know. By gosh, I wish I knew what they were, where they came from! I'll hazard a guess, though. I think they were pre-human, and that their introverted culture was driven out by the appearance of man on the planet. So they built the domes, and that incredible city, and surrounded themselves with tabus, and lived peacefully in their own way.

"They went through a period of scientific invention that must have lasted an incredible number of years. Invention just for the kick of it, too. They never passed any of it on to humanity, and only used themselves what they needed for their own comfort. Like that dingus there."

Storm indicated the huge humming mechanism in the center of the dome.

"That warms them, feeds them by direct energy, keeps their bodies alive while their minds are playing around free in space and time," he said. Queer buried sparks came in his black eyes. "I wish I could follow them," he whispered, "for a little while."

Rick leaped forward, without warning.

He threw himself flat, clutching at Storm's ankles. It was the time he had waited for—the single second when Storm's mental attention was on something other than the brain of Richard Gunn Urquhart.

Storm's blaster beam flared obliquely, almost roasting the skin on Rick's back but not quite hitting him. Rick grasped the cloth of Storm's coverall and yanked with all his might. Storm fell back on his shoulder-blades, and the blaster let off a second time, at the top of the dome.

Rick's bare feet found traction on the steps and flung him forward again, his whole weight across Storm's body. The big man lost some more breath, and Rick clawed for the blaster.

The fall must have hurt Storm, but he didn't let it stop him. He used his free hand, and his knees, and his heavy boots. He was strong. Rick was a big man, and powerful, but Storm was stronger. He beat the living daylights out of Rick, but he couldn't shake him loose from that blaster.

Rick curled his naked body up, tightened his muscles, and took it. There was only one thing in the universe that mattered—the blaster. He got hold of Storm's thumb and worked, doggedly.

It broke. It tore out of the socket in a mess of ripped flesh and tendons, and Storm screamed like a wounded horse, and that was that. Rick had the blaster.

He broke away, to get off far enough to use it. One of Storm's boots took him squarely in the abdomen. Rick rolled back down the steps and lay there, trying to retch his insides out. The blaster skidded away across the crystal floor.

Storm got up. He looked at his hand. He pulled out his handkerchief and bound it tightly, using his teeth. Then he leaned against the wall of the arch and vomited.

At the foot of the steps, Rick was trying to get to his hands and knees, and sobbing aloud.

Storm noted where the blaster was. It has skittered far away, much farther away than Rick could hope to move for some time. Storm went down on the other side, into the laboratory dome.

Mayo McCall lay in the shelter of a machine too big and heavy for her to tip over. She was tied securely, and gagged. She needed no voice to tell Storm her thoughts. Her eyes told enough.

"You can kiss him good bye—what's left of him after I'm through," he whispered.

He found the small mechanism he was looking for, placed conveniently with others he had intended to take out to the 'copter after he was done with Rick. It was a harmless-looking little gadget—a shield over a prism inside a triangle of slightly luminous metal.

Storm wasn't sure how it worked. He guessed at cosmic ray frequencies, snared by the triangle and concentrated through the prism. But he knew what it would do.

He placed his left hand carefully behind the shield, his thumb over the control stud, and went back up the steps.

Rick had crawled to within ten feet of the blaster. Storm smiled. He pressed the stud. A little gossamer thread of radiance spun out from the prism. It touched the blaster. The metal crumbled to dust and then vanished.

"Rick—Ricky!" Storm said gently.

Rick turned his head. The great central machine hummed quietly, and the Thinkers dreamed their cosmic dreams, and paid no attention to the man who crouched naked on their floor, or the black giant who stood on their steps with destruction in his hands.

"You can't kill me," Rick whispered.

Storm laughed, without sound, and pressed the stud again.

Rick moved. Where he found the strength in himself he never knew, except that it was that or die, and he wasn't ready to die. He rolled sideways. The beam missed him, eating a snaky groove in the floor. The outermost row of coffins were closed to him. He pulled himself behind the nearest one. They were solid to the floor. They offered cover, and though Storm could follow him mentally, he couldn't see to aim.

Rick started working back across the dome.

Storm followed them. He laced the coffins with the crumbling light, leaving them ruined, the bodies within them partially destroyed. The Thinkers never stirred. Their minds were too far away, to be caring what happened to their flesh.

Rick played Storm with a sort of insane mixture of cleverness and sheer courage. He stayed behind each particular coffin until the beam had eaten dangerously close. Then he rolled or slid obliquely across the crystal floor, each time in a different direction, so that he was always screened except for an occasional second. Storm might have hit him, right-handed. Left-handed, he couldn't.

Not at first, anyway. But Rick knew his luck couldn't hold forever. He felt like a plucked hen, with nothing in his hands, not even a rock.

His eyes blazed and narrowed suddenly. He began to circle, so that presently he would come back to the path they had already followed, where the ruined coffins were. Storm came doggedly after him. Storm was in no hurry. He was enjoying himself.

Rick came up to the coffin he wanted. It had been eaten away so that the plastic top was partly gone. The body inside was in two pieces now, cut cleanly through the middle. There was no blood, no viscera, no abdominal cavity. The flesh looked like sponge rubber.

Rick, crouched behind the coffin, reached up and took hold of the legs.

He waited a long moment, his brows knotted in concentration. Storm stood erect, smiling faintly, playing his disintegrator beam on Rick's shelter. Because of the arrangement of the coffins Storm's whole body was exposed to Rick's view if he looked over the top or around the right-hand end. From the left-hand end Storm's legs were hidden by the corner of another couch.

Rick whipped his unpleasant weapon down. It was lighter than human legs would have been, but heavy enough.

But Storm laughed, avoided it easily without taking his eyes from Rick's coffin. Suddenly he flicked the disintegrator beam upward, aiming above the right-hand corner.

At the same instant, Rick's head and shoulders thrust up and over the left-hand corner. He hurled the trunk section of the Thinker's synthetic body at Storm's head—and he did it left-handed.

Storm was slow, a fractional instant, caught off balance. The clumsy thing struck him. It was not heavy enough to stun him, or even do more than stagger him back against one of the coffins. But it was heavy enough to hamper him, and the dead arms went around him almost as though the reflexes still lived in their inhuman flesh.

Rick moved. He had never moved so fast in his life. Bruises, aches, weariness, the pain he carried with him—nothing mattered. He moved. He hit Storm before the carrion had slid free of his arm, or been shaken off.

Storm fired at Rick, but the beam went past him, and then

Rick's hand chopped down edgewise across Storm's wrist and the deadly little prism dropped.

Rick got his bandaged hands where he had told Hugh St. John he wanted them.

He held them there, his eyes half-closed and happy, cat-like, long after there was any need. Storm didn't die easy, but he died.

"Instinct," whispered Rick conversationally to the blackened face below his. "I'm left-handed. You didn't know that. You watched my mind figure out what I was going to do, and because you're right-handed you figured how it would be—only I'm left-handed. So you shot in the wrong place. Instinct crossed you up."

Storm didn't answer. He couldn't answer—now!

CHAPTER 16

YES, STORM WAS dead. But Rick didn't mention that to Mayo when he staggered into the laboratory dome and untied her. There aren't any words at a time like that. They clung to each other for a while, and Mayo cried a little, and Rick did too.

After a time, when the world had stopped swinging quite so wildly around them, Rick got up and began walking around, looking at the machines. He was a good mechanic. He was able to figure out what most of them were for, within reason. He was wearing Storm's black coverall. Storm's cigarettes were still in the breast pocket. Rick lighted one. His face was expressionless.

"What are you thinking, Rick?" Mayo said.

He didn't answer. Mayo got up and went slowly to the collection of mechanisms Storm had gathered together.

"He told me all about what happened," she said. "Hugh and Eran Mak will govern Mars well. Things will be good, if they're left alone to do what they've dreamed of."

Still Rick didn't answer.

Mayo picked up a small tube and aimed it at him.

"You can't have Mars," she said. "I won't let you have it, to play with."

He stood looking at her for a moment, with nothing in his eyes but a blank coldness.

"Yesterday I was in Caer Hebra," he said, as though to himself. "Kyra talked to me. I heard her."

Mayo was puzzled. She let the tube waver a little, and suddenly Rick was laughing at her.

"A tough baby, you are! And by Jaffrey, I'm not so sure you wouldn't use it, at that!" He turned away, blowing smoke at the lucid dome. "How do we get out of here?"

"I watched Storm. I know where the controls are. I can turn on the thought-projector, too, if we want to. But, Rick—what are you planning?"

"Don't you trust me?"

"No."

He went back to her.

"Now do you trust me?" he asked again, after a while.

"Less than ever. Oh Rick, won't you please—"

He stopped her words with his lips. "I haven't said anything, have I? Now let's clear out of this place."

Mayo's eyes held a cold doubt, but she nodded. Later, when she thought he wasn't looking, she slipped the tube into the pocket of her coverall.

"What about all this stuff?" she asked. "It's dangerous, Rick."

"It's been safe this long, I guess it'll keep a little longer. We'll pass the problem on to Mak and St. John and let them sweat about it."

"You're going to see them?"

"Yeah."

Rick reached into the pocket of his coverall and pulled out the little energy projector Storm had used—the prism in the shining triangle. He turned the thing over in his hands, scowling at it, and then dropped it on the pile beside Mayo.

"Where's the control, honey?"

"For this dome, it's over there on the left. Or do you want to go back through the city?"

"No," he said. "I do not want to go back through the city." Mayo went away. When she came back he put his arm around her shoulders as they crossed the dome to the hidden entrance.

They took the fuel from Storm's 'copter and carried it to Rick's and took off. Presently Rick noticed that Mayo was crying quietly.

"What's wrong?"

"I was thinking of Kyra. Storm told me all about it. He would. I'm glad you could be with her."

"Yeah," said Rick. "Yeah, she died happy."

They sighted pursuing ships several times, but nothing could stay with them. Rick lapsed into a sullen, brooding silence and snarled at Mayo every time she tried to speak. Finally she gave it up. She sat with her eyes closed, and a couple of grim, tight lines hardened into the corners of her mouth.

Presently Rick turned on his transmitter and got in touch with the Company. The switchboard operator goggled at him and then began pushing plugs frantically. In a couple of seconds Hugh St. John was looking out of the screen at Rick, with Eran Mak behind his shoulder.

They both saw Mayo at the same time, and came crowding against the screen as though they wanted to get through to her. Especially St. John. Rick watched him sourly. "That guy's crazy about her," he thought. "He's so crazy about her his blood's almost tepid. The lily!"

They hardly noticed Rick at first, until Mayo had told about Storm and the Polar Cities, and what Rick did there. Then St. John turned to him.

"I'm glad you came back," he said gravely.

"That's fine," Rick answered. "You made it so easy for me, too."

"We did what we thought was right, Rick."

"That explains it okay, then," snarled Rick. "It whitewashes the whole thing. Doesn't matter what you do to a guy as long as you think it's right. Right for whom, St. John? And if you say 'Mars' I'll beat your head off as soon as I land."

St. John's mouth tightened. Behind him Eran Mak smiled and nodded. His golden eyes were bright.

"I never thought of you as a chicken, Rick," he said. "But here you come, home to roost. Too bad you have Mayo with you. I've got a feeling it would be much simpler just to shoot you down over the field."

"Uh huh," Rick said. "That's one reason I have her with me." The bells tinkled faintly in the Martian's ears, and Rick shuddered. "You better tell all those MPP boys to clear the air for me. I'm coming down."

"Better make it the landing field," St. John said. "You ruined the 'copter deck in the compound. We'll send a car for you."

"And an armed escort?"

"And an armed escort."

"I'm coming in peace," said Rick. "How I go out again is something you can worry about then."

St. John gave him a cold and level look, and nodded. The

screen went dead. Mayo leaned back in her seat again and closed her eyes.

"Rick," she said quietly. "I love you. I'll go anywhere with you, do anything with you, except one thing. Think about it. Think hard, before you do anything."

"I've done nothing else but think, for a long time," Rick said.

They didn't speak after that. Rick swooped in to the old Company field where he had stolen the ship that wrecked Storm's plans, and made his landing. A car was waiting for them, with an escort of jeeps manned by Martian Government men. Rick submitted quietly to a polite but thorough search. They found no weapon on him. They did not search Mayo.

The car sped smoothly away toward the compound. Rick glanced up at the distant towers of Ruh on the cliffs above the sea-bottom, and his eyes were as cold and depthless as amber glass.

Martian G-men, mostly soft-muscled political office-holders, ushered them into the building St. John was using in place of the now non-existent Administration Pylon. St. John met them at the door of the office and persuaded the escort to go away. They didn't want to. They looked at Rick much as the men of Valkis had, but for a different reason. On the face of it they were outraged by the supposed sacrilege to the Collar of Ruh. In reality, they were worried about the new Union Government and what it was going to do to their jobs.

They did go away, however, leaving Rick and Mayo alone with St. John and Eran Mak. The Martian was lounging in his habitual position on the window sill, smoking and swinging the bells back and forth in his ear with a monotonous forefinger. He watched Rick through the smoke, his eyes yellow and unwinking as a hawk's.

St. John took Mayo in his arms. Rick turned away irritably, not wanting to see either of their faces. He let them talk, a few low words, while he sprawled out wearily in a big chair and got a cigarette going. He felt suddenly as old as Mars, and as tired.

"There are no words to thank you, Rick," St. John said presently. "This is a very strange situation. I'm grateful to you with all my heart, and yet I wish you weren't here. I'm afraid of you, and afraid of what may have to be done."

"At least you're honest about it," Rick said.

"There's no point in deception." St. John sat down behind a desk piled high with papers. He looked at the mess and sighed. "Forming a new government out of what we have to work with is no easy job. I've been over to Kahora several times, and Mak's been wearing his legs off running back and forth to Martian headquarters. I've stayed here because it seemed to be the focal point of all the trouble and I thought I could handle things better if I did. Also, the Company had to be taken care of. My heavens, the things Storm had been doing!"

Rick glanced almost lazily at St. John. "Yeah. You haven't got recognition and charter yet from the Interplanetary Authority, have you?"

"Not yet. But there's no question that we will, considering the circumstances."

"That is, all the circumstances but one," replied Rick.

St. John nodded slowly. "That's what you came back for, isn't it?"

Rick jumped up. "My stars!" he roared. "What did you think I'd do? Who did all this anyway? Who was it sweated in these cursed mines, and took the beatings and the burnings and the kicks in the teeth?" He thrust his hands out. The bandages had come off, showing the raw new scars. "Was it you got pinned to the wall in Ruh, or me? Was it you that Beudach put the Collar on, or me? Was it you that talked to the Marshies and the Earthmen into fighting together, into being blood brothers from here on out? Was it you stuck your neck out there in the Thieves' Quarter, maybe to get a knife in it, and was it you stole that ship and crashed it on top of Jaffa Storm?"

His voice was making the windows rattle. His face was blank and hard with fury, the veins like whipcords on his temples. He stopped suddenly and paced back and forth a little, and when he spoke again his voice was only a tight whisper.

"By jumping jingoes, I've given too much, St. John," he said. "Blood and sweat and the fear of dying, while you were sitting on your hands, wishing. If you and Eran Mak think you can get rid of me with a crack on the head and fifty thousand credits to show for it, you're crazy!" He laughed and swung around so he could face both of them. "Would you be satisfied, St. John? Would you, Mak?"

There was a long silence. Eran Mak smoked quietly, enigmatic as the sea-bottom outside.

"No, I don't suppose I would be," St. John said slowly, at last.

"The question," said Eran Mak, "is not whether you're satisfied, but whether or not you can do anything about getting satisfied.''

Rick smiled.

''Tell 'em, about what's up there under the Polar domes, and what Storm was going to do with it,'' he said to Mayo.

She told them. But her eyes, like Eran Mak's, were on Rick.

He gave them plenty of time to think it over. They didn't like it. The thought of all that power frightened them. St. John reached out once for the telescreen, and stopped.

''No, I wouldn't trust the Marshies that far just yet, if I were you,'' Rick said with a laugh. ''All right, so there's force there. But I don't have to use it.''

''May I remind you you're a prisoner here,'' Mak said.

''Sure. So was I on the *Mary Ellen Dow*. A guy goes through a certain number of things, and he gets so he doesn't care any more. Like I said, I don't have to use it.''

He was close behind Mayo now. Quite suddenly he caught her around the neck with one arm and held her while he snatched the tube out of the pocket where she had hidden it. Then he let her go and stepped back.

He aimed the tube at a chair. A little pink tongue licked out and touched it, and there was nothing but a heap of dust.

''Disintegrator,'' said Rick. ''Now, maybe you'd better get busy with the telescreen. A planet-wide hook-up, see? Maybe you'd better tell everybody just what happened here the night of the raid.''

Mayo got up slowly and stood facing him.

''You know what that will mean,'' St. John said.

''Sure. Your geese will be pretty well fried, won't they? The fine altruistic saviors of Mars won't look so hot, will they?''

''Think a minute, Rick, before you do this,'' St. John said. ''Men fight any way they can to win what they want. Believe it or not, Mak and I are honest. You have fifty thousand credits, remember.''

''Not any more. They bought my way off the *Mary Ellen Dow*.''

Eran Mak whistled. ''So it meant that much to you!'' He slid off the sill and stood up. ''What will you take in place of Mars?''

''What could you give me in place of a world?'' countered Rick.

They stood looking at him, St. John and Mayo and Eran Mak. He scowled, his jaw set stubbornly, his eyes hooded and sulky. He was careful that he should not see Mayo's face.

St. John sighed. He reached out, slowly like an old man, to press the connection on the telescreen.

"Wait!" Rick said hoarsely.

They stiffened, staring at him. There was sweat on his face and his hand trembled slightly.

"Wait," he said. "Listen. Yesterday Kyra died in Caer Hebra. She died smiling. She said she'd live again, in the new Mars, and remember that she helped make it. Helped make it—with me! And by Jaffrey, I did do it! I pulled this messy dustball together and made it tick. Nobody else could have done it. Nobody but me!"

He paused and rubbed his hand over his eyes. "I don't know why I give a cuss what Kyra said. I don't know whether she'll live again, or remember. But if she did— Oh, rats! Mayo, come here."

She came. There was a glow starting back in her eyes.

"Listen, Mayo. Is this what the prophecy meant, my shadow over Mars? The shadow that's there now and will always be there, because I put Mars together with my two hands? I've been thinking, Mayo. I can get this world, or at least I can make a blamed good try at it. I can milk it dry, maybe, but—well, there are other worlds, and I'm young yet, and I—" He pulled her close to him. "Does that make sense, Mayo? I'd rather have you than Mars. Like I told you once, you're part of me, and if I couldn't have you, I wouldn't care what else I had. You know something? All the time I was getting away to come back here, I wasn't really thinking of Mars. I was thinking of you."

"I said you had a soul, if you could ever find it," Mayo whispered.

Rick put his lips on hers. "Bosh, for my soul. I found you." His arms tightened.

St. John and Eran Mak turned away.

"Other worlds," Rick murmured after a while. "There's always Outside—the Belt, and even Jupiter. Ships get better every year, and they need trail-breakers out there. Unless you want to stay here, without me."

She stopped his lips with hers.

Rick started to laugh. "I guess I'm crazy. Looking at St. John over there, behind that desk all stacked up with papers, already getting bags under his eyes worrying about politics and charters and chiselling bums, I'm glad I don't have to. I got to thinking about that, too. Breaking trail is fine, but building the road afterward is just a lot of hard work, and somebody else can have it."

He moved forward, holding Mayo tight in his arm. "Okay, you guys. You've got the grief. But don't think I'm through blackmailing you. I'm sticking you for the best blamed ship that flies, all fitted up, and a crew to match, and first trade rights for what I bring in from the Belt. And listen." His voice dropped and he flushed uncomfortably.

"Just in case Kyra does come back—build a good road, will you? I'd kind of like her to remember me and think that my shadow over Mars was still a good one."

FOLLOWED IN SPACE!

The *Starsong* was beginning to pass between the two huge red binaries into the thicker sprawl of stars through which the channel led. The channel was not straight, and you could not take it too fast—in that swarm of suns the fabric of a ship could be torn apart in some deadly gravity drag or vaporized in collision. The only thing was that the Orionids were still following them.

But Birrel said nothing. This was Garstang's job and he let him do it. The enormous pairs of red suns flashed past them on either side and were gone, and they were in the channel. Under his feet he could feel the *Starsong* quiver, wincing and flinching like a live thing. On either side the overhanging cliffs of stars seemed to topple toward them. He looked upward at the nebula, like a glowing thundercloud roofing the channel, and then down at the shoaling suns below.

Garstang said flatly, "We didn't get away quite fast enough. They'll be barrelling in here after us and they'll have us in range before we ever get through the channel."

"As far as I can see," said Birrel, "we've only got one way out of it."

He looked up at the screens again, at the vast glow of the nebula overhead.

Garstang was silent for a moment. Then he said, "I hoped you wouldn't think of that."

The Tor Double Novels:

*forthcoming

EDMOND HAMILTON

BATTLE FOR THE STARS

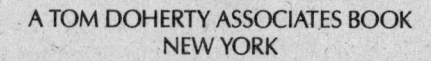

A TOM DOHERTY ASSOCIATES BOOK
NEW YORK

To E. Hoffman Price

BATTLE FOR THE STARS

Copyright © 1961 by Edmond Hamilton
Reprinted by permission of the author's estate and the estate's agent, Blassingame-Spectrum Literary Agency

A TOR Book
Published by Tom Doherty Associates, Inc.
49 West 24 Street
New York, NY 10010

Cover art by Bryn Barnard

ISBN: 0-812-55960-6   Can. ISBN: 0-812-55961-4

Library of Congress Catalog Card Number: 61-15300

First Tor edition: May 1989

Printed in the United States of America

0 9 8 7 6 5 4 3 2 1

1

IT WAS NO place for a man to be.

Men were tissue, blood, bone, nerve. This place was not made for them. It was made for fire and force and radiation. Go home, men.

But I can't, thought Jay Birrel. Not yet. My feet ache, I didn't sleep well, I want to see my wife, but I can't go home, I have to go on into this place where a human being looks as pathetic as an insect in a furnace.

Such thoughts made Birrel uneasy. He disliked imaginative thinking and imaginative people, he regarded himself as a tough, practical man. They had a job to do and that was all there was to it, and he might as well quit mooning about it. He straightened up a little more. He was always doing that, trying to gain a little height, so that when he gave an order to a man he would not have to look up to him. It seemed a little foolish to do it, but he could not quite get over the nagging consciousness that his height was only average.

He said, "Radar?"

Joe Garstang, beside him, answered without turning. "Nothing has been monitored yet. Not *yet.*"

Garstang was a younger man than Birrel, but he was so big and broad and slow-speaking that he made you think of a rock. The rock could worry, though. Birrel sensed the worry now and thought, He doesn't like this job . . . And he doesn't like having me aboard. No captain likes to be outranked on his own ship, especially on a mission like this one. Well, that is too bad, I do not like it either, but we are going ahead into that mess anyway.

He concealed his own profound distaste at the prospect they were watching. It was comparatively quiet here in the bridge, with only a muted chattering from the calc-room just aft. The place was almost like a metal-and-plastic shrine, with the broad control-banks as its mechanical altar, Venner and the two technicians their silent ministrants, and he and Garstang watching the screens like anxious suppliants.

The screens were not really windows. They were the final sensitive parts of a chain of incredibly complicated mechanisms that took hold of some of the faster-than-light radar information flowing into the ship, and translated it into visual images. But they looked like windows—windows through which smashed the light of a thousand thousand suns.

This place was cluster N-356-44, in the Standard Atlas. It was also hellfire made manifest before them. It was a hive of swarming suns, pale-green and violet, white and yellow-gold and smoky red, blazing so fiercely that the eye was robbed of perspective and these stars seemed to crowd and rub and jostle each other. Up against the black backdrop of the firmament, they burned, pouring forth the torrents of their life-energy to whirl in cosmic belts and maelstroms of radiation. Merchant ships would recoil aghast from the navigational perils here. Unfortunately, this was not a merchant ship.

There was a rift in the cluster, a narrow cleft between cliffs of stars, which was roofed by the flame-shot glow of a vast, sprawling nebula. It was the only possible way into the heart of the cluster, this channel. Had others gone in this way? Were they still in here? That was for them to find out.

He looked at the looming, overtopping cliffs of stars that went up to the glowing nebula above and down to a fiery shoal of suns below. He thought of Lyllin, waiting for him in the quiet house back at Vega. He thought that he had no business having a wife.

"Radar?" he asked again.

Garstang looked at the tell-tales and said, "Still nothing." He turned, his heavy brows drawn together into a frown, and said doggedly, "It still seems to me that if they're in here, we should have come in with the whole squadron."

Birrel shook his head. He had his own doubts riding him, but once you started showing doubt, you were through. He had made his decision, he had committed them, and now he had to look confident about it no matter how lonely and exposed he felt.

"That could be exactly what Solleremos wants. With the right kind of ambush, a whole squadron could be clobbered in this mess. Then Lyra would be wide open. No. One ship is enough to risk."

"Yes, sir," said Garstang.

"The hell with you, Joe," said Birrel. "Say what you're thinking."

"I am thinking that it was not my lucky day when you picked the *Starsong* for your flagship. That's all."

The ship moved onward through the fiery channel, toward the pair of red binary stars that marked its end. The binaries hardly seemed to change size, the swarm of stars on either side of them seemed to creep back with infinite slowness, even though the ship moved at very many times the speed of light. Once, thought Birrel, such velocities had been thought flatly impossible. Then the light-speed barrier had been cracked by the ultra-drive which altered the basic mass-speed ratio by bleeding off mass as energy and storing it, then automatically reconverting it into mass when a ship decelerated. At such velocities, Birrel felt that it was ridiculous for him to be chafing at their slowness. He always felt that, and he always chafed.

Looking at the upper screen that showed the flaring, billowing belly of the nebula above them, like the underside of a burning ocean, Birrel said to Garstang,

"Does it seem to you that the pace is speeding up? I mean, this jockeying for power between the Sectors has gone on a long time, ever since Earth lost real authority. But it seems different lately, somehow. More incidents, more feeling of something driving ahead toward a definite goal, a plan and a pattern you can't quite see. You know what I mean?"

Garstang nodded. "I know."

The computer banks back in the calc-room clicked and chattered. Relays kicked, compensating course, compensating tides of gravitic force quite capable of breaking a ship apart like a piece of flawed glass. The two red binaries gave them a final glare of malice and were gone. They were out of the channel.

A star the color of a peacock's breast lay dead ahead.

Venner, the anxious and alert young officer who stood not far from Garstang, said,

"That's the nearest star with E-type worlds, sir. We've plotted five others farther in."

Garstang looked at Birrel.

Birrel shrugged. "If they're based in here, it'd be on an E-type. Take them one by one."

Garstang gave his orders. Birrel watched the blaze of peacock-blue grow swiftly. No ambush in the channel, so now what? Ambush on the world of the blue star? Or nothing? Time

and money wasted and maybe it was all just a feint on Solleremos' part, trying to draw the Fifth here while a move was
made somewhere else.

Suddenly Birrel felt old and tired. He had been in the squadron for almost twenty years, ever since he was seventeen, and
in all these years the great game of stars, the strain, the worry,
had never let up.

It must have been nice in a way, Birrel thought, in the old
days a couple of centuries ago when the United Worlds still
governed in fact from Earth, and all the star-squadrons were
part of one galactic fleet whose struggles were only with the
natural perils of the galaxy itself. But that had not lasted long.

The trouble was that it had got too big, too fast. It should
have taken millennia to expand so widely. But the fact that on
scores of E-type star-worlds they had found peoples completely
human in every respect, had upset all calculations. The an-
thropologists were still arguing whether that was because original germinal spores of life, seeding worlds of similar type,
had produced identical chains of evolution, or whether there
had been a long-ago spread of some human stock through all
these worlds. Opinion inclined to the latter theory, but it didn't
really matter. What mattered was that finding all these star-
peoples, some of them semi-barbaric but others almost up to
the technical level of Earth, had accelerated the expected slow
expansion into a human explosion across the vast areas of the
galaxy.

Too big, too fast. The United Worlds that had been set up
back on Earth had handled it for a while, but it could not
govern that vast sprawl of stars at anything like a local level.
That was when the Sectors had been set up, the subdivisions
of the UW. And that, thought Birrel, was when things had
taken a different path.

There were five great Sectors, and there were five governors,
who headed the Sector Councils. Solleremos of Orion, Vorn
of Cepheus, Gianea of Leo, Strowe of Perseus, Ferdias of
Lyra—and all of them jealous of each other. Five great pro-
consuls, paying only a lip-service allegiance to the shadowy
UW far away on Earth, all of them hungry for space, hungry
for power. Yes, even Ferdias, thought Birrel. Ferdias was the
man he served, respected, and even loved in a craggy sort of
way. But Ferdias, like the others, played a massive game of
chess with men and suns, moving his squadrons here and his

undercover operatives there, laboring ceaselessly to hold on to what he had and perhaps enlarge his Sector just a little, a small star-system here and a minor cluster there. . . .

And the game went on, and this mission was part of it. Ferdias wanted to know if Orion ships were secretly basing in here where they had no business to be. This cluster was no-man's-land, part of the buffer zones that were supposed to reduce friction between the Sectors. Actually, stellar wildernesses like this one were the scenes of frequent, nameless little struggles that were never reported at all. Birrel hoped, not too strongly, that he was not about to start another such.

"We're getting close," said Garstang.

Birrel shook himself and got down to business. There followed a few minutes of activity on split-second timing, and then the *Starsong* was shuddering to the vibration of her mass-reconverters as she plunged toward a bright world almost dangerously close to her. There was still no sign of any enemy, and the communicators remained silent.

An hour later by ship's chrono they had located the one port of entry listed for the planet and they had set the *Starsong* down in the middle of a large piece of natural desert that served well enough for what little space traffic ever came here.

It was night on this side of the planet. There was no moon, but, on a cluster world, a moon is a useless luxury. The sky blazes with a million stars, so that day is replaced not by darkness, but by light of another sort, soft and many-colored, full of strange glimmers and flitting shadows. By this eerie star-glow, through the now-unshuttered ports, a town of sorts was visible about a mile away.

Otherwise there was nothing. No ships, no base, no legions from Orion Sector.

"The ships could be hidden somewhere," Garstang said pessimistically. "Maybe halfway around the planet, but waiting to jump us as soon as they get word."

Birrel admitted that that was possible. He had put on his best dress coverall of blue-and-silver, and now he stuffed a portable communicator into one pocket. Garstang watched him dourly.

"How many men will you want?" he asked.

"None. I'm better alone on this one."

Garstang's eye widened a trifle. "I won't come right out and say you're crazy."

"Look, I know what I'm doing," Birrel said impatiently. "I was here once before, years ago, when old Volland commanded the Fifth, and I know these people. They're what you might call poor, but proud. They have a lot of traditions about long-ago splendor, how their kings once ruled the whole cluster and so one. They detest strangers, and won't let more than one in at a time."

"Fine," said Garstang. "But what if you run into trouble in there?"

"That's the reason I'm taking the porto." Birrel frowned, trying to plan ahead. "Exactly thirty minutes after I enter the town I'll contact you, and I'll continue to call at thirty-minute intervals. If I'm so much as a minute late, take off and buzz hell out of the place. It'll give me a bargaining point, anyway."

They went down to the airlock, which was open now and filled with a dry, stinging wind. Birrel paused, looking toward the distant town that was a lonely blot of darkness between the star-blazing sky and the gleaming sand. Here and there in it lights burned, but they were few and somehow not welcoming.

Garstang said, "A lot can happen in thirty minutes. Suppose you're not able to bargain?"

"Then you're on your own. But don't get yourself trapped—if it looks hopeless, you take her away."

Garstang snorted. "I'd get a fine reception from Ferdias if I went back and told him I left you here."

"Don't fool yourself," Birrel said roughly. "Ferdias would rather lose a commander than a ship, anytime. Just remember that."

He went down the ladder to the sand and began to walk.

He looked up at the incredible sky as he walked, and he thought of how wonderful that had seemed to him when he had first come here. But that had been a long time ago, he had been young and eager then and bursting with pride that he belonged to the Fifth, feeling somehow that space and stars were all his personal property.

What's changed me? Birrel wondered. I'm older, I'm thirty-seven, I'm a little tired, but it's more than that, I look at things differently now. Maybe it's the weight of command, or maybe being married, or it might be that this is something that happens to every man as he goes along, that the excitement goes out of things and, you have seen so much happen, that you glimpse the shape of possible disaster long before it ever

reaches you. The devil with it, he thought, this is no time for brooding, I had better be on my toes.

The town took shape as he approached it. The stone-built houses, mostly round or octagonal, were scattered about with no particular plan. Under the red and gold and diamond-colored stars that burned above them as bright as moons, they looked curiously remote and evil, like old wizards in peaked hats, peering with winking eyes. The dry wind blew, laden with alien scents, and, apart from the wind, there was no sound at all.

2

THE QUIET WAS only what Birrel had expected. Not a soul in this place could have remained unaware of the coming of the ship, but, with cold hostility, they were ignoring it. Nobody came out to meet him, no one moved against the scattered lights ahead. Birrel tramped on, wondering how many eyes watched him come.

Three men met him at the edge of the town. They wore pale cloaks and carried long staffs or wands of office that were tipped with horn. They were all of seven feet tall. They wore their hair high on their heads to accentuate this height, and they were slender and graceful as reeds, moving with a light, dancing step as though the wind blew them. But their faces in the star-glow were smooth and secret, their eyes as expressionless as bits of shiny glass.

"What does the man from outside desire?" asked one of them, speaking in Basic.

Birrel said, "He desires to speak with your lord about the others who have come here from outside."

But they were not going to make it that easy for him. Their faces remained impassive, and the one who had spoken said coolly,

"Others?"

Birrel retained his patience. The Sector held a great many worlds, and their different peoples varied widely in psychology, and anyone who got impatient would not get far with

them. That was all the more true here in the no-man's-land of
the cluster.

"Yes. The others," he said, and then just stood stolidly,
waiting.

Finally the tall man shrugged delicately and said, "Our lord
has wisdom in all matters. Perhaps he will understand your
words."

They fell in around Birrel and moved with him into the wide,
sandy space that went between the wandering houses. The
nerves tightened up in his belly, and his back felt cold. He
looked at his wrist chrono, carefully. Garstang would be
watching with the 'scope, but once he was in among the houses
he could no longer be seen.

That was almost at once. The tall men walked on with their
light, swaying stride, so that he had to move at an undignified
trot to keep up with them. The stone houses with their high
roofs closed in behind him, and there were only shadowy walls
and sandy ways and a few dusty, leafless shrubs. Birrel had
heard of the strange, underground cultivation these people
maintained in great caverns, but had never seen that.

He thought that this dark, poor, arid town ill accorded with
old tales of cluster-kings. Yet many of the human peoples at
far-separated stars had such legends—the persistence of the
legend, indeed, was one reason for the theory that all these
various human stocks in the galaxy, so completely human that
they could and did interbreed, had been seeded through the
star-worlds by a space-conquering people in the remote and
forgotten past.

Tall figures back in the shadows watched Birrel pass. They
said nothing, but their silence was in itself hostile. Soon, when
they were close to the center of the town, his guide stopped
beside a round, stone structure from whose open door came
light.

"Will the man from outside enter the dwelling of our lord?"

Birrel breathed a little more easily as he went through the
door. Apparently he had guessed wrong, and—

He stopped.

He had not guessed wrong at all.

The odd, square, crystal lamps in the big, bare stone room
did not really light it as much as did the soft star-glow pouring
in through the high windows. There was quite enough light to
show him the four men here. They were not the tall natives of

this world. They were men dressed much like himself and all but one of them had sonic shockers at their belts and wore upon their shoulders the insigne of Orion Sector.

The one exception, who wore only a plain coverall, stood directly in front of Birrel, a lean, dark iron-faced man with very alert eyes, and the easy, dangerous manner of one who enjoys his work because he is so admirably well fitted for it, as a cat enjoys hunting.

He smiled at Birrel and said, "My name is Tauncer."

Birrel had never seen the man before, but the name was enough to tell him the full depth of this disaster. On more than one world he had heard this name and had seen the work of this man, the most famous of Solleremos' agents.

He said, "I should feel flattered, shouldn't I?"

Tauncer shrugged. "We all do what we can, Commander. Each in his own way. Please sit down."

Birrel sat down in one of the carven stone chairs. His feet barely touched the floor, making him feel ridiculously like a child in an adult's chair. He looked toward the door, but none of the tall natives had come in after leading him neatly right into this.

He wanted to glance at his chrono, but he did not dare. Tauncer was watching him, and he did not think that those insolent, amused, black eyes missed much. The other men lounged, not watching him, not doing anything, but Birrel was sure their weapons would come out in a hurry if he grabbed for his porto. He would have to stall as long as he could.

"Just as a matter of curiosity," he said, "how did you set it up with these people? They're famously hostile to strangers."

Tauncer nodded. "That's right. Only I'm not exactly a stranger. We all, in these days, have mixed ancestry from many worlds—you have it, I have it, everyone. Well, I happen to have a trace of this people's blood. Not much, but enough."

He added casually, "By the way, Commander, you might as well look at your chrono, if you want to. I can see that you want to very much."

His white teeth showed, and Birrel felt a rising anger. Tauncer was enjoying himself. He was good at this, very good, and he was going to have fun with the honest clod he had trapped. Well, perhaps that fun could be spoiled.

He did look at his chrono, saying, "Of course, you know

that I wouldn't walk in here with my eyes shut. My men have their instructions."

Tauncer's tone was almost soothing. "I'm sure they have. And don't feel too badly about this, Commander. This was all set up on a minute study of your psychology and past record. It would have been almost impossible for you to act other than you have. All we had to do was wait."

It confirmed, for Birrel, what he had already guessed. The rumor about Orion ships basing in this cluster had been purposely leaked so that he would walk right into Tauncer's hands. He cursed himself for his bad judgment. Garstang had been right, he should have brought the squadron in.

"I suppose," he said, "that all of this is for some good reason."

"Naturally," said Tauncer. "I just want the answer to one simple question."

He walked closer and stood in front of Birrel and looked at him keenly. He asked his question.

"What is Ferdias planning to do about Earth?"

There was a long moment of complete silence, during which Birrel simply stared at Tauncer, and Tauncer probed him with a gaze like a scalpel.

On Birrel's part, it was a silence of sheer astonishment. No question could have taken him so unexpectedly. He had been prepared to be grilled about squadron dispositions, forces in being, bases, all the things that the men of Orion would like to know about Lyra. But this—

It didn't make sense. Earth was not part of the present-day star struggle. That old planet, so far back in the galaxy that Birrel had never been within parsecs of it—it was history, nothing more. It had had its day, its sons long ago had spread out to the stars and their blood ran in the veins of men on many worlds, in Birrel himself. But its great day had long been done, and the Sector governors, who played the cosmic chess-game for suns, paid it no heed at all. No, Birrel decided swiftly, the question was merely a fake, a cover-up for something else, some other line of attack.

"I'll repeat," said Tauncer. "What's Ferdias planning to do about Earth?"

"I haven't," said Birrel, "the faintest idea what you're talking about."

"Possibly," said Tauncer. "But I've been given the job of

making the inquiry, and I'll need more than your word and an expression of innocence. Where's Karsh?''

He shot out the last question so suddenly that it almost caught Birrel off guard, but he maintained his blank look.

"Karsh?"

Tauncer sighed. "Well, these formalities are just delaying us. Dow!"

One of the other men came forward. Tauncer spoke to him in a low voice and he nodded and went into another room. Birrel's pulse began to pound heavily. No more than fifteen minutes had elapsed since he entered the town. There was plenty of time left for mischief. Yet he said flatly to Tauncer,

"You must know that you don't have much time."

"All the time in the world, Commander. Your men aren't coming in after you."

"You're pretty sure."

"Yes, I'm sure. Can't you hurry that up, Dow?"

"All ready." Dow came back carrying a light tripod with a projector mounted on top of it. And now Birrel had a leaden feeling. He had seen that particular type of projector before. It was called a vera-probe and it beamed electric wave-impulses in a carefully controlled range that absolutely stunned and demoralized a man's brain, blocking off his will and making him temporarily incapable of lying or of resisting questioning.

Birrel had no information about Earth to give away and he knew nothing of the whereabouts of Karsh, who was Ferdias' right-hand man in the secret struggle of Sectors. But there were plenty of other things in his mind, things of importance to Lyra that Solleremos would be only too glad to learn.

How long now? Ten minutes more? Too long. Even five minutes would be too long, once that projector started pounding his skull. He had to do something to gain time and there was only one thing he could think of to do.

He suddenly jumped forward out of the tall, stone chair. He was quite sure that they did not want to kill him, or even to stun him yet, and he was right, for no weapon was drawn. Birrel sprang toward the projector, only five or six feet away.

Dow and the other men were on top of him almost at once, but not quite in time. He fetched the tripod a thrashing kick as they bore him down. It fell over. He could not hope that it was broken, but it would take them time to set it up again.

He tried to keep them busy as long as he could, but Tauncer

understood perfectly well what he was up to. He had his men haul Birrel back to the chair and hold him, he set Dow to adjusting the projector again, and then he spoke to Birrel with cool patience.

"You may as well spare yourself, Commander. I told you that your men are not coming in after you. They'll stir up a hornet's nest with these people if they try, and they won't even have very long to try."

"Why not?"

Tauncer smiled. "I have my mission and the military have theirs. We've had three cruisers standing off and on, well away from here and masked from radar—they got word the moment you landed and they're already on their way. Your men will soon be busy with their own affairs."

It was what Birrel had feared. He tried to keep his face composed, but something of what he felt must have showed in it for Tauncer's smile deepened.

"All this is the price you pay for fame, Commander. We picked you to question because the Fifth is Ferdias' elite squadron, and nobody gets command of it unless he's in Ferdias' special confidence and favor."

"Friendship is one thing," said Birrel hotly, "and favor is another. I don't like your choice of words."

He was just talking, words, sounds with no meaning. Inside he was thinking of Garstang and the *Starsong*, all of them unaware of destruction riding down upon them along the radar-blind cone on the other side of the planet. It was he who had led them here.

He looked at Tauncer, and he began now to hate that smiling face, that easy confidence of superiority. Perhaps it was because Tauncer really was his superior in this sort of thing that he hated him. But, Birrel thought, superior or not, Tauncer had guessed wrong on the instructions that he had left his men, and that was about the only chance he had left. Keep talking, stall as long as possible.

"Ferdias will tear your heart out for this," he said.

"Perhaps," said Tauncer. "But he may have other things to occupy his mind."

"Earth? It doesn't mean anything to him. It's only a name, and a half-forgotten one at that. Why should Earth occupy his mind? Why, Tauncer?"

How long is thirty minutes? How long does it take three

cruisers to come from Point X to Target Zero? How long does it take for a man to realize he's through at last?

Tauncer seemed to know his thought. "Time almost run out, Commander? I'm afraid that's not going to help you. Ready, Dow?"

Dow said again, "All ready."

Tauncer nodded. Dow touched a stud on the projector.

As though that touch had done it, a dull and mighty roaring echoed from out in the desert—the full-throated cry of a heavy cruiser taking off.

The men looked, startled, toward the open doorway. Desperately, Birrel tugged free of their hold, out of the unseen force that was already battering at the edges of his mind.

"You out there!" he shouted at the doorway. "The men from outside will destroy you unless I go free! Call your lord—"

Then Tauncer's men caught up to him and one of them hit him hard on the side of the jaw. Birrel shut up, hanging with blind determination to his consciousness. Forethought had provided this one chance. He would not get another.

The cruiser came low over the town. Dust sifted out of the cracks of the stone walls. The men fell to their knees, covering their heads with their hands. The floor rocked under them, beaten by the rolling hammers of concussion, as the shock-wave hit them.

3

THE RIPPED SKY closed upon itself with a stunning, thundering crash. After a minute or two the noise and the shock-wave ebbed away.

Silence.

The men began to get up again. But Birrel did not move.

The cruiser came back. This time it was even lower. Garstang must have tickled her belly on the peaked roofs. Good God, thought Birrel, he's overdoing it. This time the stones were shaking loose, the whole town rocking from that tremendous shock-wave.

When it was over, a long, thin shape came in through the

doorway. It was the leader of the tall, native men who had brought Birrel here. He was not smug and secret now. His face was a mask of fear and rage as he spoke to Tauncer.

"You said that if we helped you, you would keep all other outsiders away!"

"We will," said Tauncer. "Listen—"

"Yes, listen," mocked Birrel. "Listen to it coming back. It'll keep coming back, unless I walk out of here, until—"

Dow hit him across the mouth to silence him. The tall man stood hesitating. Then the *Starsong* roared back over, and this time it did seem as though the roof was going. When it had passed, the man's hesitation was gone. With a kind of desperate haste, he grabbed Birrel's arm and shoved him toward the open doorway.

"Oh, no," said Tauncer, starting forward. "You can't do that."

The tall man turned on him a face livid with frustrated anger, and he took that anger out on Tauncer.

"Shall the children of kings be destroyed to serve mongrels such as you? Shall I call my people in?"

Birrel, heading toward the door, saw outside it the crowd of tall, pale-cloaked men who had gathered. Tauncer saw them too and he stopped, his face dark and wary.

Still full of resentment at being so easily trapped, Birrel could not forego the gesture of flicking dust off his sleeves before he went through the door. Tauncer's dark eyes showed a gleam of amusement at this bit of bravado, but it stirred the man Dow to rage.

He cried violently, "Are we just going to stand here and let him go?"

Tauncer shrugged. "Why, yes, there are times when you just stand and do nothing and this is one of them."

Birrel went out through the door and through the scared, angry crowd outside it. They glared their hatred at him, but no one stopped him, no one followed him. He snatched the porto out of his pocket and talked fast to Garstang. Then, without trying to make a dignified exit, he stretched his legs and ran like the devil toward the desert.

The cruiser dropped down ahead of him, as black and big against the stars as a falling world. The lock yawned open, and Garstang was inside it to meet him. He started to ask what had

happened, but Birrel pushed him bodily away down the corridor, heading for the bridge.

"Get in there and do your stuff, Joe. We've got three Orionid cruisers coming this way up the planet's radar-shadow, and I don't know how close they are."

Garstang's square face got dismal, but his step quickened and his voice crackled orders as they went past the radar and calc-rooms to the bridge. The intercom went suddenly crazy and men jumped at the control-banks. The last thing Birrel heard before the howling roar of take-off drowned everything was Garstang observing complainingly that this sort of thing was hard on a ship.

They went up and away from the planet. Garstang's orders had been designed to shove them out on a course exactly opposite from the course the Orionids must be using to come in. Just as those others were using the planet's radar-shadow to sneak in undetected, so the *Starsong* was using the opposite radar-shadow to sneak out. But the cone of shadow would pinch out very soon.

"Less than a half-hour," said Garstang, looking through a filter-port at the blazing peacock sun that was sliding back as they pulled out. "It's pretty close quarters yet, but we'd better hit it and get all the start we can before they spot us—we can't jam three of them."

Birrel nodded, grimly agreeing. Ultra-light-speed missiles, with their deadly warheads, each had their own independent radar to home on their targets. A cruiser's defense against them was not armor, but incredibly powerful shafts of electromagnetic force that jammed the radar of oncoming missiles and sent them wandering astray. You could jam against the fire of one ship, maybe even two if you were lucky. You could not jam against three, they would inevitably saturate and smother your defense.

Garstang gave the order for full acceleration schedule, the sirens wailed warning. Despite the unseen autostasis that cradled frail human bodies against impossible pressures by swaddling them in a matrix of force, they felt a wrenching deep in their brains and guts as the *Starsong* plunged ahead.

At fantastically mounting speeds the ship raced toward the two red binaries that guarded the entrance to the channel. The scanners and ultra-radar had come into play, replacing normal vision, making their cunning illusion of sight. Birrel watched

the two red double stars hungrily. Then on the intercom radar-room said dismally,

"They've come on the 'scope, sir. Three N-16s, overhauling us at a five to three-point-six ratio."

Birrel glanced at Garstang. "It figures. Tauncer would have messaged them to keep right after us—they didn't have to land and then take off again."

Garstang nodded silently. Now the *Starsong* was beginning to pass between the two huge red binaries into that thicker sprawl of stars through which the channel led. He glanced at the tell-tales, then ordered their acceleration schedule cut back. There was, Birrel knew, nothing else he could do. The channel ahead was not straight and you could not take it too fast—in that swarm of suns the fabric of a ship could be torn apart in some deadly resultant-point of gravity drags, or vaporized in collision. The only thing was that the Orionids were still coming up on them.

But Birrel said nothing. This was Garstang's job and he let him do it. The enormous pairs of red suns flashed past them on either side and were gone, and they were in the channel. Under his feet he could feel the *Starsong* quiver, wincing and flinching like a live thing now and again as some new combination of gravitic forces wrenched at her. On either side of them now the overhanging cliffs of stars seemed to topple toward them. He looked upward at the nebula, like a glowing thundercloud roofing the channel, and then down at the shoaling suns below.

Garstang said flatly, "We didn't get away quite fast enough. They'll be barrelling in here after us and they'll have us in range before we ever get through the channel."

"As far as I can see," said Birrel, "we've got only one way out of it."

He looked up at the screens again, at the vast glow of the nebula overhead.

Garstang was silent for a moment. Then he said, "I was hoping you wouldn't think of that."

Birrel shrugged. "Have you got any better idea? Anyway, it's not an order. This is your ship."

"Is it?" Garstang said sourly. "If it was, we wouldn't be here now. All right." He turned back and spoke into the communicator. "New course, north and zenith thirty-eight degrees. Full autopilot."

Young Venner, over at the control-banks, flashed a startled glance before he could compose his face. I know how you feel, thought Birrel. We're all scared, you're not alone.

The *Starsong* shot upward, plunging high into an area so choked with stellar radiance that it made the channel seem like sunless space. The manual control banks went dark and dead. Now, from the calc-room back of the bridge, a new sound came, different from the normal, occasional bursts of chattering. This was a steady sound, a sound of authority, the voice of the *Starsong* speaking. She was flying herself now. The men aboard, commander and captain and crew, were her charges, dependent on her cold, mechanical wisdom and her vision and her strength. They had set up on the calculators what they wanted her to do and now there was nothing for them but to wait.

The *Starsong* spiralled higher, her radar system guiding her on a twisting evasive path between the clotted stars. Then Birrel saw a great, glowing edge slide across the fore screen and grow into a vastness of dust and cosmic drift, illuminated by the reflected glow of the half-smothered stars it webbed.

Radar reported that the three Orionid cruisers had come into the channel. But the *Starsong* was already skimming through glowing arms that reached like misty tentacles searching for more stars to entrap. Once in the cloud, she would be screened from the cruisers' long-range radar by the most effective jamming device in space—the billions of billions of scattered atoms of the nebula itself.

Effective. Yes. But potentially as dangerous as Orionid warheads. For in a place where radar would work only at frighteningly short ranges, you could be onto a chunk of cosmic drift before the beams had time to tell the computers about it. All you had in the nebula was a chance, and not even a particularly good one. But against three cruisers you did not even have that.

Birrel went to the back of the bridge and strapped himself into a recoil-chair, beside Garstang and the others. Nothing moved now within the ship. The frail, breakable organisms of breath and heart and bone had abdicated their control. This was the hour of the ship, the hour of steel and flame and the racing electron, faster than human thought.

The *Starsong* spoke to herself in the calc-room, and plunged headlong into the cloud.

The universe was swallowed up in soft light, in racing, streaming tides of dust made luminous by reflection. Like an undersea ship of old, the *Starsong* raced with the gleaming currents and burst through denser, darker deeps, where the stars were faint and far away, to leap once more into a glory of wild light, where the dust-drowned suns burned like torches in a mist. And the metallic voices in the calc-room rose to an unhuman crying as the computers strained to take in the overwhelming surge of data from the short-range radar, analyze it, and send imperative commands to the control-relays.

They had almost a sound of insane music to them, those voices, and the *Starsong* seemed to dance to the music, whirling and swaying between the fragments of drift that threatened her with instant destruction if she faltered for the fraction of a second. Three times before, in his service, Birrel had been through this ordeal, yet that did not keep him from feeling halfdazed, clinging to the chair and laboring for breath as he felt and listened. The same illusion gripped him now that had mastered him before when forced to run a nebula—the feeling that the suns and star-worlds were all gone, that he was enwrapped in the primal fire-mists of creation. Mighty tides seemed to bear the ship forward, everything was a whirl and boil of light, millrace currents seemed to rush them endlessly through infinity, with all space and time cancelled out. He wondered briefly, once, whether the Orionids had followed them in and then he forgot them. The agony, the intoxication and the terror were far too great to admit any petty worries about anything human.

But at last, with almost shocking abruptness, they broke into clear space and the cloud was behind them and they were out in the fringe-edge of the cluster. Like men enchanted waking from a dream, Birrel and Garstang stood erect again, and the voice of the *Starsong* was stilled and human voices spoke once more.

Birrel went into the com-room and made contact with his squadron far ahead. He gave orders, and then rejoined Garstang on the bridge.

"Brescnik's on his way," he said. "Can you keep clear?"

"I can," said Garstang, and ordered full power. They were passing out of the last fringe-stars of the cluster and he had nothing between him and the Pleiades now but light-years of elbow-room. He took full advantage of it.

After what seemed a long interval, radar reported that the

three Orionids had come out of the cluster by the channel, and then had turned around and gone back into the cluster.

Garstang looked at Birrel. "They didn't risk the nebula, and now they've seen the squadron coming."

Birrel thought of Tauncer, and smiled.

The squadron neared them, moving with majestic consciousness of its own power and authority. In the screens, when they joined it, there was nothing to be seen but a few far-separated flecks of metal gleaming in the light of the distant Pleiades. But Birrel saw it as it was, forty-four ships awesome in their massiveness, thousands of men, all that made up the mighty Fifth. And he felt, as he always did, both the throb of pride that he had been given its leadership and the nagging doubt that he or any man was good enough to lead it.

The hard, excited voice of Brescnik, the Vice-Commander, came rapidly as they joined.

"So there *is* an Orionid base in there! By God, we'll soon—"

"No," Birrel cut in. "There was no base in there. There was a trap, for me—but I still don't know just why they set it. Stand by."

He sat down at the coding machine and set up a message. Top secret, in the code that only the governor and the commanders of the five squadrons knew, to Ferdias at Vega, briefly detailing his encounter with Tauncer.

"*—am unable to explain interest in Earth, and your alleged plans concerning it. Suggest attempt to distract from some other objective. Await instructions. Birrel.*"

In a remarkably short time the answer came back.

"*Report Vega at once with full squadron.*" And it added, "*Unfortunately, no distraction. Ferdias.*"

Birrel sat looking at the cryptic tape for a long time after they had got under way in obedience to it. He did not understand it, could find no possible explanation for it. But all the same it made him feel, more strongly than ever, that premonition that the pace, the tempo, of the great game for suns was indeed about to step up still faster, and that that was not good, not good at all.

4

IT ALWAYS SURPRISED Birrel, the warmth and eagerness he felt when he returned to Vega Four. It was not the world itself, though it was a nice planet and he liked its people. But there were lots of nice planets and Birrel had never felt that he belonged to any particular one of them. He had never stayed at one long enough to form any attachment, for his father also had served the Lyran fleet and, from childhood, his memories were only of a succession of bases on many worlds.

But now, watching the purplish bulk of the fourth planet spin toward them through the blue-white glare of Vega, even his nagging worry about what trouble Ferdias had in store for them only a little tempered his anticipation. It still seemed a little strange to him that he should feel this glad to be getting back to a woman.

Birrel had married only three years before, and the fact that he had done so in itself still rather amazed him. For he had always had a deep bias against wives and families. His father had died in a totally unnecessary and meaningless space disaster, and the memory of his mother's sad loneliness had given him that bias. Women were fine, but not a woman. His thinking had become fixed on that point and he was pretty sure he would never have asked Lyllin to marry him, despite the way he felt about her. But Lyllin was Vegan and her people had their own customs. It was she who had quietly suggested they marry and he had fallen all over himself agreeing. He was still glad of it, and still surprised.

He watched as the purplish globe expanded into a great, misty blue mountain-and-desert world, the capital of a Sector which was, in everything but name, an empire of stars. And when the Fifth, all traffic cleared away before it, broke atmosphere and came growling and thundering down across the black mountain-chains toward Vega City, he thought that Lyllin would have heard and would be down there now in the hillside villa, looking up at the giants as they came in.

They swept over the city toward the Fifth's home base, over against the foothills of the opposite black range. In smoothly

scheduled detachments the ships made their landings, and the *Starsong* was in the first detachment.

When Birrel, a little later, walked down into the hot, stinging blue glare, Brescnik had already come over from his own ship. The Vice-Commander was a blocky, brusque and highly competent man. He was also hot-tempered and his comb of colorless hair seemed always to bristle up when he was angry.

"What the devil is all this about, Jay? Pulling the whole Fifth in as though it were a scout-detachment! What's Ferdias up to?"

"I haven't an idea," Birrel said. "But I hope to find out."

"Politics," said Brescnik disgustedly. "That's what it always is. You'll see."

A flitter, with an orderly for pilot, took Birrel away from the base toward the big city in the distance, and on the way Birrel thought of what Brescnik had said. Brescnik's attitude was typical of most officers and men of the squadrons, including himself. It was also typical of a great many other people, and that was why the legislature was wary of opposing a popular governor like Ferdias. It had been called "the starship psychology," this general, underlying feeling that one-man leadership was best in big affairs. The theory was that in the two-hundred-year spread-out from Earth, the feeling of a ship commander, who was responsible for the safety of all on board, had carried over into the matter of government. And that feeling had been reinforced by the historical example of the United Worlds, whose headless council had soon lost control over the wider sphere.

Birrel looked down at the city. This was Old Town, a place of graceful, white roofs and cupolas and golden-yellow trees and grass, and rambling, quaint (and dirty, he had to admit it) narrow streets. The native Vegans, Lyllin's people, had built it and it showed how far they had come from their fierce tribalistic-war state of centuries before. They might have got further on their own as time went on, but then the universe had crashed in upon them, the great wave that had started long ago from Earth and that was still rolling, not Earthmen only now, but all sorts of people from many worlds and of many bloodstrains, all part of the space explosion. It was these newcomers who had built New Town, whose gleaming miles of metalloy and glass dwarfed the older quarter.

They had also built the enormous, massive structure he was

going toward, the governmental buildings that flashed and glittered in the blue-white sunshine. A new building was being added to the nexus, Birrel noted. The place was always getting bigger, just as the Sector was always growing out into new star-fields, wherever it could do so. That thought brought the worry back into his mind, the uneasy apprehension that the rivalry between Sectors was getting dangerous, and his face lengthened.

He was landed on the roof of one of the buildings, and a lift took him down to a middle floor. He went through the corridors until, finally, efficient secretaries shunted him smoothly and quickly into a room few people ever entered.

It always seemed to Birrel a very tiny room to be the center of government of so many stars. For this, not the halls of the legislators, was the real center and everyone knew it.

"Stop saluting, Jay," said Ferdias. "You know you're at ease when you step in here."

Ferdias came around the desk. He limped, from the crash of a Class Nine trainer long ago. That crash had had fateful results. It had washed Ferdias out of the service, shattering his ambitions. He had had to turn all his terrific energy and drive into other channels, and he had chosen political ones. Everything other men thought necessary, a wife, a home, friends and fun, Ferdias had ignored, driving toward his goal. Birrel thought that he himself had done pretty well, to be leading a squadron at thirty-seven, but Ferdias was only six years older than that.

He was a small man. But, somehow, you never remembered that fact, nor his limp. You saw only his face and the searching, light-colored eyes, and, when you saw them, you began to understand why, at the age of forty-three, he was one of the five great Governors.

He held out his hand, smiling. Birrel sometimes felt that he was one of the few real friends Ferdias had, though why he should be he did not know. Anyway, he was not sure of it, you were never absolutely sure of anything with Ferdias.

"Now let's have it, Jay," he said.

Birrel let him have it, the full story of the trap in the cluster. And Ferdias' face got just a trifle tighter.

He said, finally, "You took foolhardy chances going in there alone. But since you got out all right, I'm glad you did it. For I'm sure now of what I only suspected before. In his eagerness

to find out how much I know, Solleremos has told me what I wanted to know.''

Birrel, frankly puzzled, said, "I just don't get it. 'What is Ferdias planning to do about Earth?' What in the world would you plan about it? Don't answer, if I'm out of line asking.''

Ferdias did not answer, not at once. He limped back to his chair and sat down, and then looked up keenly as he spoke.

"Jay, you're more than half Earth-blood, aren't you?''

Birrel nodded. "Three-quarters, to be exact. My father was straight Earth. My mother's parents were Earth and Capellan.''

And again, as so many times, he felt a passing sadness when he mentioned her. His father had died in that pile-up so long ago that he could hardly remember him, but he wished that his mother could have lived to see him commanding the Fifth. Somehow, even when you got what you most wanted, it never came out quite the way you expected.

Ferdias' voice cut into his thoughts. "Tell me, how do you feel about Earth?''

Birrel stared. "What do you mean—feel about it?''

"Just that.''

Birrel shrugged. "Why, I've never been there. You know that—I was born in a transport off Arcturus and I've never been farther back in than Procyon.''

Ferdias persisted. "I know all that, yes. But what do you think about Earth?''

Birrel frowned, then made a gesture. "Just what everybody thinks, I suppose. It was an important place, once. Starflight began there—even we ourselves began there, in a way, those of us who have Earth blood. But that's all long ago. It hasn't rated for much since its United Worlds council tried to hold all the galaxy in one government and failed. No wonder they failed—it's hard enough to hold a Sector together, let alone the whole galaxy.''

"Suppose one of the Sectors decided to go back there and take over Earth," said Ferdias.

Birrel felt a shock of astonishment. "Why, no Sector would touch the UW's little federal district for—'' He stopped, looking at Ferdias, and then he said, "Or would they?''

"Solleremos would like to," said Ferdias.

Birrel was so astounded that, for a moment, he just looked. "You mean, he wants to take Earth into Orion Sector?''

"He wants to very much indeed," said the other. "Listen,

Jay. Solleremos' pressure on our borders recently has only been cover-up. Earth is his real objective."

"But why in the world? It's a big name in history, but after all it's only one unimportant little star-system now."

"Is it so unimportant?" Ferdias' eyes, hot and flaring now, fascinated Birrel. "Materially, maybe it is—a worn-out, third-rate planet. But psychologically, it's a very important world indeed. Think of the Earth-blood mingled in all the galaxy races now. All those people have, perhaps without altogether realizing it, about the same feeling toward Earth you have. They know it no longer directs things, they know the UW council and fleet are just a shadowy sham—but still it's Earth, it's the ancient center of things, the old heart-world. Suppose one of the other governors gets Earth into his Sector, and speaks from there hereafter?"

Birrel saw it now—and he also realized, not for the first time, that when it came to galactic intrigue he was a babe in arms. It would indeed give any of the rival governors a colossal psychological advantage, to make the old center of things his seat of government. Commands that came from Earth would have a psychological potency that would be hard to withstand.

He liked the shape of it less and less, as he thought about it. He looked at Ferdias, and said,

"I take it that you're not going to let Solleremos get away with this?"

"No, Jay. I don't want Earth. But I'm not going to let Orion Sector grab it, either."

Ferdias went on, in his quick, incisive way. "Solleremos knows very well that I'll try to stop him. That's why he had Tauncer, his right-hand man, set that little trap in the cluster for you. They're quite aware that I trust you and they hoped I'd have told you just how I plan to block them."

But he hadn't, Birrel could not help thinking. Ferdias had not told him a whisper of all this until now, when it was necessary. He had let him go into the cluster without knowing the real situation, and that had been wise because what he did not know he could not tell. But, in a way, it was an epitome of their years of relationship. He trusted Ferdias, all the way. But Ferdias, knowing that, still always held his own reservations, his own secrets.

It made Birrel feel a sudden resentment. But his irritation faded when he reflected that he did exactly the same thing with

the officers and men of the Fifth. He didn't tell them everything he had in mind, he couldn't, but he expected their loyalty nevertheless and he got it, just as Ferdias got his.

Ferdias was saying, "There's a big celebration coming up on Earth soon. The two-hundredth anniversary of the first space-flight from Earth. It means a lot to them, and the UW council invited me to send an official delegation to represent Lyra Sector."

"So?"

"So I'm sending you."

Birrel stared. "Me—to Earth? But what can I do if—"

Ferdias interrupted. "The Fifth Squadron will go with you, Jay. To take part in the commemoration, the flyover."

Now Birrel began to understand. "Then if Solleremos tries anything, the Fifth will be there waiting for him?"

"Exactly." Ferdias spoke the word like a wolf-snap. "I know Solleremos' intentions. I know about when he plans his grab for Earth. Earth can't stop him, not with the small UW forces. But if the Fifth Lyra happens to be on Earth right then, it won't be so easy for him."

Birrel felt a little stunned. Fighting the hidden, border wars of the rival governors was one thing. That went on under cover, and, if a ship didn't come back from the marches of little-known space, it was officially listed as lost by accident. But a full-fledged struggle between Sectors, if it erupted back there at Earth, was quite another thing. It could rock the civilized galaxy. . . .

Ferdias was going on matter-of-factly. "You'll take off five days from now. You'll take full supply auxiliaries and transports."

Birrel looked up sharply. Transports meant the families of all personnel would accompany the squadron, and that was a thing they never did unless the Fifth was making a rotational transfer to a completely different base.

Ferdias smiled. "It's got to look peaceful, Jay, a friendly, peaceful gesture to the commemoration. That's why the transports go."

Birrel nodded, understanding now. If anyone claimed that the Fifth was going to Earth for military reasons, the fact that they were hampered with transports and dependents would argue eloquently the other way. It was a fine cover-up, shrewd planning. Yet the fact remained that they would be hampered,

and he did not quite like the idea of Lyllin going into possible trouble.

He asked Ferdias, "When we get to Earth—besides taking part in that celebration, what? What, definitely, are my orders?"

Ferdias said, "Go and look up your ancestral home."

"My—what?"

"Ancestral home. Place where the Birrels came from, on Earth. I had it searched out, and it's still standing. It's in Orville, a place near the city New York. It's the most natural thing in the world that you should go and visit it while you're there."

Birrel began to get it. "I'm to contact somebody there, for orders?"

Ferdias nodded. "Karsh."

Instantly, hearing that name, Birrel revised his conception of the scale and importance of this thing. He had only met Karsh a very few times, but he knew how important the gray, colorless little man was to Ferdias in the secret struggle between the Sectors. Like Tauncer, he was a stormy petrel whose presence usually meant big trouble.

"Karsh is on Earth?"

"Yes, Jay. He's been there for months. He bought this old house I speak of and he'll be waiting there for you. His estimate of the situation will govern your orders."

"But if Orion—"

"Don't worry," Ferdias interrupted. "You'll get warning if Solleremos moves on Earth. But Jay—one more thing."

"Yes?"

"The Fifth goes to Earth for an official courtesy visit. You're not to tell more than that to anyone. Anyone."

He repeated the word without any emphasis at all, but when Ferdias repeated something, that was emphasis enough.

Birrel, as the flitter took him back across the city, hardly saw the brilliant capital flashing by beneath. He did not like this mission at all.

He wondered whether Ferdias had thought that the whole thing might be just another clever feint by Orion, and that, with the Fifth at faraway Earth, the strongest sword and shield of Lyra would be gone.

5

THE BLUE SUN was touching the dark hills above the old part of the city, and the sky was flooded with a purple dusk when Birrel came home. His house was a fluently curved, white glimmer, behind which the flitter landed him. He went eagerly through the rooms, all cool and bare in the Vegan manner, but there was no one in them.

Lyllin had chosen to wait for him out on the terrace that looked across the soft lights of Vega City. She came toward him. She was all Vegan and looked it, her flesh showed pale as new gold, with the darker masses of her hair picking up the same tint and turning it to copper. She was dressed in the fashion of her own people, in a chiton so mistily transparent that her fine, slender body seemed to be draped in a bit of the deepening twilight itself.

He held her for a time before he told her his news. He was surprised that it did not seem to make her happy.

"To Earth?" she murmured. "Just for the space-flight anniversary? It's so strange—"

"But this time you'll be with me," he said. "Not on the voyage—you'll ride transport, of course—but on Earth, all the time I'm there."

"How long will that be, Jay?"

He did not know, and said so. He felt guilty not to be telling her the whole truth, but he knew Ferdias well enough to know that when he said "anyone" that included everyone.

Lyllin's face had shadowed subtly, but now she smiled brilliantly and said,

"I'll get you a drink."

He sat with her for a while on the terrace, watching the night come on. The lights of the city went far away and, in the distance, the great, black ranges shouldered against the stars. There was a buzz and drone of flitters in the sky. He liked this world, this place, best of all the places where he had based.

After a time he went in and called his Vice-Commander. Brescnik's face looked irritated, in the instrument.

"Yes, I got an order on it a little while ago. We'll have to

work damned fast to have transports and all ready by that time.
A real bright thing, making all this trouble for a celebration.''

"What's the matter with you?" Birrel asked. "Haven't you
got any reverence for the anniversary of star-flight?"

Brescnik answered that in some short and pungent mono-
syllables, and Birrel grinned.

"All right, you've made yourself clear. I didn't dream this
thing up. Just make sure to get things started at the base right
away. I'll be over tomorrow.''

He went back out to the terrace where Lyllin was still sitting
looking up at the star-groups. She had been very quiet, but she
had a way of silence, and he did not find that strange.

"Brescnik is burning,'' he told her. "Let him sweat. What's
the use of having rank if you can't use it to pass some of the
dirty work off onto someone else?''

She looked up at him and said, "I shall hate it at Earth."

Birrel was surprised and shocked. He had been married to
her all these three years now and yet he had never got used to
the way she would bring unexpected things out of her silence.

"Why in the world—?" he started to say. Then he said impatiently, "Lyllin, that's ridiculous! You've never seen the
place, you hardly know anything about it. You may like it."

She said, looking away across the lights, "No."

"But why not?"

For a moment she did not answer. Then she turned and
looked directly at him, her face a pale blur in the purple night.

"It's your place, your people, not mine. You'll be all right
there, but what will they think of me?" She looked away from
him again and said in a low voice, "What will *you* think of
me, there among your own people?"

Birrel was so angry that he would not speak for a moment.
Then he took hold of her with rough hands and turned her
around. He said,

"I'm ashamed of you. If you could even think a thing like
that—'' He resisted a temptation to shake her. He had learned
very early in their married life that there was a tone you could
not take with Lyllin, and so he made himself speak patiently.
"Listen to me! Earth is no more to me than it is to you. It's a
name, a place where my grandfather happened to be born.
That's all it is. Nearly everybody in space has Earth blood in
them, you know that.''

"You have more of it than anything else," she said.

"Sure," he said. "My father came from Sirius to take service with Lyra, and my mother's father happened to be an Earthman too. Does all that make me belong to a place I've never seen?"

She looked up at him and he could not clearly see her shadowed face, but he thought that she wanted to be convinced. He was not good with words and the only way he could think of convincing her was to put his arms around her.

She kissed him with a sudden, passionate possessiveness. But he did not think she was yet convinced. It suddenly occurred to him that he did not know much about Earth and could not really be sure how they would regard his Vegan wife there. She had her people's pride, and if they treated her at Earth like an alien, a freak—

Birrel was still worrying about that when he went next day to the base. But there, when he went over preliminary flight-plans with Staff, he received fresh cause for anxiety.

Ewer, the plump and usually cheerful Third of Staff, gave him disquieting news on their way to the chartroom.

"Orion's First and Third squadrons have been on the move. And we've lost them."

"What do you mean, lost them?" said Birrel.

"Just what I say. Here, I'll show you."

They had entered the vast, darkened room that contained a glittering representation of a part of the galaxy. It was only that comparatively small part which human civilization had yet reached, beyond it lay the unpictured, unexplored reaches of stars which no one had yet visited. But even this small section contained thousands of stars and worlds and nebulae all reproduced accurately by projected images of light. They looked like stars caught in spider-webs because of the reference-grid of pale lines that ran through them. Each world had a glowing symbol beside it—a symbol that said it was an E-type human-peopled world, or an E-type with alien life and so not to be bothered, or a non-E-type, or a non-habitable planet, or something else.

Ewer, using a beam-pointer, indicated a region in the extreme east of Orion Sector, nearer to distant Sol than Vega was and not far from the blue line that delimited Lyra space. His beam flicked along a broad, ragged region of dimness, all along the side of which a familiar symbol was repeated.

"A very big radio-emission area across here," he said.

Birrel nodded understandingly. The symbol was the one for so-called "hot hydrogen" clouds, attenuated atom-scatterings that emitted all up and down the electromagnetic spectrum, fouling up all communications.

"Orion's First and Third went across here—" Ewer's gleaming wand traced a course southeastward, a path that went beyond the symbol-marked dimness. "Our long-range radar watch-stations here and here and here—" The wand touched a dead star, and then the planet of a small sun with the symbol for "no oxygen, no life," and then another dead star, and Birrel thought of the lonely nature of those watchers' duty. "—tracked them that far," Ewer was saying. "But when they got behind that big area of radio-emission, we lost them. Of course they went there deliberately, to evade our watch."

"Where would you estimate they are now?" Birrel asked.

Ewer shook his head. "I can't hazard a guess on a thing like that. Somewhere in this region."

The beam he swung cut an area between Vega and distant Sol, that, in this compressed microcosm, seemed choked with stars and stellar debris. A real mess, thought Birrel, and the Fifth would have to go through it. Along one side stretched a perfect cemetery of cosmic cinders, dead suns and drift. Along the other was a parsec-long sprawl of "cool hydrogen" which normally only emitted on the 21 centimeter band. But it was riddled by vast filaments of gaseous matter, the debris of a super-nova of long ago that was moving through it, and, by collision with the atoms of cool hydrogen, would cause terrific radio-emissions.

"They could be anywhere in there, but it would take powerful short-range radar to find them," said Ewer. And he added, "If they're hiding in there, it's somewhere not too far from your flight-line to Sol."

"That," said Birrel irritably, "I'd already figured out."

"Sorry," said Ewer.

The First and Third Orion were Solleremos' crack squadrons. You did not move such forces around idly. Birrel did not like the look of it. When he thought of the transports that would be with the Fifth, and of Lyllin in one of them, he liked it even less.

"Will you have alternative flight-lines set up, and we'll go over them tomorrow?" he asked Ewer.

He went out and told his flitter-pilot to take him to Govern-

ment House. But he had to wait there for more than an hour before he got to see Ferdias.

Ferdias said promptly, "I know about the First and Third Orion. And I'm sure it's a feint by Solleremos, a threat to keep the Fifth from going to Earth."

"Suppose it's not a feint," Birrel said. "They could be waiting to hit the Fifth, and no bluff about it."

Ferdias nodded. "They could be, but I don't think so."

"With transports to protect, we'd be in a bad situation if it came to fighting," said Birrel.

"I realize it, but we have to take a calculated risk." Ferdias looked impatient. "Do we have to go over this again? I tell you, the UW won't let the Fifth come to Earth at all if it comes stripped down to battle-strength. They weren't too eager there about a whole squadron coming, and this is the only way I could get them to welcome you. Suspicious as they are, still they don't figure you'd bring your wives and children along if you meant trouble."

This was a new thought to Birrel. "Then they're suspicious of us, at Earth?"

"Of course they are. Karsh reports that Orion's agents have been busy whispering to the UW officials there. They're trying to put it across that *I* am out to grab Earth. Then Solleremos would have an excuse to step in, to prevent my wicked intentions."

Birrel liked the sound of it less and less, but there was a point beyond which you did not argue with Ferdias. He got up and looked across the desk at Ferdias and said,

"I'll do the best I can for you, on this."

"I know that, Jay."

"But I just want to say, you're sending the wrong man to handle a diplomatic tangle."

Ferdias smiled. "I know men, and I don't think so. Anyway, you'll have Karsh there to steer you."

And that, Birrel thought dourly as he walked out of the room, was a fine, comforting directive for a man going into a thing like this. The more he heard about this job, the more dubious it seemed. And he was still worried by the way Lyllin felt about it.

To his surprise and relief, when he got home that night he found Lyllin bright and gay and dressed in her finest.

She laughed at his stare. "Some of my people wanted to give us a going-away party—you don't mind?"

Birrel had counted on staying home this night, but he was too relieved by her bright spirits to object. A flitter took them down to Old Town and they walked through the rambling streets and graceful, white walls and arcades and the scattered, drowsy light of the older city. Enormous, white flowers grew between the stones, drenching the night with a sweet fragrance, and the soft, slurred Vegan speech was all around them, with hardly a word of Basic.

They were almost all purebred Vegans in the ancient court-yard-garden where they ate spicy food and drank the sweet, fruit wines. They were a volatile folk, and their talk and laughter echoed off the walls like the chatter of birds. Birrel, watching Lyllin sparkle, almost forgot his worries about the mission. He liked Lyllin's people, they had completely accepted him. After a lifetime spent, first as a child playing around family barracks, as a youngster in space academy and then in endless starships with brief worldfalls, he felt as though he had found friends and a home when he found Lyllin.

He was surprised when a laughing girl told him, "We're all going up to a Varn festival—they're being held up in the western pass villages tonight. Don't you love them?"

"I've heard of them, but I've never seen one," Birrel said.

"They're very old, and a bit foolish, but they're fun," she promised.

He had indeed heard of the Varn festivals that the Vegan folk of the high mountain villages held and had held for centuries, but somehow Lyllin had never wanted to go to them. He had had the feeling that because these folk-festivals were vestigial survivals from the old, wild past of her people, she did not want him to see them. He looked now for her to excuse them from going, but instead Lyllin smilingly took his hand and went along with the others to the flitters.

The flitters took them up into the bright starlight and away from Old Town toward the northern mountains. They landed in a chill, misty high pass, where one of the old stone villages showed in the starlight, vague against the swirling fog of the great, deep valley beyond. There were many other flitters here, and the party Birrel was with walked along the gritty, stone road to a point where the village street began and where quite

a number of Vegan folk were standing, laughing and chattering and looking expectantly toward the village.

The village lay dark and silent beneath the stars. It was as though every soul in it was asleep, but Birrel knew this could not be so on the night of the ancient festival. He knew that the people in these lofty, isolated little communities had not taken so completely to the new civilization the starships had brought as those in the lowlands. These were small landholders, miners, metal-workers, who held faster to old Vegan ways. He supposed they were all inside their houses, and he wondered what kind of a festival this was.

The chattering folk around him quieted, an expectant hush came over them. They stood in the cold mist, looking down the silent street to where it dipped out of sight into the vast valley beyond the pass. They, and the silent dark houses, all seemed waiting for something. Then a whisper of excitement, and a nervous titter, passed through them as something appeared at the far end of the street.

A figure had come up out of the valley and stood, vague in the curling mists. Blurred as it was by fog and distance, it was a figure of nightmare—a man-high, erect shape that was like a hideous travesty of humanity, a lizard-thing walking upright on bowed, powerful legs, the scaly hide glittering in the starlight, the flat head turning this way and that, the filmy eyes staring.

"Varn," said the whisper among the people around Birrel, and some of them laughed again, but the laughter was nervous.

Birrel knew that the thing was, of course, one of the villagers here masked and suited in a clever costume. But the costume was so cunningly perfect that the illusion was horrifyingly real.

There had been no Varn living on this world for hundreds of years. Long before the starships came the Vegans had fought to its end their age-long struggle against the brainless, ferocious lizard-folk who lived in the deep mists of the vaster chasms and came over the ranges to raid and rob and slay. But the memory of that terrible struggle was still strong and he could understand why a silence and a shiver ran through his companions when a second hideous figure appeared in the mist, and then a third and fourth.

Eight of the pseudo-Varn in all came into the street, ran from locked door to locked door, scrabbling and mewing. There was a hideous realism about their capering, and Birrel

felt Lyllin's small hand tighten on his fingers. Then, suddenly, the doors of houses opened.

Men emerged, dressed in the ancient Vegan style and carrying long whips. They rushed upon the pseudo-Varn. They swung the whips and the long lashes whistled and cracked, and the pseudo-monsters screeched and made mock charges and recoiled again from the whips. From inside the houses came now the fierce and rhythmic sound of an old battle-song.

Birrel felt the reaction of the people around him. There was no amused chattering, no tittering now. They leaned forward, eyes glittering, as the whips rose and fell, as the men beat back the charges of the mewing not-men. They began to shout themselves, fragmentary, half-forgotten phrases of the fierce, old anthem. They were shaking, quivering, sweating with fierce excitement, no longer at all the pleasant, gay companions of an hour before. Lyllin was shivering and her eyes were bright as she too watched, her lips moving.

Birrel thought he understood now. He did not know people the way Ferdias knew them. He knew men of his own sort pretty well, but women not at all. However, you could not live with a wife without at least partly understanding one woman.

He bent to Lyllin and said quietly in her ear, "That's enough for now. It's late."

She made no objection as they went back to the flitter. But all the way back home she said nothing, but hummed the fierce old rhythm under her breath.

In their house, she turned and smiled brightly and spoke rapidly. "Did you enjoy it? It's a little uncivilized, I know, but then we're not a very civilized people, really."

Birrel knew then he had been right. He said nothing, but stood looking at her, and in the face of his silence she rushed on, with an edge of desperation in her brittleness.

"In fact, I'm such an incurable savage underneath that I'd better stay home and wait for you. I wouldn't fit in on Earth. I'd be—"

He stepped forward and took hold of her. "No matter where we go, you'll be Lyllin. And I'll love you."

Her mouth became soft and uncertain, like a child's, and her eyes had tears in the corners of them now. And when he kissed her, her lips were bitter with those sudden tears. She said nothing more but he knew that she was still afraid, afraid

of what Earth might do to them. In the depths of his soul, Birrel cursed Solleremos and his ambitious schemes.

THE SQUADRON TOOK off and the blue flare of Vega dropped behind it. The cruisers and scouts and auxiliaries and transports, eighty-three in all, dwindled suddenly in scale from great ships to mere metal motes that huddled together in their flight through infinity. For two hundred years, humanity had been pressing outward through the stars. Now some thousands of men and women and children were taking the road back.

The course was familiar, at first. Straightaway from Vega to the Triple Crown, three white suns which were a famous star-mark in Lyra Sector. Then the Fifth bore westward and nadir, taking its sights on a dying red star to make the so-called Dark Passage between two vast dust-clouds that looked down like frowning cosmic mountains at the tiny passing ships. And now Lyra space began to narrow into a long salient between Orion and Perseus Sectors. Far away upon their left marched a distant bastion of clotted clusters and nebular mists that was like a great rampart guarding Perseus. They went on past that, and drew closer to the vague boundary between Lyra and Orion, and ahead there lay to the left the cemetery of dead suns and to the right that vast sprawl of tangled filamentary nebulae.

Birrel studied the vista on the big radar-screen. The cinder-cemetery to the left was fuzzy from minute particles of drift, so fuzzy that ships could indeed hide from long-range radar in there. The other region, that of the filamentaries, was an absolutely blind area on the screen, its terrific radio-emissions blanking out long-range radar completely.

"I *think*," said Garstang, frowning down at the screen, "that they'd be hiding in the drift, not the filamentaries. Those would foul up their own communications pretty badly."

"Not if they held a tight enough formation," said Birrel. "But it's no good guessing. I've got to send in scouts."

He called Grenard, the leader of the scout division. Those swift midgets were far out in front of and on either side of the big cruisers and transports.

Grenard, a comparatively young man, was as reckless and restless as a good scout-commander had to be.

"Fine," he said instantly. "I'll go into the filamentaries and send Nearing into the drift. If they're in there, we'll find them."

"Just a minute," Birrel said hastily. "You may find them but you won't be able to call all the way back here through that stuff. String out scouts at regular intervals—with at least one on each side close enough to pick up and relay from you and Nearing."

Grenard understood at once. "You think they may knock us off if we do spot them?"

"It's possible," Birrel answered curtly.

"Well, this begins to sound interesting," said Grenard cheerfully. "We'll set it up that way."

Birrel looked at Garstang. "Were we ever like that? Hellbent for trouble and excitement, and never mind the risks?"

Garstang said mildly, "I expect we were."

The Fifth moved onward. Its way lay down a parsec-long avenue of clear space between the filamentaries and the drift. The squadron changed formation as it went, the mighty cruisers closing in around the transports. Far ahead, darting at speeds no cruiser could reach so swiftly, the tiny scouts flung right and left toward the two radar-blind regions.

The visual screens in the radar-room came on. By means of pick-up and relay chains, what was seen by the scouts of Grenard and Nearing came through.

"Nothing yet," said Grenard's voice. "It's quite a mess, as you can see for yourself. I'm going into search-pattern. Hold on."

The screen showed little but a twisted blur of light. At moments it would take form as a vista of long, glowing filaments in the darkness. Long ago a star had exploded with inconceivable violence and sent these threads of gas flying out through the universe. They were still flying, though compared to the scout's ultraspeed they seemed to stand still. And the utterly tenuous, cool hydrogen they passed through was generating radio-emissions that kept the picture a nightmare blur despite the relays that picked it up and amplified it and passed it on.

Grenard's little ship was quartering this howling radio storm like a restless hound. He had so far found nothing. Then Nearing's voice came from the other screen and Birrel turned his attention to that.

"Not a thing but drift so far," drawled Nearing. "Molecular, most of it."

Nearing's screen showed nothing but dark space and distant stars. Transmission was better but there just wasn't anything to see, the tiny particles of the drift and the dark, cindery, dead suns being practically invisible. But Nearing's powerful short-range radar was probing, as he, too, went into search-pattern.

The Fifth moved on, down the strait between the filaments and the drift. In every cruiser, the men were at battle-stations. In the transports, they wouldn't even know there was any danger. Birrel wondered what Lyllin was doing, what she was thinking, right now, right this moment.

"Nothing yet," said Grenard's voice.

"You know," said Garstang, "both these regions are well inside Lyra space. Would Orionids really risk coming into them in force?"

"I told you," said Birrel. "The pace is stepping up. I think they would."

Nearing's voice drawled, "Nothing."

And they went on. The filamentaries marched past on one side and the dark drift on the other, and the big ships of the Fifth never slackened, but there was still a long way to go before they would reach wide-open space again.

Before they had traversed more than half the distance, Grenard suddenly yelped like an excited terrier.

"Got them! They're here, all right. Two squadrons in tight formation. Moving on intercept course."

Steel bands seemed to tighten across Birrel's chest, but he kept his face composed. He picked up the mike and asked,

"How far are you from them?"

Grenard told him, and added, "Too far for a visual, but there's no doubt at all on the radar."

"Hang on to them," said Birrel. "Keep watching them."

Garstang, suddenly stiff and tense, said softly, "Intercept, eh? They're going to hit us."

"Are they?"

Garstang stared. "Why else would they be headed to intercept us? Shall I order action-formation and transports back?"

Birrel said, "No."

"Then what?"

"We go on," said Birrel. "We just go on."

Garstang looked stricken and started to say something and then instead said, "Yes, sir."

"It's a bluff," said Birrel. "It has to be a bluff. They don't quite dare to risk open war by hitting us. But they're trying to scare us back, prevent us from going to Earth."

Garstang shrugged. "You seem pretty sure."

Birrel said, "Look, if Grenard could radar-range them, they could range Grenard. If they were really going to hit us, they'd knock out Grenard first thing. Instead, they let him ride along, watching them. They *want* him to report to us, to scare us back."

"It sounds logical," said Garstang. "But if you're wrong—"

"If I'm wrong, we're in big trouble," Birrel said. "Ferdias told me to take this risk and I'm taking it."

The Fifth moved on, no ship slackening speed or changing its place in formation. At ten-minute intervals, Grenard continued to report on the two Orionid squadrons, and his report was always, "Intercept course." Each time Birrel waited for it to be different, but it was the same.

The short hairs on the back of his neck began to bristle. The Fifth and the two mightiest squadrons of Solleremos were racing toward each other and intercept-point was less than an hour away. It began to seem as though both he and Ferdias could be wrong. It had not seemed possible that Orion would really hit them and turn the secret intriguing struggle between the Sectors into open war, for war was unthinkable and had been so for centuries. But if they were wrong, if Solleremos' ambitions had overleaped his judgment—

There was still time to send the transports back, to fall back and cover them. But he knew well enough what would happen if he did that and went back to Vega. He had to go on because to Ferdias he was expendable in a calculated risk, just as Grenard and Nearing were to him.

"Intercept course," repeated Grenard's voice.

The next ten minutes were several eternities long. When Grenard finally spoke again, he said the same thing.

Garstang looked stonily at the radar-screens and said nothing. He thinks I'm wrong, thought Birrel. And it looks as though I am, and Ferdias has miscalled it this time.

Thirty-three minutes to go and if they don't change course now it is not a bluff and we are going to be in for it. Thirty-two

Thirty-one. Speak up, Grenard, why don't you report, are you all asleep on that scout? Speak—

"Intercept course—," said Grenard, and Birrel felt his middle tighten and then he jumped as Grenard continued, "—now abandoned. New course of Orionid squadrons seventy-four degrees westward, five degrees zenith. Shall I follow?"

"No, don't follow," said Birrel. "But range their course as long as you can."

He turned to Garstang. Garstang said, "Well." And then he let out a long breath.

Birrel waited until soon Grenard reported that the Orionids had just passed out of his limited radar-range, still on the new course.

"Pull back to position," Birrel ordered, and added, "Good work."

"They've sheered off," he said to Garstang. "Ferdias was right, they're not yet quite up to attacking a Lyran squadron in Lyra space."

The Fifth went on and presently they were moving out of the strait into wide-open space. Ahead, there stretched a region with a few stars and fewer E-type worlds, and that distant region belonged to none of the Sectors but was the small area still ruled by the once all-governing United Worlds.

Garstang looked at the screen that showed the spaces behind them.

"We got by them coming in," he said. "But they're still there. How will it be when we go back?"

Birrel said nothing. He had thought of that and he did not like the thought for he had a premonition that they had been allowed to go on to Earth because they were going into a trap.

7

FAR AHEAD, LOOKING rather lonely in the midst of a great emptiness, shone a small yellow star. Birrel studied it. How should he feel about it now that they had reached it? Like a child seeing its father for the first time, or like a man returning to an ancient hearth? He could feel nothing of that. This was only another star.

He said, "Begin the deceleration schedule."

By the time the Fifth was cruising at normal approach velocity, the yellow sun was close enough so that they could study its planets. They were a barren lot mostly, only the third one was E-type. Venner said that and then he looked up startled from his instrument, as though he had only just remembered where the name "E-type" had originated. Messages now started crackling in, first formal greetings, then approval of landing-patterns. The Fifth smoothly shifted formation and went into the pattern.

Garstang touched Birrel's arm and pointed, to where far off a little gray-green planet with a stony satellite rushed to meet them.

"Earth."

The squadron sped toward it, the cruisers and supply-ships and transports, the men and women and children, strangers from the far reaches of the galaxy. And yet not quite strangers either, for the names that had come from this world were still among them, and the traditions, and in many of them the blood.

A quiet had settled on the bridge, Birrel supposed it was the same with the whole squadron, everybody staring and thinking his or her own thoughts. He wondered what Lyllin was thinking, and wished that she were here with him instead of back there in one of the transports.

Earth came closer. He could see clouds, and the white splash of a polar cap. Closer still, and there were seas, and the outlines of continents. Colors began to show more clearly, and the land became ridged with mountain-chains. Great lakes took form, and dark green areas of forest, and winding rivers. A nice world. A pretty world. Birrel eyed it sourly. Its other name was trouble.

"Why did Ferdias have to pick *us* for this job?"

Unconsciously he had spoken aloud, or loud enough for Garstang to hear. "It's only for a visit," said Garstang. "Just a celebration. What's wrong with that?" His tone was mild, without mockery.

But Birrel looked at him sharply. He knew that Garstang and Brescnik and all his other officers and men must have been talking and wondering. Wondering why the Fifth had been pulled out of its needful place and sent so far for this rather meaningless celebration.

They came down past the shoreline of a blue-green ocean,

past a big, odd-looking city that sprawled over islands and peninsulas and up an inland river valley, and then beneath them was a large spaceport. The squadron roared in to its appointed landing, bristling on its best behavior, every ship set down with masterly precision, and there was a great crowd assembled there to meet it. Flags whipped in the wind. A band blared out, playing not modern instruments, but old-style ones, a brassy music with a solemn throb of drums beneath it that was immensely stirring.

The men of the Fifth debarked and formed in order, every boot polished and every coverall immaculate, solid lines of blue and silver glittering in the soft blaze of this golden sun. Birrel felt the heat of it on his face. His heels struck solidly on the tarmac, and the wind touched him, balmily, laden with smells that were strange to him. And he thought, "This is Earth." He looked around at it.

He could see only the spaceport, and despite its size that was old and worn and poor. The tarmac was cracked and blackened, the rows of ancient shops and hangars all weathered. Opposite the Fifth were drawn up two dozen cruisers with the old insigne of the UW fleet on their bows, and with their crews standing at attention in front of them. Those old, small ships—why, they were Class Fourteens, obsolete for years! He supposed they were all that the UW had.

Two men walked toward him. One was a middle-aged civilian, the other an arrow-straight, elderly man in a black coverall that also bore the UW insigne. He stiffly returned Birrel's salute.

"Nice landing, Commander," he said. "I'm First Admiral Laney, and I welcome your squadron back."

Incredulously, Birrel realized that the old admiral was keeping up the pretense that the squadron from Lyra was still a part of the UW fleet.

It was so preposterous that it was funny. Not for a century had the UW fleet had any real authority in the outer galaxy. Its staff never sent any orders out to the squadrons of the five Sectors, any more than the UW council dared send orders to the five governors. Yet this old Earth officer was trying hard, in front of the crowd, to act as though he were really Birrel's superior officer . . .

Then, seeing the faintly desperate look in Laney's eyes, Birrel softened. After all, what difference did it make—it was only

a pretense and he felt sorry for the old chap trying to play this part.

He saluted again and said, "Fifth Lyra Squadron, Birrel commanding, reporting, sir!"

A look of grateful relief crossed Laney's face. He said uncertainly, "At ease, Commander. Let me present you to Mr. John Charteris, chairman of the council of the United Worlds."

Charteris was a gray, quiet, faintly anxious-looking man. He shook hands warmly, but his eyes were reserved, measuring. He began a little speech directed at the tele-cameras nearby. "We welcome back one of the gallant squadrons of the galactic fleet to take part in our commemoration of—"

When the speeches and handshaking and bandplaying were over, Birrel gave an order, and his men broke ranks.

Brescnik came up to him and asked, "Shall we debark our people now?"

The old admiral told Birrel, "Quarters are all ready for them near the port."

Charteris added, "But you and your wife, Commander, must be my guests." And as another man joined them, "This is my secretary, Ross Mallinson."

Mallinson was a tall and elegant young man of a type that Birrel did not like, the smooth diplomat type who always made him feel uncouth. Despite his smiling manner, Birrel got the feeling that he was tough and unfriendly.

Charteris had a car and driver waiting, and they drove back between the lines of lofty, looming ships. The women and children and babies of the men of the Fifth started coming out of the transports, and Earth officers began deftly shuttling them into cars to take them to their quarters. From beyond a fence, the big crowd of Earth folk spectators watched interestedly. And of a sudden, for the first time his men's families seemed a little outlandish to Birrel. The women and children were of so many star-peoples, so many shades of skin, so many different ways of speech and dress. He thought he detected a supercilious amusement in Mallinson's conventional smile, and he resented it.

At the transport he excused himself and went in to Lyllin's cabin. He stopped short when he saw her. He had never seen her like this. She wore an Earth-style dress of impeccable lines, was perfect in a smart, sophisticated way. She still did not look

like an Earth-woman, not with that skin and eyes and hair. But she looked stunning, and he said so.

"I'm glad I look civilized enough for your people," Lyllin said sweetly.

"My people?" Birrel drew back stiffly. "So you're still brooding on that foolishness? That's fine. I'm not in a tough enough spot here, my wife has to get super-sensitive and make it tougher."

Lyllin's expression changed. "What kind of spot?" He was silent. She looked at him steadily, her eyes searching his face. "It's something dangerous, isn't it?"

"I'd have told you about it if it were something I could tell you," he said. "You know that. Will you forget it? And forget about these people being *my* people!"

He went out with her and Lyllin went through the introductions, cool and proud. He saw admiration in Mallinson's eyes, but that did not make Birrel like the tall, young diplomat any better. Then he stepped aside from the group as Brescnik came up for orders.

"Two-day leaves for one-third of the personnel, in rotation," Birrel said. "I want duty kept up."

Brescnik looked surprised. "If you say so. But there'll be some grumbling."

"Let them grumble. Check out any necessary refitting right away. Port facilities here can take care of that."

Brescnik grunted. "I've seen better facilities on fifth-grade planets. Plenty old! But we'll make out."

Charteris' car swept them along a broad highway toward the east, the chairman explaining to Birrel that in this congested region cars were favored over flitters. While Mallinson chatted brightly with Lyllin, Charteris kept up a pleasant and wholly perfunctory conversation that gave Birrel little chance to look closely at the passing landscape.

In these flying glimpses, Earth did not look too strange or different. It was a green world, but lots of E-type worlds were that, and many of them had blue skies and fleecy, white clouds like this one. The sun, setting now behind them, seemed changing its light from soft gold to reddish and the long rays struck across tracts of conventional plastic-and-metal houses such as one might see on any modern world. Then as they went on farther, Birrel sat up straight and stared ahead. In the

blaze of sunset light there rose the most surprising city he had ever seen.

It was overpowering and at the same time ridiculous. Its starkly vertical towers were unbelievably lofty. No one built in this huddled perpendicular fashion on any world he had ever visited. But he knew this city was old and he supposed that the outmoded style of building of centuries before had just kept going by momentum—after all, they could not suddenly tear the whole place down and start again from scratch. Nevertheless, when they were actually in the streets Birrel found himself oppressed by the overhanging loom of these grotesque structures.

But Charteris' big terrace apartment, high about the myriad lights that were coming out with twilight, was pleasant. The chairman, still talking polite formalities, showed him the great UW building that towered up a mile southward of them.

"It stands on the site once occupied by the United Nations," said Charteris. "It was a great day when the United Worlds building replaced that, almost a hundred and fifty years ago. People had achieved a peaceful Earth, now they would achieve a peaceful universe."

Birrel glanced at the chairman sharply, but could detect no irony in his voice or in his quiet face.

There was a formal dinner that night presided over by Charteris' wife, who looked like a slightly weary but game veteran of many such dinners. There were toasts, and speeches, and much talk about the commemoration. Sector politics were unobtrusively avoided although there were two officials from Cepheus Sector and one from Leo, looking warily at him, but talking courteous nothings.

Birrel fretted through it all. What was Solleremos doing while they sat babbling here? Were his two crack squadrons still poised out there? Ferdias had promised he would get warning if they moved, but would that warning come in time?

Later, when the guests had gone and Lyllin had retired, Birrel sat on the terrace with Charteris and Mallinson and had a final drink. He looked at the reticulations of lights hung loftily against the sky and thought that this was as strange a vista as he had ever seen. From away to the west there was a roll of thunder, ripping across the sky and suddenly ending, as a starship came into the port. He was thinking that it was a medium-

class merchant by the sound, when he became aware that Charteris was asking him a question.

"Is Orion Sector going to send a squadron for the commemoration, too, or only a token delegation?"

Alarm rang a bell in Birrel's mind. What was behind the question? Had Charteris heard something that he had not heard, or was he just fishing for information?

He answered casually, "Why, I don't know. But surely they'd notify you of their plans."

Charteris continued to eye him, and now Birrel sensed the steely, determined man inside that quiet, gray exterior. But it was Mallinson who spoke up smoothly.

"We sent an invitation to Governor Solleremos for Orion to take part, of course," he said. "It was accepted, but we haven't yet heard what sort of delegation is coming to represent them."

Birrel thought swiftly, They're lying, they *have* heard something—and they're trying to find out if I've heard it too. But what? Was Orion already moving, were Orionid forces coming to Earth on the excuse of the celebration, just as the Fifth Lyra had done?

He would get no information from Charteris or Mallinson. It was now apparent that they and probably other high officials of the UW, of Earth, were suspicious of both Lyra and Orion. And, in spite of bringing along the transports, the coming of the whole Lyra Fifth squadron had sharpened their suspicions. Birrel, desperately afraid of making a blunder, felt himself sweating. It was true what he had told Ferdias, he was no good at this kind of intrigue, and unless he made contact soon with Karsh and got a briefing, he could easily turn suspicion into open hostility.

8

BIRREL DECIDED QUICKLY that he had better not try to fence with Charteris and Mallinson. They were experienced in this sort of thing and he was not, and was likely to make some betraying slip. The thing to do was to set it up to see Karsh as soon as possible.

Rising from his chair, he stretched and said, "It's been a long day, at that."

Charteris, instantly the courteous host, smiled. "And a few more tedious ones ahead, I fear. We have many things planned to entertain you and your officers, Commander."

That was not good news, but he would have to make the best of it. Birrel bade them good night and turned away, then turned back again as though he had suddenly remembered something.

"By the way," he said, "while I'm here on Earth I want to look up my ancestors' old home. I understand it's in a village not too far away."

Charteris nodded understandingly. "Of course. Quite a few visitors have a sentiment about their ancestors' old home world."

Mallinson set his drink down and said, with an edge to his voice, "Less sentiment and more loyalty out there is what the UW needs."

There was a moment of awkward silence, but Charteris covered it by saying, "No politics tonight, Ross. Not with a guest. Good night, Commander."

Birrel went to his room, and found Lyllin sleeping or pretending to sleep. He suspected it was the latter, that she was still so resentful that she wanted to avoid conversation with him. He was rather relieved, for he did not care to talk too much here. It seemed vulgar to suspect listening-devices, and he felt sure that Charteris would not stoop to such stratagems. But of Mallinson he was not so sure—the bitter edge to his sudden remark had betrayed deep feeling. He supposed that a good many Earth folk felt that way. They had once had, or thought that they had, all the galaxy as their backyard, with Earth to be the center of things forever. Now that was all changed, and it would be too much to expect them to like it . . .

Lying unsleeping in the dark room, he tried to plan. He could understand now why it had been arranged for him to meet Karsh in that place away from New York. Ferdias' agent could not possibly contact him here, where the brilliant spotlight of publicity played upon him, where he was Charteris' guest. He fretted to think of going through meaningless functions at a time like this, but he would have to do it and get

away as soon as possible. He braced himself for a wearing time of it next day.

The day proved wearing enough, but not quite in the way that Birrel expected. Mallinson, all smooth smiles again, appeared at ten to be his guide and sponsor. Charteris' wife had taken a fancy to Lyllin and had plans, so Birrel went alone with the tall, young diplomat.

"The UW first, of course," said Mallinson as they got into a waiting car. "You'll find it interesting."

Birrel looked with no liking at the crowded streets. The fact that the summer sunlight was golden instead of blue-white did not bother him, he was used to different kinds of sunlight. The air he breathed was the norm for an E-type world, with a pleasant snap in it from the salt ocean. But the towering cliffs of buildings, the huddle and clamor and bustle, were strange and repellent. He thought that a starman could easily get claustrophobia in this city.

The United Worlds building towered like a man-made metal mountain. The Council was in session, Mallinson told him, but inside the sweeping, pure-white lobby Birrel was introduced to a group of the secretariat. He listened to names, shook hands, smiled, and looked into politely smiling faces, and underneath the courtesy he felt the impact of their dislike.

"You'll want a look at the Council chamber," Mallinson said, taking his arm. "We'll go up to the gallery."

Birrel got a shock when he entered the gallery. Its rows of seats were only thinly occupied by spectators, but what was really shocking was the floor of the chamber.

They had dreamed and built big when they had raised this structure a century and a half ago. Too big. The domed, white amphitheater was vast, its floor holding several thousand seats. And less than a fifth of the seats, those nearest the rostrum, were occupied. The graceful name-standard that identified each section told the story. Biggest section was that of Earth, including the little industrial colonies that were all that its barren, non-E-type sister planets of this system could support. There were smaller delegations from the few of the nearby star-systems that still clung loyally to the UW—Tau Ceti, Alpha Centauri, and others. And in the other sweeping sections of empty seats, the standards were blank.

Birrel felt uncomfortable, looking down at those blank, empty sections. They had been designed to hold members from

Lyra and Orion, Cepheus and Leo and Perseus, the five great sectors of galactic civilization, in the brave, young days when everyone was sure that this hall would be the permanent center of government of the galaxy. It was not his fault, he thought, that it had not happened that way—it had all been long before he was born, but, all the same, it was an uncomfortable thing to see.

Charteris sat in the chairman's place, at the back of the rostrum, gravely listening as an elderly delegate spoke on with droning monotony about some piece of legislation that Birrel did not in the least understand.

"Impressive, isn't it?" said Mallinson.

Birrel looked down at the empty sections on the floor, and at the half-empty spectator seats around them, and then he turned and looked squarely at Mallinson. He said,

"You blame us—out there in the Sectors—for all this, don't you?"

Mallinson's face did not alter a line of its smile, but his voice had chilled steel in it. "Yes."

"My men and I are responsible for something that happened more than a century ago—something that was bound to happen?"

"Was it bound to happen?" Mallinson questioned softly. "Well, perhaps it was, perhaps there were too many stars and worlds to govern from any one place. But the way in which the Sectors' governments have come to be dominated by ambitious governors—*that* was not bound to happen."

Birrel asked bluntly, "If you people feel that way, why did you ask any of us back here for your commemoration?"

"Believe me, it was not my idea," Mallinson assured him.

They looked at each other, with frank and honest dislike. Then Birrel rose.

"Fine," he said. "We understand each other, and you can quit being the polite guide. I have to go out and check the squadron, anyway."

"The driver will take you," said Mallinson. "One more thing, Birrel. I speak for myself, not for Charteris. He still has a dream that someday the Sectors will come back to the UW."

Birrel nodded. "Thanks for setting me straight, at least." He turned and left the gallery.

He felt relief when the car was out of the city, across the river and speeding out a thruway. At least there was more room

out here. Looking at the neat, modern houses they passed, he wondered how many of the people here felt like Mallinson. A good many of them, he supposed.

The rolling thunder of a ship in take-off drew his gaze to the big spaceport ahead. Far away across it, the giant hulls of the Fifth were like a mountain-range against the sky. Their majesty dwarfed everything else on the port—the older, smaller naval cruisers of the UW, the merchant starships, the tubby ore-freighters from the harsh sister-planets. He told the driver, who stared up at the looming giants in awe, how to reach his flagship.

When Birrel went up to the bridge of the *Starsong*, he found Joe Garstang sitting with his feet up reading a flamboyant magazine. He hauled to his feet and saluted, looking dourer than ever.

Birrel nodded in the direction of the communic room. "Any messages for me from Vega?"

Garstang shook his head. "Nothing."

Birrel had expected that, but all the same it was a small disappointment.

"Do you want to call Ferdias?" asked Garstang. "I'll have the operators set it up, if you do."

"Nothing to call about," said Birrel casually.

He was lying in his teeth. There was plenty he would like to ask Ferdias about in the light of the situation he had found here. But while their code was secret, too many messages flying back and forth from the Fifth to Vega would be monitored and would surely arouse further suspicions here on Earth. That was, he knew, why Ferdias had chosen to contact him through Karsh.

He asked Garstang, "What about the refitting?"

"Didn't need much. Nearly all done already."

"How are our people getting along over in their quarters?"

"Fine," said Garstang. "Just fine—except the six of the *Starsong*'s men I have down in the brig."

"For what?"

"There was a welcome party over there last night," said Garstang. "You know—crewmen of the UW fleet welcome crewmen of the Fifth Lyra. Drinks, fun, a good time."

"So?"

"So finally one of our men felt so good he mentioned that the Fifth could mop up the whole UW fleet without raising a

sweat. That's what started it. It was quite a thing while it lasted. Never did see so many fists flying."

Birrel swore. "We come here on a good will mission and good will's the one thing lacking. I won't have any more of that."

"I don't think there'll be any more," said Garstang, with a hint of steel in his voice, and Birrel was satisfied. Then Garstang asked in a more plaintive tone, "When am I going to get to see anything of this place? Been busy with discipline and refitting up till now."

Birrel nodded. "All right, Joe. Leave Venner in charge and come along with me. But first I have to see Brescnik."

Garstang obeyed with alacrity. Presently he and Birrel, in the car, were speeding along the row of cruisers. Each time they passed a ship it was like going into the shade of a thundercloud, and then they would pop out again into the golden blaze of the afternoon sun. Brescnik's was the fifth ship in line, but the Vice-Commander was not there—a junior officer pointed across the tarmac to a distant, small hangar that was tucked in between the UW maintenance-shops and those of the merchant lines.

"They brought something in a little while ago, sir— Commander Brescnik went over to see."

Birrel had the driver take them over there and they found Brescnik, standing out in the sunlight with a small group of officers, all of them staring curiously into the small open hangar.

Brescnik saw Birrel and Garstang, and saluted, and then pointed into the hangar. "Take a look at that. Damnest thing I ever saw."

Birrel looked. Inside the hangar was a ship so small and strange that at first he did not recognize it as a ship at all. It was no bigger than a duty-boat, it was knobby and horribly designed, and it looked as though it was made out of pewter instead of modern alloys. A whole crew of men who wore the black coverall of the UW fleet were swarming over the hideous, little craft, working on it and polishing it.

"What is it?" Birrel demanded.

"That," said Brescnik, "is the pride of Earth. *Trailblazer One*, the first starship that ever flew. They've had it in a museum all this time—only brought it out once a century ago for a flight in the centenary celebration."

"You mean they're going to fly that thing?" said Birrel incredulously.

Brescnik nodded. "They say so. In the big flyover. Just a little hop, they say."

Garstang shook his head slowly. "I'd as soon run blind through a cluster as ride that old hunk of iron. How did anyone ever do it?"

Birrel was wondering that, too. He had learned all about the history of starflight, in his training. But it had all been names and dates and methods of propulsion, just facts you had to know to pass your tests. He had never really visualized the impossibly dangerous nature of those early flights—not until now. And not until now had this bicentenary seemed to him anything but another bureaucratic-inspired function to give a chance for dull speeches. But there was more to it than that, after all. He could see why it was such a big thing, to Earth.

Brescnik asked hopefully, "You taking over again?"

Birrel shook his head. "No, you're still stuck with it. They can't spare me over in that place, I'm in such big demand socially. Sorry."

"Yes, *sir*," said Brescnik, making it a dirty word.

Birrel grinned briefly. Then he asked, "You've been around here all day—tell me, have you noticed or heard of any big-scale docking preparations for expected ships?"

Brescnik frowned. "A lot of docks over on the other side of the port are being cleared."

"Enough to dock a squadron?"

"I don't know, I was only by there," Brescnik said. He looked keenly at Birrel. "Whose squadron?"

Birrel hesitated. "Well, we're not the only Sector that will be represented at this affair, you know. Could be that contingents will come in from Leo or Cepheus."

"Or Orion?" said Brescnik. And as Birrel was silent, he said grimly, "Look, Jay, if Solleremos sends a squadron here and sets it down beside the Fifth, there's going to be trouble."

"Absolutely," affirmed Garstang. "I don't think we could hold our men back—and it wouldn't be just a fist-fight, this time."

No, Birrel thought somberly. It wouldn't be a fist-fight. It would be a lot more than that. It might very well be a full-scale collision here between Orion and Lyra, and that could tear it right across the galaxy—that could really tear it.

He hesitated. He had a decision to make and he did not yet have facts enough on which to make it, but he had to make it. This was the price you paid for Commander's rank, for all the salutes and brass and deference.

He said to Brescnik, "I want you to put the Fifth quietly on Ready. I repeat, quietly."

Brescnik did not quite change expression, but something came into his face that had not been there before. He said, "You're sure you don't want full Alert?"

Birrel shook his head. "You couldn't do that without cancelling all leaves and tipping off everyone. Ready is enough." And then, turning to Garstang, he said,

"Come on, Joe, if you want to see the bright lights of Earth. You may not have much time."

9

AND THE LIGHTS were bright. With the coming of night the narrow metal-and-stone canyons of the old city became rivers of luminosity, so that the crowds in them seemed to swim in shifting radiance. Centuries before, this congested metropolis had used electric filaments, arcs, neon tubes, to challenge darkness. Now, when localized effects akin to sodium-vapor glows could make the air itself radiant, the ancient tradition of New York persisted and its central streets glowed with displays of light such as Birrel had seen on no other world.

He didn't like it. Riding through the crowded streets with a carful of gay, chattering people that included Lyllin, Garstang, Mallinson and an Earth couple whose names he hadn't even caught, Birrel stared out sourly. He was used to far more awesome lights than these—the titanic splendors of a cluster's massed suns, the sprawl and glow of vast nebulae. But you saw those from the quiet of the bridge, they changed position with godlike deliberation, they didn't whirl past you like all these lights and crowds and noises in the streets.

He wished he had not come on this excursion, but Mallinson had said that, since Charteris was occupied tonight, he was their official host. He had offered to show Lyllin some of Earth's night-life, and Birrel had felt it would be a rudeness to refuse.

Lyllin appeared to be enjoying it, though with her you could never be sure. But of Garstang there seemed no doubt whatever, he had had some drinks and was having himself a time.

Yet Birrel uneasily remembered what Garstang had said after they had left Brescnik at the spaceport that afternoon and were walking back to the car.

"Brescnik's a good officer," he said in his mild way. "Obeys orders and asks no questions. I guess that's why he made Vice-Commander."

Birrel glanced sharply at him. "Yes."

Garstang added, "And I guess that's why I'll never make Vice-Commander. I ask questions. Like, why are we going on Ready? Like, what the devil's going on?"

Birrel was about to dress him down when something occurred to him. He said,

"You heard what was said about an Orion squadron maybe coming in. What makes you think anything else than that is going on?"

Garstang shrugged. "I told you how my crewmen started a row saying we could mop up the whole UW fleet. Well, there was a reason they said that. It was some cracks the UW crewmen at that party made—about what were we doing here with a full squadron, did Ferdias have ideas of taking over Earth?"

Birrel stopped. "Has anybody else been talking that sort of thing?"

"It's been mentioned through the squadron on the way here— just a speculation."

"A real bright one," Birrel said. "Do they think we'd come on a job like that with full transports?"

"Well," said Garstang, "there's an idea that that might be just cover-up."

Birrel said a disgusted word. "Sure," Garstang agreed. "But you'll have to admit it would be like Ferdias. Anyway, I'm just as glad I've got no family to tag along with me here."

Birrel had brooded on that all the way to New York. If people were talking like that, Karsh's report to Ferdias had been accurate—there was wide-spread suspicion here of the Fifth's purpose in coming. Such suspicions might indeed have been planted by Orion's agents for their own reasons, but, all the same, they were real. Karsh, who knew the situation here better than he, could tell him how to deal with that. That is, Birrel

thought sourly, if he ever got out of this inane round of social doings and made his all-important contact with Karsh.

Mallinson had stopped the car and now he led them along the crowded sidewalks. The press was terrific, people had poured in from far distances for the commemoration. It was a motley crowd, laughing, gay, noisy, under the flaring lights. Persistent music blared, the special commemoration march. As though to top the din, a rolling thunder ripped across the sky. Birrel, listening intently, put it down as another merchant starship.

They went into a place almost as noisy as the street, softly lighted, filled with music and chatter and the rustle of many people dancing. There were other uniforms in here beside Birrel's and Garstang's—black coveralls of the UW, a sprinkling of officers from Cepheus and Leo. But they all looked at Birrel and at Lyllin, whose foreign beauty was a standout even in this crowd.

"I don't see as many of your men tonight as I expected," Mallinson said after they had a table. "I thought they'd all be in on the town."

Birrel shrugged. "We've some refitting that's keeping a lot of them busy."

"Of course," said Mallinson, smiling. "I'm sure you have much to think about and prepare for." And he turned to Lyllin and talked brightly of Earth wines and foods.

Go ahead and needle, Birrel thought. You'll not get a thing out of me, no matter what you and Charteris suspect. And where was Charteris tonight, anyway? What was it that kept him so occupied?

The music and the chatter were getting on his nerves. He looked around and saw the curious looks his party was getting. He resented them. He saw two young junior officers in the UW black, at a bar across the room, look at him and Lyllin, and then one of them said something and the other laughed. Birrel's temper flared, but at that moment he felt the small buzzing in his pocket.

"Will you excuse me?" he said to the others, and got up and walked out to the lobby of the noisy place and into a privacy-booth. Then he quickly snatched the short-range porto out of his pocket, thumbed its button, and said, "Yes?"

No one spoke and he said again, sharply, "Yes?"

He thought he heard a sound like a sigh from the porto. Then nothing. The tiny blinker on the porto went out.

Birrel stood, frowning. Only a very few people had the wavelength of his personal porto. He could not think of one of them who would do a thing like this for a joke.

But was it a joke? He did not think so. What, then? He had not the faintest idea, but he suddenly began to worry. He set his porto to Brescnik's wave and punched the call button.

Brescnik's voice came, surprised. "Did I call you? No."

Birrel asked sharply, "How are you out there?"

"Ready," said Brescnik simply.

"All right, keep it so," said Birrel, and cut off.

That, at least, removed his major worry. He thought he was probably a little too jumpy. Still, the call bothered him.

On his way back to the table, Birrel passed the bar and saw the two young UW officers who had looked at him and Lyllin and had joked and laughed. The anger that the porto call had interrupted came back to him. He went up to them and they turned, two very young Earthmen who looked startled. Birrel spoke flatly to the blond-haired one.

"You were saying something amusing. I'd like to hear it."

The young officer said, puzzledly, "What—"

Birrel repeated, "You were looking at my wife and at me a few moments ago, and remarking on us. I'd like to hear what you said."

An appalled look came into the junior officer's face. He stiffened up, though, and said, "I wasn't speaking to you, sir."

"All the same, let's hear it," suggested Birrel, in an edged voice.

The young officer glanced at his companion, then back into Birrel's hard face. His face became pink and he breathed with difficulty and finally he spoke with a sort of desperation.

"Since you insist, sir. I said, 'Look at the damn Lyra commander swanking in to show off his brass.' "

It was so unexpected, and so exactly the kind of thing that Birrel himself would have said when he was a wet-nosed junior officer, that he suddenly laughed aloud. The frightened young Earthman gaped.

"All right, I asked for that," said Birrel. "I'll buy a drink."

"Yes, sir," gasped the other.

He tossed down the drink, shook hands with them, and

turned and left them staring incredulously after him. He was still chuckling when he got back to the table.

"It's good to see you're getting along so well here, Commander," said Mallinson, plainly curious.

"Isn't it?" said Birrel, and looked at the two young officers who were now rapidly departing, and chuckled again.

Then, meeting Lyllin's dark, steady gaze, Birrel felt less amused. He had an idea that Lyllin guessed perfectly well why he had a chip on his shoulder, though he hoped she did not.

He had another drink, and another, and watched her dancing with Mallinson and listened to meaningless chatter from a dozen voices. More of Mallinson's friends had joined them, there was a babble of questions about Lyra from them, and though he could hardly hear over the beat of the music, Joe Garstang answered them, lying with expansive magnificence.

The table trembled slightly.

Birrel stiffened, but then he decided that it was only the clamor of music and the dancing feet that had caused the vibration.

Then, even as he started to relax, it trembled again, more strongly, and a sound came into the room. It was a faraway sound, but so big, so deep, so strong, that it dominated the immediate brassy din like a growl of distant thunder.

Distant, but getting closer fast, very fast. Joe Garstang looked startledly at Birrel. Birrel kept his face unmoved but under the edge of the table his fist clenched and unclenched as the whole place, the whole city, began to vibrate to that awesome thunder. It was rolling over them, shouting and echoing and then starting to slide away toward the west.

Garstang's lips moved without saying the words aloud. "Class Twenty."

Birrel nodded. There was no other ship that made that kind of sound in worldfall, but a modern battle-cruiser. He waited.

Again, thunder ripped from the high, eastern sky and crossed above them and faded westward. And again. And again.

Birrel was sweating now. How many more? If this was a full squadron, there was no doubt about it at all, it could only be one of Solleremos' squadrons and the fat was in the fire.

A fifth shock-wave rolled down its giant voice to them. He saw Mallinson and Lyllin coming back to the table. The music had stopped.

There would not be any more, Birrel told himself. Five was all. There would not be—

The sixth cruiser thundered past.

Mallinson's eyes had a bright mockery in them, fastened upon Birrel's face.

Now the seventh cruiser would come and then the rest of the Orionid squadron and that would be it.

The thunder ebbed away, and there was no seventh. The music took up again. Mallinson sat down, smiling.

"That will be the official delegation from Perseus," he said. "Mr. Charteris is at the spaceport to welcome them."

Birrel gave him a hot, hungry stare. He was thinking that Mallinson had enjoyed watching him sweat. All right, he had sweat, he was still sweating. But this had done it. He would go it blind no longer in this accursed tangle. He saw a chance in this, and quickly took it.

"I'm sure the chairman will be busy with these new visitors," he said. "It seems a good time for me to take that little trip I mentioned."

Mallinson looked honestly puzzled. "Trip?"

"You remember—I said that I wanted to visit my ancestors' old home here. I think that Lyllin and I will go up there tomorrow."

Lyllin gave him a swift glance of surprise. She did not change expression, but of a sudden she seemed as remote as the edge of the galaxy. Birrel knew what she was thinking. All right, let her think it, at least until he got away from here.

Mallinson said heartily, "Why, of course, I remember now. I'll have a flitter to take you."

"A ground-car is enough, if I can borrow one," Birrel said. "I'd rather drive and see more."

Mallinson agreed instantly to that, too. He's glad to get me away from here right now, Birrel thought. But why?

Maybe Karsh could tell him why. He hoped so. He hoped he would not find out the hard way.

10

DRIVING NORTH FROM New York next day, Birrel almost regretted his refusal of a flitter. It seemed ridiculous for a man who could lead a squadron across a big part of the galaxy, but the traffic frightened him.

He had not driven cars very much, and certainly not on highways like this big, northern thruway. On Earth, people apparently still used cars in great numbers for short distances, and they drove fast. Automatic safety-controls triggered by proximity radar prevented collisions, if you stayed within a certain speed limit, but none of these people appeared to worry about the limit. It was not until they branched off on a subsidiary highway that held much less traffic that Birrel's tension relaxed.

Lyllin had hardly said a word to him since their start. He turned now toward her and said,

"I want to explain about this ancestral home business—I didn't want to talk about it last night in Charteris' place."

Still looking composedly ahead, Lyllin said, "But you don't have to explain. It's perfectly natural that you should want to see the place your people came from."

"Will you stop behaving like a woman and listen?" he said irritatedly. "*My* people, again. What in the world would I care where my great-grandfather lived? I'm doing this because Ferdias ordered it." He added, "I wasn't supposed to tell you even that much, but it wouldn't look natural to leave you behind, so it seems I have to."

Lyllin's face cleared and she turned now and looked at him. "Ferdias' order? But why—" She stopped. Her mind was quick and after a moment she said, "You're to meet someone at this place, is that it?"

"Yes."

"And I'm not supposed to know what it's all about?"

He nodded. "That's it."

He thought that Lyllin looked somehow relieved. She said, "I don't mind, you don't have to tell me. I'm worried, I wish I knew, but it's all right."

He understood. Her relief was because she had found out that he did not really care about Earth ancestors or ancestral homes, that that was only a cover-up.

They turned off the secondary highway onto even less travelled roads. These back roads were old and rambling, twisting accommodatingly around hills and ponds, and bordered most of the way by big trees. A few of the trees Birrel knew, for their seeds had in the past been taken to other worlds, but others were totally strange to him. It was the same with the houses—some of them were modern plastic-and-metal villas such as you would see on any civilized planet these days, but there were also antique stone houses, and once he and Lyllin both exclaimed when they saw a very old house that was built all of wood.

It seemed to Birrel that this countryside looked as old-fashioned in its own way as did the city New York in a different way. They passed a steepled church mantled thick with ivy, stone fences with moss upon them, smooth fields that looked as though they had been tilled for ages. In some of the fields, quite modern driverless tractors were trundling about, doing the cultivation they were programmed for without need of any direction. Apparently this was mostly farming country, and that at least did not surprise Birrel. On every planet people still farmed, for the convenient synthetic foods never quite satisfied human hungers altogether. It was the obsolete look of the farms and homes and villages that surprised him.

He remembered now something Charteris had told him as they looked from the latter's terrace at New York. "You'll find us very old-fashioned in some ways. It's really an emotional attachment to the past, to the times, even after star-travel began, when Earth was still the center of the universe." Birrel had not fully understood that then, but now he was beginning to, it did explain why these people were so loath to give up old customs, old habits of thought, old ways of living that went back two centuries to the days of Earth's pre-eminence and glory.

A brilliant bird flashed across the road and he and Lyllin argued what it way. "A robin, I think," Birrel said doubtfully. "In school, when I was little, we had an old Earth poem about Robin Redbreast. I didn't know then what it was."

"Not nearly so splendid as a Vegan flame-bird," Lyllin said.

"But the red of it, with these green trees and blue sky. . . . It's a pretty world, in a way."

They rolled finally down a little hill and over a bridged stream into the town of Orville. It was only a village, with a number of shops, some modern plastic and others quite ancient in style, around an open square. There was a time-corroded statue of a soldier at the center of the park, and benches on which old men sat in the sun.

Birrel asked directions of a merchant standing in front of his shop, a chubby man who stared open-mouthed at the two visitors. And Birrel suddenly realized how strange indeed they must look in this sleepy, little Earth village—he in his blue-and-silver starman's coverall, his face dark from foreign suns, and Lyllin whose beauty was a breath of the alien.

A rag-tag of curious, small boys had gathered around by the time he got his directions. He was glad to drive on out of the village by the designated road.

"You would think," said Lyllin, "that it would all be more modern. After all, this is where it all started. But so many old-fashioned buildings, roads . . ."

Birrel nodded. "I guess they poured most of what they had—men, money, materials—into the effort to conquer space. A lot of people have gone out from here and not come back. It doesn't have as many people now as it used to."

This road was an even narrower and more rambling one, looping casually along the side of a wide, shallow valley whose neat farms and fields and patches of woods lay silent in the blaze of the soft golden sun. They met no other cars, though an occasional flitter hummed across the blue sky. The farms looked well-worked and prosperous, but most of the houses were old. Birrel kept counting them, and when he had counted six houses he turned into a lane and stopped.

This house was of field-stone, an ancient, brown, dumpy structure that had a forlorn and deserted look. Under the tall, stiff, dark-green trees in its front yard—were they the trees called "pines"?—the grass was high and ragged. The lane went on past the house, past an orchard of gnarled trees heavy with green fruit, to a big old barn. There was no one in sight and no sign that anyone was here.

"Are you sure it's the place?" asked Lyllin.

He nodded, getting out of the car and starting toward the porch. "It's the place. Ferdias' agent bought it a while ago, so

we'd have this secluded place to make contact. There should be someone here."

There was a bell-push at the door, but no one answered it. Birrel tried the door. It swung open, and they went in.

They went through a dark, entry hall into a room such as they had never seen before. Its walls were of painted wood, instead of plastic. The furniture was wooden, too, and of archaic design, the whole effect to Birrel's eyes being one of slightly dismal ugliness. He stood, looking uncertainly around. The room, the house, were very silent.

"Look at this," said Lyllin, in tones of surprise.

She was touching a chair, and the chair rocked back and forth on its curved bottom. "I thought it was a child's toy, but it's too big for a child."

He shook his head. "Beyond me. And it's beyond me too why Ferdias' man isn't here."

He called, but there was no answer. He went through all the rooms, and there was no one.

Birrel felt a mounting alarm. Had something gone wrong with Ferdias' careful plans? Where was Karsh, who should have met him here with the information and orders he must have? Suppose Karsh didn't come—who then could give him warning of Solleremos' strike, if Orion did strike?

His dismay and anxiety increased by the moment. He stood, irresolute. Finally, he said,

"We'll have to wait. Ferdias' man is bound to be along soon, he must have left the place unlocked in case we came."

"You mean—perhaps stay here all night?" said Lyllin. "But food—and beds—"

"We'd better look around," he said unhappily.

They found new blankets on the old-fashioned beds. And in the kitchen cupboards there was food in modern self-heating plastipacks.

"We can make out," he said. "But it's a devil of a thing."

While Lyllin prepared their supper, he went out and restlessly walked around the place. The weedy yard ran into brushy, unused fields and nearby woods. The old barn was empty, and the other outbuildings were shabby and forlorn.

He did not think much of Earth, if this was a sample. He went back inside, and helped Lyllin solve the puzzle of an ancient sink. Even the reddening sunset light pouring through

the windows could not make the wooden walls and timeworn cupboards look less dingy. He said so, and Lyllin smiled.

"It's not so bad. We'll eat out on that back porch—it's less musty there."

The porch was not screened, and gregarious buzzing insects dropped in upon them as they ate, and Birrel slapped and swore. The whole western sky was a flare of crimson, great bastions of cloud building ever higher. Under the sunset, beyond the fields, the ragged woods brooded darkly.

A small animal came soundlessly out of the high grass near the barn and stopped and stared at them with greenish eyes.

"What is it, Jay—a wild creature?"

He looked. "It's a cat, that's what it is. An Earthman in the *Stardream* had one for a pet, kept it at base. He called it Tom." He tossed a bit of food onto the step. "Here, Tom."

The cat stalked carefully forward, eyed them coldly for a moment, then bent to the food. After a moment it turned its back on them and departed.

Darkness fell. Birrel began to feel a thin edge of desperation. Karsh had not come. What if he didn't come at all? How long could he wait in this forgotten backwater place, not knowing what was going on out there in deep space, whether the Orion squadrons were still poised there or whether they were moving? He could not stay away from the Fifth forever and he did not wish to call Brescnik from here unless it was vitally necessary.

Lyllin said, "Is it possible that your man is waiting in that village, Orville—that he missed you and doesn't know you're here?"

"It could be, I suppose." He grasped at the straw. "I'll go down to the village. If he's there, I'll soon find him. Do you mind waiting here—just in case he does come?"

She said she didn't mind. But he took the compact shocker from his coverall pocket and left it for her before he went out.

11

HE DROVE RAPIDLY back along the dark, lonely road to the village. The little town looked lonely and dark, too, when he

got there. There was a scattering of inadequate street-lights, but the shops were almost all closed and he saw only a few people. It all seemed quiet and sleepy under the warm summer night. In the shadows at the center of the square, the old iron soldier stood at stiff attention.

The lights of a tavern caught Birrel's eye, and he went toward it. It seemed about the last place where Karsh might be, but it was almost the only place open and he felt that he could use a drink anyway. He went into the place, a long, poky, dimly-lit room with less than a dozen men in it. There had been a buzz of voices, but the talk suddenly fell silent as he entered. He went to the bar, and the men farther along it and the men at the tables followed him with their eyes. The tavern-keeper, a bustling, skinny man, hurried up and tried to act as though a deep-space starman was no unusual visitor at all.

"Yes, sir, what'll it be?"

Birrel's eyes searched the rack of unfamiliar bottles. "You pick it. Something strong and short."

"Yes, sir. Here you are."

It was a tawny liquor of fiery content that Birrel did not much like. But he drank it, letting his eyes wander over the other men in the place as he did so. He had seen when he first entered that Karsh was not here. Most of these men looked like farmers or mechanics, hearty-looking, sunburned men, a couple of the younger ones tall and gangling. There was one very old man with a wrinkled face, who stared shamelessly at Birrel with bright, beady eyes. They did not on the whole seem unfriendly, but they seemed aloof. Birrel had an idea that he would get very little information out of this insular bunch. He might as well go.

But, as he set his glass down and turned to go, the old man limped forward, peering bright-eyed and inquisitive at him.

"You're the fellow who was asking directions to the old Birrel place today," he said, in an almost accusing tone.

Birrel nodded. "That's right."

The old man was obviously waiting for an explanation as though he was entitled to one. It occurred to Birrel that he had better take this opportunity to give one, if he didn't want the whole countryside wondering why a starman had come here. The last thing he wanted was to get everyone curious about him.

So he said, "Birrel's my name. My great-grandfather, a long

time ago, came from here. I'm just looking up the old place, that's all.''

He turned again to go, feeling that he was wasting time here. But, to his surprise, one of the middle-aged Earthmen came toward him with hand outstretched.

"Why, if your folks came from here originally, that sort of makes you an Orville boy, doesn't it? What do you know about that! Vinson's my name, Captain."

"Commander," Birrel corrected, and shook hands. "Glad to know you. Guess I'll be on my way."

"Say, now, not without me buying you a drink," boomed Vinson. "Not every day one of our own boys comes back from way out there. You're with that Lyra squadron that came for the bi-centenary, aren't you? Think of that!"

There were outstretched hands and hearty words of welcome as Vinson made introductions. Birrel stared at them, dumbfounded by this sudden thaw. Then he got it.

All through the galaxy the pride of born Earthmen was proverbial—and so was their clannishness. He had met it more than once and he didn't like it. He was therefore all the more astonished now, that they should suddenly accept him as one of their own. Four generations, and this place he had never seen until today, yet they claimed him as "one of our own boys." To Birrel, who had never seen Earth until two days before, it didn't make sense.

He wanted to get out, he had found no trace of Karsh here and time was passing, but it was not easy to leave. More men kept coming into the tavern, as word got around, to shake hands with and buy a drink for the "Orville boy" from far-off Lyra. Vinson, a jovial master of ceremonies, rattled on with introductions that Birrel only half heard—"Jim Hovik, who lives up north of your folks' old place"—"here's Pete Marly, who can remember when some of the Birrel family still lived here"—and on and on. Not all of these men, Birrel found out, were farmers. At least three of them had made star-voyages in various capacities. Earth looked so poky and old-fashioned that you forgot how many starmen came from here.

Finally, Birrel managed to thank them and shouldered his way to the door.

"Have to go, my wife's waiting," he said, and a friendly chorus of voices bade him goodnight. "I'll ride with you as

far as my own place—I'm just down the road from you," said Vinson.

Birrel was sweating as he drove out of the village. A fine way to conduct a secret mission, with the whole village bawling his name! And it had got him nowhere—

Vinson's house was the fifth farm on the road. As he got out of the car he said, "Sure does beat all, your coming back from so far. Shows what a small world it is."

"It's a small galaxy," Birrel said gravely, and Vinson nodded. "Sure is. Well, I'll be seeing you. Drop over any time. Goodnight."

As Birrel drove on, he was faintly startled by an upgush of light that silhouetted the bending trees ahead. A great segment of warm silver was rising in the sky. Then he realized—it was that moon that they had passed on their way in to their landing.

The moon of Earth. The "Moon" of the old Earth poems that people still read in Basic. Not too impressive, but pretty. But how the threads of almost everything you had read and heard kept subtly running back to this old planet! He supposed some of the flowers whose fragrance he could smell on the warm, night air were "roses." It was odd, how much you knew about Earth that you didn't realize you knew, even though you had never been here before.

The old road drowsed beneath the rising moon. He glanced up at the star-pricked sky. Had the Birrel, who was his great-grandfather, all those years ago, looked up at the starry sky as he walked along this same road? He must have. He had looked too long, and finally he had gone out to that sky and had not come back here.

The house was dark when he turned in at the lane, but he saw the dim figure of Lyllin sitting on the porch.

"No. No one came," she said, as he sat down beside her.

"And no sign of Karsh in the village," Birrel said. "A fine thing. We'll have to wait."

They sat a while without speaking in the soft, warm darkness. All sorts of small, unfamiliar sounds came out of it, buzzings, and cheepings and monotonous stridulations. Birrel felt increasingly uneasy. They couldn't wait here forever. Brescnik was competent, but the Fifth was his own responsibility and he could not stay away from it indefinitely . . .

Strange, glowing little sparks of light drifted across his vision, and he became suddenly aware that the whole, dark yard,

and the meadow and woods beyond it, were swarming with such floating sparks. They winked on and off, in a fashion he had never seen, dancing and whirling under the dark trees and above the high, rank grass.

"What are they?" asked Lyllin, fascinated.

"Fireflies?" Birrel said doubtfully. "I remember that word, from somewhere . . ."

Then he suddenly started and exclaimed, "What—"

A small sinuous body had suddenly plopped into his lap. Two green eyes looked insolently up at him. It was the cat.

"It's very tame," said Lyllin. "It must have been somebody's pet."

"Probably belonged to the last people who lived here," Birrel said. "It's tame, all right." He stroked the furry back. The cat half-closed its eyes and emitted a rusty, purring sound. "Like that, eh, Tom?"

Tom settled down cozily in his lap, in answer. Lyllin laughed, and reached to stroke his head.

With startling swiftness the cat recoiled from her. It leaped off Birrel's lap, stared green-eyed back at them, and then started across the lawn.

Birrel turned, laughing. "Crazy little critter—" He stopped suddenly. "Lyllin, what's the matter?"

She was crying, and he had rarely seen her cry. "Did it scratch you?"

"No. But it feared me and hated me," she said. "Because it knows I'm alien here."

Birrel said, "Oh, rot. The wretched beast is just afraid of strangers."

"It wasn't afraid of you. It could sense that I'm different—"

He put his arm around her, mentally cursing Tom. Then, as he looked angrily after the cat, Birrel tensed.

Tom had started across the lawn toward the dark brush nearby. But the cat had stopped. And as Birrel looked, Tom recoiled from the brush, and then went away from the dark clumps, running in long bounds.

Birrel's thoughts raced. The cat had recoiled from those clumps of brush, exactly as it had recoiled from Lyllin. For the same reason? Because someone alien, not of Earth, was hiding in those shadows?

He listened, but could hear no suspicious sound. Yet his

muscles were suddenly strung tight. Karsh would not approach this appointed rendezvous so secretly. If non-Earthmen were skulking in those shadows, it could only mean one thing.

Birrel rose and stretched and said casually, "Come on in the house and forget it, Lyllin. I could stand another drink—"

She silently went in with him. But the instant they were inside, Birrel dropped his casual pose. He made a lunge into the nearest bedroom and grabbed for the blankets there. Running back into the living-room, he tossed one of the blankets to the bewildered Lyllin with frantic speed.

"Wrap it around your head—*quick!*"

She was intelligent. But she was not used to obeying orders instantly and without question. She started to speak, but there was no time for explanations, if what he suspected was true. He grabbed the blanket out of her hands and started wrapping it many times around her head, speaking rapidly as he did so.

"Out there. Someone. If they want to be quiet about it, they're sure to use a heavy-duty sonic shocker. Hurry—"

He pulled her to the floor. The blanket swathed her head. He wrapped the other blanket around his own head, fold after fold. They lay tense, not moving, waiting.

Nothing happened.

He thought how foolish they would look, lying on the floor with their heads swathed, if nothing at all did happen.

He still did not move. He waited.

A series of small sounds began in the back of the house, just vaguely audible through the blanket-folds. A chattering of windows, the creaking and rattling of beams, the clink of dishes in the cupboards.

The sounds came slowly through the house toward them. *Chatter, rattle*—leisurely advancing. He knew then that he had guessed rightly. The sonic beam itself was pitched too high to hear, of course. But it was sweeping the house.

It hit them. Lyllin stirred suddenly with a muffled exclamation and Birrel gripped her arm, holding her down. He knew what she was feeling. He was feeling it himself, the sudden shocking dizziness, the buzz-saw sensation inside his head. The sonic beam, sound-impulses of high frequency pitched above normal hearing limits, worked nevertheless through the auditory nerve-centers, striking them many times a second and so overloading them that the kickback produced unconsciousness. Even through the many swathings of thick blanket, the

beam could make itself felt. Without protection, they would both already have been out cold.

The shock passed. The beam was sweeping on to the front of the house. Birrel remained on the floor, his arm holding Lyllin down so that she could not get up. He had used sonic beams himself and he had a pretty good idea of how this one would be used.

He was right. After a minute the small, half-audible sounds of the house and its contents shuddering came back toward them.

Chatter—clink. Rattle—clink—

It hit him again, and he set his teeth and endured it. And again it passed them, and once more the dishes in the kitchen cupboards started talking.

Birrel suddenly thought of the unsuspecting Earth folk in the nearby farms, people like Vinson and the others, sleeping peacefully in their old houses without ever dreaming of what was going on in their quiet countryside. How could they suspect that people from far-off stars were among them tonight, pitted in secret struggle?

12

THE RATTLING AND clinking sounds shut off abruptly. At once, Birrel unwrapped his head and twitched at Lyllin until she did the same. He made a warning motion to her, to keep down, and he himself crawled forward to the hall into which the front door opened. He had taken the little shocker back from her and he had it in his hand now.

There was a grotesque old table in the back corner of the hall. He got down behind it and waited. There was no sound at all.

Then there was a sound. Footsteps, on the porch outside—coming quickly and confidently toward the door.

A man came through the door. He wore a dark jacket and slacks, he carried a shocker, and he walked like a dancing panther. Birrel knew him, though it had been a long way off, on another world, that he had seen him last.

His name was Tauncer.

Behind Tauncer came an older man, as gray and solid and rough at the edges as an old brick. He looked like an Earthman. He was loaded down with a long-range porto-communicator and some other pieces of equipment stowed in a carrying case that hung from his shoulder.

Taking no chances at all, and allowing himself to feel a deep and vicious pleasure, Birrel aimed the shocker and triggered it.

Even so, warned by some faint sound or perhaps only by the instinct of the hunter, Tauncer swung toward him in the instant before the shocker-beam—a short-range version of the big sonics—struck him. The impetus of Tauncer's turn made him hurtle halfway down the little hall to hit the floor headlong.

The brick-like man was slower. He had only managed to open his mouth and lift his hand halfway toward his pocket when Birrel's second burst dropped him quietly where he stood.

Birrel got up. He found that he was shaking slightly. He looked down at Tauncer and remembered a mocking voice on a distant world and he flexed his fingers in a hungry way, thinking how easily a man could die. Lyllin came into the hall and he said angrily,

"You were to stay back there."

She looked at the sprawled bodies. "Are they dead?"

"We're not out on the Sector frontier," Birrel growled. "I wish we were. No, they're not dead."

"Who are they?"

"They're agents of Orion," he said. "That one there is the man who nearly caught me in the cluster. I've brought you into bad trouble."

He rummaged the house until he found a coil of insulated wire, and bound the hands of the two men very securely behind them. Then he searched them. He did not find any documents, which was no surprise. He removed a shocker from the brick-like man, and took it and the porto and the heavy carrying-case far out of reach.

The carrying-case contained a vera-probe projector with its tripod collapsed. Possibly the same one Tauncer had tried to use on him on the cluster world. Tauncer seemed extremely fond of the vera-probe, which must indeed be highly useful in his business. Probably he never travelled without one.

He gave Lyllin the shocker that Tauncer had dropped. "Watch them. Back in a moment."

He went out and rapidly, carefully, searched the grounds of the old farmhouse. He found the sonic device, squatting heavily behind a bush. He stood by it for some moments, perfectly still, listening, but there was no sound except the monotonous stridulations of insects. There did not seem to be anyone else around. Tauncer and the Earthman must have come alone. Birrel frowned. He picked up the heavy sonic device and shoved it into a new hiding-place in the brush, and then stood for a second longer, uneasy and baffled. There was no sign of a flitter. They must have landed back in the woods to avoid betraying themselves by noise. But he could not search the whole woods, not tonight.

He went back to the house.

"They're coming around," said Lyllin. She was sitting in a chair in front of the two bound men, watching them. She rocked back and forth in a rhythmic motion, making the old floorboards squeak. "Look," she said, in a voice that was just a little too high, "I found out what this queer chair is for. It's rather pleasant."

"I don't find it so," said Tauncer suddenly. "The creaking irritates me." He opened his eyes, and Birrel had the feeling that he had been keeping them closed for some time, shamming, while he took stock of the situation.

"Well," he said to Birrel. "I'm an acknowledged expert with the sonic beam. Just as a matter of curiosity, would you mind telling me how you did it?"

Birrel said, "We had warning—a friend of mine named Tom."

Tauncer looked puzzled, but let it go. He looked up at Birrel with an insolent lack of fear.

"How did you know I was here?" Birrel demanded.

"We followed you," said Tauncer. "It was easy."

Birrel shook his head. "No. You didn't follow us here. If you had done that, you wouldn't have waited half the night to act. You found out about this place somehow, and came here. How did you find out?"

Tauncer smiled.

Birrel thought rapidly. No one had known about this old farm selected for their rendezvous except Ferdias and he, himself, and Karsh. And the inexorable mathematics of that simple equation admitted of only one solution. Karsh had not come to the rendezvous. And that aborted call the night before on

his personal porto wavelength, that strange sigh and silence—
it all added up to the same thing.

A rage began to grow in Birrel. He had not met Karsh many
times, in the past. He was certainly not his friend, for Ferdias'
chief agent could not afford the luxury of friends. But, all the
same, he had liked the gray, quiet, dedicated man.

He looked down at Tauncer and he tried to control his anger.
It would not get him anywhere and he needed to think clearly,
now of all times. Now, he saw, the Earthman had regained
consciousness, too, and was looking up at him, scared, wary,
and as viciously resentful as a trapped rodent.

"You've got no right to do this to me," he told Birrel loudly.
"I'm a citizen of Earth, and you're an alien here."

"Shut up, Harper," said Tauncer boredly. Harper swallowed, but he shut up.

Birrel said suddenly, "You caught up with Karsh last night,
didn't you?"

Tauncer was too skilled in tricks to show the slightest emotion. He said mildly, "Did we?" But the Earthman, Harper,
was not so good. His face changed for a fleeting moment, and,
to Birrel, that was proof enough.

He was quite sure that Karsh was dead. Tauncer, who must
have come to Earth before the Fifth ever arrived, had won his
years-long duel with Ferdias' agent. The vera-probe would have
emptied Karsh of all his knowledge, and there would have been
no reason then to leave him alive.

Birrel felt the disastrous impact of it. He had depended on
Karsh to tell him what his course was to be in this dangerous
and highly complicated situation. There would be no one to
tell him anything now, there was no use calling Ferdias for
orders for Ferdias could not possibly estimate things from faraway Vega. He would have to think out his own decisions and
he would have to do it quickly. The very fact that Tauncer had
made this attempt proved that the crisis was sharpening fast.
There might be very little time left before the blow-up.

He said to Tauncer, "Now you can tell me some things."

Tauncer's eyes looked up brightly at him, the contemptuous
eyes of the adroit and wily man measuring the honest clod for
another defeat.

"You'll get no more from me than I got from you, Birrel—
and you know it."

Birrel said grimly, "I'm pressed for time. I'll get it out of you."

"With the vera-probe? You don't know how to operate it."

"That's true," said Birrel. "But there are other ways." He took the shocker from Lyllin's hand and motioned to her to get up. "Go on into the other room, dear. I don't think you'd enjoy this."

She looked at him as though he was someone she had just met and was not sure she liked.

"Try to understand," he said. "I don't do this sort of thing every day."

"Of course," she said. She went into the next room, and he shut the door behind her. He came back to the two men.

Tauncer laughed. "Bluff."

"You're sure of that?"

"Quite sure. You're a good fighting man, but you haven't the stuff in you for this kind of work. If nothing else, the way your wife looked at you just now would stop you."

Birrel nodded. "I think a lot of my wife. But I think a lot of something else, too, and that's the Fifth squadron. So you're going to tell me things, Tauncer. Like the present position and plans of the Orionid First and Third squadrons."

"It won't work," Tauncer said decisively. "I don't want to boast, but I'm plenty tough in my own way. To make me talk you'd have to do things that no decent, honorable dolt like you *could* do. I feel quite safe."

Birrel looked with grim meaning at the Earthman, Harper. "He doesn't look as tough as you."

Tauncer chuckled. "Oh, Harper's just the ordinary two-for-a-cent traitor you can buy on any planet to help you—he doesn't know anything. Go ahead and work him over, if you don't believe me."

Harper's voice rose angrily. "That's a fine thing to say!"

Birrel felt an increasing frustration. Tauncer lay there, bound and helpless, and yet the man had a boundless self-confidence, as though he held all the cards in his hands. What made him so confident? And why, after he had learned of this rendezvous from Karsh, had he come here? To kill Birrel, after questioning him with the probe—to demoralize the Fifth by suddenly removing its commander, a stroke timed to coincide with the appearance of Solleremos' squadrons?

He had to know where those squadrons now were and what

they were going to do and when. Tauncer knew that, and must be made to tell, as quickly as possible. There was only one way Birrel could see to make him.

He went into the next room and closed the door. Lyllin flashed a glance at him from where she sat.

"I was bluffing," he said. "And it didn't work."

He took out his porto, set it to Brescnik's wave, and pressed the call button. Brescnik answered almost at once.

"Something has come up," said Birrel. "I don't think there's a lot of time."

"Shall I go on Alert?"

Birrel hesitated. He wanted to say, Yes. He desperately wanted every man in the Fifth at his post, right now. But he dared not order an Alert, not without some proof of Solleremos' intentions that he could show Charteris and Mallinson. Otherwise they would surely interpret the Alert as evidence that Ferdias was indeed planning a grab for Earth.

"No," he said, after a moment. "Not yet. I need a man up here. Someone who can use a vera-probe."

A brief silence indicated Brescnik's puzzlement, but heroically he refrained from asking questions.

"There should be someone among our technicians," he said. "I'll find one."

"Send him up here as fast as you can," said Birrel, and gave directions. "Keep on Ready."

He turned off his porto and then swung around to Lyllin. "I have to stay here a while longer. I want you to go back to New York."

She said evenly, "No."

He started to get angry. But he stopped. There was a certain look on Lyllin's face that he knew.

"All right, but you're making it tougher for me," he grumbled, and left her and went back to the other room.

Tauncer and Harper lay where he had left them, Harper looking a little scared, but Tauncer's eyes still bold and confident.

"So you're having Brescnik send up a vera-probe operator?" said Tauncer.

Birrel was for an instant thunderstruck, wondering how Tauncer could have overheard, and Tauncer laughed at his expression. Only then did Birrel realize that the other had merely made a logical estimate of what he would do.

It shook him, all the same, to realize that even though he was a prisoner, Tauncer was thinking away ahead of him.

"Clever of you," Birrel said grimly. "Thanks for reminding me of just how clever you are."

He went into the dusty, back rooms of the old house. One had been a bedroom and still contained two beds with old-fashioned, ornate metal frames. Birrel eyed them, then went back and picked up Tauncer by the shoulders and dragged him roughly to the bedroom. He shoved him onto one of the beds and then went and got the coil of insulated wire.

"This solicitude for my comfort—" began Tauncer mockingly, but then he stopped. Birrel, with a length of the wire, was tying his feet together. He then lashed the bound feet to the bottom frame of the bed, and secured Tauncer's shoulders with another length of wire he ran under the bed itself. He then dragged Harper in and tied him onto the other bed in the same way.

"I think that'll hold even a very clever man, for a little while," said Birrel.

For an instant, a vicious anger flashed in Tauncer's eyes. It was the first time Birrel had penetrated the mocking self-confidence of the man, and it pleased him immensely.

He went back to Lyllin.

"How long?" she asked him.

"Several hours, anyway," he said. "Brescnik will find a man fast, but it'll take time for him to get up here." He added gloomily, "Too long. But we'll have to wait."

Lyllin glanced at the window. A pallid light was streaking the dark sky outside.

"Go get some sleep," he said. "One of those rooms upstairs."

She did so. Birrel sat and watched the gray light strengthen, going every now and then to look in at the two captives. Harper eyed him a little frightenedly, each time. But the third time he looked, Tauncer was either sleeping or shamming sleep. He thought it was real sleep, and it betokened a confidence that nagged Birrel with worry.

Why should Tauncer be so confident—because he counted on help coming? Were others beside Harper in on this with him? Birrel took to walking around the house, peering out the windows in turn.

The sun rose, washing the ragged fields and woods with

golden-yellow light. He saw no one out there. Twice, he sprang to the front window as he heard a motor, but once it was a ground-car that went casually by, and, the other time, a heavy farm-truck.

Lyllin came down a couple of hours later. "You didn't sleep," he said accusingly.

She smiled. "No. I'll get some breakfast."

The mid-morning sun was warm and they ate on the porch again. As though he had been waiting for them, the black cat came out of the shrubbery and strolled up onto the steps, insolently expectant.

"Get out of here, you little pest," said Birrel.

"Oh, feed him," said Lyllin. "After all, he did give you your warning."

Birrel grunted, and tossed the leftovers onto the step. He was just turning to go and have another look at Tauncer and Harper, when there was the unmistakable sound of a car pulling up in front of the house.

"Your man?" said Lyllin, but Birrel shook his head swiftly.

"No, he couldn't get here this fast. Wait here."

He grabbed the shocker out of his pocket and ran to the front of the house.

13

THE CAR HAD stopped in the front lane and a man was getting out of it. Birrel's grasp tightened on the shocker. But then an ample-figured, middle-aged woman got out of the car also. He looked back again at the man, and now he recognized the broad, ruddy face of the man he had met in the tavern the night before, the one who lived just down the road. Vinton. No— Vinson. He and the woman were coming toward the house.

"Is it trouble?" asked Lyllin's quiet voice from close behind him.

Birrel turned quickly. "No, just a neighbor, one of these farm people. You meet them. I'll be back in a moment."

He ran back along the hall to the back room where Tauncer and Harper lay bound to the beds. Tauncer had his eyes open now. Birrel hastily inspected the insulated wires to make sure

both men were still fast. Then he went out, closing the door of the room. He came through the hall and closed the hall door tightly, too. He didn't think his captives could be heard, even if they yelled. If they did make themselves heard, he could always say he had a drunken friend back there and go back and silence them with the shocker. But, with a vera-probe operator on the way, he did not want to put them out for that long, if he could help it.

When he got back into the living-room, Vinson greeted him jovially in his booming voice.

"A little early for a call, Commander, but we were going by and Edith wanted to meet you folks. Hope you don't mind."

Yes, he minded, Birrel thought exasperatedly. He minded like the very devil, but there was nothing he could do but smile, and shake his head, and go through the introductions.

Lyllin was aloof and hesitant again with these Earth folk. But Mrs. Vinson did not seem to notice that. She stared at Lyllin with open marvel and admiration.

"You came all the way from Vega with your husband—think of it! Why, lots of women here on Earth have had their husbands go away into space, but not many ever went that far to stay with them."

Birrel, chafing inwardly, asked them to sit down. Immediately Vinson began talking about the problems of farming, the high cost of automatic tractors and auto-harvesters, the fact that weather-control was still not all that it should be and related subjects about which Birrel knew nothing and cared less.

He began to feel caught in a minor nightmare. To sit here in an ancient farmhouse on Earth, listening to the gossiping of these worthy, but totally strange folk, while the conflict between Orion and Lyra could be rushing toward its climax, seemed insanely impossible. It was like one of those dreams, where you were trapped and tangled in ridiculously frail webs and watched disaster approaching you.

Birrel became aware that Vinson's booming voice had stopped and that the man was looking at him questioningly.

"I'm sorry, I was thinking of something else," he said.

"I was just saying," Vinson said, "that when I called on that chap who bought this place, he told me he wasn't going to live here, but was buying it for someone else. But I sure didn't figure that someone would be one of the old Birrel family!"

Birrel stared. Of course Karsh would have said something

like that—and naturally everyone here would now assume that he was the new owner. And he could not contradict that assumption without a lot of explanations that he was in no position to make.

"About working your land here," Vinson went on. "The fields aren't too good, but they could be got in shape again. I'll be glad to help on that."

"Why, thanks," stumbled Birrel, "but you see, we'll be leaving very soon, going back to Vega—"

"Oh, sure, I know that," Vinson said heartily. "But, of course, you're planning to come back here or you wouldn't have bought your folks' old farm. Might as well get some profit and use out of the place till then. Now, we'll go over the land together and figure."

Birrel did not know what to say to that. No one had dreamed that such ridiculous but real problems as this would come up when this old farm had been bought as cover for a rendezvous. In fact, they never would have arisen, if Karsh had met him here as planned. The doing away with Karsh by Tauncer had pulled the foundation out from under everything.

Vinson misinterpreted Birrel's silence, and said quickly, "I didn't mean right now. Just dropped in for a social call but I thought I'd mention it. I'll come back later and walk over it with you."

He rose to his feet and Birrel felt sharp relief, as he and his wife went to the door.

"Sure would like to have you come over for dinner sometime before you leave," Vinson said.

His wife added coyly, "You're our celebrities here now, you know. In the village they're talking about having a Welcome Home celebration for you."

When the two had left, Birrel turned and looked blankly at Lyllin. "A Welcome Home celebration. For God's sake, that's all I need right now."

He hurried back to the rear room, to find Tauncer lying quietly and Harper squirming restlessly.

Tauncer smiled. "You look worried, Commander. Things not going well? I'm afraid you're a little beyond your depth."

Birrel looked at him steadily, and asked, "Who's coming, Tauncer?"

Tauncer's smile faded into a wary look. "What do you mean?"

"You're expecting someone to help you or you wouldn't be so cocky," Birrel said. "Who?"

"I haven't an idea what you're talking about," Tauncer said lightly. But his smiling stopped.

Birrel's forebodings deepened. He prowled the house and grounds more vigilantly than ever, and every time a car hummed down the road or a flitter buzzed over, he stopped and listened.

The hot noon hours went by. The sun passed its zenith and now big clouds began to build in the western sky. Birrel began to chafe restlessly at this waiting. He realized it would take Brescnik a little while to find among the technicians of the Fifth a man who could operate a vera-probe. But, even so, he should have been able to get one up here by fast flitter by now.

The bastions of cloud in the west swelled higher, and the humidity became intolerable. Birrel went out and looked around again. From a distance came the sound of Vinson's auto-tractors lumbering about the fields on their appointed programs. The sky darkened, and Birrel thought that a storm was building. He came back to the house to find the black cat sitting on the porch and looking at him with an insolent air of ownership.

Lyllin met him at the door. "No one?"

"No one," he said. "What's the matter with Brescnik? A flitter will have trouble locating this place, if a storm comes up, and—"

A flash and then a crash of thunder interrupted him. Birrel swore. "That's fine."

"It won't last long, will it?" said Lyllin.

He gloomily said that he wished he knew. At that moment they heard a scratching and mewing outside the door.

"The cat," said Lyllin. "I think it's scared of the storm and wants in."

"Let it go to the barn," he said.

Lyllin smiled, and went to the door and opened it. The black cat stalked in, keeping well away from her, with its tail erect and a general look of being annoyed at the delay in answering the door.

Birrel started to say that for sheer insolence the cats of Earth took the palm, but another crash interrupted him and this time the old house shook to its foundations. The thunder came closer quickly, and now the flashes of lightning outside the rain-dashed windows were blinding.

Then as the uproar lulled for a moment, he thought he heard the buzz of a flitter close overhead. He raced back through the kitchen to the porch, and by another world-illumining flash he glimpsed the flitter making a rough landing between the house and the barn.

Birrel waited for the next flash. It showed two men climbing out of the flitter. He raised his shocker.

The two were running toward him through the rain, but it was too dark to see their faces. Why didn't another flash come? Then one did, and he saw them clear and close.

One was Joe Garstang. The other was a young officer with the badge of a Technic-First-Class, who looked a bit scared as they ran up onto the porch out of the smashing rain. Garstang shook himself and growled,

"I've seen worse storms on other worlds, but I never saw one come up so bloody quick."

"What are you doing here?" demanded Birrel. "Why aren't you with your ship?"

"Brescnik told me to come along. By the way, this is your vera-probe operator. Vathis, T-first-class."

"Why did Brescnik send you? What's wrong?"

Garstang waited until the reverberations of another crash of thunder died away, and the old house stopped shaking. Then he said, with a puzzled look on his broad face,

"We're not sure anything's wrong. But Brescnik's worried. Traffic—normal merchant traffic—is only running one way down at that spaceport. Ships keep going out, but none come in."

He paused, then added, "Brescnik thinks that the UW authorities are quietly evacuating the spaceport."

Birrel thought of that, and he did not like the shape or sound of it.

He asked, "You haven't any evidence why?"

Garstang shook his head. "Not a glimmer. All we have is a guess. You know what that guess is."

Birrel knew. If Charteris and Mallinson and the rest had some foreknowledge that Orion squadrons were on their way to strike, they'd get their ships off the spaceport. And if that was what it was, he had better get the Fifth off too.

But he would be going blind, if he took off now, with no information as to Orion's plans. His worries had suddenly in-

creased tenfold, but he had to delay long enough to probe Tauncer.

He told Garstang rapidly about Tauncer. Without waiting for Garstang's reaction to that, he turned to young Vathis.

"You come along. I want the probe set up and used as quickly as possible."

They went to the living-room. Lyllin sat composedly there and Birrel noticed that the cat was sitting across the room from her, pricking up his ears at each crash of thunder. Garstang went over to speak to Lyllin, but Birrel took the young technician to the vera-probe in the corner.

"How long will it take you to set it up?"

Vathis looked over the apparatus. "It seems a conventional hook-up. Fifteen minutes."

"Make it ten," said Birrel. Then he said, "Make it five."

At that moment, in the comparative lull between the crashes of the receding storm, there came a clangorous peal from the old-fashioned doorbell.

"You expecting somebody else?" said Garstang.

"Oh, Lord," said Birrel. "That'll be Vinson, he said he'd come back. A neighbor here. You go ahead and get the probe ready, I'll get rid of him."

He hurried to the door and opened it. But the man standing outside it was not Vinson.

It was Mallinson. And despite the fact that he wore a streaming slicker, the tall, young bureaucrat looked as elegant as ever. He walked coolly in past the stricken Birrel, saw Lyllin and bowed to her, and then turned around. He said,

"So this is Ferdias' little spy-nest on Earth? Very clever, Commander."

There was, Birrel realized, not the slightest use in lying. Mallinson's glance through the open door of the next room, at Joe Garstang and the uniformed young technician and the partly set-up vera-probe, had ended the possibility of that. There was nothing Birrel could say. But there might be something he could do.

He reached into the pocket that contained the shocker. Mallinson, who was taking off his wet slicker, did not turn toward him but said casually,

"Perhaps I should say that I have a number of men outside. I'm afraid they're getting pretty wet."

14

BIRREL TOOK HIS hand away from his pocket. He knew now that he was in real trouble and that force would not get him out of it. He had to talk fast and make the other believe him, but he did not know how much chance there was of that.

Mallinson was looking around the room and its old-fashioned furniture.

"The old, ancestral home," he said. "How natural that you should want to see where your people came from on Earth. What a laudable sentiment!"

His voice suddenly became cutting and his bitter hostility came through. "I never did buy that, Commander, not for one minute. And when we got a report that officers of your squadron had come up here to huddle with you, I knew I was right—that your sentimental pilgrimage was just to cover up while you stabbed Earth in the back."

Birrel got angry. "No one is stabbing Earth in the back. At least, none of us."

"Ah, yes," Mallinson said ironically. "Lyra is wholly innocent. It's Orion that has intentions on us and you're trying to protect us. Isn't that your line?"

Birrel controlled his anger. Shouting was not going to get him anywhere.

"It's not just my linc, it's the truth," he said. "I was just going to prove it, when you came. I would have called you as soon as we had proof to show you."

"Proof of what?"

"Proof of what Solleremos is planning. We've caught Tauncer, his ace agent. We're going to use the vera-probe to question him."

"We'll do the questioning ourselves, in New York," Mallinson said grimly. "After we've dealt with you and your squadron."

"Dealt with—" Birrel stopped, feeling a chill as though a cold hand had grasped him. He asked evenly, "What do you mean? About dealing with the Fifth?"

"Your squadron is going to be disarmed," Mallinson said

incisively. "It's not going to carry out the mission Ferdias gave you. We've brought in missile-launchers all around the spaceport and have cleared away all traffic. Tonight your officers will be given ten minutes to evacuate all ships—oh, yes, we're well aware that you're on Ready—and if they don't comply, the Fifth Lyra will be destroyed."

"Talk," said Birrel between his teeth. "You wouldn't dare. You know it would mean instant war between the UW and Lyra."

"Is that what you call peace?" Mallinson demanded harshly. "A powerful task-force coming to Earth under pretext of a friendly call, and preparing to take over our planet?"

"Damn it, we've no such plans, it's Solleremos who plans that," Birrel exclaimed. "And if you disarm the Fifth and Orion's squadrons come—"

He could not finish. The words he spoke brought him such a nightmare vision of the Orionid ships sweeping in, of the disarmed cruisers and transports of the Fifth disappearing in a storm of smoke and fire, that he could not go on.

"We're taking no chances," Mallinson was saying implacably. "The Fifth Lyra will be disarmed. You and everyone else in this house are in custody, as of now."

"You're taking no chances," mocked Birrel, raging. "You're throwing away your planet, that's all. Good God, man, think! If I'm right, if Orion is planning a grab, you're paralyzing the only force that might be able to stop them."

"There's the UW fleet—," Mallinson began, but Birrel interrupted savagely.

"Solleremos will eat it up, and you know it. No matter how loyal you are to Earth, you've got to admit that her fleet can't face two heavy Orionid squadrons for ten minutes."

A look of anxiety shaded Mallinson's face for a moment. But he said doggedly,

"We'll have to do what we can. We'll fight enemies if they come, but we'll make sure first we're not attacked from behind."

He went toward the door. "I'm calling my men in now. There will be no violence, unless you provoke it."

Birrel sprang desperately after him and caught him by the arm. "Mallinson, listen! Forget for now what you think of me. Just think of this: If Orion has mounted a strike against you,

can you wait till we get back to New York to find out? A few hours could be too late!''

Mallinson looked around at him sharply. ''What are you getting at?''

''This—we've got Tauncer in there. We've got a vera-probe and a man to operate it. Don't you want to know right now what's coming from Orion? Or would you prefer to take the chance of being clobbered?''

Mallinson hesitated, with indecision in his attitude for the first time. ''What the devil can you lose?'' Birrel demanded.

Mallinson decided. ''All right, we'll question this man you say is an agent of Orion. But one of my own men will operate the probe.''

He went to the door and called outside. The storm had receded to a dull, distant rumble, but clouds still darkened the sky and a drizzling rain still fell. A hard-looking Earthman in a slicker came up onto the porch, and Mallinson spoke with him, and he nodded and went out into the grounds again.

Mallinson turned. ''Let's see this man.''

When they went into the rear bedroom, Tauncer's eyes flew to Mallinson. Birrel almost admired the lightning speed with which Tauncer reacted.

''Secretary Mallinson!'' he exclaimed. A look of shaky relief crossed his face. ''Thank God you've come! This Lyran commander must be crazy—he attacked us, tied us up here—''

Mallinson interrupted, saying flatly, ''He claims that you're Orionid spies.''

''Spies?'' Sheer astonishment showed in Tauncer's face. ''I don't know what this is all about.''

Harper said loudly and aggrievedly, ''I'm a UW citizen! Are you going to let him do this to one of your own citizens?''

Birrel was prepared to see Mallinson waver, but there was tougher stuff in this young diplomat than he had anticipated.

''If you're innocent, you'll be out of here soon,'' he told them. ''But, first, you're going to be probed.'' And as a middle-aged Earthman came in with the vera-probe he said to him, nodding at Tauncer, ''This one first.''

''I protest this!'' cried Tauncer. ''Use of a probe on an unwilling subject is forbidden by every law in the galaxy!''

''Lots of things are against the law,'' Mallinson said coolly. ''Go ahead, Kane.''

Kane, the Earthman, touched the switches. The projector started buzzing.

Tauncer could not move his body, but he rolled his head back and forth rapidly. But Kane was an expert operator. He kept the invisible beam of the probe swivelling to follow Tauncer's movements.

Tauncer's face was briefly strained and then it went slack and his eyes lost their keen brilliance, becoming vague and unfocused.

"Under control," said Kane.

"Tauncer," said Mallinson sharply. "Can you hear me?"

"Yes."

"Is Solleremos planning to take Earth into his Sector?"

Some dim vestige of a censor barrier seemed to survive in Tauncer's mind, because there was a long delay and Mallinson asked the question again, more loudly. But when the answer came, it was clear enough.

"Yes."

"How long has he been planning this?"

"Years."

"But he's going to move now?"

"Yes."

"Why right now?"

"Because," answered Tauncer's stiff voice, "if he doesn't, Ferdias will grab Earth first."

There was a long silence. Mallinson turned and looked at Birrel with a fiery light in his eyes. Birrel exclaimed,

"He's lying, the probe's not completely efficient—"

Kane, the operator, looked up from the projector and said coldly, "It's one hundred per cent."

Mallinson, after that long, furious look at Birrel, turned back to the man on the bed. He asked,

"How will he do it?"

"Direct attack. The UW naval forces are negligible. Lyra's Fifth Squadron will be caught surprised and disorganized by absence of command."

"Absence of command," repeated Mallinson. "That's why you're here, then?"

"Yes."

"You were going to probe Birrel and then kill him?"

"Yes."

Mallinson hunched forward a little as he asked the next question, and his voice was sharp and penetrating.

"What is Orion's attack plan? From what direction will those two squadrons come in to Earth?"

They waited tensely for the answer to that. But Tauncer replied readily in the monotonous voice,

"I don't know."

Birrel exclaimed, "He's lying! I told you control wasn't complete. He has to know—"

Kane said stiffly, "I know how to use a probe. He's under complete control."

"But—" Birrel began. Mallinson waved him back. "Let me do this, Birrel. If you *please*."

He spoke sharply to Tauncer again. "Why don't you know the attack plan, when you've been here as advance agent for it?"

"Because," said Tauncer, "it would be too risky. If I were caught and probed, it would give the whole thing away."

Mallinson drew back. He looked at Birrel and said, "It makes sense. And we can't get out of him what he doesn't know."

"All right," said Birrel. "So he doesn't know. Still he had to get word to the Orion force that things here are clear, that my squadron is immobilized. How was he going to get word to them if he didn't know where they were? Ask him that."

Mallinson asked him. And Tauncer answered.

"The long-range scout-craft that brought me secretly to Earth has been waiting to come and take me off again, hiding a good way out in space—"

Mallinson interrupted. "Hiding? How could it hide from our radar watch?"

"Easily. It's been lying up against the asteroid Hermes. It—it—"

Tauncer stuttered and fell silent. Kane, the man operating the probe, spoke stiffly to Mallinson.

"I can't guarantee responses if you interrupt the subject's answers, sir."

"Sorry," muttered Mallinson. He waited a moment, then asked, "Go ahead, Tauncer. How were you to contact the Orion force?"

Tauncer mechanically repeated his former statement first. "The long-range scout-craft that brought me secretly to Earth

has been waiting to come and take me off again, hiding a good way out in space. After I swept this house with the sonic beam, I called the scout by long-range porto last night. It's to come tonight and take me off. It will take me to the task-force.''

So that was it, Birrel thought. That was who Tauncer had been expecting, and waiting for. But—

Birrel rudely thrust past Mallinson and fired a question before the angry, young diplomat could prevent him.

"How would the scout find you here—how would it know where to land, Tauncer?"

"It will come in on a homing beam from our flitter. I was—to turn it on—tonight—"

"Where is the flitter? Exactly where?"

"It—it is under trees—near clearing in woods—we landed—we landed—"

Tauncer's monotonous voice trailed away. His chin sunk on his breast.

"Tauncer!"

"It's no good," said Kane disgustedly, shutting off the projector with a snap. "Interruptions, then change of questioner, they're enough to disrupt the whole process. We'll get nothing more from him this time. He'll be out for at least two hours."

"It's enough," said Birrel. His mind was racing. "The officers of that Orion scout that's coming—they'll know the position and course of Solleremos' two squadrons. If we grab them, the probe will soon get it out of them—and we'll know where and when it's coming."

"Forget that 'we,' " said Mallinson crisply. "You're not going to exploit this crisis with Orion, Birrel. What I said goes. The Fifth will be disarmed, or destroyed."

The rage that Birrel had repressed before began to burst his control. It seemed to him that in all history, stupidity had caused more irretrievable disasters than anything else and now he was up against it himself and did not seem to be able to do anything at all about it.

"You are being a damned fool," he said to Mallinson. "You—"

Garstang caught his arm. He said nothing, but Birrel understood. If he blew up now, he was lost.

He said to Mallinson, "I apologize for that. Please listen to

me one moment. If I can convince you utterly that my orders are only to defend Earth, not to grab it, will you let me take the Fifth out?''

"You could talk all night without convincing me,'' Mallinson said contemptuously. "We're wasting time.''

Birrel found it hard to say what he had to say. It would mean putting himself temporarily out of the whole thing at a time when the crisis was rushing upon them, no one knew how near. Yet it was his only card and he had to play it.

"Would you believe me if I talked under the probe?'' he said.

Mallinson looked a bit startled. "You're offering to be probed?''

"How else can I convince you?'' Birrel said rawly. "Yes. I'll take the probe.''

"All right,'' said Mallinson, after only a moment's hesitation. "Sit in the chair there. Go ahead, Kane.''

Birrel sat in the chair and as Kane re-adjusted the projector he thought desperately, Hours—I'll be out for hours, maybe, if anything goes wrong and maybe it'll be all over when I come out of it, maybe it'll be too late, damn Mallinson, damn all suspicious Earthmen—

The shocking radiation of the probe hit him. It was as though great winds swept through his brain, bearing him away toward darkness. He had asked for this, but all the same he instinctively tried to fight it, to keep his will, to think, to see.

He saw as through a red mist. Lyllin had come into the room, though he had not seen her come. She was screaming, a sound he could not hear, and she was trying to reach Mallinson and the man at the projector, and Joe Garstang was holding her back. No more. The winds of darkness took him completely.

15

THE NOT KNOWING, the not feeling, the not caring. A nothingness so complete that you were only aware of it when pain began to drag you out of its comfort.

Pain in his head, like lances thrusting repeatedly through his

skull. The pain of feeling again, of hearing again. And what he heard was a soft sobbing, but what he felt was a pair of hands roughly shaking him.

"Come on, Jay, come out of it." That was Garstang's voice, with an edge of desperation in it.

Another voice said, "It's passing off."

"That's easy for you to say," mumbled Birrel. "It's my head."

The way the words dribbled off his lips disgusted him, and he made a determined effort to open his eyes. He succeeded.

He was lying on a couch in the living-room. It was twilight now, the windows dark and lights on. Lyllin hung beside the couch, with the marks of tears on her face. He thought they were tears of rage rather than anything else. Joe Garstang had knelt and was shaking him.

Kane, the operator of the probe, stood by looking uncomfortable. He said loudly, as though exculpating himself,

"I told them to let you be. I told them you'd have a bad headache if they woke you too soon."

"It's over an hour now, he'll have to stand the headache," retorted Garstang. He shook Birrel again. "Come on, snap out of it."

For the moment, Birrel hated Garstang and his rough hands and his monotonous voice. Then what he had heard penetrated to his brain. More than an hour? It was too long to be lying here like a log, much too long.

He trued to sit up. Garstang helped him, saying, "That's the boy."

"For God's sake spare me your hearty clichés," said Birrel, and then he said, "Sorry, Joe. Thanks."

The man Kane had gone out of the room. Almost at once Mallinson came into it. He came over to where Birrel sat shakily on the couch and looked down at him with sour dislike.

Birrel looked up at him. "Well? You probed me?"

"Yes."

"Then you know now that I'm not here to make any grab for Earth, but to keep Orion from doing it."

"I'll admit this," said Mallinson slowly. "That those are your orders at present."

"What do you mean by that?"

"I mean," said Mallinson, "that Ferdias could send you

other orders, as soon as Orion is disposed of. I still don't trust Ferdias one bit more than Solleremos."

"Good God!" cried Garstang. "Does that mean you're still going to disarm the Fifth? After what you've heard?"

Birrel looked at Mallinson, whose mouth was pursed obstinately. He said, "You know this much for sure now, Mallinson—that I will take the Fifth out and fight beside the UW fleet against Orion's squadrons. You know it, don't you?"

"Yes, I know it," Mallinson said doggedly. "It's what happens after that I'm thinking about."

"There won't be any after to worry about if your UW fleet meets two heavy squadrons alone," said Birrel. "And you know it."

Mallinson's face got longer. After a moment, he said,

"I don't have authority to make such a decision. We'll put it up to Charteris when we get back to New York. And we'd better get started."

Birrel stared at him. "What do you mean—get started? We can't leave here! Have you forgotten that the Orionid scout is coming here tonight—in a few hours—to keep its rendezvous with Tauncer?"

Mallinson replied, with a hint of complacency, "I've taken care of that. I sent word to Admiral Laney. There'll be two cruisers waiting for that scout that will grab it before it ever reaches Earth."

Birrel looked at him, and then he looked at Joe Garstang, who stared back strickenly.

"He took care of it," said Garstang. He spoke a profane word. "He took care of it fine."

"What's the matter with you two?" demanded Mallinson. "You wanted that scout captured—its commander will know where the squadrons of Orion are. This way we make sure of capturing it."

Again, Birrel had to master his anger before he spoke. He said slowly,

"Look, Mallinson. You know a lot more about some things than I do, but you don't know navy or you'd never have sent that order. It will destroy any chance of capturing the scout."

"Why will it? It can't get away from our cruisers."

Birrel nodded grimly. "No, the scout can't get away. And its captain knows Orion's attack plan, and he will know that if he surrenders it'll be probed out of him. So what will he do?"

Mallinson thought about that, and the angry flush on his face began to fade.

"He'll fight," Birrel continued. "Suicidal, of course—but no officer would let himself be captured and give away a whole, big operation like this one."

He said nothing more, for a moment. He gave Mallinson time for it to sink in. And it did. Almost imperceptibly, Mallinson's expression changed from tough self-confidence to worry.

Again, when he spoke, the young bureaucrat surprised Birrel. He said levelly,

"I can see I made a mistake. What do you suggest?"

"Call off your fleet," Birrel said instantly. "Let that scout come through. We'll find Tauncer's flitter and turn on its homing-beam and the scout will land here. Then we'll grab them, and if we can take their captain alive the probe will get out of him what we want to know. How many men have you got here?"

"Six," said Mallinson. "I could call more, but it might be too late now—"

Birrel glanced at the windows. The twilight was deepening into darkness now.

"It's a lot too late," he said, and added bitingly, "You had plenty of time to call them when I was blacked out, if you'd been thinking. We'll have to do with what we have. Joe and Vathis and I make three more—ten against fifteen or sixteen in the scout. Not bad odds, if we can surprise them."

Mallinson said, "I'll call the fleet and have the two cruisers recalled. The porto's in my car."

He hurried out, and Birrel got hold of Garstang's arm and dragged himself to his feet. Lyllin came to support him on the other side, and he walked shufflingly back and forth across the lamplit room between them, feeling his motor-centers regain control of his limbs. But his head still felt as big as a balloon, and all painful.

He said finally, "I'm all right now." But Garstang and Lyllin kept close to him as he walked unsteadily out onto the porch.

It was full darkness now, but the west wind was blowing the clouds off in scattered tatters. Stars were showing, and among them he saw the blue flare of Vega. He thought of Ferdias

there. He thought what a mess of things he had made here and what Ferdias would say about that.

Mallinson's men—a knot of dark figures—were gathered out by his car in the lane. Mallinson came hurrying back to the porch.

"We're ready to start hunting for that flitter. You've got shockers?" Then, as he made out Lyllin in the darkness, "Hadn't your wife better get out of here?"

Birrel had been looking off into the darkness, back toward the slightly deeper shadow that was all that could be seen of the ragged woods behind the fields. He had been thinking.

"Wait, Mallinson," he said. "I've been in that woods, a little. We could flounder around in it all night without finding Tauncer's flitter. All we know is that he landed it in a small clearing and pushed it under trees. We need a guide to find it. If we can force Harper to lead us to it—"

Mallinson interrupted, and his voice was unhappy. "I sent Tauncer and Harper down to New York under guard, while you were still out. I supposed we'd be following them right away."

Birrel would have liked to swear again but, with time running out, he could not afford the luxury. He said, after a moment,

"Then that's out. But we still need a guide. There's a neighbor just down the road—a man named Vinson—who should know those woods. We'll go get him."

He took hold of Lyllin's hand and led her down off the porch with him. "You're going too, Lyllin. You can stay in Vinson's house a little while."

It was one of the few times he had ever given Lyllin a direct order. She would do anything for him, but she would not be ordered. For an instant she hung back, but then she came quietly along. Her pride was such that she would not make a scene about it, but he felt that he would hear about it later.

Mallinson drove, barrelling the car dangerously fast down the narrow road. Above the bordering trees, the stars gleamed all across the sky. Whatever else Earth might or might not have, Birrel thought sourly, it certainly had capricious weather.

When they pulled into the lane beside Vinson's big stone farmhouse, Birrel saw that the lights inside were dimmed. But, almost at once, Vinson and his wife came out onto a side stoop, while from behind them the bright, artificial dialogue of a Tri-V program continued to chatter.

"Why, it's Commander Birrel," said Vinson. "And his wife. Hi, neighbor! Come right on in—"

"There's a little trouble," Birrel interrupted. "I wonder if Lyllin could stay here with your wife an hour or so? And I want to talk to you."

Vinson's wife enveloped Lyllin like a motherly hen and bustled her into the house. Vinson, looking puzzled, came down off the step.

"This is Ross Mallinson, secretary to John Charteris," Birrel told him. "Listen, you know the woods behind our fields?"

Vinson goggled, and Birrel had to repeat the question before he answered.

"Why, sure. But what—?"

Birrel told him, as rapidly and concisely as he could. Presently Vinson went back up onto the step and called and his wife came out.

"What's the trouble?" she asked. "I was asking Mrs. Birrel, but she—"

Vinson interrupted her, saying in a wondering, half-incredulous tone, "They say a war may start. And the first fighting is going to be right here, tonight."

"Don't worry, I only need your husband to guide us in the woods," Birrel told the woman. "I'll send him back before anything happens."

Vinson suddenly spoke in a loud and emphatic tone. "The hell you'll send me back! This is my world, same as yours. I've got an old hunting-shocker. Back in a minute."

He raced into the house, with his wife hurrying after him, and, in the splash of dim light from the window, Mallinson looked at Birrel and said ironically, "His world, the same as yours."

Birrel shrugged. "I'm a local boy in a way, remember?"

Vinson came running out, carrying an old shocker of nonlethal type, and climbed into the back of the car. As they rocked back along the country road, he talked excitedly.

"There's three—maybe four—little clearings back there where a flitter could set down. But one of them hasn't got any trees near it that would be big enough to hide a flitter under."

"Then forget that one and take us to the others, as fast as you can," said Birrel, as the car slewed sharply into the lane where Mallinson's men and Garstang and Vathis were waiting.

Mallinson started to lead the whole group back toward the fields and the woods beyond, but Birrel hung back.

"Wait a minute," he said. "Tauncer had a heavy-duty sonic shocker and we'll need that. It's in the bushes—"

One of the dark figures interrupted. "We found that. We have it."

"All right, then, let's move," said Birrel. He felt a little better about their prospects. Mallinson's men—UW security agents, he supposed—seemed to know their business.

Vinson led as they tramped back across the ragged fields, their feet crushing the Queen Anne's Lace and ironweed and tall grass, their knees raked by blackberry briars. They had no light, but the stars were out and, after a little while, Birrel's night vision cleared and he could make out the dark, low wall of the woods just ahead of them.

He turned sharply as from the north came an eerie sound of barking that sounded like witch-laughter.

"Just a fox," said Vinson. "This way. Past that big clump of sumac."

The field had been dark, but the woods were a tangled darkness. There was brush that tripped them, and thorn-apple trees, whose sharp spikes clawed at their faces. They made as little noise as possible, but, when Vinson stopped to get his bearings and they all stopped behind him, sudden silence was a sharp contrast.

This was, Birrel thought, a devil of a way to begin the long-feared, long-awaited struggle with Orion. Not out in open space, not in some mighty cluster of suns, as he had always supposed the first real clash would come. No, it had to be here in the nighted woods on this old planet, fossicking about amid thorns and briars and brush, with a farmer to guide them.

Tiny insects he could not see in the darkness hummed and buzzed in his ear and he felt himself stung in face and hands as by small needles. One of the Earthmen swore under his breath and then was silent.

"Over here," said Vinson. "Got lost for a minute—don't often come here in the dark."

His voice was high and excited, though he tried to keep it down. He led them through a mass of tall weeds, a sort of brushy meadow, into a grove of big trees.

"No," he said after a moment. "There's no flitter here."

"Try the other places," Mallinson said. "And hurry."

They worked through more brush, splashed rather noisily across a small stream, and finally emerged into another clearing of high weeds.

"Wait," said Vinson's voice suddenly from ahead.

"Anything?" asked Mallinson sharply.

"The sumac and milkweed are all crushed down here. Let me look."

They waited, fighting the tiny, stinging insects, while Vinson moved off into the darkness. They heard him groping and fumbling, and then heard nothing.

Birrel's headache, which he had almost forgotten during the urgency of the search, returned to plague him. It made him feel irritable. When Garstang slapped his cheek and muttered, he turned to tell him to shut up. But he did not, there was no use in taking his headache out on Joe.

There were rapid, heavy footsteps and Vinson came blundering back out of the darkness. His voice was a high, triumphant whisper.

"Found it! Over in that grove of beeches—they set down here and hauled it under cover—"

Mallinson cut him off. "Take us to it."

In the shadows, beneath huge trees that had curiously smooth bark, the light flitter gleamed dully. Mallinson said, "Kane!" The man who had operated the probe hurried forward and got into the open cockpit of the flitter and squatted down. There was the gleam of a small light, quickly hooded.

After what seemed a very long few minutes, Kane spoke up.

"It's here. Simple oscillator to send out a beam that'll be almost entirely masked by the ordinary Tri-V frequencies. It's a clever—"

"Never mind that," Mallinson interrupted. "Turn it on."

They heard nothing, saw nothing, but Kane presently scrambled out of the flitter. "It's on."

Mallinson looked around and then after a moment he said, "Birrel."

Birrel stepped closer to him. "Yes."

"You know what this Orionid scout will be like and what it will do, better than we," said Mallinson. "Will you set up the ambush?"

"Do I give the orders in the attack?"

"Yes. Of course."

"All right," said Birrel. "Let's go back to that clearing. That's where the scout will come down."

In the starlit, brushy, open space, he stopped and tried to figure. Posting the men strategically around the meadow was not difficult, but it was the heavy-duty shocker that worried him. They were going to have to rely on it a lot, and they would not have time to bundle it around much.

He finally kept Garstang and the shocker with him, at a point on the edge of the clearing nearest the hidden flitter. Mallinson stayed with him as a matter of course and he retained Vinson, too—he was afraid that, in his excitement, Vinson would give the whole show away.

They squatted down beside the shocker, then.

They waited.

16

AT THREE MINUTES and fourteen seconds before midnight a small, fast spacecraft, with the insigne of the striding warrior on her bows, dropped down out of the starlight like a humming shadow. It could not have been heard far by human ears, but the farm dogs up and down the valley heard it and set up a startled barking. The scout came down, landed in the brushy meadow and was silent. And presently the distant dogs also fell silent.

Birrel stood up, whispering as he did so to Garstang, who remained crouched with the heavy shocker, beside Vinson and Mallinson.

"All right, you know what to do, and for God's sake make it fast when you move."

He walked boldly out into the dark meadow. The scout lay black and brooding, its fish-tailed bulk a vague, darker silhouette against the brambles and weeds and pale, white blossoms of Queen Anne's Lace. Birrel stepped toward it, and as he did so he took out a tiny pocket-lamp and flashed it briefly, once.

He was sweating now. If Tauncer had arranged a specific recognition signal, he would be cut down before he took ten more steps. He had to gamble on the chance that the homing-

beam from the flitter would be the only signal. It had seemed like a good gamble, until now. Now it did not seem so good.

Several eternities went by while he took four more steps forward. Then there was a familiar grinding sound and a door in the side of the scout opened, showing, inside it, a small airlock, illuminated by the faintest of blue light.

Birrel swallowed hard. His gamble had paid off. He was going to live—but maybe only two minutes more, if things went wrong.

A uniformed man appeared in the faint, blue light of the airlock, and stood in a waiting attitude. That would be the captain of the scout-vessel, Birrel thought—he surely would be there to meet Tauncer on a mission so important as this one. He did not see anyone else, but he knew very well that one crewman would be standing just inside, at the airlock panel.

Birrel walked forward in the darkness. He raised his voice, in as good an imitation of Tauncer's as he could muster, speaking in sharp complaint.

"You should have been earlier! Don't show any lights—we've got to get out of here fast!"

"Earlier?" said the man in the airlock. "Why, you said yourself—"

Birrel drew the shocker from his pocket and let go with it, at eight paces distance. The man who was speaking shut up and fell.

Now was the time, the decisive moment. Birrel ran forward the few yards to the airlock, his feet almost tripping in the briars. He ran into the lock just as an Orionid crewman with an incredulous expression on his face stepped in from the other side, staring at the officer lying on the floor. Birrel dropped him with a burst from the shocker and leaped over him as he fell, heading for the inner door.

His luck suddenly ran out. There was another crewman in the corridor, just beyond the lock panel, and he was drawing his side-arm. Birrel fired and ducked. He did not duck fast enough and the burst from the other's shocker grazed his right side and that whole part of his body went numb and he started to fall.

He would not fall, damn it! He lurched against the smooth metal wall, leaning to support himself. The shocker had fallen from his hand, and, while he had dropped the man in the corridor, he could hear voices, somewhere beyond, now raised in

alarm. Where were Garstang and the others? What were they doing out there, anyway?

Then he heard them in the darkness outside, thrashing like cows through the brush and high grass. He also heard an alarm siren go off forward in the scout. He ought to do something, to move, but, for the moment, he was as helpless as an old woman, leaning against the wall and trying not to fall down on the unconscious man, who had done this to him.

Garstang and Vinson came pounding into the lock, carrying the heavy shocker between them. Garstang looked professionally worried, but Vinson was the excited amateur at fighting, his eyes popping.

"Get it in here!" Birrel said. He meant to shout it, but his voice came out as a croak.

The big shocker was no more use in the airlock than it would have been from outside. Even a small scout had enough shielding in its hull to stop stuff like this, and the shielding in any ship was continued through the inner wall of its airlock.

"Are you hurt?" said Vinson. "What—"

Garstang said, "Come *on!*" He hauled Vinson after him, the heavy squat machine precariously carried between them, past Birrel and the sprawled figure on the floor.

He slammed the thing down on the floor, with its projection-grid facing down the corridor, and flipped the switch. As though they had timed it for that, two men, who wore the striding warrior on their jackets, popped into the farther end of the corridor. They had weapons in their hands, but did not use them. They seemed to skate and slide majestically forward before they crumpled up under the soundless and invisible blast.

With an effort, Birrel croaked to Garstang, "Sweep it, Joe, what's the matter with you?"

"The damn thing's heavy, didn't you know?" panted Garstang. The shocker was still on, still humming, and Garstang was trying to pivot it around so that its blast would sweep the interior of the whole scout, through the light bulkheads that could not shield against it. Vinson was trying to help him, but he did not understand exactly what Garstang was doing and he was more hindrance than help. Birrel tried to get down to help, but his numbed leg instantly gave way under him and he sat down and thought what a ridiculous leader he made, sitting here on his backside, in the corridor. Then, as Mallinson's men came running in from outside, he got his voice enough to yell at them,

"Help Garstang!"

Kane understood instantly what Garstang was doing. He sprang forward, shoving Vinson out of the way, and grabbed one side of the big shocker. He and Garstang rocked and tilted the heavy thing.

In the farther parts of the scout-craft there was bedlam going on, a sound of things breaking and men's voices raised in inarticulate cries. A tall man, with a lieutenant's tabs on his shoulders, came at a staggering run into the passage. Vinson raised his old shocker, but there was no need, the man fell and lay still. Birrel, struggling to scramble again to his feet, felt the metal floor and walls quivering with the jarring force that was blasting through the whole ship.

He said in a moment, "That should be enough. Shut it off and go on in. You help me, Vinson."

Garstang and Kane and the rest of Mallinson's men went down the corridor in a rush. Mallinson himself was behind Birrel, looking a little white-lipped, as though violence was a new and upsetting thing to him, but looking determined, also.

Vinson was shaking a little as he helped Birrel up and steadied him with a husky arm. He kept babbling,

"Have we done it? Have we taken the ship?"

"Depends if the big shocker caught them in time," said Birrel. "Help me forward."

There were sounds from forward and overhead, men's voices calling, but whether they were the voices of Mallinson's men or of Orionids he did not know.

"Up this companionway," he told Vinson. "Damn this leg!"

Vinson and Mallinson helped boost him up the companionway and Birrel could not help thinking what a totally unheroic leader of an attack force he made. "I should have a sword to wave," he thought disgustedly.

Up in the communications room behind the bridge of the scout, two of the Orionid crew lay sprawled where they had fallen from their chairs. There were splinters of glass and plastic where the sonic wave had shattered equipment.

"The question is, did it stop these communic men in time?" said Birrel. "If they got a flash off to their parent squadrons—"

Mallinson ran back out of the room, shouting for Kane. When the technician came, he was puffing and looked excited and triumphant.

"I think we've swept the craft," he said. "Two men still half-conscious, but they couldn't do anything. The boys are searching—"

Mallinson interrupted. "Look at this communic stuff. Was a message being sent when we hit them?"

Kane lost some of his excitement and went over and started to examine the bank of controls in front of the two empty chairs. They waited, Birrel leaning heavily on Vinson.

Kane said finally, "No. The settings show they didn't even have a carrier wave on yet."

"All right," said Birrel. "You'd better secure all prisoners before they come around. Mallinson, you might look through the log, though I doubt you'll find anything there to help us. What we need to know is probably in that captain's brain and nowhere else."

As Mallinson nodded and hurried out, Birrel turned to Vinson. "Help me into one of those chairs."

Vinson, as he did so, said excitedly, "We did all right, didn't we?"

Birrel looked at him and managed to grin. "We did fine. You did fine."

Joe Garstang, still sweating from his exertions, came in. He said, "Those lads weren't playing, their shockers were all set on lethal. It's a good thing you only caught a graze."

"I've had enough good things tonight to last me," Birrel said sourly. "Rub my side."

Garstang did so, and, after a number of minutes, the stunned nerves recovered enough so that Birrel could stand on his own. With Vinson and Garstang, he limped back down through the scout to the airlock. The Orionid captain, senseless as a log, was propped in a sitting position against the wall and two of Mallinson's men were watching him.

Birrel looked at him for a moment. Then he went outside. It was somehow astonishing, after the noise and fighting and running inside the ship, to find that the dark woods were as silent as ever. The breeze blew soft with the unfamiliar smells of Earth, and far away, across the starlit valley, a farm dog was still yelping querulously.

Birrel took the porto out of his pocket and talked into it for a few minutes. Then he put it back, and limped back to the blue-lighted airlock.

Mallinson was there now. "Not a thing in the papers." He

glanced at the unconscious Orionid captain. "But he'll know how and when those squadrons plan to come. We'll get him down to New York and probe him there, fast."

Birrel nodded. "I'll go with you. I've just called my squadron. The Fifth is going on Alert."

Mallinson looked up sharply. "Oh, no. Not without Council sanction. I've made it clear that we don't trust Lyra one bit more than Orion, and it will be up to the Council whether you're allowed to act in this."

"Council be damned," Birrel said. "My squadron is not going to be caught flatfooted. Our scouts will take off in an hour. Our light cruisers in two."

Mallinson said grimly, "If any of your ships attempt to take off without permission, they'll be hit by our missiles."

"They will take off," Birrel said. "You can accept that as a constant in your calculations. You'd better get on to Charteris and tell him so and have him send new orders to those missile-batteries."

Mallinson looked at him, and then a fine sweat began to come out on his forehead. He said, "I can't do that."

"If you don't," Birrel said unyieldingly, "you'll have a first-class battle with the Fifth right there on the spaceport. You may clobber us. But if you do, all Solleremos' squadrons will have to do is come in and pick up the pieces."

Mallinson's control snapped and he gave way to a white anger. "You think, because there's a crisis, you can issue ultimatums—"

Birrel broke in harshly. "The ultimatum was yours. And I'm calling it. Get one thing straight. The Fifth is not going to be caught down. I'll repeat that. *The Fifth is not going to be caught down!*"

Whatever was in his voice finally got through to Mallinson. He looked at Birrel, a look of trapped frustration and pure dislike.

"I'll call Charteris," he said finally. "It'll be up to him."

Birrel nodded. "I'd make it all very clear to him, if I were you."

He went back out into the soft darkness, and Vinson and Garstang followed him. He said to Vinson,

"You don't mind my wife staying with you a little? I don't want her alone here."

"Lord, no, she's welcome," said Vinson. "But you—"

"I'll be busy for a while," said Birrel, and added, "One way or another."

Now began hurried movement around the scout. Kane's voice could be heard ordering some of the men to get flitters and bring them to this place, giving others instructions for the securing of the senseless men inside the scout.

Birrel waited.

Mallinson finally came to him.

"Well?"

"I told Charteris," said Mallinson. "It's up to him. If he considers Lyra a bigger threat than Orion, your ships will be hit when they take off."

Joe Garstang said a coarse word. "In my eye! You won't take on us and Solleremos too!"

Mallinson said nothing to that. He said stiffly to Birrel, "You're to return with us to New York. The flitters will be here in a minute."

He strode away, and looking at his stiff, unyielding back, Birrel wished he was as confident as Garstang. There was an obstinacy about these Earthmen that he was beginning to recognize, and it worried him so deeply that, for a moment, he considered calling Brescnik and cancelling his order.

No. Somewhere, out there in the starry sky, Solleremos' sneak strike must be on its way, and no one knew how near. The Fifth was going out to meet it, even if it had to fight its way out.

17

No MISSILE HAD been fired.

The scouts of the Fifth had taken off, and later the light cruisers, and the deadly launchers that ringed New York spaceport had remained silent. Now the scouts were well outside the system of Sol, quartering like restless hounds, while the light cruisers moved, in tight formation and at reduced speed, beyond the big ball of poison-and-ice that was called Saturn, all of them waiting for orders.

Birrel was beginning to think that there would be no orders for anyone, if the argument went on much longer. He had been

in this room high in the UW tower for almost an hour, expostulating, pleading, reasoning, and he had got nowhere. He was tired. His head still ached and his side was still half-numb. He was not sleepy, pills had taken care of that, but he felt sore and worn out. He was beginning to have a conviction that Earthmen were foredoomed by their own pigheadedness and that it would bloody well serve them right.

He looked along the table and saw hard unfriendliness and distrust in every face. Not only in the faces of Charteris and Mallinson but also in those of old Admiral Laney and his staff. He could understand politicians being stupid enough to sit around a table and gabble, even in a crisis like this. He could not understand naval officers doing such a thing. No wonder, he thought, bitterly, that the United Worlds had failed to maintain its sway, if this was the way it had faced up to crises.

"The answer, again, is no," Charteris said stonily. "The Fifth Lyra will act under UW command, or it will not act at all."

"It's not a question of command," said Birrel. "It's a question of strategy."

"We will determine the strategy," Charteris said.

Birrel pushed his chair back and got up from the table. He repressed the things he wanted to say. He turned his back on them and went over to the window and looked out, fighting for self-control. If he blew his stack now, they were all in trouble.

It was two-forty-five in the morning, but the streets of the old city still glowed with vari-colored light, stretching away beneath the UW tower like a vast gridiron of gleaming lines. The pleasure places would be jammed again with the crowds that had flocked here for the commemoration. They had not the faintest idea what this commemoration was going to be like. Not one word of the situation had gone out in the newscasts.

Just as well, Birrel thought. These Earth folk would not believe it anyway, they were so armored in obstinate pride. They thought of their world as the start of everything, the fountainhead, and they resented the fact that the outer worlds had fallen away, they disliked the Sectors. But they had never dreamed that one of the Sectors might turn against them, any more than a father dreams that his children may turn and attack him. Well, in a way, it was a true analogy. That thought took some of the rage out of Birrel and he turned back to the hostile, silent group around the table.

He went past them to the big depth-chart of the Solar system and its immediate stellar environs, which filled the whole end of the room. Sol and its planets and the nearer stars were perfectly projected, so that, when Birrel stepped into the chart, he was like a giant shouldering through the galaxy.

There was a line of red light in the chart, beginning out in the direction of Scorpio and extended toward Sol. The captured Orionid captain of the scout had talked, under the probe. The big computers two floors down had taken the coordinates he had yielded, and had extrapolated from them to show the approximate course of the two squadrons that were coming. The red line was like a dagger pointed at Earth's heart.

"They've made a long circle around," Birrel said. "They're coming in from directly opposite the direction of Orion, the least expected direction—"

Admiral Laney interrupted. "We've gone over that. We'll meet them. But this is the UW's fight and your squadron will obey UW orders, if it goes with us."

Birrel looked into the old admiral's frosty eyes and said, and meant it,

"Sir, I would be proud to fight under you. But facts are facts. The UW fleet, no matter how long and honorable its history, cannot meet and match an Orionid squadron. This is a fact. Another fact is that there are few miracles in warfare. If your fleet and the Fifth meet the Orionids head-on, the odds are that we'll lose. I am just as proud of the Fifth Lyra as you are of your fleet and its traditions, but I still say we'll lose. We've only one chance to even the odds and that is surprise."

"Surprise, in these days of long-range radar?" said an officer incredulously.

"It can be done," Birrel said steadily. "It has been done, more than once, out in the fringe-clusters between the Sectors."

He turned around to the depth-chart again and pointed to a blurred and speckled area lying between the orbits of Mars and Jupiter.

"Here you seem to have a natural *chevaux-de-frise*, to borrow an ancient term. I'd like to make use of it. Do you know your way around in it?"

"The Asteroid Belt?" said Laney. "Yes, we know it."

"If you could bait the Orionids in there, entangle them in the drift—" Birrel began.

The old admiral interrupted. "Do you suppose that they're that simple? To follow us in there, knowing that the Fifth Lyra is somewhere on their flank?"

"They won't know that, if we can work it right," Birrel said earnestly. He left the chart and came back to the table. "The Fifth's heavy cruisers will take off. Presently long-range radar will show the whole Fifth heading outside this system toward Orion as though to intercept a possible direct attack from that direction."

"But—"

"But it won't be the Fifth they range," Birrel continued. "An equal number of ships—merchant-freighters, ore-tubs, anything you can grab together fast, will assemble beyond your fifth planet and move out *impersonating* the Fifth. Long-range radar can't tell the difference. And half of our fast scouts will go with this dummy squadron to keep Orionid scouts from getting close enough to use short-range radar."

Charteris looked at Laney, a question.

"It might be done," said Laney. "The dummy squadron, I mean. Let's have the rest of it."

"Simple," said Birrel. "Your UW fleet baits the Orionids so that at least a significant portion of their strength is tangled in the drift. The Fifth Lyra—" he strode back to the chart, his hand plunging in just above the gleaming globe of Sol—"will be lying up here, effectively masked from radar. When you have them hooked—"

He made a downward, slashing motion with his hand.

Charteris looked again at the admiral. "Well?"

Laney grudgingly admitted, "It might work."

"Do you formally recommend it as a plan of defensive action?"

Laney did not equivocate now. "Yes."

"Very well," said Charteris, and Birrel began to breathe a little more easily, and then he heard Charteris saying, "But the Council ruling still applies, the Fifth Lyra will be under your direct command, Admiral."

Birrel gave up. He had done his best to convince them and it had not been good enough, and that was that. But then he heard Laney saying to the chairman,

"No. In an operation like this, the Fifth Lyra will have to have independent command. You just can't coordinate such a

strike by prearranged order, and direct communication with the Lyrans won't be possible in their radar-hide."

Charteris looked dubious. "If you say so—"

"I do say so."

Charteris stood up. "I have to have full Council approval for this. They're waiting."

He went out. Birrel looked at Laney, but the admiral's eyes were as hard and unfriendly as they had been and he did not say "Thanks" as he had intended.

"The Council will approve," Laney said brusquely. "I suggest we get down to working it out."

Two hours later, Birrel rode with Garstang in a fast car that took them through the city, heading for the spaceport. The canyoned streets were dark and quiet now, the old metropolis slept. There was little traffic and the car hummed between the dark towers toward the river, waking echoes.

Birrel still could not quite believe that this was it, the start of the long-feared clash between Lyra and Orion. Both Sectors were so far away that their stars were mere points of light in the sky of this ancient, sleeping city. And again he thought that even when things you expected happened, they never happened in the way you expected.

He was tired and he was getting sleepy as the pills wore off, but he had to snap out of it when they reached the spaceport. The looming black hulls of the big cruisers were alive. Men went up and down the gangways, orders were bawled over the sound of cars that dashed between the ships.

In the bridge of the *Starsong*, he went over it with Brescnik and Hallet, the third in command.

"That's about it," he finished. "Anything?"

Brescnik showed his teeth in a mirthless smile. "Only that your choice of an ambush hide is going to make it plenty interesting, even before things begin."

Birrel stood up. "It will. Lift out when you get the word from UW's staff, they'll time it with the dummy squadron's movements. I'm going to get some sleep."

Northward, the fields around Orville brightened with a new day. In the meadow, behind the Vinson house, Lyllin stood, shivering a little in the slight chill, looking to the south and listening. A flitter buzzed across the sky to the west, but there was nothing else. Then a far-off roll of thunder crossed the

sky. She knew that thunder and what made it. She listened, as one thunder-roll after another pulsed and muttered.

She had had one short call from Birrel. *Wait there, I'll come back.* Now the muttering thunder in the south seemed like the receding footsteps of everything she had ever loved, passing out over the distant hills.

She turned slowly, and went back into the house.

18

THE SKY SCREAMED light. The sun, Sol, its atoms ceaselessly riven and then reborn, shrieked raving energy, magnetism, electricity, light, radiant heat, a rage across the heavens, a cosmic storm, flinging up wild plumes and spindrift of violet calcium, of yellow sodium, of blue and green and red flame.

Over it, as over a limitless fiery ocean, hung the shoal of silver ships. Tossed and twitched by storms of radiation, wrenched by the claws of the titan magnetic field, scorched by the blaze of the star that sought to overcome their shielding, the ships of the Fifth fought to hold position. Their formation wavered, sagged, reformed and wavered again, and still they held together, fighting against the star.

The flagship, the *Starsong*, had it a little easier. It was much higher above the sun, far enough out from the storm of force so that its long-range radar functioned, at least partially. By that same token, it could be ranged by radar, while the squadron, though itself blind radarwise, could not be ranged.

Birrel sat in the communic-room of the *Starsong*, eating a sandwich. He did not want it, his stomach was tight with tension and he was not hungry at all, but he had learned long ago that if a commander showed excitement in a tight situation everyone under him would let his own excitement ride him. He chewed his sandwich and watched stolidly as Garstang and Venner hung over the big radar-screens that yielded an approximation of the results of long-range radar information, in a form most quickly comprehended.

Garstang swore. "Out again."

The screens had suddenly all blazed a useless white, even the powerful rays that served them wrenched and cut by a

sudden outburst of solar activity. The ship shuddered and rocked momentarily.

"There's nothing yet anyway," said Birrel. He thought, My God, what a fake I am, I'm the most jumpy man in the squadron and I have to sit here and pretend. He wanted to jump up and run to the screens, but he forced himself to sit still and finish the sandwich. Already it was giving him a gut-ache.

He got up then and walked over to the screens. They had come back on again, but they did not show much.

One was ranged west and zenith. It showed a swarm of tiny flecks moving far outside the System of Sol, heading out in the direction of the star Saiph. It looked for all the world like a full naval squadron, with its scouts out screening it, its light cruisers flanking the central heavy columns. Birrel hoped it looked that way to the Orionids. Only the scouts were for real, the rest of that swarm was merchant ships, ore-freighters, everything the UW had been able to gather together and throw out as a dummy. If Orionid scouts got close enough to use short-range radar and detect the imposture, it was going to be their last flight.

He looked at another screen. That one plotted the rim of the asteroid belt, a blur of dots that were rock fragments, dust, pebbles, the streams of debris between Mars and Jupiter. Beyond the rim of that stony jungle, five ships moved slowly, behaving like a normal patrol. The remainder of the UW fleet was hidden among the asteroids and no radar could detect them there.

"Why don't they come?" fretted Garstang. "Do you suppose that captain had it wrong? That plans were changed?"

The screens suddenly blazed white again. The *Starsong* shuddered and heeled as the wave of solar electricity overloaded and affected relays in its control system. The automatic corrections in the circuits functioned almost instantly, and the fabric of the vessel stopped shivering.

Birrel shrugged. "We should soon know."

"It had better be soon," muttered Garstang. "The boys can't sit on that star forever."

The storms of force that intermittently rocked the *Starsong* were bad enough. But on the squadron, hiding much closer to the solar corona, it must be rougher. A lot rougher. Brescnik had so far kept them together, but neither ships nor men could take that sort of thing for too long. Birrel, watching the screens

with perfectly faked stolidity, prayed inwardly for the Orionids to come.

They did not. Time passed. He began to sweat. He did not think he could keep up this pretense of calm much longer.

Suddenly Venner caught Garstang's shoulder. "There!" he said. He leaned forward and pointed his forefinger at the screen.

Out of the depths toward Scorpio came a swarm of tiny flecks that might have been nothing more than bits of cosmic drift. They moved together, very fast. They swept in toward the System of Sol with a rush and they came almost exactly on the course that that red dagger in the chart had foretold. Two full squadrons of Solleremos' fleet, on planetary approach.

The five UW ships on patrol, out beyond the Belt, abruptly wheeled around in perfect formation and moved out to meet them.

Birrel's mouth was dry. Runnels of sweat crept down his temples, down his body. The palms of his hands were clammy.

The *Starsong* rocked again and Garstang uttered an oath. The radar was out again, the screens were blank. Then they cleared.

The five UW ships had not gone far out. Suddenly they wheeled again, seemingly abandoning formation. But Birrel knew they were running a firing pattern and his fists·clenched tight. The five leaped in formation again and cracked on speed and ran back toward the Belt.

One in the great swarm of flecks, one of the Orionid cruisers, vanished silently from the screen.

Garstang shouted, and, as though at a signal, the screen went out again.

Birrel ran his uniform sleeve over his face, and kept still. There were so few of the UW ships, and so many of the others, something more than double the strength of his own squadron. Far below, Earth lay naked, stripped, utterly without defense. Birrel thought of Lyllin, and the old house with the dusty road in front of it. He thought of the dark woods and the meadow where they had fought in the night, and curiously enough he thought of the cat. Insolent little beast . . .

He waited for the screens to clear, and watched.

A number of Orionid ships detached themselves from the main fleet and raced after the UW patrol. They were much faster, they could only be light cruisers, S-4s. The long arm

of Solleremos was reaching swiftly now, and one of the UW ships winked off the screen. The other four reached the Belt.

The Orionid advance plunged in after them.

"Now," whispered Garstang. "Now—now—"

The eight Orionid light cruisers apparently detailed to mop up this patrol sped down a deceptively open "lead" through the asteroid drift. The lead pinched out in a cul-de-sac of radar-specks that were actually wildly gyrating rocks. The Orion cruisers did a fast about, practically on each other's heels, but, before they were finished, the four UW ships and nearly a dozen others appeared from nowhere all around them, coming into view on the screen as they left the radar shelter of the asteroids they had perilously hugged.

"Hit them," muttered Garstang. "Oh, hell, get onto it and *hit* them!"

They hit them. Of a sudden, in quick succession, two of the UW ships and five of the Orionids vanished off the screen.

"That hurt them," said Birrel, and unclenched his fists. "They're hooked—"

Garstang turned and looked at him and then picked up the mike of the intercom. He did not speak into it, he looked at Birrel and waited. Birrel bent forward, his eyes on the screen.

Down there in the Asteroid Belt, the trap had been sprung. And now the Orionids knew they had the whole UW fleet, such as it was, to deal with—a force too small to stop them, but too formidable to leave on their flank and rear. All depended on their movements now. If they had been fooled by the dummy Fifth that had gone out, they would move one way and, if they had not, they would move another.

An anguish grew in Birrel as the swarm of specks that were the main body of the Orionid squadrons came on. The strata-gem had been too transparent, too clumsy. He should have known that and yet he had talked Laney and Charteris into it, and—

He held his breath. The swarm of flecks was changing pattern, and altering course. They heavy central columns of the Orionid squadrons were forming into a cone-shaped formation that moved toward the UW ships which hovered, in apparent doubt, above the fringes of the drift. The heavy cone moved in to make contact, with its cloud of scouts driving furiously all around it like a thinner, larger outer cone.

Garstang was looking at him, almost pleadingly. No, thought Birrel. Not yet. Not quite yet.

He waited until the van scouts of the Orionids were five times missile-range from the drift. Then he nodded to Garstang.

"Commander to Vice-Commander," said Garstang rapidly. "Rejoin!"

The Fifth rejoined its flagship fast, glad to get farther from the glare and danger of Sol, and soon the ships came onto visual screens as well as radar.

Down there, at the fringe of the Belt, contact had been made. Dots were vanishing, faster and faster. Birrel's throat was dry. Nobody had ever fought a fleet action before, there had been individual cruiser-skirmishes out on the vague, stellar frontiers, but nothing like this. There was no precedent and the action-plan he had prepared could prove utterly foolish. Throw away your doubts and worries, he thought, you're hooked yourself now and there is only one thing you can do, so you might just as well be heroic about it.

He said, "All right, let's go down," and the Fifth Lyra swooped out of the sun.

19

IT SEEMED TO Birrel that they had been fighting by the Belt for several eternities.

But was this fighting? Standing here, in the bridge of the *Starsong*, and looking up at the screens, while the ship groaned and quivered like a living thing?

The screens showed dark space, with the torrents of rushing stone of the Belt only a distant, slanted blur across the upper sector, the blur slipping and heeling over as they changed course. Nothing but that and the occasional fleeting glint of polished metal as a neighboring ship in their column momentarily caught the light, and no sound, but the pounding throb of power.

Then far out, on the left of one screen, a blinding little nova burst into being. It flared, and died, and there was darkness

again and nothing to show that a ship had vanished in nuclear explosion.

"We're making contact again," said Garstang. Standing in the captain's place, his face was dark and still as iron, but with sweat shining on the edges of it. "Where the hell are those UW ships anyway?"

"Laney was hit hard," said Birrel. "We've got to keep punching while he regroups in the drift. He'll come out again soon."

He hoped.

He hated to go back to the radar room, where you could see nothing but flecks on a screen, but he had to, it was the commander's place in battle.

Battle? This was not battle the way he had envisaged it—this moving forward in parallel columns groping for an enemy who was using all his devices to blind and confuse radar, two forces clawing for advantageous position here, just outside the Belt's whirling jungle of drift.

It seemed like anti-climax, after their first attack. They had plunged down from their ambush above the Sun on full ultra-drive acceleration. Using ultra-drive in planetary neighborhoods was so risky as to approach the suicidal. But the Fifth had gone down on carefully plotted acceleration and deceleration schedules, first building up a terrific velocity and then instantly decelerating to a manageable speed. It had worked, the Orionids had not had time to disperse their formation in defensive evasion. The Fifth had crashed down through the middle of their line like a flying axe-blade.

It had been like that in Birrel's mental picture, but not like that in reality, there was no shock, no crash, the enemy ships hardly even saw each other. Even in their comparatively tight formation, the Orionids were separated by enough open space that the whole two columns of the Fifth had cut down between them without even a near-collision. Nevertheless they had hit the Orionids, and hit them hard, for their attack had been analogous to the classic, old sea-navy tactic of "crossing the T." The concentrated missile fire of Birrel's ships upon each end of the broken Orionid cone they raced through had been more than jamming-defenses could hold against. The missiles had smothered the ships closest them, as they raced past, and Solleremos had lost three heavy cruisers and two light ones right there.

On down, nadirwards from the shattered Orionid line, the Fifth had flashed around and formed in shorter columns spread out from each other and drove back up at the enemy. The UW ships had come boiling out of the Belt, like angry hornets, to hit them from the other side. It had looked as though it would be decided in minutes. It would have been, except for one thing—the Orionids knew how to fight, too.

They were still as strong as both the UW and Fifth together. Whoever commanded them knew his business. The UW ships were nearest, and the Orionids had slid into a front that faced the Belt and that turned all their fire on the hornets from that direction. It was more than the UW fleet could take, and, after losing four ships within seconds, Laney had pulled back into the Belt. Solleremos' commander had had just time enough to face around as the Fifth Lyra came up at him from nadir.

Birrel had been fanning out his columns to form the cone that would flank the ends of the Orionid formation, roll it up into a concentrated target. It was too late for that. With Laney knocked back to the Belt, he would have been "coned" himself if he had persisted. He had ordered them back into columns and had started a rapid-fire, one-two-three punching all along the line to keep the Orionids from maneuvering to envelop him.

He did not think he could keep punching this way for very long. Unless Laney came out of the drift and drew off at least a part of the superior forces facing him, it was only a matter of time until the heavier weight told.

Looking down at the shifting pattern on the radar screen, Birrel said sharply into his throat-mike,

"Brescnik is moving his column too wide. Tell him."

"Yes, sir." The communic officer's reply came thinly through the din. On the screen, in a moment, their left column drew back a little.

The *Starsong* creaked, shivered and jumped as it swerved this way and that on the evasive pattern it was following. The generators were droning in their highest key, furnishing every possible ounce of power for the missile-jamming broadcast that was their defensive armament.

"A C-22 in right column out, sir," said Venner.

A dot in the shifting pattern had disappeared. A ship of the Fifth Lyra and its crew had vanished in a flare, as a missile got through its jamming.

Birrel's eyes flew to that part of the screen and now he noticed a significant change in the pattern of the Orionid formation.

"They're shifting ships to smother the head of our right column," he said.

He hesitated, knowing this to be the pivotal crisis. The move could be a feint, inviting him to move forces to his right, so that the Orionids could suddenly smash at their weakened left and center. But if it wasn't a feint, their right would take an equally disastrous punch. What it came down to was that they were outnumbered and losing the initiative because of it. Where the hell were the UW ships? Laney had had time enough to regroup.

He set his teeth and gave the order. "Formations three and five to area sixteen—"

"*Sir!*" yelled Venner, interrupting.

Birrel swung on him furiously. To interrupt a commanding officer's orders during an action was so monstrous an offense, as to be incredible.

Venner did not seem to care. He pointed at the screen and babbled, "They're coming out—the UW—look at them!"

Laney had suddenly burst out of the shelter of the Belt. Those flying flecks, tight-bunched on the radar screen, were the UW's little fleet. Disregarding all defensive evasion tactics, it was careening at highest planetary speeds toward the left end of the Orionid formation.

The Orionid flecks shifted swiftly to form front and meet this reckless flank punch. But two of the flecks winked out as missiles hit them and through the gap in their formation Laney flung the UW fleet.

It was a suicidal attack that could not possibly persist for long against the superior Orionid weight. But it kept on going, the UW tight formation like a sword that was being thrust right into the bigger fleet. The Orionids started to bunch around that sword, to destroy it within the next few minutes by a concentrated missile fire that could not possibly be jammed.

But Birrel had instantly realized the one reason why Laney had made his desperate sortie. It was up to the Fifth to do the rest.

"Cone out!" he ordered into the mike that carried his voice to every ship in the Fifth.

The columns of the Fifth seemed to explode, on the radar

screen. They flew apart, the individual ships racing toward the bunched-up enemy and, at the same time, shifting into a new formation. The cone—a gigantic candle-snuffer speeding toward the Orionid mass.

The Orionid commander had not time enough to disengage with Laney and fan out defensively. The Fifth's cone was almost upon him. The Orionid ships recoiled from the threat, toward the edge of the Belt. The UW cruisers, hanging on like dogs to a bear, went with them.

The Fifth was committed, and Birrel ran out of the radar room to the bridge. The *Starsong* heeled over, its generators screaming now and its fabric shuddering, and Birrel pitched and stumbled into the bridge where the screens were now alive with light.

Garstang's face flashed, wild and sweaty. "We're crowding them into the Belt. They can't disengage in time—by God, look at those Earthmen!"

They were in such comparatively close contact now that the view-screens, drawing upon short-range radar to build their visual images, showed the whole scene.

The fight had barged into the fringes of the Belt. Drift was all around them, from particles of sand that tapped and banged and clattered against the *Starsong*'s hull, to massive boulders that came at them like juggernauts of stone. The automatic proximity-warnings kept up a schizophrenic screeching in the calc-room, and their imperative orders to the control-relays constantly contravened the human helmsman. All around them the ships of the Fifth were similarly floundering, weewawing, and then pressing forward again in a staggering, crazy battle. The Orionids, drawing back as they frantically sought to re-form, were even more deeply entangled in the drift and could not re-form.

Witch-fires of unholy brilliance began to flare here and there through the tangle, great bloomings of nuclear flame that paled the stars and then winked out. Birrel, appalled, thought at first that both sides must be losing ships at an incredible rate. Then he glimpsed a fifty-ton boulder, that came whirling down on the *Starsong*, suddenly explode in a white fury that blanked out all the screens. It had been hit by a missile, and that Orionid missile had undoubtedly been intended for their ship.

"Those aren't ships that are getting hit—most of the hits are

on the drift," muttered Garstang. "How the devil can you fight in a mess like this?"

"Laney and his boys are doing it," Birrel said. "Keep pressing them."

Starships—the majestic giants of the far galaxy intended to operate in the endless parsecs of deep space—were out of their element in the Belt. That went for the Fifth Lyra as well as their enemy. The smaller, old-fashioned UW ships had an advantage here in maneuvering, and they were taking it to the full.

They couldn't stay in here, Birrel thought. They'd all smash up, something had to give, to break—

The Orionids did.

There was no change in the wild confusion on the visual view-screens, but Venner yelled suddenly from the radar room. Birrel ran back there.

"Pulling up zenithward," babbled Venner. "Look, they—"

Birrel saw for himself. Ceasing their futile efforts to re-form in the drift, the flecks that were Orionid ships were individually bolting up out of the Belt.

"Follow them, before they can re-group," Birrel ordered. "Zenith, all ships."

The Orionids were already re-grouping, he saw an instant later. But they were doing it while going at accelerating speed away from the Belt and the whole system of Sol.

The Fifth Lyra and the UW ships came fast up out of the drift after them. Falling into a ragged formation of short parallel columns, they moved zenith and west until they were high above the curious, big, ringed planet—Birrel could not remember its name, at the moment—when a message came from Laney. It gave Birrel a sharp pleasure to hear the old admiral's voice.

"Are they really pulling out?"

"I think so," Birrel answered, looking at the radar screen. The Orionid ships were, he estimated, building up a long-jump acceleration program. "Yes. Their surprise strike failed, and they got hurt. We'd better start pursuit."

Laney demurred to that. "Not without authorization from the Chairman. I'll set up a three-way visual circuit. Hold on."

Birrel chafed at the delay. He wanted to start the pursuit-acceleration at once, the chance would not be there for long.

But he had lost three light cruisers and one heavy one, as well as half a dozen scouts, and, without the UW ships, he would not be able to bring sufficient fire-power to bear on the Orionids when he did catch up to them.

"Politicians," he muttered. "Why do they always have to meddle in a fight?"

When he faced both Laney and Charteris on a split screen a few minutes later, his forebodings were justified. Charteris, looking as though he had had as bad a time waiting as they had had fighting, spoke firmly.

"No pursuit. Keep watch out there until it's certain that they're on their way back to Orion."

"And we just let them go?"

Charteris nodded. "We do. This thing isn't generally known yet, though there are rumors. I shall announce that an unidentified force of ships, apparently from some totally unknown power beyond the civilized galaxy, attempted to attack Earth and were repelled by the UW fleet and the Fifth Lyra."

"For God's sake!" cried Birrel. "You're giving Solleremos an out—deliberately!"

"Yes," said Charteris.

"But why?"

"We've had to fight a battle," said the chairman. "Thanks to your help, we won it. But we don't want to have to fight a war."

20

FOR FORTY-EIGHT HOURS, while they kept watching beyond the system of Sol, Birrel raged. During that time messages came in to New York from one Sector capital after another, pledging aid and assistance in case the unknown attackers should return.

"Unknown," said Birrel furiously. "Every capital in the galaxy knows where they came from. And listen to this—this one tops everything."

It was the message—a bit belated—that Solleremos had sent to the United Worlds. Orion was shocked by the mysterious attack on Earth. Orion would use every resource to attempt to

learn the origin of the attackers. The Governor of Orion solemnly promised his aid against them, if they came back—

Birrel broke off and said a profane word.

"I don't know," said Garstang hesitatingly. "Maybe it was better at that to give Solleremos this way to cover up. Without it, this thing would go on and on."

Birrel turned on him angrily. "So you think Charteris was right to snatch the battle away from us just when we'd won it?"

Garstang shrugged. Then he quit being diplomatic and said doggedly, "We haven't had a war since the old days before space-travel. We don't want one, even if we have to let Solleremos off easy to prevent it. Do we?"

Birrel started a hot answer, but stopped. He realized, hard as it was to admit it to himself, that what Garstang said was simple truth.

"Oh, hell," he said, turning away, "everyone knows my job better than I do."

Even though Charteris and Garstang might be right, even though the old demon of war, that had been kept caged for many generations, should not be let loose, what was Ferdias going to say to this? The Fifth had carried out Ferdias' mission, had prevented Solleremos' grab at Earth. But he could have weakened the power of Orion to do further mischief if he had been able to maul those two squadrons more, and he had not done so. He worried about it.

He was still worried when they finally returned to Earth, leaving a strong guard of UW scouts out on watch. But when the Fifth followed Laney's fleet in, and touched down at New York spaceport, Birrel got a surprise.

It was twilight and the ships of the Fifth loomed up like scarred, battle-weary giants in the dusk. Birrel, walking along the side of the *Starsong* with Garstang, saw the scars in the side of the great hull. They were not from enemy action—a ship hit by a missile was just annihilated—but from the drift. Every pebble in the Belt seemed to have left its mark, one compartment had been holed twice and only its automatic bulkheads had saved the ship. But the *Stardream*, next in line, was worse hit than that. A sizable chunk of stone had got through its proximity-radar defenses and had smashed in some of the armor near its stern like tin.

Four major ships gone, with all their crews, and six scouts, and a lot of damage to repair—Birrel felt a reaction of weari-

ness and distaste. He heard a distant uproar of voices over in
the part of the spaceport where the even-more-battered ships
of the UW had landed, but it was not until he and Garstang
had passed the *Stardream* that they could see what caused the
growing noise.

Men—hundreds of men in the black UW uniform—were
running towards the ships of the Fifth. They were utterly without discipline or organization, they were nothing but a yelling
mob, and Birrel, tired as he was, felt shock as he contrasted
them with his own disciplined crews marching out of their
ships. What were they doing, what was the matter with their
officers to let them behave like this—

He stared. The UW men were heading, all along the mighty
line of the Fifth, toward his own debarking crews. The Earthmen reached the Lyrans. They hit them with their fists. They
grabbed them and wrestled them to the ground. They pounded
their backs, shook their hands, yelled at them, their voices
wild, their faces shining in the twilight.

"What the devil—"

"They're just saying hello," said Garstang. His voice was
mild, but he was grinning. "We fought a battle together, and
we won it. Remember?"

Birrel saw that the discipline of the Fifth was crumbling.
His crews were breaking ranks under the assault of the rejoic-
ing Earthmen, they were yelling back, striking hands, pounding the backs of the Earthmen in their turn.

"This," said Birrel, "is a fine way for trained men to act."
There was no conviction at all in his voice.

A quartet of officers in black came toward him and he recognized Laney. The admiral's face was stony, but there was a
fire in his eyes that he could not conceal.

He shook Birrel's hand and said stiffly, "My congratula-
tions, Commander. Very well handled. Very."

Birrel said politely, "Well, I must admit that that suicide
charge you put on made it a *little* bit easier for us."

They looked at each other poker-faced for a few moments
and then they both began to laugh, and shook hands again.

Venner pushed his way into the group and spoke to Garstang. And in a moment Garstang, suddenly on his best military behavior, came up to Birrel.

"Sir," he said, "*Starsong* requires your presence aboard."

Birrel's nerves made a high-jump and then froze. Garstang's

face was perfectly impassive, and so was Venner's, but there was only one reason why *Starsong* would suddenly require him back aboard now. The long-awaited message from Ferdias must be coming through.

He turned back to Laney. "Excuse me, sir?"

Laney waved him away. "We all have many things to attend to." He glanced out over the yelling, cheering mob of men in black and blue uniforms and then he said absently, before turning away, "Do you suppose we should tell the men to stand at ease?"

Birrel went back to the ship with Garstang and Venner.

There were two messages. One was in open code, and addressed to the whole Fifth Lyra. *Well done*, it said. *Lyra Sector and I personally are proud. Ferdias.*

The second one was in closed code, for Birrel alone.

He took it to his quarters and looked at it stonily for a time before he started to decipher it. He was still worrying about the non-pursuit of Solleremos' squadrons, and the open message to the Fifth did nothing to reassure him. Naturally, Ferdias would congratulate all hands. There was nothing else he could, or would, do. But the private message to the Commander might not be so friendly. It might even conceivably be something like, *You are hereby replaced in command by—* At this end, Birrel felt that he had no choice but to go along with the orders of the UW Council. But from where Ferdias sat, it might look different.

Birrel sighed and began his decoding.

The first sentences relieved his worries. *Who says you're not a diplomat? Good work, Jay.*

But the next sentence started his worries all over again, but in a different way.

Take a rest at Orville till further instructions.

Why should Ferdias want him to go back to Orville?

Wasn't this over now? Hadn't the battle been fought and won? What was there left for him to do now, but take part in the commemoration flyover and go home?

Why bother with Orville?

A vacation, perhaps. Reward for a job well done. Go and relax in the country, look over your ancestral fields, forget all about ships and stars.

Maybe.

Maybe it was only because the other things were so fresh in

his mind, so strongly connected with the place at Orville that the mere mention of it made him uneasy—Karsh and Tauncer, secret meetings, intrigue and treachery and sudden death.

But that was ridiculous. Karsh was dead, Tauncer was in whatever place the UW people maintained for such as he, and the threat of Orion was thoroughly disposed of as far as Earth was concerned. What was between Orion and Lyra was another matter and had nothing to do with Orville. It was foolish to suppose that Ferdias was suggesting another assignation with some agent there. Birrel shook his head. He was just tired, imagining things. Ferdias was pleased with the way he had handled things and was giving him a leave, and that was all there was to it.

That was fine, only why should Ferdias care where he spent his leave?

Take a rest in Orville. Coming from Ferdias, a suggestion like that was an order.

A cold foreboding settled upon Birrel. There was something wrong here, something hidden. But what?

For no reason at all, there came into his mind the memory of Tauncer, lying rigid with the vera-probe playing on him, saying mechanically in answer to Mallinson's question, "—if he doesn't, Ferdias will grab Earth first."

Birrel told himself he was a fool. Just because Ferdias had further instructions for him did not mean that he had any plans like that. Ferdias had told him that he didn't want Earth.

Ferdias had told him . . . Yes. But wouldn't he have told him that even if his plans were quite different? Just as he had let him go into the cluster without telling him the real score until later?

Hell, thought Birrel. I'm building all this up because I'm tired and jumpy. I need sleep.

He was not to get it for a while. Mallinson came. There was a brief and slightly awkward silence, and then Mallinson said stiffly,

"The Chairman is waiting for you."

He paused, looking over Birrel's head, his mouth set as though he tasted something bitter.

"I would be glad," he said, "if you would accept my personal apology for past suspicions."

Birrel shrugged. "None is needed."

And on the way back to New York with Mallinson he

thought, Why should you of Earth trust Lyra more than Orion, or Leo, or any of the others? Why should you, even now? You don't know what Ferdias may have up his sleeve. *I* don't know, yet.

New York was blazing. The big crowds that had gathered for the commemoration had something else to commemorate tonight, the victory over the "unknown invaders" that everyone knew had been from Orion. The streets were wild and even Mallinson's official car had trouble getting through.

"The town will belong to the fleet personnel tonight," Mallinson said. "Your men as well as ours, Commander."

Birrel said gloomily that he hoped people would not get all of his crews drunk.

Mallinson smiled, for the first time. "I can practically guarantee that they will."

They went into the UW tower by a back entrance. Charteris was waiting in a little office. He did not look calm or stony now. He looked, all at the same time, older and careworn and excited and eager.

"Well," he said. "The Council will want to tender you our formal thanks later, Commander. Right now I wanted to say—" He stopped and looked blank and then said, "I'm not sure just what I did want to say. Maybe just the same thing. Thanks, that is."

Almost shyly, he stuck out his hand.

Then he said, "Sit down, Commander. I can well imagine you're tired. Fortunately, there'll be time enough before the commemoration to give you a rest, and to repair the damage you've suffered."

He went on, when Birrel had sat down, "I had a message today from the governor of Lyra."

Birrel's nerves went hard and tense. "Yes?"

"A very warming message," Charteris said. He paused. "I'm considered a bit of a dreamer, you know. But I still cherish the idea that someday the Sectors will return to us. Perhaps this is the beginning of new and better things. Who knows?"

Birrel's tension relaxed not at all. He was thinking that this might indeed be the beginning of new things, but that Charteris might not like the new things very much.

Charteris misinterpreted his silence, and sprang to his feet. "I'm detaining a weary man with babblings. I won't keep you

longer now, and I apologize for bringing you all the way in here.''

Birrel rose too. He said, ''That's all right. I'm going on back up to the farm in Orville—my wife's still there.''

Charteris looked at him curiously. ''You really like that old place, don't you?'' His eyes brightened. ''Well, then that's something the UW can do to show its gratitude to you. We'll have the recent sale of that place voided, it having been made for what you might call illegal purposes. It will be bought in your name. Consider your old, ancestral home your own property, Commander.''

Birrel, startled, began to protest, but his protests were waved aside.

''Forget it, Commander. It's a pretty trivial, little piece of Earth to give you in return for what you've done for us—but it seems to mean something to you.''

On his way down with Mallinson, Birrel still felt vexed. He didn't really care anything about the old place, it was all a misunderstanding. He didn't want even a trivial piece of Earth.

Ferdias might feel differently. Ferdias might want it all.

21

VINSON CAME ACROSS the fields in the middle of the next morning. He looked as though he had waited as long as he could, but just could not wait any longer. He came up onto the sunny porch, where Birrel and Lyllin had lingered over late breakfast, and he stood looking at them awkwardly and grinning.

''Hear you had quite a fight out there,'' he said, in an elaborately offhand way.

Birrel shook his head. ''A brawl in space is just radar and computers. It's not a real fight where you can see the men you're fighting, like the one we had back in those woods.''

Vinson turned dull red with pride, but he said nothing to that as, at Lyllin's invitation, he sat down. He looked at the black cat that sat on a chair near Lyllin.

''Picked up a cat, I see,'' he said. ''Well, there's nothing like a good cat to keep down pests.''

Birrel looked sourly at the small, black animal that sat there

with such insolent self-assurance, as though he owned the whole place and they were merely his guests.

"I haven't seen this one doing anything useful," he said.

Lyllin laughed, and reached and stroked the sleek back. Tom looked boredly away, as though he only permitted this as a mark of special favor.

Birrel thought how surprised he had been when he had arrived the night before and found Lyllin sitting on the porch waiting for him, with the cat in her lap. He had had, for a moment, a slightly eerie feeling of sudden recognition, as though he, who had never been here before the past few days, could remember other women in the past, sitting on the porch of this old house and waiting for their men to come home.

Lyllin's eyes had clung to his, but she had merely said, lightly,

"I've been accepted."

"You've been bribing the beggar with food," he had accused. "His sides are bulging."

She had only laughed and stroked Tom, as she was doing now, but when he had bent and kissed her, her lips had been trembling.

Vinson was saying, "I promised to go over the fields with you, remember? Wondered if you would like to do that now." He added eagerly, "You know, I was thinking that, with my equipment, I could work these fields into pretty good shape for you. There's plenty of time for clearing before fall. And you need to bring these fields back as soon as you can."

Birrel had forgotten all about Vinson's promise, but he remembered now and he hastily tried to squirm out of this.

"Thanks," he said. "Thanks a lot. But you see, I'm liable to be going back to Lyra any time now. I'm afraid I won't have time to do anything with this place."

"Don't worry, I can do it all for you," Vinson said. "My machinery stands idle half the time, anyway. Then, when you come back, you'll have a lot better property here."

Birrel gave up. The man was obviously so anxious to do him a favor, that it would be churlish to object further.

"All right," he said, getting up. "We'll look it over."

They went out into the bright, hot day and Vinson started to talk about the old barn and how it needed roofing, and how the orchard should be pruned, and other things so remote from Birrel's experience that he did not understand them at all. He

pretended to listen and he nodded intelligently as they went along, but his thoughts were very far from Vinson's talk of auto-tractors and weather-control taxes and the like.

He kept wondering how soon Ferdias' orders would come. He didn't see why they had just not been given him in that coded message. Yet codes had been broken before, and if Ferdias' orders were a potentially explosive secret, he might not have wanted to risk that . . .

His mind was brought back to the immediate present by Vinson stopping. They had walked along the edge of one of the fields, an edge that was a tangle of encroaching saplings and briars.

"You have to keep fighting back stuff like this," Vinson was saying. "First thing, I'll program an auto-dozer to clear off all this brush."

Some of the briars had dark berries on them, oddly faceted like the eye of an insect. Birrel asked what they were.

"Just wild blackberries. They're a pest—right now they're ripe, though." And Vinson picked a handful and handed them to him.

The berries stained Birrel's hand, but he found them sun-warmed and pleasant-tasting—not sweet, but with a sharp tang.

"They're good," he said. "Thanks."

Vinson stared. "For what? They're your blackberries."

His blackberries. His field, that Vinson led him across, talking of atomic-synthesized fertilizers and the necessities of draining. It made Birrel smile, a little. A star-captain in the service of Lyra had a lot of use for an old farm on Earth.

But he continued to nod intelligently as Vinson led the way around the fields. The sun was hot now, swinging overhead in the blue sky. Great clouds sailed like majestic ships, and the warm air had a drowsy feeling to it and yet, at the same time, had a peculiar, tingling quality that seemed to touch something deep inside you with every breath you drew.

They circled around the edge of the fields and then went along the fringe of the woods. Birrel asked the names of the trees that were unfamiliar to him, and Vinson told him.

"Just scrub stuff, not good for much of anything," he said. "Can't clear it away and farm it, for the creek backs up through here at high water."

He added, a little farther along, "This is where the line goes

through—weeds on this side are yours. That old path leads to a pretty good fishing-place on the creek.''

It grew hotter, and Birrel mopped his brow, as they went on along the rustling, green fringe of woods. Birds flashed away in front of them, and once Vinson pointed up at a slowly circling speck in the blue sky and said that it was a hawk. They passed a small stream, a delightful thing with a series of tiny waterfalls and little curves of pebbly beach under miniature rock ledges covered with a feathery green growth that he learned were ferns.

Walking back across the fields toward the house, Vinson swept his arm this way and that to emphasize his points.

''All this should be turned over this fall and the sod left to rot down. In the spring I can really start getting it into shape.''

That's fine, Birrel thought. But where will I be when my fields are in good shape again? And what will you and the rest of Orville be thinking of me? You may be out here sowing my fields with salt instead of tenderly caring for them.

Aloud he said, ''That sounds good. Of course, I don't know the first thing about it.''

''You'll learn,'' Vinson said.

Birrel suddenly stopped as they approached the house. A car was pulling up in front of it. Then he saw a woman getting out of it. She was a tall, bony woman of middle age, who proceeded to help a very old woman out of the car.

''Oh, Lord,'' said Vinson. ''That's old Mrs. Sawyer. Good old soul, but she'll talk your leg off.'' He added, with a grin, ''I'm deserting, I've heard her too many times. See you later.''

He strode off hastily in the direction of his own home. Birrel went forward a bit uncertainly, as Lyllin came out of the house. The old woman was now, in a shrill voice, superintending the removal from the car of what appeared to be a bundle of big, thick and clumsy-looking books.

The bony woman took the books to the porch and then smiled at Birrel and Lyllin and held out her hand. ''I'm Netta Sawyer,'' she said. ''Mother simply had to come and see you. I hope it's not an inconvenient time.''

Birrel, noting her anxious look, assured her that it was not. The old woman came toward them, making a great show of fussing and tottering. She said,

''You look like one of the Birrels. You've got the same ugly

chin." She turned and peered at Lyllin. "And you're his wife?
I hope he doesn't beat you like Nicholas did."

"Mother—" began the younger woman unhappily, but was
completely ignored.

"Nicholas?" said Birrel.

"Nicholas Birrel," said the old woman. "They always said
he beat his wife. I was only a child then, but I remember the
talk. Why don't we go inside where a person can sit down?"

Birrel started to lead the way to the door, but was stopped
by a sharp command from the old woman.

"Pick up those albums and bring them. Why do you think
I came here?"

Birrel was wondering that, but resignedly picked up the
bulky, old books. When they were seated in the living room,
the daughter explained anxiously,

"Mother has all the old, family pictures—your family—and
thought you would like to see them."

"Why—that's very nice," said Birrel. "Then it was your
family, too, I take it?"

"Not mine—not a drop of Birrel blood in me," said the old
woman, as though triumphantly refuting an accusation. "But
Sawyer's mother was a Birrel, and I've always saved his old,
family pictures, though I don't know why I did it. They were
all a cross-grained lot."

She turned and said to Lyllin, with a sort of deeply sympa-
thetic understanding, "I expect you've had your troubles with
this one. I know what they're like, Sawyer took after his
mother."

"It hasn't really been so bad," Lyllin murmured, without a
trace of a smile, but was ignored as the bright, old eyes turned
back on Birrel.

"Yes, you've got that sulky, Birrel look. They all had it.
Here, I'll show you."

She had disposed herself in the center of the sofa and she
now proceeded to hold a small court there, turning the leaves
of the old albums and uttering her sharp comments while Birrel
and Lyllin sat uncomfortably on either side of her and stretched
their necks to see. From the absolute seriousness of Lyllin's
face, Birrel knew that she was rather enjoying his entrapment,
and he steamed.

"Here's Nicholas," said the old woman. "I don't remember
him too well myself, but I don't doubt that he did beat his

wife, as people said. Here's his father—let's see, that was John Birrel—no, James—''

The commentary continued, and the time-yellowed photographs flipped past, entirely meaningless to Birrel until one name drew him out of his polite inattention.

''—Cleve Birrel, that went off to Sirius or somewhere. That would be your great-grandfather—''

Birrel was a little startled that the picture was of a young man, not an old one—though he realized that his surprise was quite illogical. In fact, the Cleve Birrel who had gone off to the stars had been a good bit younger than he himself was now. It was a good, young face, distinguished only by an eager quality in the eyes.

''You look a good bit like him,'' said Mrs. Sawyer, as though it was no compliment.

Birrel saw no resemblance, though he did not say so. But to his surprise, Lyllin agreed with the statement.

''Yes, there's something in the expression—''.

The old woman nodded satisfiedly. ''Just what I said. The same ugly chin.''

It was an hour later before she suddenly got to her feet and announced that she had no more time to give them and must go. Now all her tottering and fussing had disappeared and she went briskly out to the car, disdainfully refusing support from her daughter and Birrel.

''I'm leaving the albums with you, but only as a loan,'' she said severely to Birrel. ''I've saved those pictures a long time and I don't want them flying out to stars away off. Remember, now.''

Birrel solemnly promised, and then shook his head as he and Lyllin watched the car go down the road.

''Fine,'' he said. ''Now we'll have all the people around here dropping in.''

''I don't think so, Jay,'' said Lyllin. ''I got to know these people a little better while you were gone. I believe they'll respect your privacy, even though they're all tremendously grateful to you.''

''They've nothing to be grateful to me for,'' he said, almost roughly. ''I was just obeying orders.''

She looked at him, a little bit startled, but said nothing.

Her prediction was borne out, and that day passed without anyone else coming. Unreasonably, Birrel began to chafe at

the sleepy silence of the place. In the afternoon he and Lyllin went for a walk, heading westward up the gentle slope of the wide, shallow valley.

They first went by the path Vinson had pointed out, through the woods to the creek. It was shallow in this summer season, a mere flat ribbon of water studded with big stones. Graceful drooping trees grew along it, their dependent branches trailing thin spear-shaped leaves almost to the water. Birrel remembered what Vinson had called them.

"They're willow trees," he said, and felt a touch of complacence in his knowledge. "Those bigger ones are elms—no, oaks."

They crossed the stream by jumping from stone to stone, and went on by another well-marked path, through more woods and then up a long, grassy slope. When they reached the ridge there was a breeze blowing, and they stood for a while looking out across the broad valley with its fat-looking fields and its old farmhouses half-hidden in clumps of trees.

"That's the Bower farm," said Lyllin, pointing. "I met them at the Vinsons' while you were gone. And that white place north of it is the Hovik farm, and I think the Menzels live just beyond it."

Then she turned and laughed and said, "I think that pays you back for your willows and oaks."

Birrel laughed, too. They stood for a while longer, the wind ruffling Lyllin's hair. Then his restless impatience made Birrel move on again.

No one came the rest of that day, but that evening there was a call from Brescnik.

"We're getting the damage fixed pretty fast," he reported, and gave details. He added, with a rasp in his voice, "But we're having plenty of personnel trouble. Over there, in New York, it's a night-long celebration every night."

"I expected that," said Birrel. "Have Joe Garstang handle the problem."

Brescnik snorted. "Garstang? I had to dress him down myself this morning when he got back from the city."

Birrel grinned briefly. "Tell him to stop that sort of thing. Anything else?"

"Message from Vega that four S-Fifteen scouts from the Second squadron are on their way to help replace our losses," Brescnik said. "The Second's scout and light-cruiser divisions

were cruising well eastward, so those four should be here in a few days.''

''Report as soon as they get in,'' Birrel said, and switched off.

He stood, frowning and thinking. This would be it, these scouts Ferdias was sending. In one of those ships would be someone bearing the instructions that Ferdias did not want to risk in a communicator message. The scouts should arrive just before the commemoration, and then he would know where he stood and just what it was that he still had to do . . .

Birrel could not get to sleep that night. The dark house was silent, only the sound of a light breeze in the pines outside, and Lyllin's breathing was easy and relaxed, but he twitched and turned until he gave it up and quietly put on his clothes and went down the stairs. He bumped into the newel post at the bottom of the stairs, muttered a curse at it, and then put his shoes on. It seemed warm and stuffy in the lower rooms, so he went back through the kitchen and went out and sat down on the steps of the back porch.

The night was dark, no stars showing. The warm wind blew up from the west, from the direction of the woods and the creek, and it brought sounds and smells. The sounds were of far-off dogs gossiping, and the periodic hooting of some night-bird, and the tiny, stridulating voices of insects. The smells were fragrant ones from the old flower-bushes in the yard, mixed in with the heavier rankness of the bursting vegetation in the weedy fields and woods.

Birrel suddenly realized the highly seasonal nature of this planet. It was funny that he had not thought of it before—planets where the inclination of the axis from the ecliptic produced seasons, were not so common. He usually noticed and disliked seasonal planets, their sharp changes of climate being distasteful compared to the even weather of a normal world like Vega Four. He wondered why he hadn't thought about it here. Of course it was summer now, but the fantastic rapidity with which vegetation grew and matured was obvious. It must be strange, he thought, to live here in a place where presently all that bursting growth would wither and die and be covered by snows, and then, months later, be triumphantly reborn. . . .

He turned suddenly as something brushed lightly against him. It was the cat. From somewhere Tom had appeared, stalking soundlessly across the porch and sitting down by Birrel's

side, looking out into the whispering darkness with bright green eyes. He did not look up at the man, or paw him, or demand attention, Birrel noticed. He sat in a sort of cool, detached companionship, until one of the small sounds out in the night caught his interest. Then he rose and stalked down the steps and into the darkness, without a backward glance.

"Going hunting," Birrel thought. "They stay wild, in a way, yet they live with people, too. Damned odd—"

He sat for a while, but he saw nothing more of the cat. After a time the endlessly-repeated, small noises against the quiet of the night soothed away his restlessness. He yawned, and then took off his shoes and went back up to bed.

For the next two days, nothing happened. Birrel and Lyllin rambled and explored the place, and sat nights on the porch, and all the time he was ticking off the interval required for a fast scout to get to Earth from an indeterminable point inside the frontiers of Lyra space.

The commemoration was near, and when he went back down to New York with Lyllin to check on how the damage-repair was coming, they found the city even more crowded now and blazing with decorations. People along the streets, who happened to glimpse his Lyran blue-and-silver uniform in the passing car, waved enthusiastically to him.

The wounded ships were almost repaired, Brescnik told him, and would be ready for the flyover.

"When will those four scouts from the Second get in?" asked Birrel.

"Should be in any time now," said Brescnik. "We've had no word from them since the first report."

Then, Birrel thought, within a day or so at the most he would know what Ferdias intended.

It was late afternoon by the time they got back to the farmhouse, and, soon after they did so, there was a call from Vinson. He had plans for renovating Birrel's fields and buildings all drawn up—should he bring them over?

"I'll come over," Birrel told him. "Right after dinner."

So later he left Lyllin tidying the kitchen and went out. He looked back at her for a moment, thinking how queer it was that somehow she did not seem at all strange or out of place in that old-fashioned room performing that ancient task.

He started across the ragged fields, but stopped after he had gone a little way and stood looking at the sky. With the utter

capriciousness that seemed to characterize all Earth's weather, the blue-and-gold day had suddenly changed into a garish, red sunset. The clouds, high in the eastern sky, still caught the dazzling sunlight. But, lower down, they shaded into pink and crimson and cinnabar, and, below these, there was a narrow band of clear sky which was pure lemon in color. Against that band of light the farther ridge of the shallow valley stood out, each distant tree or building-roof sharply silhouetted.

The light, washing across the fields in which he stood, changed by the minute. All the briars and weeds around him caught that glory, and put on a fantastic beauty. Far away, across the red western sky, two hawks quartered their way, planing and circling and effortlessly lifting. The soft, evening breeze murmured in his ear, as though trying to whisper secrets.

Birrel shook his head wonderingly. This place never seemed the same twice.

He started on toward Vinson's, and then he stopped. A voice was calling his name.

He turned around, and there was a man following him across the weedy field. The man did not come very fast, for there was a slight limp in his gait as he came across the uneven ground. Birrel stood stock-still for a moment. Then he went back to meet Ferdias.

22

THE LIGHT STRIKING across the field in long, level rays could not account for all of the glow in Ferdias' face. There was a sort of radiant eagerness about him, that showed in his eyes, and his step, and the way he grasped Birrel's hand.

"Well," he said, "this is quite a place to meet again. I find Lyllin sweeping the floor in that quaint house, and you walking around the fields like an old farmer."

He laughed. Then he looked around the sunset-reddened landscape, his tawny eyes, as always, seeming to take in every detail.

"So this is what Earth is like, away from the spaceports and cities? Not much, is it? But interesting."

"I take it," said Birrel, "that your visit here is an unofficial one."

Ferdias nodded in his quick way. "You know it is. Unofficial *and* top secret. That suspicious bunch at the UW would take alarm if I came here openly. So I slipped in one of those replacement scouts from the Second, and had Joe Garstang bring me up to this place. Surprised you, didn't I?"

"You did," said Birrel. "I thought you were still at Vega."

Ferdias shook his head decisively. "Oh, no—not with everything riding on this thing. Officially, I've never left Vega Four. But actually, for the last week or so I've been with the Second, cruising a good part of the way to Earth and waiting to see how things came out."

He slapped Birrel on the shoulder. "They came out pretty good, thanks to you, Jay."

Birrel said, "I'd have followed them up and made it better than pretty good, if I'd been able."

He told of Laney and of Charteris' decision. Ferdias listened intently and then shook his head again.

"Charteris was wrong. You can't avoid a war by pretending it isn't happening. Of course Solleremos is covering up now, but sooner or later he'll try it again. Whereas if those two squadrons had been completely shattered—"

With no impulse at all to defend Charteris, but with a certain testiness, Birrel said,

"I ought to point out that shattering them was no foregone conclusion, even if we'd mounted pursuit as I wanted to. They still had plenty of fight left in them and still matched our strength."

Ferdias said understandingly, "And if you had let the UW ships hang back and taken up pursuit yourself, you'd have been overmatched. There was nothing else you could do, but go along with Charteris. But it complicates things—"

He broke off, looking thoughtfully at the red-smoldering western sky. In the east, dusk was advancing in a slow tide of deepening gray. The hawks were gone now, but a bat came low over them, flitting jerkily this way and that in the twilight.

Birrel felt that Ferdias was going to say something he did not want to hear, something that he had worried about all these past few days. He had a feeling that time was running out on him, and it made him speak up before Ferdias could continue.

"We'll have all damage repaired before the commemora-

tion," he said. "So right after that's over, we'll be ready to take off for Vega."

Ferdias shook his head. "The Fifth isn't going back to Vega, Jay—not right away, that is."

The twilight seemed suddenly chill and heavy to Birrel. He knew, now. He had expected this ever since he had received Ferdias' message, but he had kept hoping that he was wrong, that there was some other explanation. Now there was no doubt at all. He looked across the dusking valley, where the lights of farms were now showing here and there, and he felt a sadness, a regret that things had had to turn out this way.

Ferdias made one of his quick, incisive gestures as he continued. "The transports can go back, under escort, but the fighting strength of the Fifth has to stay at this system until we're sure Solleremos won't try another grab."

Birrel said incredulously, "You don't really think he would? Not with the setback he's had, and the damage to his crack squadrons—"

Ferdias interrupted. "Maybe not right away, but he'll try it again, sooner or later—he, or Gianea or Strowe or old Vorn. We've stopped this grab, but, if we go away now, we'll leave Earth wide open for another one any time."

"So the Fifth stays around indefinitely?" said Birrel. "What is the UW going to say to that?"

Ferdias answered promptly, "I intend to offer the UW an offensive-defensive alliance, mutual citizenship with Lyra Sector, with complete autonomy in all their own local affairs."

"It sounds fine," said Birrel. "A real, fine offer. They'll throw it right back in your face."

"No, they won't," said Ferdias. "They can't, the spot they're in."

Birrel said earnestly, "Look, Ferdias, I don't know politics the way you do. But I've got to know the people here a little bit. They won't go along with your idea. They'll fight, if necessary."

"There won't be any fighting," said Ferdias. "Oh, sure, the UW Council will object and argue for a while, but, in the end, they'll accept the alliance with Lyra."

His voice hammered with confident emphasis, as though he sensed Birrel's inner reluctance.

"Jay, they have to, there's no other way out for them! The UW knows now that the time has come when one of the Sec-

tors will absorb it. Solleremos' try has shown them that. With him, or with Strowe or Gianea, it would be just a straight, brutal take-over. I'll be offering them an alliance of equals, with my only request a full fleet-base on Earth and an alignment of their foreign policy with Lyra's. It's better than they'd get from any of the other Sectors.''

Ferdias was speaking the truth about that, Birrel knew. But how long had this truth been in his mind? Had it been there when, at Vega Four, he had said that he had no designs at all on Earth? Had it?

"You don't like it," Ferdias was saying. "Well, neither do I, really. But if I hold back now, I'm just making a gift of this world to one of the other Sectors. Would the people here prefer that to an alliance with us?''

"No," Birrel admitted. "An alliance would let them keep their pride. But—''

"There are always a million 'ifs' and 'buts' in a thing like this," said Ferdias. "But now, when the UW has just had a frightening object-lesson, is the time to push this alliance. We've got to plan, and plan fast.''

He started walking with Birrel back across the dusky fields toward the softly glistening lights of the old farmhouse. The weeds were crushed beneath their boots and the now familiar, bitter smell of the Queen Anne's Lace came to Birrel's nostrils as they walked.

"The whole Fifth will lift out the day after the commemoration," Ferdias said. "The transports, as I said, can go straight back to Vega under light escort. How long can your cruiser force stand by and be supplied by your own auxiliaries?''

"Stand by—where?" asked Birrel. "It makes a difference, you know.''

"Well outside this whole system of Sol," said Ferdias. "We don't want you anywhere near Earth, it would seem entirely too much like blackmail pressure and that's the last thing I want when I offer the alliance.''

"Standing by a parsec or two out there—say three-four weeks," said Birrel, after running over the logistical problems in his mind. "Any longer time than that would make necessary a supply-stop on the way back to Vega later.''

"Three to four weeks," repeated Ferdias thoughtfully. "It should be enough to put the alliance proposal across. If necessary, you could stretch that out a little?''

Birrel shook his head irritatedly. This was the sort of thing you always came up against when people tried to make political considerations override military and logistical ones.

"Sure I could stretch it out," he said. "But we'd be in a low state of supply if we stretched it, even for a few extra days—and that would make it tough for us, if we got into a fight."

"Oh, forget that, there's not going to be any fight," Ferdias said impatiently. "We'll say four weeks, definite. If all goes well, you won't have to go back to Vega then—we'll have a base here and you can come back and resupply right here."

Birrel hated sketchy planning, it had a habit of coming back and hitting a commander in the face, but he knew Ferdias well enough to know that he would have to make the best of that. He did ask,

"What about the escort for the transports? Remember, Solleremos doesn't exactly love us right now. But if I detach enough force from the Fifth to make an adequate escort all the way to Lyra space, I'll weaken my squadron seriously."

"I thought of that," said Ferdias. "An escort force from the Second will come in far enough to convoy the transports back—your detachment will only have to see them on the first leg of the way."

More possible hitches, Birrel thought—but he did not raise objection now for they had reached the farmhouse and Lyllin and Joe Garstang were sitting on the porch.

"Relax," Ferdias said as Garstang scrambled to his feet. "Jay and I have some things to go over. And I need a drink."

"I'll get you one," Birrel said, nodding to Lyllin also to stay seated.

She gave him a look from unfathomable eyes, but said nothing. She and Garstang smell what's in the wind, Birrel thought, anybody would with Ferdias himself coming here secretly, and she doesn't like it. Well, I don't like it either, none of us do.

He followed Ferdias into the lamplit living-room, and went on back to the kitchen for a bottle. He came back with it to find Ferdias looking around the room.

"Charming, in a way," said Ferdias. He touched the rocking chair, looked at the wooden walls, and glanced into the big, old photograph albums lying on the table.

Birrel thought, as he went back to the kitchen for glasses,

I'd better get those albums back to the old lady before we leave here, I promised I would.

He brought back the glasses. Ferdias had sat down and his hands were grasping his knees in a familiar gesture.

"Here's the way we'll lay it out," he said. "The commemoration is day after tomorrow—all right, the Fifth can pull out right after it. I'll have left before then, of course, and, as soon as you've cleared Earth, I'll have the formal offer of alliance messaged to the UW from Lyra Council. You'll proceed with the Fifth on out of this system to wait, after detaching the transports—"

Birrel, as he poured out the drinks, was listening carefully. This was going to be a sticky enough job and he could not afford to fog up any details. But, as he stood listening, he became aware of a curious thing happening to him.

He was shaking a little. A feeling had come up in him that he did not even recognize at first, but it was so blindly hot and strong that it seemed to grasp his whole mind and body, leaving his will no control at all. Standing there gripped by that overmastering emotion, Birrel heard himself speaking, yet it seemed to him that his lips spoke without any command at all from his mind. He heard himself saying,

"I'm not going to have any part in it, Ferdias."

He had never astonished Ferdias before. He did so this time. Ferdias stared blankly, stopping in mid-sentence.

"You—what?"

Birrel carefully set down the half-filled glass. "Your grab for Earth. I'm having no part in it. None."

And now, as he spoke the words, Birrel knew what it was, that overpowering feeling. It was an anger so deep that it completely possessed him. All the time out there, in the twilight, that he had been talking of logistics and ships and routes, he had been trying to ignore that anger, to thrust it down into his subconscious and forget it. He could not keep it down any longer, it had suddenly broken through and taken hold of him and he was shaking with it.

Ferdias had leaped to his feet. His blank astonishment had been replaced by the look with which he always faced a challenge.

"What's the matter with you, Jay? I've explained that this alliance isn't a grab—"

"You explained to me before," Birrel interrupted harshly.

"Back at Vega Four, remember? You said, 'I don't want Earth, all I want is to keep Solleremos from grabbing it.' "

Ferdias nodded, with a sort of dangerous calmness. "Yes, I said that."

"Was it true, Ferdias? Or was that just talk for my benefit, so I'd come on this mission full of noble ideas about how we were protecting Earth, not threatening it?"

"Listen to me, Jay—" Ferdias began, but Birrel went on.

"Just as you're talking to me now about friendly alliances and how it's all for the good of Earth—when, what you really mean is, that now Solleremos has been repulsed, we can grab it for ourselves!"

Ferdias almost never lost his temper. But his iron control over it slipped a bit now, and he said, violently,

"What's all this talk about truth and lies and intentions? Do you suppose that the game for stars is played according to Sunday school rules?"

"Play it any way you want to," said Birrel. "I don't mind your lying, if you want stars that badly. But I object to your making a liar out of me. And you've made me one, for the first time in my life. Ever since I got to Earth, I've been telling everyone we had no hidden intentions, telling them that all we wanted to do was help them. All right, I refuse to be a liar any more, if you go ahead and do this, I'll have no part in it."

Ferdias' eyes were flaring, but he kept his temper now. He stood looking into Birrel's face and, after a moment, he said,

"You're resentful, because you think I didn't trust you with the truth. But there's more to your resentment than that."

"Isn't that enough?" demanded Birrel. "To send a man on a job and not even tell him where he stands?"

"No, there's more to it than that," said Ferdias, eyeing him. "You wouldn't blow up like this for that alone. You've worked up an emotion about the old home-world, Earth. Haven't you?"

"Oh, hell," said Birrel, "if you think I care a curse one way or another about this world—"

"Who's doing the lying now?" asked Ferdias, in a voice like a whiplash.

Birrel started to answer, then did not. What Ferdias said was ridiculous, and yet . . . Was it possible for a man to be snared by nostalgia? Could such trivial things as trees and fireflies, birds and sunsets, a forlorn, old farm under the moon, could things like that reach and touch something in the subconscious

of a man, something which he had inherited, but never knew he had? No, it was foolish to suppose so, Ferdias was just talking, and talk was not enough this time. He said, with an edge to his voice,

"I'm sure of one thing. I will not give the Fifth any orders to attack or intimidate the UW fleet or Earth."

Ferdias looked him in the eye. He said flatly, "As of this moment, you're relieved of all command. Brescnik will take over."

And the blow had fallen and to his secret amazement, Birrel did not seem to feel it at all, his hard resentment and resolve were quite unchanged. He said calmly,

"Brescnik's a good officer. He'll obey your orders. But will the Fifth obey *him*, if he orders potential action against Earth?"

"They're not all as sentimental as you, Jay," said Ferdias. "They'll obey."

"Will they? Why don't you ask Joe Garstang?"

Ferdias frowned at him. Then he went to the door and called Garstang in.

Garstang listened and his face, respectful and awed at first, became increasingly unhappy.

"Well?" said Ferdias impatiently.

"I don't know," said Garstang painfully. "Of course, no-body's going to disobey direct orders. But still—"

"But still—what?" demanded Ferdias.

With an heroic effort, Garstang looked into his eyes. "The UW fleet helped us clobber Solleremos, you know. They fought beside us and they more than pulled their weight. Nobody would like turning against them—though of course, orders—" His rambling stopped, and he looked almost desperately around and then added, "Too, the big part of us came from here, I mean away back. Nearly everybody's got some sentiment—"

"Give me a direct answer," Ferdias ordered curtly. "Would the ranks of the Fifth carry out such orders, if they were nec-essary?"

Garstang, scared and sweating, looked at him. He said, in a tone little above a whisper,

"Honest to God, sir, I don't know."

Ferdias looked at him for a moment, in silence. Then he went over and looked out the window into the darkness, saying nothing. His face was the face of a man who has fought his

way through many foes to the moment of victory, only to find his sword breaking in his hand.

He said after a while, without turning, "I should have foreseen this. Earth is important in galactic politics, because of the psychological influence it has on men's minds. But I forgot that the thing would cut both ways, would affect my own men all the time they were here—"

He was silent, as though the irony of that was too bitter on his lips to utter. Birrel and Garstang looked at him and said nothing. Finally, he turned back toward them. His face was hard, dark and stony, but his voice was composed.

"Very well. The Fifth will take part in the commemoration and then return to Vega as scheduled. You'll forget that I was here."

For just one moment, his control slipped again and his voice flared. "There'll be another time, and I'll take care—" Then he stopped, and turned toward the door.

Birrel said, "I'll turn over command to Brescnik tonight."

Ferdias stopped at the door, and looked back at Birrel. He was an ambitious man, a ruthless man, and an unscrupulous man. But he was not a small man.

"You served me long and faithfully, Jay, though you did go weak on me in the end. You'll return to Vega in command, and will resign two weeks later, with full honors. I think that pays any debt I owe you."

Birrel felt so strong a tug of old loyalty, old comradeship, that he almost wanted to deny all that he had said, to make it between himself and Ferdias as it had always been. He could not quite do it. But he held out his hand.

Ferdias struck his hand away. "The hell with that," he said, and went out into the darkness.

Garstang, stricken, came to life and tumbled after him.

Birrel stood still. It seemed to him that at this moment he should be feeling crushed, shattered, by the impulsive jettisoning of his life, his career, almost everything that had meant much to him. Yet he did not feel so.

He looked around at the old room and the things in it and at the windows, outside which the trees bent and whispered. What had he to do with this place? How could he have been such a fool? And even more bewildering, he did not feel like a fool.

Then, as he heard Lyllin come in from the porch he turned slowly to meet her gaze. He could not read her eyes.

"You heard?" he said.

Lyllin nodded. "I listened."

He thought of the villa on Vega Four, of Lyllin's friends and family there, of the blue sun going down behind the mountains. He said miserably,

"All right, go ahead and say it."

"What have I to say?" Lyllin said. "Except that you did right. And that you know you did."

"But to throw everything away—"

"If you'd done what Ferdias wanted you to do, you might have thrown *me* away," she said. "And don't look so worried. You would have retired from space duty in a few years anyway, and I don't think a desk would suit you."

She looked musingly around the room. "I think we'll like it here, when we come back. We could make some changes in the house. And if you don't like farming, I'm sure the UW would be glad to have you."

He grasped her wrist. "Lyllin, understand this: I'm not taking you away from your own world."

She looked up at him. "We've lived a good while on my world. But you, Jay—you never had a world until we came here. Now you have one, and that means it's mine too."

"Why in the world," said Birrel exasperatedly, "must everyone assume that I'm so crazy about this musty, old planet that I want to come back to it?"

"Don't you?"

He started to answer, and then he stopped, and looked around at the lamplit room and out the door at the dark trees. After a moment he said,

"Well, I don't know. We'll see."

Lyllin smiled.

And the commemoration blazed. The lights, the bands, the parades and the speeches, and finally the flyover—with the battered ships of the UW leading the way, and the mighty giants of the Fifth following them. Then, while everybody held their breath and kept their fingers crossed, that grotesque relic, the first of all starships, lurched, coughed and wobbled up into the sky, and labored bravely around the planet, and by some miracle came down safe again.

The night after it ended, Vinson and his wife stood out in the darkness behind their house and watched the sky. A west wind was hurrying big clouds across it and there was nothing to be seen but clouds that suddenly unveiled stars and then swiftly veiled them again. The wind finally brought them the sound for which they listened, the far roll of thunder across the sky. It was faint, for the wind came from a different direction, but they stood listening as it was repeated again and again until the last mutter faded, and the Fifth was gone.

"I do hate to see them go," said the woman, as they turned back toward the house.

"Won't be long till they're back," said Vinson. Then he chuckled, as he opened the door. "I was just thinking of that cat they took with them. Won't *he* be glad when they bring him home again?"